THE COUNT OF MONTE CRISTO:
THE DEFINITIVE MODERN VERSION

THE COUNT OF MONTE CRISTO:
THE DEFINITIVE MODERN VERSION

DAN EBERSOLD

Copyright © 2025 All rights reserved.

All rights reserved. No part of this publication may be reproduced, distributed, or transmitted in any form or by any means, including photocopying, recording, or other electronic or mechanical methods, without the prior written permission of the publisher, except in the case of brief quotations embodied in critical reviews and certain other noncommercial uses permitted by copyright law.

ISBN 979-8-9924513-1-3

For my parents,

Their love, support, and unwavering belief in me have shaped everything I do. Without them, the toughest moments in life would have felt impossible to face.

Love you both!

PREFACE

Originally published as a serialized novel, *The Count of Monte Cristo* captivated its 19th-century audience much like a modern-day soap opera. Released in installments between 1844 and 1846 in the French newspaper *Le Journal des Débats*, each segment left readers on a thrilling cliffhanger, eagerly awaiting the next chapter. Alexandre Dumas expertly crafted twists, betrayals, and revelations, ensuring his audience stayed hooked.

Much like today's episodic television dramas, these regular publications sparked communal excitement and discussion, with readers eagerly speculating on the fate of Edmond Dantès and the vivid characters in his world of revenge, justice, and redemption. Similarly, just as modern popular TV shows extend their storylines due to success, this story will at times follow a similar pattern. Think of each volume as a season and each chapter as an episode, with pacing that may shift or moments that feel drawn out—much like a long-running series on Netflix or HBO.

This is the same story as the original book: the same names, people, places, chapter titles, and terms as they were in the original version. However, this modernized version has updated the language in certain parts to contemporary usage, simplified the archaic expressions, and ensured the tone resonates with a modern audience while still preserving the essence of the original story.

My goal for this publication is for you to enjoy this version—perhaps even more than the original—while still gaining a deep understanding of the story. By the end, you won't just recognize key plot points and characters, but truly grasp the themes, motivations, and intricacies that shape the narrative. Whether for casual discussion or a high-stakes *Jeopardy!* question, you'll be prepared to dive into any conversation about the original text with confidence.

To preserve the authenticity of the source material, certain terms that are either antiquated or lack a precise English equivalent may have been retained in the text. The first time such a word or phrase appears, a footnote at the bottom of the page[*] provides the closest modern interpretation or explanation.

If you enjoy this version, you may find it worthwhile to explore the original text as well. That said, this adaptation is only around 100,000 words —a much more concise take compared to the original's staggering 460,000 words. The full text is a massive undertaking, packed with intricate details, subplots, extended passages, and drawn-out conversations that can be overwhelming for some readers—including me! That's exactly why this adaptation exists: to offer a more accessible and enjoyable experience.

Fortunately, since the original version is in the public domain, you can access it for free through numerous sources, including online libraries and eBook platforms. Whether you want to compare versions or experience the story in its original form, it's readily available at no cost.

Enjoy!

---

[*]Just like this.

TABLE OF CONTENTS

VOLUME ONE..1

Chapter 1: Arrival in Marseilles...................................3
Chapter 2: Father and Son..6
Chapter 3: The Catalans..15
Chapter 4: Conspiracy..20
Chapter 5: The Wedding Feast...................................26
Chapter 6: The Deputy Procureur du Roi...................37
Chapter 7: The Examination......................................41
Chapter 8: The Château d'If......................................44
Chapter 9: The Evening of the Betrothal...................47
Chapter 10: The King's Closet at the Tuileries...........50
Chapter 11: The Corsican Ogre..................................52
Chapter 12: Father and Son..55
Chapter 13: The Hundred Days..................................58
Chapter 14: The Two Prisoners..................................60
Chapter 15: Number 34 and Number 27.....................63
Chapter 16: A Learned Italian....................................67
Chapter 17: The Abbé's Chamber...............................69
Chapter 18: The Treasure...72
Chapter 19: The Third Attack....................................74
Chapter 20: The Cemetery of the Château d'If...........77
Chapter 21: The Island of Tiboulen............................81
Chapter 22: The Smugglers..84
Chapter 23: The Island of Monte Cristo.....................87
Chapter 24: The Secret Cave......................................90
Chapter 25: The Unknown...96
Chapter 26: The Pont du Gard Inn.............................100
Chapter 27: The Story..103

VOLUME TWO...107

Chapter 28: The Prison Register.................................109
Chapter 29: The House of Morrel & Son....................113
Chapter 30: The Fifth of September...........................116
Chapter 31: Italy & Sinbad the Sailor.........................119
Chapter 32: The Waking...122
Chapter 33: Roman Bandits..125

Chapter 34: The Colosseum..128
Chapter 35: La Mazzolata..132
Chapter 36: The Carnival at Rome..135
Chapter 37: The Catacombs of Saint Sebastian...........................138
Chapter 38: The Rendezvous..142
Chapter 39: The Guests..145
Chapter 40: The Breakfast..148
Chapter 41: The Presentation...151
Chapter 42: Monsieur Bertuccio..154
Chapter 43: The House at Auteuil...158
Chapter 44: The Vendetta...162
Chapter 45: The Rain of Blood..165
Chapter 46: Unlimited Credit...168
Chapter 47: The Dappled Grays..175

VOLUME THREE...181

Chapter 48: Ideology..183
Chapter 49: Haydée..187
Chapter 50: The Morrel Family..190
Chapter 51: Pyramus and Thisbe..194
Chapter 52: Toxicology...197
Chapter 53: Robert le Diable..201
Chapter 54: A Flurry in Stocks..205
Chapter 55: Major Cavalcanti...209
Chapter 56: Andrea Cavalcanti...213
Chapter 57: In the Lucern Patch...217
Chapter 58: M. Noirtier de Villefort..221
Chapter 59: The Will...224
Chapter 60: The Telegraph...227
Chapter 61: How a Gardener May Get Rid of the Dormice
     That Eat His Peaches..231
Chapter 62: Ghosts..235
Chapter 63: The Dinner..239
Chapter 64: The Beggar...243
Chapter 65: A Conjugal Scene...247
Chapter 66: Matrimonial Projects..250
Chapter 67: The Office of the King's Attorney.............................254
Chapter 68: A Summer Ball..257
Chapter 69: The Inquiry..260
Chapter 70: The Ball...264
Chapter 71: Bread and Salt..268

Chapter 72: Madame de Saint-Méran..................................272
Chapter 73: The Promise..276

VOLUME FOUR..279

Chapter 74: The Villefort Family Vault..............................281
Chapter 75: A Signed Statement.......................................285
Chapter 76: Progress of Cavalcanti the Younger...............289
Chapter 77: Haydée..292
Chapter 78: We hear From Yanina....................................295
Chapter 79: The Lemonade..301
Chapter 80: The Accusation..304
Chapter 81: The Room of the Retired Baker.....................307
Chapter 82: The Burglary..310
Chapter 83: The Hand of God...314
Chapter 84: Beauchamp..317
Chapter 85: The Journey..320
Chapter 86: The Trial..324
Chapter 87: The Challenge...328
Chapter 88: The Insult..333
Chapter 89: The Night..338
Chapter 90: The Meeting..342
Chapter 91: Mother and Son..346
Chapter 92: The Suicide...350
Chapter 93: Valentine...355
Chapter 94: Maximilian's Avowal......................................359
Chapter 95: Father and Daughter.....................................364

VOLUME FIVE...369

Chapter 96: The Contract...371
Chapter 97: The Departure for Belgium...........................376
Chapter 98: The Bell and Bottle Tavern............................380
Chapter 99: The Law..384
Chapter 100: The Apparition..388
Chapter 101: Locusta...393
Chapter 102: Valentine..398
Chapter 103: Maximilian..402
Chapter 104: Danglars' Signature....................................406
Chapter 105: The Cemetery of Père-Lachaise..................410
Chapter 106: Dividing the Proceeds.................................414
Chapter 107: The Lions' Den..418

Chapter 108: The Judge..........422
Chapter 109: The Assizes..........426
Chapter 110: The Indictment..........430
Chapter 111: Expiation..........434
Chapter 112: The Departure..........439
Chapter 113: The Past..........445
Chapter 114: Peppino..........449
Chapter 115: Luigi Vampa's Bill of Fare..........453
Chapter 116: The Pardon..........457
Chapter 117: The Fifth of October..........461

VOLUME ONE

Chapter 1: Arrival in Marseilles

On February 24, 1815, the lookout at Notre-Dame de la Garde spotted the *Pharaon*, a three-masted ship returning from Smyrna, Trieste, and Naples. Immediately, a pilot was dispatched, guiding the vessel between Cape Morgiou and the Rion Island toward Marseilles.

The ship's arrival created a buzz along the waterfront. Sailors and onlookers gathered at Fort Saint-Jean, craning their necks to get a glimpse of the approaching ship. The *Pharaon* was a local pride—built, outfitted, and owned by a well-known businessman from Marseilles.

As the ship glided through the straits, its slow progress stirred unease. It was clear to experienced sailors, however, that the ship wasn't damaged. Everything about its approach was deliberate and expertly managed. The anchor was ready, sails adjusted, and the first mate stood beside the pilot, issuing precise commands and ensuring every order was executed flawlessly.

One of the onlookers, too impatient to wait, jumped into a small boat and rowed out to meet the ship. The young first mate, noticing the man's approach, stepped forward. Tall, slim, and confident, with dark eyes and jet-black hair, the mate exuded calm authority despite his youth.

"Edmond Dantès," the man called from the boat, "what's going on? Why is the ship moving so slowly?"

"We've had a loss, M.* Morrel," Dantès replied, his voice heavy with sorrow. "Captain Leclère passed away during the voyage."

"And the cargo?" asked Morrel, the ship's owner, his business instincts kicking in.

"The cargo is safe and intact," Dantès assured him. "But losing Captain Leclère has been hard for all of us."

"How did it happen?" Morrel pressed.

"He died of a fever, sir, three days of agony before he passed. We buried him at sea, near El Giglio Island."

As they spoke, Dantès seamlessly directed the crew to bring the ship into the harbor. "Lower the topsails! Adjust the jib!" he called out. The crew moved with practiced precision, clearly respecting their young leader.

"And you?" Morrel asked. "Did you take command?"

"Yes, sir. It was my duty as first mate." Dantès paused, his tone growing somber. "Captain Leclère left specific orders before he died. He asked me to deliver a package to Marshal Bertrand on Elba."

"Elba?" Morrel said, his voice dropping to a whisper. "Did you meet anyone there?"

Dantès hesitated. "I did, sir. While delivering the package, I was introduced to the emperor himself."

"Napoleon?" Morrel's eyes widened. "You spoke with him?"

"He asked a few questions about the ship and our voyage," Dantès said matter-of-factly. "Nothing out of the ordinary. He mentioned knowing your family, sir. Said he served with a Morrel while stationed in Valence."

---

*"M." is shorthand for Monsieur, and used as we use "Mr."

Morrel's expression softened. "That would have been my uncle, Policar Morrel. He would be touched to know the emperor remembered him."

The conversation was interrupted as customs officers and health inspectors approached the ship. "Excuse me, sir," Dantès said, stepping away to oversee their arrival. "Prepare to drop anchor!" he shouted. The chain rattled as the anchor plunged into the water. As Dantès busied himself with his work, another man on board, Danglars, was walking up to Morrel.

Danglars, in his mid-twenties, had a calculating air about him. He also had a reputation for trying to frequently use flattery to gain approval of his superiors while alienating his peers.

"Dantès is quite the leader, isn't he?" Morrel said, watching the young mate in action.

Danglars smirked. "Perhaps too much so. He's ambitious, that one. Took command the moment the captain died and made an unnecessary stop at Elba. Cost us a day and a half."

"He was following orders," Morrel replied sharply. "Captain Leclère trusted him, and so do I."

Danglars' expression darkened, but he said nothing. Nearby, Dantès approached, his duties momentarily complete. "Is there anything else you need, sir?" he asked Morrel.

"No, Edmond," Morrel said warmly. "You've done well. Let's finish the customs paperwork, and then you can rest. You've earned it."

As Dantès walked away, Danglars' eyes followed him, his gaze full of jealousy and malice.

Chapter 2: Father and Son

We leave Danglars, who is struggling with hatred and trying to make the shipowner suspicious of his friend. Instead, let's follow Dantès, who, after walking down La Canebière, turned onto Rue de Noailles*, and entered a small house. He quickly climbed up four flights of dark stairs, holding the railing with one hand and pressing his heart with the other. He stopped in front of a half-open door and looked into the room, where he saw his father.

His father, unaware that the ship *Pharaon* had arrived, was standing on a chair, happily trimming the flowers and vines growing on the trellis by the window. Suddenly, he felt an arm around his waist, and he heard a familiar voice behind him: "Father, *dear father!*"

The old man cried out and turned around. When he saw his son, he fell into his arms, pale and trembling.

"What's wrong, my dear father? Are you sick?" Dantès asked, worried.

---

*"Rue de Noailles" translates to "Street of Noailles," which in everyday English would typically be phrased as "Noailles Street." This book uses "Rue de [blank]" throughout.

"No, no, my dear Edmond, my boy, my son! I didn't expect you, and the joy of seeing you so suddenly... Oh, I feel like I might faint," the old man said.

"Come on, cheer up, my dear father! It's really me. They say joy doesn't hurt, so I came without warning. Smile, please! Here I am back again, and we're going to be happy!"

"Yes, yes, my boy, we will be," the old man replied, "but how can we be happy? Will you never leave me again? Tell me, what good fortune has come your way?"

"God forgive me," said the young man, "for being happy at the misfortune of others, but Heaven knows, I didn't ask for this luck. It just happened, and I can't pretend to feel bad about it. The good Captain Leclère is dead, father, and with the help of M. Morrel, I will probably take his place. Do you understand, father? Just imagine—me, captain at twenty, with a hundred franc pay, and a share of the profits! Isn't that more than a poor sailor like me could ever have hoped for?"

"Yes, my dear boy," said the old man, "that's very fortunate."

"Well, when I get my first money, I'm going to buy you a small house with a garden where you can plant clematis, nasturtiums, and honeysuckle. But what's wrong, father? Aren't you feeling well?"

"It's nothing, nothing," said the old man. "It will pass soon." But as he said this, his strength failed, and he fell back.

"Come on, a glass of wine will make you feel better," Dantès said, quickly. "Where do you keep your wine?"

"No, no, don't worry. I don't need it," the old man answered.

"Yes, yes, father, tell me where it is," Dantès opened several cupboards.

"There's no wine," the old man said.

"What? No wine?" said Dantès, his face going pale as he looked at his father's gaunt face and the empty cupboards. "No wine? Have you been without money, father?"

"I don't need anything now that I have you," said the old man.

"But..." stammered Dantès, wiping sweat from his brow, "...but I gave you two hundred francs three months ago."

"Yes, yes, Edmond, that's true. But you forgot a little debt we owed to our neighbor, Caderousse. He reminded me that if I didn't pay, M. Morrel would pay for you. So, I paid him."

"But..." cried Dantès, "I only owed Caderousse one hundred and forty francs."

"Yes," said the old man.

"And you paid him from the two hundred francs I left you?"

The old man nodded.

"So, you've lived on sixty francs for three months?" Dantès muttered.

"You know how little I need." the old man said.

"God forgive me!" cried Edmond, falling to his knees before his father.

"What are you doing?"

"You've hurt me!" Dantès said, his voice full of emotion.

"Never mind, my boy. Now that I see you again, everything's fine. It's all over."

"Here I am," said the young man, "with a promising future and some money. Here, father!" he said, throwing some gold coins, five-franc pieces, and smaller change onto the table. The old man's face brightened.

"Who does this belong to?" he asked.

"To me, to you, to us! Take it! Buy some food, be happy, and tomorrow we'll have more."

"Easy, easy," said the old man, smiling. "Let me use the money slowly, or people might think I've been waiting for you to come back so I could buy things."

"Do as you like, but first, get yourself a servant. I won't leave you alone like this. I've got some fine coffee and tobacco in the hold, which you'll get tomorrow. But wait, someone's coming."

"It's Caderousse," the old man said. "He's heard you're back and no doubt he's come to congratulate you."

"Ah, lips that say one thing, but hearts that say another," murmured Edmond. "But never mind, he's a neighbor who helped us once, so he's welcome."

At that moment, the black-bearded head of Caderousse appeared at the door. He was a man about twenty-five or twenty-six and was holding a piece of cloth, as he was a tailor and had just returned from the market.

"Well, is it you, Edmond, back again?" he said, grinning broadly and speaking with a strong Marseillaise accent.

"Yes, as you see, neighbor Caderousse. I'm here and ready to help you any way I can." replied Dantès, trying to hide his coolness with forced civility.

"Thank you, thank you! But I'm fine, and sometimes there are others who need me." Caderousse said. Dantès made a questioning gesture. "I'm not talking about you, my boy. No! No! I lent you money, and you paid it back. We're square."

"We're never square with those who help us." Dantès replied. "When we don't owe them money, we owe them gratitude."

"What's the point of talking about it? What's done is done. Let's talk about your happy return, my boy. I went to the quay* just now to buy some cloth, and I ran into our friend Danglars.

'Are you really back in Marseilles?' I asked him—'Yes, for a little while.' he said.

'I thought you were in Smyrna.'—'I was, but I'm back now.'

'And where's the dear boy, Edmond?'—'With his father, I suppose.'

So, I came here as quickly as I could to congratulate you." Caderousse added.

"Good old Caderousse!" said the old man. "He's so fond of us."

"Yes, indeed," said Caderousse. "I love you both because honest people are rare. But it seems you've come back rich, my boy." he added, glancing at the gold and silver on the table.

Dantès noticed the greedy look in Caderousse's eyes. "Eh," he said casually, "this money isn't mine. I was just telling my father that I was worried he didn't have everything he needed while I was away, and to prove it, he emptied his purse. Come, father," he added, "put the money back in your box—unless Caderousse needs something, in which case, it's his."

"No, my boy, no," said Caderousse. "I'm not in need, thank God. I live within my means. Keep your money—keep it, I say! One never has too much. But I appreciate your offer as if I had taken it."

"It was given with good intentions," Dantès replied.

"Of course, of course. Well, I hear you're doing well with M. Morrel, eh? You sly dog!"

"M. Morrel has always been kind to me." Dantès said.

"Then you were wrong to refuse his invitation to dinner."

---

*Local market

"Did you refuse to dine with him?" asked the old man. "After he invited you?"

"Yes, father," Edmond smiled at his father's surprise at the honor shown to him.

"And why did you refuse?" asked the old man.

"So I could see you sooner, dear father," the young man answered. "I was eager to see you."

"But surely M. Morrel must have been upset?" said Caderousse. "And since you're about to be captain, it wasn't wise to offend the owner."

"I explained to him why I refused," Dantès replied. "I hope he understood."

"Yes, but to be a captain, you must flatter your superiors,"

"I hope to become captain without that," Dantès said.

"Good for you—good for you! Nothing will make your old friends happier. I know someone down by the Saint Nicolas citadel who'll be pleased to hear this."

"Mercédès?" asked the old man.

"Yes, father, and now that I know you're well and have everything you need, I'd like your permission to visit the Catalans."

"Go, my dear boy," said the old man. "And may Heaven bless you and your wife, as it has blessed me with my son!"

"His wife!" said Caderousse. "She's not his wife yet, is she?"

"No, but she will be soon, I think." said Dantès.

"Yes, yes," said Caderousse. "But you were right to return quickly, my boy."

"Why?" asked Dantès.

"Because Mercédès is a very beautiful girl, and pretty girls always have admirers. She has plenty, especially from the city."

"Really?" Dantès replied with a smile, though a hint of worry showed in his eyes.

"Yes, indeed," said Caderousse. "And great offers too. But you'll be captain, and who could refuse you then?"

"Meaning," Dantès asked, trying to hide his concern, "that if I weren't going to be captain?"

"Eh, eh!" said Caderousse, shaking his head.

"Come now," said Edmond, "I have a better opinion of women in general, and Mercédès in particular, and I'm sure that whether I become captain or not, she will remain loyal to me."

"Good for you," said Caderousse. "When you're about to marry, there's nothing like full trust. But go now, my boy. Go tell her everything."

"I will," said Dantès. After kissing his father and nodding at Caderousse, he left the room.

Caderousse stayed for a moment, then said a good-bye to Dantès father and left to reunite with Danglars, who was waiting for him at the corner of Rue de Senac.

"Well?" asked Danglars. "Did you see him?"

"I just left him," said Caderousse.

"Did he talk about becoming captain?"

"He mentioned it as if it were already decided."

"Really?" said Danglars. "He seems too eager."

"It seems M. Morrel has promised him the job."

"So he's very excited?"

"Yes, and actually a bit arrogant about it. He even offered me money, like he's some big shot."

"You refused?" asked Danglars.

"Of course! Though I could've taken it, since I loaned him his first money, but now he doesn't need help. He's about to be captain."

"Ha!" said Danglars. "He's not one yet."

"God willing, he won't be," said Caderousse. "If he becomes captain, we won't be able to talk to him."

"What do you mean?"

"Nothing. I was just thinking out loud. Is he still in love with the Catalane girl?"

"Head over heels," said Caderousse "But if I'm not mistaken, things might get complicated for the future captain."

"Explain." Danglars demanded.

"Why should I?"

"It's more important than you think. You don't like Dantès, do you?"

"I never liked those who rise too quickly."

"Then tell me what you know about the girl from Catalane."

"I don't know much for sure," Caderousse started to explain "but I've seen things that make me think that Dantès might find some trouble with the Catalans."

"What have you seen? Tell me!" Danglars demanded again.

"Every time I've seen Mercédès coming to town, she's seen with a tall, dark-eyed Catalan who's got a fierce look. She calls him her cousin."

"Really? And you think this cousin is making advances on her?"

"I can't be sure, but what else could a big guy of twenty-one mean with a pretty girl like her?"

"And Dantès went to the Catalans?"

"Yes, he left before I came downstairs."

"Let's go that way. We can stop at La Réserve and drink while we wait for news."

"Fine," said Caderousse, "but you'll pay for the wine."

"Of course," said Danglars, and they went quickly to the winery, ordered a bottle of wine, and waited.

Chapter 3: The Catalans

Beyond a weathered wall, a short walk from where the two friends sat, sipping wine and talking, lay a small village known as the Catalans. This isolated community had originated from a group that, centuries ago, left Spain for a coastal area on the outskirts of Marseille. No one knew exactly where they came from, or the language they spoke, but the village had been granted to them by the city as a place to settle. Over time, a small town had risen from nothing, with houses and people who maintained their old ways—living with traditions, customs, and a language that was theirs alone.

We'll walk through the only street in this small village, entering one of the homes, which was built from sun-bleached stone that had aged to a warm, earthy color. Inside, the walls were painted white, the rustic interior evoking the charm of an old Spanish inn. A young woman stood near the window, absentmindedly picking flowers from a bunch of wild heath that she had gathered earlier. Her movements were fluid and graceful, her dark hair cascading over her shoulders, and her eyes, deep and intense, had the softness of a gazelle's. She wore a loose dress that exposed her bare, sun-kissed arms, and her feet tapped restlessly against the floor.

Sitting nearby, at a small, worn-out table, was a young man—Fernand Mondego—his posture tense as he watched her, a mixture of frustration and longing in his expression. He was in his early twenties, tall, and muscular, but there was a vulnerability about him that showed through the hardness in his eyes.

"You see, Mercédès," Fernand began, his voice betraying his impatience, "it's Easter again. Do you think it's the right time for a wedding?"

"I've told you a hundred times, Fernand," Mercédès replied, without looking up from her flowers. "You should know by now. You can't keep asking me."

"Please, tell me again. Tell me, once and for all, that you reject me. I've spent ten years dreaming of marrying you, of making you my wife. But now, it feels like that dream is slipping away. Do my feelings mean nothing to you?"

Mercédès sighed, carefully placing the flowers down. "I've never encouraged you, Fernand. I've always said I love you like a brother. But don't ask for more, because my heart belongs to someone else. Isn't that clear?"

Fernand's face tightened. "Yes, it's clear. You've been honest with me, cruelly so. But you know the customs of the Catalans. We're supposed to marry within our community. It's not just tradition—it's a law."

Mercédès shook her head. "That's not a law, it's just a custom. And don't bring that up to me. You're in the military, Fernand. You're conscripted. You can be called to serve at any time. And what would you do with me, a poor orphan, with nothing to offer but my family's old house and some broken fishing nets? I've been living on charity for months now. I can't depend on you, Fernand."

"You could have a better life, Mercédès. I want you by my side. I'll work harder. I'll be a fisherman or find another job. We can build a life together," Fernand pleaded.

"Don't be naïve, Fernand. You're a soldier, not a fisherman. If you stay here, it's because there's no war. I can't promise you anything more than friendship. That's all I have to give," she replied, her voice firm but kind.

"But I'll be more, Mercédès. I'll be a sailor. I'll wear a sailor's uniform, a striped shirt and a navy jacket. Would that please you?"

Mercédès looked up, her eyes flashing. "What are you saying, Fernand? I don't understand."

"I mean," he said, his voice bitter, "that you're expecting someone else, someone like that—someone in a sailor's uniform. But he might not come back. The sea is treacherous, you know, not to mention plenty of temptations in port for a young sailor."

Mercédès's face paled. "Fernand," she said, her voice low with anger, "how dare you? You're accusing him of being unfaithful, of abandoning me. But if he doesn't return, I'll never stop loving him. I'll mourn him. And I won't let you drag his name through the mud. I can't bear to think of what you're suggesting."

She stood up, trembling with emotion. "I will wait for him, Fernand. And if he doesn't come back, I'll die waiting. I'll never love anyone else."

At that moment, a voice called from outside. "Mercédès!"

Her face lit up with joy, and she rushed to the door. "It's him!" she exclaimed, beaming. "It's Edmond! He hasn't forgotten me!"

Fernand recoiled, his face pale with anger and jealousy. As Edmond stepped into the doorway, Mercédès threw herself into his arms. They embraced, oblivious to the world around them.

"Mercédès, Edmond, what's going on here?" Fernand asked, his voice tight, his body stiff with rage.

"Fernand," Mercédès said, pulling away from Edmond to look at her cousin, "this is Edmond, the man I love. Do you remember him?"

Edmond smiled and reached out a hand to Fernand. "Of course, we've met before, I think."

Fernand, however, didn't take the offered hand. Instead, he stood frozen, unable to speak. Edmond dropped his hand to his side.

"Mercédès, is this a joke? Why does this man in your company not shake my hand in return? Do you have an enemy here in your company?" Edmond asked, looking at Fernand in confusion.

"An enemy?" Mercédès repeated. "There's no enemy here, Edmond. Fernand is my family. He's my cousin, my brother, and I trust him. He's not an enemy."

Fernand stood there, trembling with rage, but he said nothing. Finally, he turned and rushed out of the house, his fists clenched, his mind racing.

Outside, he encountered two men—Caderousse and Danglars—who were outside of the winery, sitting under a tree, flanked by chairs with a small table between them, enjoying a drink.

"Fernand, you're running like you're being chased!" Caderousse called out. "What's going on, man? Why the long face?"

"I'm fine," Fernand muttered, his voice hollow.

"We noticed. You're acting like a man whose love has been rejected," Caderousse joked, grinning widely.

Danglars leaned forward, his eyes sharp. "Is that so, Fernand? I thought you'd be the last one to lose out in love."

Fernand glanced between the two men, his mind swirling with thoughts of revenge, but he didn't speak. He sank into a chair and buried his head in his hands, overwhelmed.

Caderousse chuckled. "Well, we all have our problems, eh, Fernand? But let's drink to the wedding. Edmond Dantès is back, and Mercédès will marry him. I can't wait to see it."

Danglars sneered. "Yes, Edmond's back. And I wonder if he'll be the one to become captain of the *Pharaon*," he said, his voice dripping with sarcasm.

Fernand clenched his fists so tightly his nails dug into his palms. "I'll get my revenge," he thought, as the men around him continued to speak, oblivious to the storm brewing in his heart.

As the night went on, Fernand's hatred burned hotter. He would do whatever it took to get what he wanted. But Edmond, for now, was the man of the hour. And Fernand was just a shadow in the background, his dreams slipping further away with each passing moment.

Chapter 4: Conspiracy

Danglars watched Edmond and Mercédès walk together until they disappeared around the corner of Fort Saint Nicolas. As they left, he turned and noticed Fernand, pale and shaking, sitting in his chair. Caderousse, meanwhile, was drunkenly mumbling the words to a drinking song.

"Well, it seems this marriage isn't making everyone happy," Danglars said to Fernand.

"It's driving me insane," Fernand replied, his voice full of despair.

"Do you love Mercédès?" Danglars asked.

"I worship her!" Fernand said, his eyes burning with emotion.

"How long has this been going on?" Danglars probed.

"As long as I've known her... always," Fernand answered.

"And here you are, sitting around, moping, instead of doing something to change things," Danglars said with a shrug. "I didn't think your people were ones to just sit idly by."

"What do you want me to do?" Fernand asked helplessly.

"How would I know? It's not my problem," Danglars responded casually. "I'm not in love with Mercédès. But if I were you, I'd take action. You know what they say: 'Seek and you shall find.'"

"I already found something," Fernand muttered darkly.

"What's that?"

"I would kill the man," Fernand said, his voice cold, "but Mercédès told me that if anything happens to Edmond, she'll kill herself."

"Pfft! Women say things like that, but they never mean it," Danglars scoffed.

"You don't know her," Fernand snapped. "What she says, she'll do."

"Fool!" Danglars muttered under his breath. "Whether she kills herself or not doesn't matter, as long as Dantès doesn't become captain."

"Before Mercédès dies," Fernand replied with a voice full of determination, "I would die first."

"That's what I call love!" Caderousse interrupted, his words slurring as he giggled. "That's love, or I don't know what love is."

"Come on Fernand," Danglars said, "you seem like a decent guy, and I have to admit, I want to help you—however..."

"Yeah, how could you help this young man?" Caderousse chimed in out of curiosity, still half-drunk.

"Listen," Danglars replied, "you're three sheets to the wind. Finish off that bottle and you'll be completely gone. But then you can stop worrying about this conversation—it takes clear minds to plot, not foggy ones."

"I—drunk? Me?" Caderousse laughed, raising his glass. "I could drink four more bottles like this. They're no bigger than cologne bottles. More wine, waiter!"

He knocked his glass on the table.

"You were saying..." Fernand said urgently, eyes wide with hope.

Danglars sighed. "What was I saying? Oh, that's right. This drunkard has made me lose track of my thoughts."

"Drunk, if you like. So much the worse for those who fear wine," Caderousse grumbled, beginning to sing:

"All the bad guys drink water; This has been proven by the flood."

Danglars ignored him. "I was saying... there's no need to kill Dantès."

"I don't care," Fernand said bitterly. "But if you have a way of stopping his marriage to Mercédès without him dying... then tell me."

Caderousse, whose head had dropped onto the table, lifted it again, bleary-eyed, and mumbled, "Why kill Dantès? Who said anything about killing him? I won't have it! Dantès is my friend, and this morning he offered to share his money with me, just as I shared mine with him. He's a true friend."

"No one said anything about killing him, you idiot," Danglars said, irritated. "We're just having a little fun. Drink to his health, and shut up."

"Yes, yes, Dantès' health!" Caderousse slurred, raising his glass. "Here's to Dantès! Health—hurrah!"

Fernand looked at Danglars, impatient. "So what's the plan? How do we stop him from marrying her?"

"Have you any ideas yourself?" Danglars asked.

"No!" Fernand snapped. "That's why I'm asking you!"

Danglars leaned back, rolling his eyes. "This is why the French are superior to the Spaniards. Spaniards chew on things for hours, while the French—well, we come up with ideas."

"Then think of one already!" Fernand growled.

Danglars called to the waiter, "Pen, ink, and paper."

"Pen, ink, and paper!" Fernand repeated, his voice growing more desperate.

"Yes," Danglars said with a smirk. "A supercargo* needs his tools: pen, ink, and paper. Without those, I'm useless."

Fernand gestured impatiently. "Bring them here."

The waiter brought the requested items to the table.

Caderousse, half-conscious, placed his hand on the paper. "You know, a pen, ink, and paper can do more to kill someone than any sword or gun," he muttered, blinking slowly.

"He's not as drunk as he looks," Danglars observed. "Give him some more wine, Fernand."

Fernand obliged, filling Caderousse's glass again, who eagerly grabbed it and drank.

When Caderousse's head slumped again, Danglars pressed on, "Now, let's consider this. After Edmond's recent voyage—where he stopped at the Island of Elba and spoke with the exiled emperor—someone could denounce him to the king's prosecutor as a Bonapartist† agent."

"I'll denounce him!" Fernand said urgently.

"Hold on. But if you do, you'll have to sign your statement and face Dantès when he's arrested. I'll give you everything you need to support your claim. I know the facts. But Dantès won't stay in prison forever. And when he gets out, woe to the one who's responsible."

"Then let him come after me. I'll take him on."

"Mercédès will hate you for it. Even if you just scratch Dantès' skin, she'll detest you."

"True," Fernand said bitterly.

---

*A supercargo is a merchant ship officer who is responsible for the commercial aspects of a voyage.
†Someone working to get the exiled Napoleon back in power.

"No, no," Danglars continued, "it's better to do this carefully. We'll take this pen, dip it in ink, and write with the left hand, so the handwriting can't be recognized. We'll create a fake denunciation."

Danglars began to write, and soon handed the paper to Fernand, who read it aloud:

"To the honorable prosecutor, A friend of the throne and religion informs you that one Edmond Dantès, the first mate of the *Pharaon*, recently arrived from Smyrna, having stopped at Naples and Porto-Ferrajo, was entrusted by Murat* with a letter for the usurper Napoleon, and then by the usurper with a letter for the Bonapartist committee in Paris. Proof will be found upon arrest, either on him, his father, or in his cabin aboard the *Pharaon*."

"Well," Danglars said, leaning back, "now the plan makes sense. There's no danger to you. The situation will take care of itself."

"Very good," Caderousse muttered, still half-dazed. "But it's an ugly, filthy thing to do. I won't stand for Dantès being hurt."

Danglars sneered. "No one's hurting him. We're just having a bit of fun... just a joke."

He crumpled the paper and threw it into the corner. "See? No harm done."

Caderousse frowned, his last bit of clarity kicking in. "If you're joking, why not just throw it away? I don't like this."

"Fine, let's just drink some more," Danglars said, dismissing him. "We've said our piece."

"Not me," said Caderousse, trying to stand. "I've had enough, let's go. I'm going up the bell tower of the Accoules."

---

*Joachim-Napoléon Murat, who was the brother-in-law of Napoleon Bonaparte. Murat held many titles, including Marshal of France and Grand Admiral of France while Napoleon was in power.

"I'll take your bet," Danglars replied. "But tomorrow. Right now, we should head back to Marseille."

"Fine. Let's go," Caderousse agreed, still slightly unsteady on his feet.

As they walked, Danglars noticed Fernand picking up the crumpled paper from the ground. Fernand stuffed it into his pocket and rushed off toward Pillon.

"That's strange," Caderousse remarked. "He said he was going to the Catalans, but he's heading toward the city."

Danglars chuckled. "Oh, he's just taking the longer route. You can never trust wine to make you see straight."

"Well, wine makes you see a lot of things," Caderousse said. "But it's still treacherous."

Danglars smiled to himself. "Let's just let it play out. It's all in motion now."

Chapter 5: The Wedding Feast

The morning sun rose, bright and clear, casting a golden glow over the ocean, its shimmering waves reflecting the light in hues of ruby.

The feast was prepared on the second floor of La Réserve, the same venue with the charming arbor that you've already encountered. The room was spacious, filled with natural light from numerous windows, each adorned with golden letters bearing the name of a major French city. Below these windows, a wooden balcony stretched the length of the building. Though the event was scheduled for noon, by 11 a.m., the balcony was already crowded with eager guests. These included the favored crew members of the *Pharaon* and close friends of the groom, all dressed in their finest to honor the occasion.

Rumors circulated that the *Pharaon's* owners might attend the wedding feast, but no one truly believed it could be true.

However, Danglars, accompanied by Caderousse, confirmed the rumor. He had recently spoken with M. Morrel, who had personally assured him of his intention to attend the celebration.

Moments later, M. Morrel arrived, greeted by a chorus of cheers from the *Pharaon's* crew, who saw his presence as confirmation that the man who would marry today would soon be promoted to captain. As

26

Dantès was beloved by all aboard the ship, the crew couldn't hide their excitement at the prospect of his advancement.

With the arrival of M. Morrel, Danglars and Caderousse set off to find the groom and let him know the important guest had arrived. They hurried to relay the message, but before they could reach him, they spotted the bridal party approaching. It consisted of the engaged couple, a group of young girls accompanying the bride, and Dantès' father. Bringing up the rear was Fernand, his usual sinister smile in place.

Neither Mercédès nor Edmond noticed the strange look on Fernand's face. They were so caught up in their happiness that all they could feel was the warmth of the sun and the joy of each other's company.

Once the message was delivered and Edmond received their hearty handshake, Danglars and Caderousse took their places beside Fernand and old Dantès—who, to the surprise of everyone, garnered much attention.

The elder Dantès was dressed in a glistening watered silk suit, trimmed with polished steel buttons. His thin but sturdy legs were clad in richly embroidered English stockings, and from his three-cornered hat hung a long knot of white and blue ribbons. He walked with the aid of a carved cane, his face radiating happiness, almost like a dandy from the late 18th century, parading in the newly opened gardens of Paris.

Caderousse, who had reconciled with the Dantès family in hopes of partaking in the feast, walked alongside him, though his mind still held onto a vague recollection of the events from the previous night, as if the memory were a fading dream.

As Danglars approached Fernand, he shot him a look full of hidden meaning. Fernand, walking slowly behind the joyful couple, appeared pale and distracted. Occasionally, his face flushed, and his features contorted in discomfort. He often glanced nervously toward Marseilles, as though anticipating something significant.

Dantès, on the other hand, was simply dressed in the merchant sailor's uniform—a mix of military and civilian attire—and with his handsome face glowing with joy, he looked every bit the picture of a young, contented man.

Mercédès, with the beauty of a goddess, had bright eyes and full, coral lips. She moved with the grace of a dancer from Arles or Andalusia. Unlike other women, who might have hidden their blushes behind a veil or cast their lashes down to shield their eyes, she smiled openly, her expression saying, "If you are my friends, celebrate with me, for I am truly happy."

When the bridal party arrived at La Réserve, M. Morrel stepped down to meet them, followed by the soldiers and sailors assembled there. He had promised the crew that Dantès would be promoted to captain, and they greeted his arrival with excitement. As Dantès approached his patron, he gently linked his fiancée's arm with M. Morrel's, who then led her up the wooden steps to the banquet hall, the guests following behind. The structure creaked under their weight, groaning as the floorboards trembled.

"Father," said Mercédès to the elder Dantès they reached the center of the table, "sit at my right. On my left, I'll place the man who has always been like a brother to me," she said with a warm smile, gesturing toward Fernand. The words seemed to wound him deeply. His face turned pale, and his features tightened in distress.

Meanwhile, Dantès, seated at the opposite end of the table, had placed his most honored guests. M. Morrel sat to his right, Danglars to his left. At a signal from Edmond, the rest of the guests took their seats as they wished.

The meal began with a variety of delicious dishes: spicy Arlesian sausages, lobsters in bright red shells, large prawns, sea urchin with its spiky exterior, and the clovis, a delicacy from the South compared favorably to the finest oysters. The feast overflowed with seafood—considered the "fruits of the sea" by grateful fishermen.

"A strange silence indeed!" remarked the old father of the groom, raising a glass of bright, topaz-colored wine, which had just been placed in front of Mercédès. "Would anyone believe this room is filled with a merry party, eager to laugh and dance the day away?"

"Ah," sighed Caderousse, "one cannot always feel joy, even on the eve of a wedding."

"That's true," said Dantès. "I'm too happy for noise or amusement. Sometimes, happiness is as heavy as sorrow."

Danglars casually glanced at Fernand, whose nerves betrayed every change in his emotional state, and looked visibly anxious.

"What's wrong?" asked Danglars, bringing his attention back to Dantès. "Are you expecting something bad? You should be the happiest man alive right now."

"And that's exactly what worries me," Dantès replied. "Man wasn't meant to enjoy unbroken happiness. It's like a fairy tale palace, protected by dragons and monsters, waiting to be conquered before victory can be ours. I feel unworthy of this honor—the honor of being Mercédès' husband."

"Oh, come now!" said Caderousse, laughing. "You haven't earned that honor just yet. Try acting like a husband, and see how she reminds you that the time isn't here yet!"

Mercédès blushed, while Fernand, tense and agitated, wiped sweat from his brow.

"Well, never mind that, Caderousse. It's not worth arguing over. It's true that Mercédès isn't my wife yet, but," Dantès continued, pulling out his watch, "in an hour and a half, she will be."

A murmur of surprise swept around the table, except for old Dantès, whose smile revealed his perfectly white teeth. Mercédès beamed with delight, while Fernand's grip on his knife tightened.

"In an hour?" Danglars asked, pale with shock. "How so?"

"It's simple," Dantès replied. "Thanks to M. Morrel, to whom I owe everything, every obstacle has been cleared. We've received permission to bypass the usual waiting period. At half-past two, the Mayor of Marseilles will be waiting for us at city hall. Since it's already a quarter past one, I think I'm safe in saying that in an hour and a half, Mercédès will officially be Madame Dantès."

Fernand closed his eyes, a sharp pain coursing through his forehead. He gripped the table to steady himself, fighting to stay upright. Despite his efforts, he couldn't hold back a deep groan, but it was lost in the loud congratulations around him.

"Good heavens!" the old man exclaimed. "You waste no time, do you? Arrived just yesterday, married by three o'clock today! A sailor sure knows how to get things done quickly!"

"But," Danglars hesitated, "what about the formalities—the contract, the settlement?"

"The contract," Dantès replied with a laugh, "was easy. Mercédès has no fortune, I have none to give her. So, our papers were simple and inexpensive." This comment drew another round of applause.

"So, what we thought was just an engagement party turns out to be the wedding?" Danglars asked.

"No, no," Dantès corrected him. "I'm not going to leave you hanging like that. Tomorrow, I head to Paris. Four days for the journey there and back, a day to complete my task, I'll be back by the first of March. On the second, we'll have the real wedding celebration."

This announcement sent the guests into another fit of joy, with the elder Dantès, who had initially noted the silence at the start of the dinner, now struggling to find a moment of calm to toast the new couple amidst the raucous chatter.

Dantès, noticing the fondness in his father's gaze, gave him a grateful look, while Mercédès glanced at the clock and silently signaled Edmond.

The room was filled with the usual lively energy of such a gathering, where everyone, free from the constraints of social propriety, spoke over each other, each person content with sharing their own thoughts.

Fernand's paleness seemed to have spread to Danglars. As for Fernand himself, he appeared tortured, unable to sit still, and was among the first to leave the table. Seeking to avoid the jubilant chaos, he silently paced the far side of the room.

Caderousse approached Danglars, who had been observing the celebration a corner.

"Dantès is a good fellow," Caderousse said, his words softened by the wine and the warm treatment he had received from Dantès, making him forget any jealousy. "Seeing him with his beautiful wife, I think it would have been a shame to do him in like we planned yesterday."

"There was no harm intended," Danglars replied. "At first, I worried about what Fernand might do, but when I saw how well he controlled himself, even sitting right across from Dantès, I knew there was no risk."

Caderousse looked closely at Fernand, who had successfully been avoiding both him and Danglars—his face was ashen.

"Of course," Danglars added, "the sacrifice was significant, considering the bride's beauty. That future captain is a lucky man. I just wish I could take his place."

"Shall we go?" Mercédès's sweet voice cut through the noise. "It's already two o'clock, and we're expected in fifteen minutes."

"Of course, let's go!" Dantès eagerly replied, rising from the table.

His words were echoed by the others with loud cheers.

At that moment, Danglars, who had also been watching Fernand closely, saw him stagger, then slump back into a chair near an open window. At the same time, a faint sound from the stairs reached his ears, followed by the heavy tread of soldiers, their swords clinking. The room fell into a hush, and curiosity replaced the earlier chatter. Soon, an almost oppressive silence took over.

The sounds outside grew louder. Then three knocks came at the door. The guests exchanged worried glances.

"I demand admittance in the name of the law!" a voice called from outside. With no one stopping them, the door swung open, revealing a magistrate in full official attire, flanked by four soldiers and a corporal. Panic swept through the room.

"I must ask," M. Morrel said, addressing the magistrate, who was clearly someone he knew, "is there some mistake here?"

"If so," the magistrate replied, "I assure you we'll make it right. But I'm here with an order of arrest. Though I regret the necessity, I must do my duty. Who here is Edmond Dantès?"

All eyes turned to Dantès, who, despite the shock, stepped forward with calm dignity and said, "I am he. What do you want with me?"

"Edmond Dantès," the magistrate declared, "I arrest you in the name of the law!"

"Me?" Edmond asked, his face paling. "Why?"

"I'm not at liberty to explain," the magistrate said, "but you'll be informed during the preliminary examination."

M. Morrel recognized that further protest was futile. He knew the magistrate was just doing his job, and there would be no use pleading for mercy. But old Dantès, driven by fatherly love, rushed forward, pleading with such emotion that even the officer seemed moved.

"Don't worry, my friend," the officer said gently, "your son likely just overlooked a small formality related to his cargo. It's probably a simple mistake. He'll be released once he clears it up."

"What's going on?" Caderousse asked, looking at Danglars, who appeared as confused as everyone else.

"I don't know," Danglars said, "I'm just as bewildered as you. I can't make sense of this."

Caderousse looked for Fernand, but he was nowhere to be found.

The events of the previous night came rushing back to Caderousse. His memory, once foggy from the wine, now returned with sharp clarity.

"So, this is part of the trick you were planning?" Caderousse quietly asked Danglars. "If so, it's a terrible move, and it could backfire badly."

"Nonsense," Danglars replied. "I told you, I had nothing to do with it. And I definitely tore up that paper."

"No, you didn't," Caderousse retorted. "I saw you throw it aside."

"Shut up, idiot! What do you know? You were drunk!"

"Where's Fernand?" Caderousse asked.

"How should I know?" Danglars said. "He's probably gone to handle his own business. Don't worry about him. Let's focus on what we need to do for our friend."

Meanwhile, Dantès, having shaken hands with his friends, quietly submitted to the officer's arrest, telling them, "It's just a little misunderstanding. I'll clear it up quickly. I probably won't even need to go to prison."

"Oh, yes," Danglars said, now joining the group nearest Dantès, "just a misunderstanding. I'm sure it'll all be sorted out."

Dantès was escorted out, the magistrate and soldiers leading him down the stairs. A carriage was waiting outside, and he climbed in, followed by the officer and two soldiers. As it pulled away, Mercédès, from the balcony, cried out, "Goodbye, Edmond! We'll meet again soon!"

The words reached Dantès as a cry of heartbreak, and he leaned out of the coach, calling back, "Goodbye, Mercédès—we'll meet again soon!" Then, the carriage turned the corner, disappearing from sight.

"Wait here," M. Morrel called to the others. "I'll catch the next carriage to Marseilles, talk to the magistrate, and bring you news of how things are going."

"Of course!" the group responded, eager for updates.

As M. Morrel left, a heavy silence fell over the room. The old man and Mercédès, each lost in their own grief, eventually looked at each other and rushed into each other's arms.

Meanwhile, Fernand returned, his hands shaking as he poured himself a glass of water. He quickly drank it, then sat down near Mercédès, who had collapsed, half-fainting, from the emotional weight of the situation. Instinctively, he pulled back his chair.

"He's the cause of all this misery—I'm sure of it," Caderousse whispered to Danglars, never taking his eyes off Fernand.

"I don't think so," Danglars answered. "He's too stupid to be behind this. I just hope the consequences fall on whoever is truly responsible."

"And not those who helped," Caderousse added.

"Certainly not," Danglars said. "One can't be blamed for every unlucky turn of events."

"You can when it leads straight to someone's head," Caderousse murmured.

The discussions in the room continued over the next hour, while the guests waited for news, but the mystery of Dantès's arrest weighed heavily on everyone.

"What do you think of all this, Danglars?" one of the guests asked.

"Well," Danglars replied, "it's possible Dantès was caught with some contraband. It wouldn't surprise me."

"But how could you not have known, Danglars? You were the supercargo on board!"

"I only knew about the cargo I was told about," Danglars explained. "Cotton from Alexandria, some goods from Smyrna. I didn't need to know more, and I don't wish to discuss it further."

Old Dantès spoke up. "My son mentioned he had some tobacco and coffee for me."

"There it is," Danglars said. "The custom house probably found those hidden items."

Mercédès, however, ignored the explanation. Her grief overflowed into a violent fit of sobbing.

"Come now," the old man said gently. "Be comforted, child. There's still hope."

"*Hope?*" Danglars scoffed.

"Hope!" Mercédès echoed softly, her voice filled with despair.

"Good news!" cried one of the party in the balcony. "Here comes M. Morrel!"

Mercédès and old Dantès rushed to meet him, but M. Morrel immediately waved them away.

"I've learned that it's all a misunderstanding," M. Morrel said. "There's no contraband involved."

"But why? What happened?" Dantès's father asked.

"We don't know yet. But it seems they'll take him to the Château d'If."

"Prison?" the old man asked, barely able to understand the meaning of the word.

"Don't worry," M. Morrel continued. "I'm going to Paris, and I'll come back to explain the situation within the next few days. Edmond will be released. There's no cause for alarm."

The news did little to ease the pain for the Dantès family, and despite the reassurance, the weight of the situation seemed too much to bear.

Chapter 6: The Deputy Procureur du Roi

In one of the grand mansions built by Puget on Rue du Grand Cours, across from the Medusa Fountain, another wedding feast was underway. This celebration was strikingly different from the one hosted by Edmond Dantès. Instead of a lively mix of sailors and humble townsfolk, the attendees here were the elite of Marseilles society. Magistrates who had resigned during Napoleon's reign, officers who defected to the royalists, and young nobles raised to despise the man who had once ruled over half the world, and was now exiled to a tiny island with a mere six thousand subjects.

The conversations around the table reflected the divisive passions of the time. The magistrates discussed politics, the officers recounted their campaigns at Moscow and Leipzig, and the women debated Napoleon's divorce from Josephine. Their joy wasn't just over the fall of a man, but the collapse of the Napoleonic idea, which they believed promised a brighter political future for themselves.

The host of this exclusive gathering was Gérard de Villefort, a young man who had recently been appointed Deputy Procureur du Roi[*]. Villefort was ambitious, charming, and cunning, traits that had secured

---

[*]Assistant District Attorney would be the most closest translation. " Procureur" literally translates to "Prosecutor" in English, and is seen throughout this book.

37

his rapid ascent in the legal world. He was also deeply in love with Renée de Saint-Méran, his beautiful and well-connected fiancée. Their marriage symbolized a union of legal authority and aristocratic power, a perfect match for Villefort's career ambitions.

At that moment, a servant entered the room and whispered something in Villefort's ear. He immediately excused himself, citing urgent business, and left the table. When he returned a short while later, his face was lit with delight. Renée watched him lovingly, her gaze full of admiration. His handsome features, now animated and glowing, seemed almost designed to captivate her.

"And why were you called away just now?" asked Mademoiselle de Saint-Méran with concern.

"For a matter of grave importance—one that may well end at the executioner's block."

"How dreadful!" gasped Renée, her face turning pale.

"Can it be true?" asked several others, their curiosity piqued.

"It appears so," Villefort replied. "If the information I've received is accurate, a Bonapartist conspiracy has just been uncovered."

"Am I hearing this correctly?" exclaimed the marquise[†].

"I'll read you the letter of accusation," said Villefort. He unfolded the note and began:

"'The king's attorney is informed by a loyal subject, devoted to the throne and the religious institutions of France, that Edmond Dantès, first mate of the ship *Pharaon*, has recently arrived from Smyrna, with stops in Naples and Porto-Ferrajo. He is accused of carrying a letter from Murat to the usurper, as well as another letter from the usurper to the Bonapartist club in Paris. It is believed that the evidence can be

---

[†] "Marquise" is the feminine form of "Marquis", which is a noun that translates to "nobleman" or "title of nobility" in English. The rank was below that of duke, but above a count.

found on his person, at his father's home, or in his cabin aboard the *Pharaon*.'"

"But," Renée interjected, "this letter is anonymous. It's not even addressed to you—it's for the king's attorney."

"That's true," Villefort admitted. "But with the attorney away, his secretary opened the letter and, judging it important, sent for me. When I wasn't available, he took it upon himself to have the accused arrested."

"So this man is already in custody?" asked the marquise.

"Yes, but let's not call him guilty just yet," Renée said gently. "We can't pass judgment before the facts are proven."

"He's in custody," Villefort confirmed. "And if the evidence is found, I doubt he'll be free again—unless it's under the executioner's escort."

"And where is this poor man now?" Renée asked softly.

"At my house," Villefort replied.

"Then you mustn't delay," the marquise urged. "You are the king's servant, after all. Duty calls."

"Oh, Villefort!" Renée cried, clasping her hands and looking at him with pleading eyes. "Please, on this special day, show mercy."

Villefort moved to her side, leaned down, and said tenderly, "For you, my dear Renée, I'll show all the leniency I can. But if the charges are true, you'll have to allow me to do my duty—even if it means his execution."

Renée shuddered at the word "execution."

"Don't worry about her, Villefort," the marquise interjected briskly. "She'll grow out of such foolishness."

With that, Madame de Saint-Méran extended her hand, and Villefort kissed it respectfully. But as he did, he glanced at Renée, his eyes silently conveying, I'll imagine it's your hand I'm kissing, as it should have been.

"This is such a somber beginning to a betrothal," Renée murmured sadly.

"Really, child!" the marquise exclaimed, exasperated. "What does your sentimental nonsense have to do with matters of state?"

"Oh, mother," Renée whispered, her voice trembling.

"Madame," Villefort said, stepping in to defend her, "forgive this little traitor. To make up for her sentimentality, I'll ensure my actions are as strict as required." He cast an affectionate look at Renée, silently reassuring her: For you, my justice will always be tempered with mercy.

Renée returned his look with a grateful smile, and with his heart lightened by her approval, Villefort departed, feeling as though he carried paradise within him.

Chapter 7: The Examination

An hour later, Villefort arrived at his office. Though he had meticulously practiced his judicial expression, like an actor perfecting a role, his thoughts betrayed him. Despite his authority and success, he couldn't completely separate himself from the shadow of his father's Bonapartist past, a legacy that could jeopardize his own ambitions.

Standing at the threshold of his office, Villefort was met by the police commissary. The man's presence abruptly grounded Villefort from his reflections on personal happiness back to his duty. "I have read the letter you sent me in Marseille," Villefort said, masking his apprehension. "You were right to arrest this man. What have you uncovered about the conspiracy?"

"Not much, monsieur," replied the commissary. "All relevant documents have been sealed and placed on your desk."

Villefort nodded curtly and dismissed the man. Entering his office, he took a moment to compose himself before calling for Edmond Dantès. The young sailor entered, his anxiety barely hidden under a composed exterior. Villefort's sharp gaze studied him, noting his earnest expression and the honesty in his tone as he spoke.

"Edmond Dantès," Villefort began, his voice steady, "you stand accused of carrying a letter intended to aid Napoleon Bonaparte in reclaiming power. Do you understand the gravity of these charges?"

Dantès' eyes widened. "Monsieur, I swear I'm innocent. I was only fulfilling my captain's dying wish to deliver a letter. I had no knowledge of its contents."

Villefort leaned forward, feigning concern. "Do you have any idea who this letter was addressed to?"

"No, monsieur," Dantès replied earnestly. "I simply followed my captain's instructions."

Villefort opened the sealed letter and scanned its contents. His stomach churned as he recognized the recipient's name: Noirtier, his own father. For a fleeting moment, panic gripped him, but he quickly masked it, knowing that his next actions could determine his future.

"This is a serious matter, Dantès," Villefort said, his voice laced with false sympathy. "The evidence against you is compelling, but I will do my best to ensure a fair investigation."

"Thank you, monsieur," Dantès said, his voice trembling with a mixture of relief and fear.

Villefort dismissed the young man, instructing the guards to return him to his holding cell. Once alone, he paced the room, the incriminating letter still in his hand. He understood the stakes: destroying the letter would safeguard his career and his impending marriage into the influential Saint-Méran family, but it would also condemn an innocent man.

After a moment of hesitation, Villefort strode to the fireplace. With a determined expression, he tossed the letter into the flames, watching as it disintegrated into ash. "Forgive me, Dantès," he murmured. "But I have too much to lose."

Having made his decision, Villefort composed himself and prepared to draft his report. His mind was already strategizing the next steps to ensure his actions remained hidden.

His ambition had won, and Edmond Dantès' fate was sealed.

Chapter 8: The Château d'If

As Edmond Dantès walked through the antechamber, two gendarmes flanked him, one on each side. The commissary of police led the way, and a heavy door connecting the Palais de Justice to the prison opened before them. They entered a series of dim, labyrinthine corridors, their oppressive atmosphere enough to unsettle even the bravest soul.

The Palais de Justice and the prison were conjoined by necessity, the latter being a grim structure whose barred windows faced the clock tower of the Accoules. After numerous twists and turns, Dantès found himself standing before a door with an iron grille. The commissary struck the door three times with a mallet, each resounding blow echoing like a hammer against Dantès' heart. When the door swung open, the gendarmes gently but firmly urged him forward. Behind him, the door shut with a reverberating clang, sealing him within the prison's suffocating air.

The chamber he was shown to was modest but secure, with barred windows and a sturdy iron door. Its simple furnishings did little to allay Dantès' fears. Yet, Villefort's earlier assurances still echoed in his mind, offering a faint glimmer of hope.

The hours crawled by. Night fell, engulfing the room in darkness. Every creak and shuffle in the corridor made Dantès' heart leap. He rushed to the door at each sound, hopeful that freedom was near, but every time, silence followed. As despair began to take hold, the sound of approaching footsteps broke the stillness. A key turned in the lock, and the door creaked open, flooding the chamber with torchlight.

Four gendarmes entered, their weapons glinting in the flickering glow. Dantès, initially hopeful, hesitated at the sight of their imposing presence.

"Are you here for me?" he asked.

"Yes," one gendarme replied.

"On Villefort's orders?"

"I believe so."

The confirmation of this name calmed Dantès. He stepped forward and allowed the escort to surround him without resistance. Outside, a carriage awaited. Its windows were grated, and a police officer sat beside the coachman.

"Is this for me?" Dantès asked.

"It is," another gendarme confirmed.

Without protest, Dantès climbed inside and took a seat between two guards. The carriage jolted into motion, its heavy wheels clattering against the cobblestones. Through the grated windows, Dantès recognized familiar streets—Rue Caisserie, Rue Saint-Laurent, Rue Taramis—before the carriage veered towards the quay. In the distance, the lights of La Consigne shimmered faintly.

As the carriage rolled to a stop, Dantès tried to peer through the darkened grates to discern his location. The doors swung open, and the gendarmes motioned for him to step out. Before him loomed a shadowy silhouette: the Château d'If, its imposing walls standing as a monument to despair.

"The Château d'If?" Dantès asked, his voice tinged with disbelief. "Why are we here?"

The gendarmes offered no explanation as they led him toward the entrance. The reality of his situation began to settle like a weight on his chest. The Château d'If—a fortress-turned-prison—was notorious, a place where hope went to die.

Inside the gates, the guards handed Dantès over to the prison officials. The heavy wooden doors creaked shut behind him, leaving only the muffled sounds of waves crashing against the rocky island. As he was led deeper into the fortress, Dantès' mind raced, clinging desperately to Villefort's assurances of his eventual release.

But as he descended into the cold, dark depths of the Château d'If, that fragile hope began to falter. For the first time, Dantès truly felt the isolation and despair that would define his days to come.

Chapter 9: The Evening of the Betrothal

Villefort hurried back to Madame de Saint-Méran's home in the Place du Grand Cours. When he arrived, the guests he had left dining were now gathered in the salon*, enjoying coffee. Renée and the rest of the company were anxiously awaiting his return. His entrance was met with a flurry of curious exclamations.

"Well, Decapitator! Guardian of the State! Royalist! What's the news?" one guest teased.

"Are we on the brink of another Reign of Terror?" another asked.

"Has the Corsican ogre escaped again?" a third joked.

Villefort approached his future mother-in-law, the Marquise, bowing respectfully. "Madame, I must apologize for leaving so abruptly. Marquis," he added, turning to his future father-in-law, "may I request a private word?"

The Marquis noted the tension in Villefort's demeanor. "Ah, this is serious, then?" he asked, following him out of the room.

In the privacy of the library, Villefort did not waste time. "I must leave for Paris immediately. The matter is urgent."

The Marquis raised an eyebrow. "Is it that grave?"

---

*Living or sitting room

"It is," Villefort confirmed. He hesitated for a moment before continuing. "If I may, Marquis, do you have significant investments in government securities?"

"Why, yes," the Marquis replied. "Nearly my entire fortune."

Villefort's tone turned grave. "I strongly advise you to liquidate your holdings immediately. Events are unfolding that could have catastrophic consequences for the financial markets."

The Marquis blinked, surprised by the urgency. "You're certain?"

"Beyond any doubt," Villefort insisted. "Write to your broker tonight, instructing him to sell without delay."

The Marquis wasted no time, drafting a letter to his broker and handing it to Villefort for delivery. "I trust your judgment," he said, sealing the envelope.

Villefort slipped the letter into his pocket and exhaled. "There is one more favor I must ask, Marquis. I need a letter of introduction to someone in Paris who can help me gain an audience with the king."

The Marquis's expression turned cautious. "You're moving in powerful circles, Villefort. Are you sure this is wise?"

"I must act decisively," Villefort replied. "The security of the realm could depend on it."

The Marquis nodded and penned the second letter, handing it over without further question. "Be careful, my boy. These are dangerous times."

Villefort thanked him and returned to the salon, where Renée greeted him with a mix of relief and concern. "You're leaving again?" she asked, her voice trembling.

"Only for a few days," Villefort assured her. "Duty calls."

Renée's eyes filled with tears, but she nodded. "Be safe."

"I will," Villefort said, his voice softening. "For you."

As he departed, Renée watched him go, her heart heavy. Around her, the festivities continued, but for her, the evening felt overshadowed by uncertainty.

Chapter 10: The King's Closet at the Tuileries

As Villefort raced towards Paris, urgency and ambition spurred him on. His carriage clattered along the roads, bypassing villages and fields at breakneck speed. Meanwhile, the focus shifts to the Tuileries, the magnificent palace in Paris that had seen the rise and fall of empires.

Inside the Tuileries, Louis XVIII sat in his private study, a modest yet elegantly adorned room known for its arched window overlooking the gardens. This chamber, favored by both Napoleon and the king, bore witness to many pivotal moments in history. Louis XVIII, with a penchant for intellectual pursuits, was seated at a walnut desk he had brought from Hartwell, England. A volume of *Horace* lay open before him, annotated with philosophical musings from the king himself.

Opposite the king stood the Duke of Blacas, a man of aristocratic bearing and steadfast loyalty. His silvered hair and dignified demeanor added to his aura of wisdom.

"So, Duke," the king began, a faint smile playing on his lips. "What brings such a somber expression this morning? Has a vision of seven lean cows troubled your dreams?"

Blacas allowed himself a brief smile at the jest but quickly returned to his serious tone. "Your Majesty, I fear a storm is brewing in the south. Whispers of unrest grow louder by the day."

The king leaned back in his chair, seemingly unperturbed. "Ah, Blacas, always the harbinger of storms. Tell me, what do these whispers say?"

Blacas hesitated, then pressed on. "Sire, reports suggest that Bonapartist sentiments are gaining traction. The people's loyalty is uncertain."

Louis XVIII set down his quill and regarded the duke thoughtfully. "You think the south is unsettled? Perhaps. But I've heard no such discontent. Are you certain your sources are reliable?"

"With all due respect, sire," Blacas replied, "your Majesty's position allows for optimism. I urge you to send trusted men to verify the situation. Better to act now than to regret inaction later."

The king sighed and returned his attention to the book before him. "Very well, my cautious duke. We shall inquire further. Select a few reliable men and dispatch them to Provence and Languedoc. Their findings will, I trust, either confirm or dispel your concerns."

Blacas bowed deeply. "Thank you, sire. Your foresight is always exemplary."

As the duke departed to carry out his orders, the king's expression grew pensive. He turned to the window, his gaze drifting over the manicured gardens. The weight of leadership rested heavily on his shoulders, but Louis XVIII had faced many trials before. Whatever lay ahead, he was resolved to face it with the same measured calm that had defined his reign thus far.

Meanwhile, Villefort's carriage continued to speed through the countryside, drawing ever closer to the heart of power. Ambition burned within him, and as the city's skyline came into view, he steeled himself for the challenges ahead. The stakes were high, and Villefort's future hung in the balance.

Chapter 11: The Corsican Ogre

The atmosphere in the king's chamber was tense. Louis XVIII sat at his desk, visibly shaken. Before him stood the Minister of Police, Baron Dandré, pale and trembling. The king leaned back in his chair, his expression a mix of alarm and exasperation.

"What is it, Baron?" Louis demanded, his voice edged with impatience. "Why do you look as though you've seen a ghost? Does this have anything to do with the troubling news M. de Blacas shared with me?"

The baron hesitated, his lips trembling as he struggled to speak. Finally, with an air of despair, he blurted out, "Sire, the usurper has left Elba. He landed in France, near Antibes, on the first of March."

The king's face turned a shade paler. "The usurper? Bonaparte?" he asked, his voice rising. "And you've only learned this today? Two days after the fact? This is unacceptable!"

"It's true, sire," Dandré stammered. "I… I cannot forgive myself for the delay."

Louis XVIII pushed his chair back abruptly, rising to his feet. "In France," he muttered, pacing the room. "Bonaparte dares to set foot in my kingdom? And so close to Paris? How could this happen?"

The Duke of Blacas, standing nearby, stepped forward cautiously. "Sire, this is not the fault of Baron Dandré alone. We have all underestimated Bonaparte's cunning."

Louis turned sharply to Villefort, who had remained waiting and silent from his arrival until now. "What do you think, Monsieur de Villefort? Speak your mind."

Villefort bowed, choosing his words carefully. "Sire, it seems evident that Bonaparte has allies within France. His landing was no random act; it was calculated. We must act decisively to secure your throne."

The king's expression hardened. "Allies? Treachery? This cannot be tolerated. What would you suggest, Villefort?"

"Immediate action, sire," Villefort replied. "Troops must be mobilized, and loyal officials dispatched to key regions. The people need reassurance that their king is in control."

Louis nodded slowly, absorbing Villefort's counsel. "You're right. We must act swiftly. Dandré, summon my ministers and military advisors at once. This is a crisis that requires all our attention."

As Dandré hurried to carry out the king's orders, Villefort stepped forward. "Sire, if I may, I would like to personally oversee efforts in the south. My loyalty to the crown compels me to offer my services where they are most needed."

The king regarded Villefort with a mix of gratitude and approval. "You have shown great devotion, Monsieur de Villefort. Very well. Go to the south and ensure that order is maintained. Report to me directly on any developments."

Villefort bowed deeply. "Thank you, sire. I will not fail you."

As Villefort left the chamber, his heart raced. This was his moment—a chance to prove his loyalty and secure his future. But as he descended the grand staircase, a nagging thought crept into his mind. The situation was more volatile than even the king realized, and the road ahead was fraught with danger.

Chapter 12: Father and Son

The room was dimly lit, with only the soft glow of a solitary lamp casting long shadows on the walls. Gérard de Villefort paced anxiously, his mind racing. Suddenly, there was a knock at the door. Villefort's servant entered, announcing a visitor who refused to give his name. Before Villefort could react, the door swung open, revealing a tall, dark figure with sharp eyes and an air of command.

"Father!" Villefort exclaimed, recognizing M. Noirtier. His initial surprise gave way to an uneasy composure.

Noirtier stepped inside, his movements deliberate. He closed the door behind him, bolted it, and then turned to face his son. "Gérard," he began, his voice firm, "you don't seem pleased to see me."

Villefort forced a smile. "On the contrary, Father. Your visit is unexpected, but I'm always glad to see you."

"Unexpected?" Noirtier echoed, seating himself comfortably. "I might say the same about your presence in Paris. The last I heard, you were preparing for your wedding in Marseille. Yet here you are, without so much as a word of warning."

Villefort sat across from his father, leaning forward. "Father, I came to Paris because of urgent matters—matters that concern both of us."

Noirtier's sharp eyes narrowed. "I'm listening."

"Have you heard of the Bonapartist club in the Rue Saint-Jacques?" Villefort asked.

"I've heard whispers," Noirtier admitted, his tone measured.

Villefort lowered his voice. "Father, the king's spies are closing in on Bonapartist sympathizers. Your name has been mentioned. If they find evidence linking you to the club, it could mean exile—or worse."

Noirtier's lips curled into a faint smile. "And what evidence might they find, Gérard? Surely, you don't believe your own father would be so careless."

Villefort hesitated. "I don't know, but I couldn't take the risk. That's why I'm here—to warn you."

Noirtier leaned back, his gaze unflinching. "And what do you propose I do?"

"Leave Paris," Villefort urged. "Go somewhere safe until this blows over. I'll ensure your name is cleared."

Noirtier chuckled softly, a sound devoid of humor. "Gérard, you've always been a cautious man. But you forget—I've faced greater dangers than this. If the king's men wish to come for me, let them try. I've survived revolutions; I'll survive this."

Villefort's frustration bubbled to the surface. "Father, this isn't about bravery. It's about survival. If they arrest you, there's nothing I can do."

Noirtier's expression softened, but his resolve remained firm. "Gérard, I appreciate your concern, but I won't run. If the time comes, I'll face my accusers with dignity. You, on the other hand, must tread carefully. Your future depends on it."

Villefort stood, his fists clenched. "I can't just sit back and do nothing."

"Then don't," Noirtier said calmly. "Do what you must to protect yourself. But don't let fear dictate your actions. Remember who you are."

For a moment, the two men stared at each other, their shared determination evident. Finally, Villefort nodded. "I'll do what I can."

"Good," Noirtier replied, rising from his chair. He placed a hand on his son's shoulder. "Take care, Gérard. The path you've chosen is fraught with peril. But you're strong enough to navigate it."

As Noirtier departed, Villefort remained in the room, his mind racing. He knew his father's defiance was both his greatest strength and his greatest weakness. And as much as he admired it, he couldn't shake the feeling that they were both walking a tightrope over an abyss.

Chapter 13: The Hundred Days

M. Noirtier's prediction proved accurate. Events unfolded swiftly, just as he had foreseen. The history of Napoleon's return from Elba is well known—a feat unparalleled in its audacity and effect.

Louis XVIII's efforts to mount a resistance were feeble at best. The fragile monarchy he had pieced together crumbled under the weight of Napoleon's swift and decisive advance. At the mere sight of the emperor, the patchwork structure of ancient traditions and modern ideas collapsed like a house of cards.

Villefort's situation grew precarious. While the king's gratitude and the Legion of Honor had once seemed advantageous, these accolades now placed him under suspicion. Napoleon's restored regime viewed royalists with disdain, and Villefort's position as deputy procureur hung by a thread. Only the influence of his father, Noirtier, kept him in office. The man who had once been Villefort's greatest threat now became his unlikely protector.

Meanwhile, Edmond Dantès remained forgotten in his dungeon, oblivious to the seismic political shifts outside. The fall of Louis XVIII, followed by the subsequent collapse of Napoleon's empire, reached him only as distant, unintelligible echoes through the stone walls.

During Napoleon's brief resurgence, known as the Hundred Days, M. Morrel made two attempts to secure Dantès' release. Each time, Villefort placated him with empty promises. Following the Battle of Waterloo, Morrel abandoned his efforts, realizing that further action could jeopardize his own standing.

When Louis XVIII returned to the throne, Villefort seized the opportunity to distance himself from Marseille and its troubling associations. He petitioned for and obtained the position of King's Procureur in Toulouse. Soon after, he married Mademoiselle de Saint-Méran, whose father had risen even higher in the royal court.

Elsewhere, the fates of Dantès' betrayers unfolded. Danglars, haunted by the prospect of Dantès seeking vengeance, sought refuge in Madrid, where he initially faded into obscurity. Fernand, consumed by guilt and jealousy, joined the imperial army. Caderousse was, like Fernand, enrolled in the army, but, being married and eight years older, he was merely sent to the frontier. Old Dantès, who was only sustained by hope, lost all hope at Napoleon's downfall. Five months after he had been separated from his son, and almost at the hour of his arrest, he breathed his last in Mercédès' arms. M. Morrel paid the expenses of his funeral, and a few small debts the poor old man had contracted. Mercédès, left alone in Marseille, endured her grief with quiet dignity.

Through it all, Dantès languished in the darkness of his cell, abandoned by friend and foe alike. The young sailor, once so full of hope and ambition, became a phantom in the minds of those who had wronged him—a distant memory relegated to the shadows of their guilt and ambition.

Chapter 14: The Two Prisoners

A year had passed since the restoration of Louis XVIII, and the prisons remained a grim testament to the fragility of human freedom. One day, a rare visitor arrived at the Château d'If: the inspector-general of prisons. His visit brought an unusual stir to the otherwise silent fortress, and Edmond Dantès, confined in his isolated dungeon, noticed the faint echoes of activity. For a man accustomed to the silence of stone walls and dripping water, the sounds hinted at something extraordinary.

The inspector, escorted by the governor, moved methodically through the cells. The prisoners, desperate for reprieve, eagerly voiced their complaints about the abysmal food, the harsh conditions, and their endless longing for freedom. The inspector listened, though his face betrayed no sympathy. For many, the visit ended with little more than a perfunctory nod and a vague promise of review.

When asked if there were any particularly dangerous prisoners, the governor hesitated. "There is one," he said. "A man believed to be both dangerous and mad. He's been in solitary confinement for nearly a year."

The inspector's interest was piqued. "Let's see him," he ordered.

Descending the narrow, damp stairway into the bowels of the prison, the inspector remarked on the oppressive conditions. "He can survive a year down here?" he muttered.

"Just barely," the governor replied grimly. "This one is a former sailor, Edmond Dantès. He's accused of conspiring with Bonapartists. He's clever and resourceful, but solitary confinement has taken its toll."

The group reached Dantès' cell. At the sound of the key turning in the lock, Dantès sprang to his feet. The light from the torches revealed a gaunt figure with piercing eyes, his face etched with years of despair.

"Who are you?" the inspector asked.

"My name is Edmond Dantès," he replied. "I am an innocent man, imprisoned here because of a conspiracy against me."

The inspector glanced at the governor, who handed him a file. The sparse notes were damning yet vague: *Edmond Dantès. Bonapartist conspirator. Extremely dangerous.*

"Do you any evidence of these claims?" the inspector asked the governor, flipping through the papers.

"None beyond testimony from a letter intercepted on his person," the governor admitted.

Dantès seized the opportunity. "I was framed! Please, investigate further. I beg of you. My life has been stolen from me for a crime I did not commit."

The inspector frowned, conflicted. Turning to the governor, he said, "Add this case to my report. I will review it in Paris."

For the first time in years, Dantès felt a glimmer of hope. Yet, days turned into weeks, and no word came. The inspector's promise faded into a cruel memory, leaving Dantès to confront the unrelenting despair of his confinement.

With time, Dantès resolved not to let despair consume him. He marked the days on his cell wall and began to focus his thoughts. Somewhere in the endless solitude, he found strength—a will to survive and, perhaps, to seek justice for the wrongs done to him. The fire of revenge began to smolder within his heart.

Chapter 15: Number 34 and Number 27

The Château d'If, a bleak fortress in the sea, housed fifty prisoners in total. Each was stripped of their identity, referred to only by the number of their cell. Edmond Dantès, once full of hope and promise, was now merely Number 34.

In the darkness of his cell, Dantès endured the torment of despair. At first, his pride and the conviction of his innocence sustained him. But as days stretched into months, and months into years, doubt crept in. He questioned everything, even his own innocence, wondering if he had unknowingly committed some crime worthy of this punishment.

As the weight of isolation bore down, Dantès sought relief in small, desperate ways. He begged to be moved to another cell, reasoning that even a darker, more confined space might offer the distraction of change. He asked for books, writing materials, and fresh air. Each request was denied, but he continued to ask, if only to hear the sound of his own voice. At times, he spoke to his jailer, a man even more reserved in speech than his predecessor, just to break the silence.

In his former life, the thought of associating with thieves and murderers would have revolted him. Now, he longed for such company—a glimpse of another face, a voice, any reminder that he was not entirely alone. He even asked for a companion, mad or sane, but his request was deemed too risky and summarily rejected. Left with no one to turn to, Dantès finally turned to God.

The prayers his mother had taught him as a child returned, each word imbued with a new and profound meaning. In the past, these prayers had seemed little more than rote recitations. Now, they were his lifeline. He prayed aloud, no longer fearing the sound of his own voice. He poured out his soul, laying bare his anguish and pleading for forgiveness for trespasses, even as he struggled to forgive those who had wronged him.

Time dragged on, and Dantès' isolation deepened. He counted the days by scratching marks into the stone walls of his cell. Six years of monotony was finally interrupted by a faint sound: a scraping, almost imperceptible. Pressing his ear to the wall, he listened intently.

"Who is there?" he whispered.

A pause. Then, a reply: "Who speaks?"

"A human voice!" he exclaimed. For years, Edmond had only heard his jailer, a mere barrier of flesh enforcing his captivity.

"In Heaven's name," Edmond called, "speak again. Who are you?"

"Who are you?" the voice echoed.

"A prisoner," Edmond replied.

"Your name?"

"Edmond Dantès."

"How long have you been here?"

"Since February 28, 1815."

"And your crime?"

"I am innocent—accused of aiding the Emperor's return."

"The Emperor? He is no longer on the throne?"

"He abdicated in 1814. How long have you been here?"

"Since 1811," the voice replied.

Edmond shuddered. This man had endured four more years in prison than he had

"Tell me about your tunnel."

"It's hidden behind my bed, but I must have made a mistake," the voice admitted. "I miscalculated and ended up far from the outer wall. I hoped to escape into the sea and swim to safety, but now all is lost."

"Who are you?" Edmond pleaded.

"I am No. 27," the voice replied.

"I know you don't trust me," Edmond guessed. "But I swear I'll never betray you. Please don't abandon me!"

"How old are you?"

"Nineteen when I was arrested. I must be nearly twenty-six now."

"At that age, you cannot be a traitor. Very well. I will not leave you. Wait for my signal."

"You won't leave me? Together, we can escape—or at least talk of those we love."

"I have no one," the voice said.

"Then love me," Edmond replied. "If you're young, I'll be your friend. If you're older, I'll be your son. My father and a girl named Mercédès are all I have. I'll love you as I love them."

"Tomorrow," the voice said with sincerity.

Edmond, overjoyed, passed the day pacing, imagining freedom—or, at least, companionship. That night, he waited in vain for the voice to return.

The next morning, three knocks broke the silence.

"Is it you?" Edmond asked eagerly.

"Yes. Is your jailer gone?"

"For the day. We have twelve hours."

"Good. I can work."

Suddenly, the floor gave way as stones and earth crumbled beneath Edmond's hands. From the opening emerged a man, who climbed lightly into the cell.

Chapter 16: A Learned Italian

The man introduced himself as Abbé Faria, an Italian scholar, clergyman, and prisoner of the Château d'If. Despite his frail appearance, he exuded an air of wisdom and confidence. His hair was streaked with white, his eyes shone with intelligence, and his thin face bore the marks of years of hardship. He had dug the tunnel from his cell to Edmond's, a task that had taken him years of patient effort.

Overcome with gratitude and amazement, Edmond helped the abbé settle into his cell. Faria explained that he had hoped to dig his way to freedom but had miscalculated and ended up in Edmond's cell instead.

"Fate has its plans," Faria said with a faint smile. "Perhaps it intended for us to meet."

The two men quickly formed a bond. Faria's sharp mind and vast knowledge were a revelation to Edmond, who had been starved for human connection and intellectual stimulation. The abbé, for his part, was invigorated by Edmond's youth and curiosity.

"You have suffered greatly," Faria said one day. "But suffering can be a great teacher. Let me share what I know with you. Together, we can rise above this place."

Over the weeks that followed, Faria taught Edmond languages, mathematics, philosophy, and history. He shared stories of his travels and his studies, and even explained his theories about politics and human nature. Edmond, in turn, absorbed this knowledge like a sponge, his mind awakening to possibilities he had never imagined.

The Abbe also revealed a secret that made Edmond's heart race: he claimed to know the location of an immense treasure hidden on the island of Monte Cristo.

"I am no fool," Faria said. "I have verified its existence through many sources. If we ever escape, that treasure can change your destiny."

For the first time in years, Edmond dared to hope for a future beyond the prison walls. Together, he and Faria began to plan their escape, pooling their intelligence and resources. Edmond's despair transformed into determination, and his once-broken spirit began to heal under the guidance of his remarkable new friend.

In the dim light of their cells, amid the cold stone and iron bars, a spark of hope flickered—a testament to the resilience of the human spirit.

Chapter 17: The Abbé's Chamber

After having passed with tolerable ease through the subterranean passage, the two friends reached the further end of the corridor, into which the abbé's cell opened. Dantès, full of anticipation, scanned the room for the treasures his friend had hinted at but saw nothing out of the ordinary.

"You won't be disappointed," Faria reassured him. "We still have several hours—it's just after noon."

"How can you tell the time without a clock?" Dantès asked, puzzled.

Faria pointed to a ray of sunlight on the wall, intersecting a series of carefully traced lines. "The sun and Earth never fail in their paths. By observing the light's movement along these lines, I can calculate the hour more accurately than any watch."

Dantès marveled at the ingenuity. "Let me see your treasures," he urged eagerly.

Faria smiled and led him to an old fireplace. Using a chisel, he pried up a stone to reveal a hidden cavity containing several items wrapped in linen. He began unveiling his collection: a manuscript about the monarchy of Italy written on strips of cloth, tools crafted from scraps of metal, and even a makeshift lamp powered by fat he had rendered from prison food.

As Faria explained each creation, Dantès was awed by his friend's resourcefulness. However, Dantès couldn't help but wonder aloud, "What would you have achieved if you had been free?"

Faria's response was somber. "Perhaps nothing. Misfortune often sharpens the mind, like pressure igniting gunpowder. Captivity has forced me to focus."

Their conversation shifted to Dantès' story. At Faria's urging, he recounted his life up to his arrest and imprisonment. Faria listened intently, connecting the dots Dantès had overlooked. By the end of the tale, Faria was convinced of Danglars and Fernand's betrayal, aided by the drunken tailor Caderousse.

"Danglars wrote the letter accusing you," Faria concluded. "Fernand's jealousy of Mercédès gave him motive. And Villefort burned the letter to protect his father, Noirtier, the true recipient."

Dantès was stunned. "Villefort's father?!"

"Yes. The magistrate destroyed evidence to save his family's reputation. Your fate was sealed by ambition, greed, and fear."

Faria's insight filled Dantès with a burning desire for justice. Observing this, Faria remarked, "I fear I've awakened a dangerous passion in you—vengeance."

Dantès avoided the topic, insisting they focus on their escape plan. Together, they worked tirelessly to dig a tunnel beneath the prison gallery. They would loosen a stone, causing the guard to fall, and escape through a window using Faria's rope ladder.

After months of labor, their preparations were nearly complete when disaster struck. Faria, while carving a peg for their ladder, collapsed in agony. His face turned pale, his body convulsed, and he gasped, "It's happening again. Fetch the phial from my bed!"

Dantès helped him back to his cell and retrieved the small bottle containing a red liquid. Faria explained, "When I'm motionless, force my teeth open and pour eight drops down my throat. But be careful—if I cry out, the guards may catch us."

Faria's convulsions grew more violent, and Dantès muffled his cries with a blanket. After hours of torment, Faria fell still, cold, and rigid. Dantès forced open his jaw, administered the drops, and waited anxiously. Slowly, Faria stirred, his color returning.

"You saved me," Faria whispered. "The last attack I had, lasted but half an hour, and after it I was hungry, and got up without help; now I can move neither my right arm nor leg, and my head seems uncomfortable, which shows that there has been a suffusion of blood on the brain. The third attack will either carry me off, or leave me paralyzed for life."

Dantès reassured him. "You'll recover fully, and we'll escape together."

But Faria shook his head. "This attack was worse than the last, and I fear the next will be fatal."

"I'll carry you," Dantès insisted. "We'll escape together, or not at all."

"Thank you, Edmond," Faria said, deeply moved. "If I can't escape, I will at least die knowing I had a true friend."

With their escape plan delayed, Faria instructed Dantès to fill in the tunnel to avoid detection. "Tomorrow, I'll share something important with you," he promised.

Dantès worked late into the night, his loyalty to Faria unwavering. Whatever the future held, he resolved to face it by his friend's side.

Chapter 18: The Treasure

When Edmond Dantès returned to Abbé Faria's chamber the next morning, he found the old man seated, looking composed and calm. In the pale light streaming through the narrow window, Faria held a rolled-up piece of parchment in his only functional hand. The paper, aged and brittle, unrolled unevenly as if reluctant to reveal its secrets.

Faria smiled and gestured toward the parchment. "Look," he said simply.

Edmond took the document and examined it closely. The paper was partly burned and covered in faded Gothic script. "What is this?" he asked, unsure of its significance.

Faria's smile deepened. "This," he said, "is the key to a treasure. A treasure so immense it defies imagination. And from this day forward, my dear Edmond, half of it is yours."

Dantès staggered at the revelation, unsure how to respond. For years, he had avoided speaking of the treasure, fearing it might be a delusion of the abbé's fevered mind. Now, faced with this bold declaration, he struggled to reconcile his respect for Faria with his skepticism.

"Your treasure?" Edmond asked hesitantly.

"Yes," Faria replied. "Do not doubt me. This treasure exists. It is hidden on the Isle of Monte Cristo. I have never spoken of it before because I needed to trust the person I would share this secret with. And you, Edmond, have proven your worthiness."

Edmond's mind raced. The treasure sounded too fantastical to be real. Yet, Faria's eyes shone with conviction, and the story he told was detailed and logical. Faria explained how he had come to possess the parchment: it was a bequest from Cardinal Spada, the last member of a wealthy and powerful family whose fortune had vanished into legend.

Faria went on to recount how he had deciphered the cryptic map and its instructions. The treasure, he claimed, was hidden in a cave accessible only by following a series of precise directions. "I had hoped to recover it myself," he said, "but my imprisonment here has made that impossible. Now, it is up to you."

Overwhelmed, Edmond tried to process the implications. If the treasure were real, it could change his life entirely. But even as hope stirred within him, doubt lingered. What if it was all a fabrication?

Faria seemed to sense his unease. "Edmond," he said, "I understand your hesitation. But believe me, this treasure is as real as the walls that confine us. And it is not just wealth—it is freedom, justice, and the power to shape your destiny."

Edmond nodded, feeling a flicker of hope. For the first time since his imprisonment, the possibility of escape seemed within reach. More than that, the treasure represented a chance to reclaim his life and exact justice for the wrongs done to him.

Together, they spent hours studying the map and discussing how to recover the treasure. With each detail Faria shared, Edmond's doubts began to fade. By the end of the day, he was no longer merely a prisoner; he was a man with a purpose, driven by the promise of a brighter future.

Chapter 19: The Third Attack

The prison walls seemed even colder and more foreboding than usual as Edmond Dantès sat by the frail figure of Abbé Faria. The man who had become his mentor and friend was now reduced to a shadow of his former self, his brilliant mind still alive but trapped in a body that was failing with every passing day.

Over the past weeks, Faria had shared every detail of his grand secret: the location of an immense treasure hidden on the island of Monte Cristo. To Edmond, the treasure represented more than wealth; it was freedom, power, and the means to right the wrongs done to him. But as Faria's health deteriorated, their shared dreams of escape seemed to slip further out of reach.

One morning, as Edmond prepared their meager meal, Faria's voice, weaker than usual, interrupted his thoughts. "Edmond," he said, his tone heavy with both urgency and resignation, "I fear my time is drawing to a close. You must listen carefully."

Edmond immediately dropped what he was doing and rushed to Faria's side. The older man's pale face was drawn, but his eyes burned with determination. "Now," Faria began, "you know everything I know about the treasure. If we escape together, we share it. But if I do not survive, it is yours alone. Use it wisely, Edmond—for justice, not vengeance."

Edmond nodded, though the weight of Faria's words felt almost unbearable. "You're not going to die," he said firmly. "We will escape together, just as we planned."

Faria smiled faintly, but said nothing. Instead, he gestured weakly for Edmond to bring him the crude map they had sketched together. It showed the location of Monte Cristo, a desolate, rocky island off the coast of Corsica. Faria's instructions for recovering the treasure were as precise as ever, despite his evident fatigue.

Over the following days, Edmond worked tirelessly, tending to Faria while secretly continuing their escape preparations. But fate seemed to conspire against them. The guards, noticing their increased activity, began reinforcing the crumbling sections of the prison's outer walls, blocking off key areas that Edmond had been counting on for their plan.

One evening, as Edmond sat beside Faria, the older man suffered the third attack. This time, it was far worse than the previous ones. Edmond's heart pounded as he tried everything he could to help—massaging Faria's limbs, praying, even shouting for the guards, though he knew they would not come. When the attack subsided, Faria lay motionless, his breathing shallow but steady.

"Edmond," Faria whispered, his voice barely audible. "Do not lose hope. The treasure… it is your key to freedom. Promise me… you will not let this place break you."

Tears streaming down his face, Edmond swore he would honor Faria's wishes. The older man gave a faint nod and closed his eyes, as if finally at peace.

The next morning, Faria was gone. Edmond sat silently beside his friend's lifeless body, the weight of grief and despair pressing down on him. But even in his sorrow, a spark of determination flickered within him. Faria had given him the tools he needed—not just the knowledge of the treasure, but the hope and resilience to fight for his future.

Edmond solemnly made his way back through the tunnel and into his cell before the guards came to remove the body of his friend. His mind was already racing. He would escape this prison. He would find the treasure. And he would make the name Edmond Dantès mean something again.

That night, as the prison fell silent, Edmond began to put the final pieces of their plan into motion. Faria's death was a devastating loss, but it had also given Edmond the opportunity to slip away unnoticed. For the first time in years, he felt a glimmer of hope—a chance to reclaim his life and rewrite his destiny.

Chapter 20: The Cemetery of the Château d'If

The dim light filtering through the tiny cell window barely illuminated the somber scene in the abbé's chamber. On the bed lay a canvas sack, its contents unmistakable: the rigid form of Abbé Faria, now lifeless and still. Edmond Dantès stood motionless, the weight of the moment pressing down on him like the stone walls of the prison itself.

The man who had been his mentor, his confidant, and his link to hope was gone. Faria, with his boundless intellect and unyielding spirit, had been the lifeline that kept Edmond's soul afloat during the darkest years of his imprisonment. Now, that light had dimmed, leaving Edmond alone once more—alone to face the silence and the void.

He lowered himself onto the edge of the makeshift bed, his head in his hands. Memories of Faria's teachings flooded his mind—the stories of a hidden treasure on Monte Cristo, the lessons in science, history, and philosophy, and, most importantly, the quiet encouragement that had rekindled Edmond's will to live. But now, those memories felt distant, overshadowed by the cold reality of loss.

"Is it better this way?" Edmond wondered aloud, his voice barely above a whisper. "To leave this world—to escape this prison of flesh and stone?" The thought of following Faria into death lingered, dark and seductive. For a fleeting moment, Edmond considered giving in to despair,

77

to end his suffering and reunite with his only friend in whatever lay beyond.

But then, a spark of defiance ignited within him. Faria had not taught him to surrender; he had taught him to fight, to endure, to dream of freedom. Edmond's grief gave way to determination. "No," he muttered, his voice firm. "I will not let this be the end. I will live. I will escape. And I will make them pay."

His gaze fell on the canvas sack. An idea began to form, one so audacious it sent a shiver down his spine. What if Edmond took Faria's place? The plan was both brilliant and perilous, but it was his only chance.

Dantès' plan was clear and calculated. Here's what he intended: if the grave-diggers realized they were carrying a living body instead of a corpse, he wouldn't give them a chance to figure it out. With one swift slash of his knife, he planned to slice open the sack from top to bottom. In the confusion that followed, he would seize the moment to escape. And if they tried to stop him, his knife would ensure they regretted it.

If they carried him to the cemetery and placed him in a grave, he would let them bury him. Once the grave-diggers turned their backs—especially under the cover of night—he intended to claw his way through the loose soil to freedom. He hoped the weight of the earth wouldn't be too much for him to push through.

But if he was caught in the act, or if the soil pressed too heavily upon him, suffocation would follow. And in that case? So be it. It would mean the end of his suffering.

He worked quickly, his hands steady despite the adrenaline coursing through his veins. He carefully moved Faria's body into the secret tunnel they had dug together, covering it with loose stones and debris. Then, he climbed into the sack himself, pulling the rough canvas over his body and tying it shut from the inside. The damp, suffocating enclosure was a grim reminder of the stakes, but Edmond's resolve did not waver.

Hours passed before he heard footsteps approaching. The sound of voices echoed in the stone corridor, followed by the metallic clink of keys. The cell door creaked open, and rough hands lifted the sack. Edmond remained perfectly still, his heart pounding in his ears. The guards carried him through the winding passages of the prison, their gruff conversation the only sound breaking the oppressive silence. The crashing of waves against the rocks that supported the prison grew louder, echoing clearly in Dantès' ears as they proceeded.

"Rough weather tonight," one of the men carrying him remarked. "Not exactly the best evening for a swim."

"True," the other replied with a cruel chuckle. "The abbé's likely to get soaked." Their laughter, harsh and mocking, rang out in the night.

Dantès didn't understand their grim humor, but an icy dread crept over him, making his hair stand on end.

"At last, we're here," one of them announced.

"A bit further," the other corrected. "Remember the last one? He got caught on the rocks, and the governor chewed us out the next day for being careless."

They climbed five or six more steps. Suddenly, Dantès felt them grab him—one by the head, the other by the legs—and begin to swing his body back and forth.

"One," one of them intoned, followed by, "Two... Three!"

Before he could react, Dantès was hurled into the air, like a bird struck mid-flight, plummeting downward with terrifying speed. The weight tied to him hastened his descent, but to Dantès, the fall felt endless, stretching into eternity.

Finally, with a bone-chilling splash, he plunged into the frigid water. The icy waves swallowed his shriek as soon as it escaped his lips, the sound silenced by the crushing embrace of the sea.

Dantès had been thrown into the ocean, dragged downward into its cold, dark depths by a thirty-six-pound weight secured to his feet.

The sea is the cemetery of the Château d'If.

Chapter 21: The Island of Tiboulen

The icy shock of the sea gripped Edmond Dantès as he plunged beneath the waves, the weight tied to his feet dragging him deeper into the abyss. Darkness closed around him, but his instincts took over. His right hand, clutching the knife he had concealed, slashed at the sack's fabric. He freed one arm, then the other, and with a desperate twist, severed the ropes binding his legs. The lead weight sank into the depths as Edmond surged upward, his lungs burning for air.

Breaking the surface, he gasped deeply, the salt spray stinging his face. Above him, a stormy sky churned with clouds, the faint light of a few stars slipping through the darkness. Behind him loomed the shadow of the Château d'If, its jagged silhouette like a specter reaching out to reclaim him. On its highest rock, the glow of a torch illuminated two figures. The guards were watching.

Fear jolted Edmond into action. He dived beneath the surface again, swimming in the direction of freedom. His movements were powerful but deliberate, honed by years of practice in the Marseilles harbor. When he surfaced again, he was fifty paces from the fortress. The torchlight had vanished. Whether by luck or by fate, he was invisible to his captors.

Edmond paused to get his bearings. The nearest islands, Ratonneau and Pomègue, were inhabited—too risky. Tiboulen and Lemaire, desolate and unguarded, lay farther out but offered a safer refuge. He oriented himself by the light of the Planier lighthouse, shining like a distant star. By keeping the light to his right and swimming left, he could reach Tiboulen.

Faria's voice echoed in his mind: "Dantès, never allow your body or spirit to weaken. One day, your strength will mean the difference between life and death." The old man's words spurred him on, even as the waves grew higher and the night colder.

The journey was grueling. The sea's relentless rhythm battered Edmond, and exhaustion tugged at his limbs. But he refused to yield. Every stroke of his arms and kick of his legs pushed him closer to the freedom he had dreamed of for fourteen years. His thoughts oscillated between the faces of those who had betrayed him and the image of Mercédès, the woman he had loved and lost.

Hours seemed to stretch into eternity before Edmond spotted the faint outline of Tiboulen. The island's rocky shore loomed ahead, jagged and unwelcoming, but it was salvation. With a final burst of energy, he swam toward it, his hands scraping against the sharp rocks as he pulled himself onto land. Waves crashed around him as he collapsed onto the cold, wet stone, gasping for air.

For a long while, Edmond lay motionless, the reality of his escape sinking in. He was free. The prison that had been his hell for so many years was now a distant shadow on the horizon. But freedom was only the beginning. Ahead lay the task of reclaiming his life and seeking justice against those who had stolen it.

As dawn broke, the first light of day revealed the barren beauty of Tiboulen. Edmond surveyed his surroundings, his body battered but his spirit unbroken. He knew that the journey ahead would be fraught with danger, but he welcomed it. For the first time in years, he was the master of his own fate.

Edmond Dantès, the man who had been wronged, was gone. In his place stood someone new, someone stronger. The storm-tossed waters of the Mediterranean had not only given him freedom but also the resolve to claim what was rightfully his.

Chapter 22: The Smugglers

Edmond Dantès flagged down a passing ship and played the role of a shipwrecked sailor expertly. He had spent only a day aboard *La Jeune Amélie* when he began to understand the type of men he was now traveling with. The captain, a shrewd and cautious man, spoke an array of languages common to the Mediterranean, from Arabic to Provençal. This ability allowed him to communicate with a wide variety of people: sailors, fishermen, and those shadowy figures who roamed seaports without identity or official occupation. It quickly became clear to Dantès that he was among smugglers.

The sharp scent of salt hung in the air as the smuggler's vessel cut through the azure waves of the Mediterranean. Edmond Dantès stood at the stern, watching the coastline of France fade into the horizon, replaced by the vast expanse of open sea. Around him, the crew moved with practiced efficiency, their rough voices mixing with the creak of the ship's timbers and the snap of sails in the wind.

These were men of the sea, hardened by a life of risk and reward, and Edmond had quickly discerned their trade. The furtive glances, the coded phrases, and the carefully concealed cargo left no doubt. These were smugglers, and he was now one of them.

Their leader and captain, a wiry man named Jacopo, was as shrewd as he was cautious. Initially, the captain was wary of Edmond, suspecting he might be an undercover customs agent. However, Edmond's expertise in navigating the vessel won the captain over. When the distant boom of cannonfire marked Edmond's escape from the Château d'If, the captain viewed him with a mix of curiosity and awe, assuming his arrival heralded some grand destiny. Edmond, for his part, remained mysterious, offering no more than necessary about his past while recounting enough details of Naples and Malta to convince the crew of his nautical experience.

One evening, as the sun dipped below the horizon and bathed the sea in hues of orange and gold, Jacopo approached Edmond. "You handle yourself well," he said, his tone more curious than complimentary. "Not your first time at sea, I take it?"

"No," Edmond replied simply, his eyes fixed on the distant horizon.

Jacopo nodded, seemingly satisfied, and walked away. The exchange was brief, but it marked a turning point. Edmond was no longer an outsider; he was part of the crew.

Their journey took them to a secluded cove where the smugglers planned to unload their cargo. The rocky shoreline rose sharply from the water, its jagged cliffs providing the perfect cover. The men worked quickly and silently, their movements choreographed by years of experience.

Edmond, eager to prove his worth, threw himself into the work. He hauled crates and barrels with the rest of the crew, his strength and determination earning him approving nods. Yet, even as he labored, his mind remained sharp, observing every detail of their operations. He noted the signals they used to communicate, the hidden compartments in the ship, and the routes they favored. Knowledge was power, and Edmond intended to gather as much as he could.

When the last of the cargo was ashore, the men gathered around a fire to share a meal. The mood was light, the tension of the day's work giving way to laughter and camaraderie. Jacopo passed Edmond a flask of rum, his gesture one of acceptance. Edmond took a sip, the fiery liquid warming him against the cool night air.

As the others drifted off to sleep, Edmond remained by the fire, staring into the flames. This life of shadows and secrecy was far removed from the one he had known, yet it offered him something he desperately needed: freedom. Here, among these outlaws, he could rebuild himself, piece by piece.

The next morning, as the smugglers prepared to set sail, Jacopo approached Edmond once more. "We're heading south," he said. "There's a stretch near Monte Cristo where we can lay low for a bit. Ever heard of it?"

Edmond's heart quickened at the mention of the island. He nodded. "I've heard of it."

Jacopo clapped him on the shoulder. "Good. It's as good a place as any to disappear for a while."

As the ship set its course, Edmond stood at the bow, the wind whipping through his hair. The island of Monte Cristo lay ahead, its rocky shores promising more than refuge. It was the gateway to a future Edmond had only begun to imagine.

Chapter 23: The Island of Monte Cristo

By a stroke of fortune, Edmond Dantès had finally secured an opportunity to land on Monte Cristo without arousing suspicion. One more night, and he would be on his way. That night, however, proved restless. Edmond's mind swirled with visions—some hopeful, others haunting. Whenever he closed his eyes, he saw Cardinal Spada's letter burning in fiery script on a cavern wall. In fleeting moments of sleep, he dreamt of marvelous grottos filled with treasures beyond imagination: floors of emeralds, ruby-studded walls, and ceilings glittering with diamond-like stalactites. In these dreams, pearls dripped like water, and he eagerly filled his pockets with the radiant gems. Yet, upon returning to the surface, the treasures would transform into mere pebbles.

When morning came, the clarity of daylight tempered Edmond's feverish imagination. He now focused on forming a practical plan. By nightfall, preparations for departure were underway. Edmond, having earned the trust and respect of the crew through his sharp instructions and steady leadership, was treated more like a commander than a mere sailor. Even the old captain, recognizing Edmond's natural superiority, saw him as a potential successor.

At ten past seven, the ship doubled the lighthouse as its beacon was lit. The sea was calm, and under a sky studded with stars, the crew rested at Edmond's command. The solitude of the night invigorated Edmond. Floating on the vast, silent sea, he felt both isolated and alive, his thoughts illuminated by dreams of the treasure that awaited him.

The next day, Monte Cristo's jagged silhouette came into view, its rocky peaks glowing in the sunset. Edmond watched intently, his face a canvas of emotions—hope, anxiety, and determination. By nightfall, they anchored at the island. Despite his usual composure, Edmond couldn't restrain his excitement. He was the first to leap ashore, his heart pounding as he touched the ground. He resisted the impulse to kiss the earth like a pilgrim reaching a holy site.

The island was familiar to the crew, one of their regular smuggling haunts. For Edmond, however, this was uncharted territory. He had sailed past it during his merchant voyages but never landed. That night, while assisting with the unloading of cargo, Edmond felt torn. He longed to reveal the secret burning within him, but he knew any mention of treasure would jeopardize his plans. His solemn demeanor, a remnant of his years in prison, masked his restlessness and deterred suspicion.

The next morning, armed with a shotgun and supplies, Edmond told the crew he intended to hunt wild goats. Jacopo, a loyal crewmember, insisted on accompanying him. Edmond reluctantly agreed, wary of drawing attention. After they had ventured a short distance, Edmond killed a kid and urged Jacopo to return with it to the others, instructing him to prepare the meal and signal him when it was ready.

Freed from observation, Edmond continued deeper into the island, scanning the terrain for signs of human activity. He found faint marks etched into the rocks, hidden beneath layers of moss and tufts of myrtle. The sight filled him with renewed hope. These markings, he reasoned, must have been left by Cardinal Spada to guide his heirs to the treasure. Yet doubts crept in—could others have discovered and looted the treasure?

As he followed the trail, the marks abruptly ended at a massive, round boulder. Edmond concluded this was the beginning, not the end, of the path.

He returned to the crew in time for the signal. Once he was within eyesight, he carefully staged a dramatic fall. The crew, led by Jacopo, rushed to his aid, finding him sprawled and bloodied.

Feigning severe injuries, Edmond refused to be moved, claiming the slightest jostle caused unbearable pain. The captain, torn between loyalty and obligation, considered postponing their departure. Edmond, however, insisted they leave, requesting only basic supplies: a gun, powder, biscuits, and a pickaxe.

"Go, go!" exclaimed Dantès.

"We shall be absent at least a week," said the captain, "and then we must run out of our course to come here and take you up again."

"Why," said Dantès, "if in two or three days you hail any fishing-boat, desire them to come here to me. I will pay twenty-five piastres for my passage back to Leghorn. If you do not come across one, return for me." The captain shook his head.

Jacopo offered to stay behind, sacrificing his share of the venture to care for Edmond. Touched but resolute, Edmond declined. After much hesitation, the crew sailed away, leaving Edmond alone. From a high rock, he waved a final farewell before watching their ship vanish into the horizon.

Once the ship was out of sight, Edmond rose, agile and determined, his injuries forgotten. Grabbing his gun and pickaxe, he returned to the boulder marked by the trail. Gazing at it, he murmured, "Now, Open Sesame!"

Chapter 24: The Secret Cave

The sun was nearly at its peak, its scorching rays beating down on the rocks, which seemed to radiate the heat like living things. Grasshoppers chirped incessantly from their hidden spots in the bushes, creating a dull, monotonous background hum. The myrtle and olive trees swayed gently in the breeze, their leaves rustling softly. With each step Edmond took, brilliant green lizards, shimmering like jewels, scurried away into the shadows. In the distance, he caught glimpses of wild goats leaping from rock to rock, graceful and sure-footed. Despite the signs of life around him, Edmond felt utterly alone, as though he were the last man on earth, guided only by fate.

A creeping unease prickled at the edge of his mind—a strange dread brought on by the oppressive daylight, as if the open sky itself might expose him to prying eyes. The feeling was so overwhelming that, just as he prepared to begin his work, he paused. Setting down his pickaxe, he grabbed his gun and climbed to the highest point on the island. From this vantage, he scanned his surroundings, his gaze sweeping over land and sea.

Edmond's eyes roamed across the distant landscapes. He saw Corsica, its clustered houses visible even from here. To the south lay

Sardinia's rugged coastline, and farther still, the Island of Elba, its storied past stirring his thoughts. Beyond these, the faint, practiced eye of a sailor could just make out the Genoese coastline and the bustling port city of Leghorn. Yet Edmond's focus was not on these landmarks. His eyes were drawn instead to two ships: a brigantine*, now vanishing into the Strait of Bonifacio, and a tartan vessel, sailing in the opposite direction, rounding the Corsican coast.

The sight of the ships reassured him. Feeling a renewed sense of purpose, Edmond descended cautiously, his steps deliberate on the rocky incline. The island's solitude enveloped him once more as he traced the markings carved into the rocks—a trail that guided him toward a small, concealed cove. Hidden like a secret sanctuary, the inlet's narrow mouth widened into a deeper basin, large enough to shelter a small vessel while keeping it perfectly out of view.

Edmond's mind raced, piecing together the possibilities. The clues from Abbé Faria's map seemed to fit perfectly. He could picture Cardinal Spada guiding his ship into this secluded harbor, following the marks etched into the rocks to this very point, where the treasure was said to rest. But one question troubled Edmond: how had the massive circular stone, weighing several tons, been positioned over the site without the help of many hands?

The answer struck him like a lightning bolt. "Not raised," he whispered to himself. "Lowered." Excited by the revelation, he jumped down to inspect the rock's base. His sharp eyes quickly discerned a sloped groove, a channel carved into the earth where the stone had been rolled into position. It rested there, stabilized by a wedge of stone and covered with layers of dirt and foliage, which had grown thick with time. Moss clung to the surface, and myrtle bushes had rooted themselves firmly in the soil, creating the illusion that the rock had always been there.

---

*A two-masted sailing vessel

Edmond worked swiftly, clearing the dirt around the base of the rock with his hands. The task was arduous, but his determination never faltered. At last, the wedge of stone that secured the massive boulder was exposed. Edmond gripped his pickaxe and struck at the barrier, loosening it bit by bit. After ten minutes of relentless effort, the wedge shifted, revealing a gap just large enough for him to insert his arm.

But the rock remained immovable, its weight far beyond Edmond's strength to lift alone. He stepped back, his gaze falling on a sturdy olive tree nearby. With practiced efficiency, he cut a thick branch, stripped it of its leaves, and fashioned it into a lever. He wedged it into the opening, straining with every ounce of his strength, but even the makeshift tool couldn't budge the massive stone. Frustrated but undeterred, Edmond realized he needed another solution.

His eyes fell on the horn of gunpowder Jacopo had left him. A wry smile played across his lips. "If I can't move it by force, I'll move it by fire," he muttered. Using his pickaxe, he dug a narrow trench beneath the stone, creating a small mine. Carefully, he packed the channel with powder and fashioned a fuse from his handkerchief, which he had soaked in saltpeter. He lit the makeshift fuse and retreated to a safe distance.

The explosion shattered the stillness of the island. A deafening roar echoed off the rocks, and when the dust settled, the massive stone lay dislodged. Pieces of the smaller rock beneath it had been blasted apart, and insects and a large snake fled from the disturbed crevice, disappearing into the shadows.

Edmond approached cautiously, his heart pounding. The once-imposing boulder now tilted precariously toward the sea. Gripping his makeshift lever, he placed it into a crevice and strained against the rock. Already weakened by the blast, the stone teetered on its base. With a final, monumental effort, Edmond pushed it free. The boulder tumbled down the slope, crashing and splintering as it went, until it disappeared into the ocean below.

Where the stone had once rested, a flat, square flagstone now lay exposed, an iron ring set into its center.

Edmond's breath caught as he stared at the iron ring embedded in the flagstone. A surge of triumph coursed through him. Every detail, every clue, had led him to this exact moment. He knelt down and ran his fingers over the cool metal, feeling the weight of centuries in its touch. His heart pounded as he slipped his lever through the ring and pulled with all his strength. At first, the flagstone resisted, but with a groan, it shifted, revealing a dark, narrow staircase descending into the earth.

For a moment, Edmond froze, peering into the shadowy depths. A sudden wave of hesitation swept over him. "What if this is all for nothing?" he whispered. He steadied himself. "No," he muttered. "I've come too far to stop now."

Summoning his courage, Edmond gripped the lever tighter and descended the steps. The air grew warmer as he went deeper, carrying the faint scent of earth and stone. Light seeped into the grotto from narrow cracks in the walls above, casting a dim, bluish glow. To his surprise, the space was neither as dark nor as suffocating as he had feared. The granite walls sparkled faintly, their surfaces flecked with minerals that reflected the light like tiny stars.

Edmond's pulse quickened. He remembered the instructions from the Abbé's map: *In the farthest corner of the second opening.* This grotto, while impressive, was just the beginning. He turned his attention to the walls, examining them carefully for signs of another hidden passage. His hands traced the rough stone, and his pickaxe sounded out each surface until a hollow echo caught his attention. Excitement surged through him as he struck the wall again, harder this time. Pieces of a plaster-like coating flaked away, revealing a layer of white stone beneath.

The discovery renewed Edmond's energy. He attacked the surface with vigor, breaking through the false wall until a second, smaller chamber appeared beyond it. The air here was thicker, carrying the stale, heavy scent of a place long sealed. He waited briefly for fresher air to filter in from above before stepping inside.

The second grotto was darker and lower than the first, its atmosphere oppressive. A corner at the far end drew Edmond's attention immediately. "This must be it," he said aloud, his voice echoing in the confined space. With renewed determination, he began to dig at the ground. Each strike of the pickaxe sent up small clouds of dust, but Edmond hardly noticed. His focus was absolute.

Then, with a metallic clang, his pickaxe struck something solid. His breath hitched. He knelt and brushed the dirt away with trembling hands, uncovering the edge of a wooden chest bound with iron. The sound of his own heartbeat filled his ears as he worked faster, revealing the entirety of the coffer. Its steel bands were ornately carved, and a silver plate on its lid bore the unmistakable crest of the Spada family—a sword set against an oval shield, crowned by a cardinal's hat.

"It's real," Edmond murmured, his voice barely above a whisper. All doubt fled as he ran his hands over the chest, confirming its solidity. This was no illusion. The treasure was here.

Edmond grabbed the chest's handles and tried to lift it, but its weight was immense. Undeterred, he inspected the locks and padlocks securing it shut. With no key in sight, he wedged the sharp end of his pickaxe into the seam of the lid. Using the tool as a lever, he applied all his strength. The wood splintered and groaned before the locks gave way with a loud snap.

The lid fell open, and Edmond's world seemed to tilt. Inside, three compartments lay filled with unimaginable riches. One held stacks of gold coins, their surfaces gleaming even in the dim light. Another was packed with rough bars of gold, their unpolished surfaces hiding the wealth they represented. The final section glittered with jewels—diamonds, rubies, and pearls that tumbled together with a sound like soft rain.

Edmond froze, overwhelmed by the sight. His mind struggled to grasp the enormity of what lay before him. For a moment, he doubted his own senses. Was this real, or was it a dream conjured by exhaustion and hope? Slowly, he reached into the chest, letting the cold metal of the coins and the smooth edges of the jewels anchor him to reality.

A rush of exhilaration overtook him. Edmond leapt to his feet, his joy spilling over in wild cries that echoed through the cavern. He climbed back out into the open air, standing atop a rock to gaze out over the sea. Alone on this remote island, he felt the weight of his discovery—treasures beyond his wildest dreams, all his.

Yet as the initial euphoria subsided, Edmond's mind turned to practicalities. He returned to the chest, carefully counting and inspecting the fortune within. There were gold ingots, countless coins bearing the effigies of long-dead rulers, and an assortment of jewels that dazzled him with their brilliance. The chest's wealth surpassed even his most optimistic hopes.

As the sun dipped below the horizon, Edmond finally emerged from the grotto. Exhausted but exhilarated, he set up a small camp near the cave entrance, his gun within arm's reach. The night passed in a haze of restless joy and vigilance, the stars above bearing silent witness to his newfound fortune.

Chapter 25: The Unknown

The day Edmond Dantès had long anticipated finally arrived. As the first light of dawn crept over Monte Cristo, he resumed his work. Returning to the grotto, he carefully inspected his treasure, filling his pockets with a few of the most dazzling gems. After securing the box and covering its hiding place with sand and stones, he meticulously disguised the site by planting fast-growing vegetation like wild myrtle and flowering thorn. His work erased any trace of disturbance, leaving the area as rugged and untouched as when he first arrived.

Though he felt a deep attachment to the island and its treasure, Edmond's heart burned with a stronger desire—to rejoin humanity, wield his newfound wealth, and reclaim his place in the world.

Six days later, the smugglers returned. From a distance, Edmond recognized *La Jeune Amélie* by her distinct rigging and sails. As the ship approached, he limped toward the shore, pretending to still suffer from his "accident." His companions greeted him warmly, expressing regret that he had missed their recent voyage.

The crew recounted how they narrowly escaped capture by a guard ship from Toulon, evading pursuit only by sailing through the night around Corsica. Despite the danger, their trip had been profitable, yielding a share of fifty piastres for each man.

Edmond, maintaining his stoic demeanor, feigned disappointment at missing the venture but joined the crew aboard *La Jeune Amélie*. They sailed to Leghorn, where Edmond wasted no time putting his plans into action.

In Leghorn, Edmond sold four small diamonds to a jeweler for five thousand francs each. Though he worried that such wealth might arouse suspicion, the jeweler, eager for profit, asked no questions.

The next day, Edmond purchased a fishing boat for Jacopo, gifting him not only the vessel but also one hundred piastres to outfit it with a crew and supplies. In exchange, Edmond asked Jacopo to sail to Marseilles and gather news about an old man named Louis Dantès and a young woman named Mercédès.

Jacopo was overwhelmed by Edmond's generosity, but Edmond explained it away with a fabricated story. He claimed to be a wealthy heir who had joined the smuggling crew out of a whim and a desire to spite his family. Jacopo, believing this explanation, readily agreed to the task.

With his term aboard *La Jeune Amélie* complete, Edmond bid farewell to the crew, who wished him well and hoped he would stay in touch. Leaving Leghorn, Edmond traveled to Genoa, where a sleek new yacht caught his eye. The vessel had been commissioned by an Englishman but was not yet delivered. Edmond offered the builder sixty thousand francs for immediate possession—a price the builder eagerly accepted.

Edmond requested a hidden compartment to be constructed in the yacht's cabin, a secure place for his wealth. The builder completed the modifications overnight, and Edmond set sail the next day. The yacht, expertly crafted by the Genoese, glided through the water with unparalleled grace, responding to Edmond's touch as if alive.

As Edmond navigated the Mediterranean, onlookers speculated about his destination—Corsica, Spain, Africa—but none guessed the truth. Guided by his resolve, Edmond steered his yacht back to Monte Cristo.

Arriving at the island, Edmond began transferring his treasure to the yacht, carefully storing it in the secret compartment. Each piece of gold and every sparkling gem symbolized his new power. Over the following week, Edmond honed his skills with the yacht, familiarizing himself with its capabilities.

On the eighth day, Jacopo returned, his fishing boat anchoring alongside Edmond's yacht. Jacopo's news was somber: Louis Dantès had passed away, and Mercédès had disappeared.

Though Edmond received this news with outward calm, he was deeply shaken. He requested time alone to process the loss and retreated to the island's solitude. When he returned, he brought Jacopo and two of his men aboard the yacht to assist him in navigating to Marseilles.

As they approached Marseilles, Edmond stood at the helm, gazing at the familiar port where his life had been upended. The memories were overwhelming—each street and tree reminded him of his former life. Anchoring near the spot where he had been taken to the Château d'If, Edmond steeled himself for the task ahead.

Disguised under the name "Lord Wilmore," Edmond walked the streets of Marseilles, testing whether time had altered his appearance enough to avoid recognition. A chance encounter with a former sailor from the *Pharaon* confirmed that no one recognized him.

Visiting the house where his father had lived, Edmond was overwhelmed with emotion. The plants his father had lovingly tended were gone, and the small rooms bore no trace of his presence. The new tenants, a young couple, watched in silence as Edmond wept for the father he could not save.

Edmond purchased the house under his alias, offering the tenants their choice of rooms in the building at no additional cost. His actions baffled the neighborhood, sparking countless rumors. Later that evening, Edmond visited the Catalan village, where he gifted a fisherman's family a new boat and equipment in gratitude for answering his questions.

As Edmond rode out of Marseilles, the sun dipped below the horizon, casting long shadows over the city. His heart was heavy with grief, but his mind burned with resolve. The world that had wronged him would soon know the full force of his transformation.

Chapter 26: The Pont du Gard Inn

In the sun-drenched countryside of southern France, midway between Beaucaire and Bellegarde, stood a small, weathered inn called the Pont du Gard Inn. Its name was proudly displayed on a tin sign, clattering in the relentless Mistral wind. Behind the inn, the Rhône river flowed lazily, a contrast to the barren, dusty road that stretched endlessly in both directions.

The inn's "garden" was little more than a dry patch of land, dotted with struggling olive and fig trees, their twisted branches bent permanently by the fierce wind. A lone pine tree, tall but visibly weathered, stood sentinel at the corner of the garden, its dried and cracked needles a testament to the punishing sun.

For nearly a decade, the inn had been run by Gaspard Caderousse and his wife, Madeleine. Once a prosperous tailor, Caderousse now clung to the remnants of his livelihood, forced into innkeeping by circumstances he often cursed. His once-proud posture was now bent, his dark complexion further bronzed by endless hours spent at the inn's entrance, scanning the horizon for travelers who seldom appeared. His wife, pale and frail, bore the marks of a life filled with disappointment and toil.

Business at the inn had dwindled ever since the construction of a nearby canal, which rerouted traffic and trade. Now, the Pont du Gard Inn was a relic of a bygone era, its empty rooms and barren surroundings a stark reminder of its former glory.

One sweltering afternoon, the monotony of their lives was broken. A figure approached from the direction of Bellegarde, a lone traveler on horseback. As he drew nearer, Caderousse squinted, his eyes narrowing against the sun. The rider, dressed in the somber garb of a priest, dismounted with practiced ease. He tied his horse to a makeshift post near the inn's sagging entrance and approached the door, his footsteps muffled by the thick layer of dust on the ground.

Caderousse, recognizing the opportunity for business, rushed forward with an exaggerated smile, brushing his hands against his worn apron. "Welcome, Father," he said, his voice laced with forced enthusiasm. "What brings you to our humble inn on such a blistering day? Please, step inside and rest."

The priest nodded, his expression calm but inscrutable. As he entered the dimly lit room, his eyes swept over the modest furnishings before settling on Caderousse with an intensity that made the innkeeper shift uneasily.

"You are Gaspard Caderousse, are you not?" the priest asked, his voice accented with the melodic lilt of the Italian south.

Caderousse froze, his forced smile faltering. "Yes… yes, that's me," he replied cautiously. "How may I assist you, Father?"

The priest's gaze remained steady. "I've heard you have an interesting story to tell—a story about a man named Edmond Dantès."

At the mention of the name, Caderousse's eyes widened. Memories of a life he had tried to bury surged to the surface. He hesitated, but the priest's calm yet commanding presence made it clear that evasion was not an option.

Caderousse motioned for the priest to sit, his mind racing. He knew this encounter was no coincidence, and as he poured a glass of wine for his guest, he wondered whether the secrets of his past had finally caught up with him.

Chapter 27: The Story

The small, dimly lit room of the inn was quiet, save for the soft creak of the wooden floorboards as Caderousse shifted uneasily in his chair. Across from him, the priest, cloaked in a calm and commanding presence, sat with hands folded, waiting for the truth to spill forth.

Caderousse hesitated, his gaze darting nervously around the room before locking onto the priest's steady eyes. "First, Father," he said cautiously, "you must promise me something."

"And what is that?" the priest replied, his tone firm but patient.

"You must swear that no one will ever know I told you this. The people I'm about to mention are powerful, dangerous. If they find out, I'll be as good as dead."

The priest nodded solemnly. "I am a man of God," he said. "What is shared with me remains between us and the Lord. Speak without fear, and tell the truth."

Caderousse exhaled shakily and leaned forward. "All right. You asked about Edmond Dantès? Let's begin with his father."

The priest's expression didn't waver, though his eyes sharpened at the name. Caderousse launched into the tale, starting with the arrest of

Edmond and the devastation it brought to his father. The old man, consumed by grief, had wasted away, refusing food and comfort. His life, once filled with the anticipation of his son's return, became a slow descent into despair.

"He loved Edmond more than anything," Caderousse said, his voice thick with guilt. "When Edmond was taken, it broke him. He barely ate, barely slept. Mercédès tried to help, but the old man wouldn't leave the house. He kept saying, 'Edmond will come back. He'll need me here when he does.' But… Edmond never came."

The priest remained silent, his face unreadable, as Caderousse detailed the chain of betrayals that led to Edmond's downfall. Danglars, envious of Edmond's promotion, had plotted with Fernand, who coveted Mercédès. Together, they orchestrated a scheme to frame Edmond as a Bonapartist conspirator. Villefort, eager to protect his political ambitions, had sealed Edmond's fate.

"And you, Caderousse?" the priest asked, his tone suddenly sharp. "You were there. You saw all this happen. What did you do?"

Caderousse's face darkened. "I was a coward," he admitted. "I should've stopped it, but… I didn't. Danglars and Fernand made it seem like a harmless joke. I told myself it wasn't my business, and I let it happen. I've regretted it every day since."

As the story unfolded, the priest's calm exterior began to crack. His knuckles whitened as he clenched his fists, and his voice took on a steel edge. "And what became of those who betrayed Edmond?"

Caderousse smirked bitterly. "They thrived," he spat. "Danglars became a baron, a millionaire. Fernand—he's Count de Morcerf now, married to Mercédès, of all people. Villefort? He's a powerful prosecutor. They all climbed higher, while Edmond rotted in prison."

The priest leaned forward, his voice low and intense. "And you, Caderousse? What did you gain?"

"Nothing," Caderousse said, his shoulders slumping. "I've lost everything. My wife is dying, my business failed, and I live in misery. It's like God is punishing me for my silence."

The priest stood abruptly, his chair scraping against the floor. "Perhaps He is," he said. "Or perhaps He sent me here to balance the scales."

From his robe, the priest withdrew a small leather pouch. He placed it on the table, the dull glow of its contents spilling into the dim room. "This diamond," the priest said, "was meant to be shared among Edmond's friends. But he had no true friends—only you. Take it, Caderousse. Let it lift you out of your despair."

Caderousse stared at the diamond, his mouth agape. "For me? Truly?"

The priest nodded. "But let it serve as a reminder. Redemption comes not through wealth, but through actions."

As the priest turned to leave, Caderousse called after him, his voice choked with emotion. "Thank you, Father. I swear, I'll use it wisely."

The priest paused at the door. "See that you do," he said, his voice a mixture of warning and hope. And with that, he disappeared into the night, leaving Caderousse alone with his thoughts—and the weight of his choices.

VOLUME TWO

Chapter 28: The Prison Register

A man in his early thirties, dressed in a sharp blue coat, beige trousers, and a crisp white vest, arrived at the mayor's office in Marseilles. He had the air and accent of an Englishman.

"Good day," he began, "I am the chief clerk of Thomson & French, a firm based in Rome. For the past decade, we have been closely associated with Morrel & Son of Marseilles. We currently have about a hundred thousand francs invested with them, but concerning rumors about their financial troubles have reached us. I've come to you for clarification."

The mayor adjusted his glasses and replied, "Indeed, sir, misfortune has plagued Monsieur Morrel these past few years. He's lost several ships and been hit by a few bankruptcies. However, as a creditor myself, I'll only say this: Monsieur Morrel is a man of utmost integrity. He has honored every obligation with unwavering punctuality. If you're looking for more detailed information, I recommend speaking to Monsieur de Boville, the inspector of prisons. He has a more significant investment of two hundred thousand francs with Morrel's firm and might be better informed. His office is at 15 Rue de Noailles."

The Englishman nodded, appreciating the mayor's discretion, and left for the inspector's office with a brisk and purposeful stride.

Upon entering Monsieur de Boville's office, the Englishman's expression momentarily flickered with recognition, but the inspector—visibly preoccupied—did not notice. The Englishman introduced himself in much the same way as he had to the mayor.

Monsieur de Boville sighed deeply. "Sir, your concerns are valid. Morrel & Son's situation is dire. I've entrusted them with two hundred thousand francs—my daughter's dowry. She's set to marry in two weeks, and I urgently need those funds. Monsieur Morrel visited me just this morning to warn that unless his ship, the *Pharaon*, arrives by the 15th, he won't be able to fulfill his obligations."

"That sounds like a potential default," the Englishman remarked.

"It's worse than that," Boville lamented. "It's outright bankruptcy."

The Englishman paused thoughtfully before saying, "If that's your assessment, I'm prepared to buy your claim."

"Buy it?" Boville asked, astonished.

"Yes, for the full two hundred thousand francs."

"No discount?"

"None."

The Englishman produced a bundle of banknotes. Boville's eyes lit up with a mix of relief and skepticism.

"Sir," Boville cautioned, "you might recover only a fraction of this amount."

"That's of no concern to me," the Englishman replied coolly. "I'm acting on behalf of Thomson & French, who may have their reasons for this purchase. All I ask in return is a small favor."

"A favor? Name it," Boville said, eager to finalize the deal.

"As the prison inspector, you oversee the registers of all inmates, correct?"

"Indeed."

"I'm searching for information about a former prisoner—an Abbé Faria. He was reportedly held in the Château d'If."

Boville's brow furrowed. "Ah, the abbé. Yes, I remember him. A peculiar man, believed to be insane."

"What sort of insanity?" the Englishman inquired.

"He claimed to know the location of a vast treasure and offered large sums to the government for his release."

"And he's deceased?"

"Yes, he died about six months ago—last February. His death was… unusual."

"How so?" the Englishman asked, feigning casual interest.

"The abbé's cell was near that of another prisoner—a dangerous Bonapartist named Edmond Dantès. They managed to dig a tunnel to communicate. Faria died unexpectedly from a seizure, which Dantès used to attempt a daring escape."

"Intriguing," the Englishman mused.

Boville continued, "Dantès replaced Faria's body in the burial sack, hoping to be carried out and buried. Unfortunately for him, the Château d'If has no cemetery. Dead prisoners are weighted and thrown into the sea."

"What happened to Dantès?"

"He was flung into the ocean, weighted with a cannonball."

The Englishman raised an eyebrow. "Remarkable."

"Indeed," Boville chuckled, evidently pleased with the resolution of his financial and professional concerns.

"And these records?" the Englishman pressed.

Boville led him to his study, where the registers were meticulously organized. He provided the Englishman access to the files related to the Château d'If. As Boville read his newspaper, the Englishman sifted through the records, finding the details on Abbé Faria and Edmond Dantès.

After discreetly pocketing a key document—an accusation letter—the Englishman closed the register. "Thank you, Monsieur de Boville. I now have everything I need. Here's the payment for your claim."

Boville quickly drafted the necessary paperwork, and the Englishman handed over the banknotes. As he left, a faint, knowing smile played on his lips.

Chapter 29: The House of Morrel & Son

A few years ago, the Morrel & Son warehouse in Marseilles bustled with life. The air hummed with the sounds of busy clerks, jovial banter among porters, and the constant flow of goods in and out. Now, the scene had drastically changed. The corridors were silent, the offices nearly empty, and a heavy air of despondency hung over the once-thriving business. Of the many clerks who had worked there, only two remained: Emmanuel, a young man devoted to Monsieur Morrel's daughter, and Cocles, a loyal, one-eyed cashier nicknamed "Cock-eye" by the former staff.

Cocles' role had evolved—he was now both the cashier and a servant, though his steadfast devotion to the company remained unchanged. His unyielding confidence in arithmetic led him to dismiss any notion of financial ruin. For twenty years, he had seen every payment made on time and believed this consistency would never falter.

However, Monsieur Morrel's reality was starkly different. Recent months had been a struggle. To meet the last round of payments, he sold family jewels and silverware. Now, with no assets left to liquidate and no credit to rely on, he faced insurmountable debts: 100,000 francs due this month and another 100,000 francs the next. His only hope lay with the *Pharaon*, his last remaining ship, whose return was overdue.

It was in this bleak context that a man from Thomson & French, a reputable firm in Rome, arrived at the Morrel offices. Emmanuel, ever wary of creditors, intercepted the visitor but was told the matter required Monsieur Morrel's personal attention. Reluctantly, Emmanuel summoned Cocles to guide the stranger upstairs. On their way, they encountered Julie, Morrel's beautiful and worried daughter. She anxiously asked if her father was in his room. The stranger reassured her, introducing himself as a representative of Thomson & French.

The stranger entered Morrel's office, finding the merchant poring over his ledger. Time and hardship had aged Morrel; his once-confident demeanor was replaced by one of resignation. He rose to greet his visitor, who observed him with a mixture of curiosity and empathy.

"Monsieur Morrel," the stranger began, "I am here on behalf of Thomson & French. Our firm holds several bills bearing your signature, which have recently come due."

Morrel's heart sank as he wiped perspiration from his brow. "What is the total amount?" he asked, struggling to maintain composure.

"Two hundred thousand francs," the stranger replied, producing documents. "Additionally, we have 32,500 francs in bills assigned to us by other creditors and 55,000 francs from other houses. In total, 287,500 francs."

Morrel's despair was palpable. "For the first time," he murmured, "I fear I cannot honor my commitments."

The stranger's tone softened. "Monsieur, your reputation for integrity is well known, but rumors suggest your business is on the brink of collapse. Is this true?"

Morrel hesitated but then spoke with quiet determination. "If the *Pharaon* arrives, I will meet all my obligations. If not, I will be ruined."

The stranger's expression hardened with resolve. "Let us speak plainly. Do you require more time to pay?"

"A delay would save my honor—and my life," Morrel admitted.

"Very well," said the stranger. "I will extend the deadline by three months. Today is June 5th; you will have until September 5th to repay."

Overwhelmed with gratitude, Morrel thanked the man profusely. "You have given me hope. I shall repay you, or I shall be no more."

As the bills were renewed, Cocles entered with heavy news: the *Pharaon* had been lost at sea. The crew had been saved, but the ship was gone. The sight of his daughter Julie and wife weeping moved Morrel to profound sorrow, but he maintained his composure. "God has spared the lives of the crew," he said. "I accept this as His will."

The sailors, led by the grizzled Penelon, who had followed Cocles into the room, shared their harrowing tale of survival. Despite their plight, they insisted on reducing their wages to ease Morrel's burden. Their loyalty brought tears to his eyes.

After dismissing the sailors and sending his family away, Morrel turned back to the stranger. "You have witnessed my misfortune. Words cannot express my gratitude for your kindness."

The stranger's gaze was steady. "Monsieur Morrel, your honesty and resilience are admirable. Hold on to hope, for brighter days may yet come."

As he left, the stranger encountered Julie on the staircase. "Mademoiselle," he said gently, "one day, you will receive a letter signed 'Sinbad the Sailor.' Follow its instructions, no matter how unusual they may seem."

Julie, startled but trusting, promised to do so. The stranger offered her a rare smile before disappearing into the streets of Marseilles, leaving behind a glimmer of hope for the beleaguered Morrel family.

Chapter 30: The Fifth of September

The unexpected reprieve granted by the agent of Thomson & French was a beacon of hope for the hard-pressed Morrel family. For the first time in weeks, they dared to believe that their misfortune might finally be easing. Morrel shared the news with his wife, Emmanuel, and Julie, and their household was momentarily uplifted. Yet, beneath this relief lay an undeniable truth: the family's situation was still precarious.

Despite the generosity of Thomson & French, Morrel faced other creditors who were far less understanding. Payments continued to come due, and while Coclès diligently managed the accounts, the mounting pressure weighed heavily on Morrel. His funds were dwindling, and even the smallest setback could spell disaster. Each day was a battle to maintain appearances and honor obligations.

The merchant's relentless efforts did not go unnoticed. Rumors circulated throughout Marseilles. Many believed that Morrel's solvency was a temporary illusion, a delaying tactic before the inevitable collapse. Yet, to everyone's astonishment, he met his obligations at the end of July with the same punctuality as always. His reputation, though battered, remained intact.

As August progressed, Morrel made a desperate trip to Paris, seeking help from Danglars, a former acquaintance who had risen to immense wealth and influence. Morrel's hope was that Danglars, indebted to him for past kindnesses, might provide the lifeline he so desperately needed. However, his hopes were dashed when Danglars coldly refused his request. Returning to Marseilles, Morrel shared the grim news with his family. Their financial ruin seemed inevitable.

Julie and Madame Morrel, devastated, called upon Maximilian, Morrel's son, for support. Maximilian, a young officer with a reputation for integrity and strength, returned home to lend his aid. His presence bolstered the family's resolve, though it was clear he, too, understood the gravity of their situation.

The night of September 4th was restless. Morrel remained awake, pacing his room in deep agitation. Julie and Madame Morrel kept vigil, their hearts heavy with worry. In the early hours of the morning, Morrel finally succumbed to exhaustion. At breakfast, his demeanor was calm but resigned. He embraced Julie tenderly, expressing an affection that felt like a farewell.

Shortly after, Julie received a mysterious letter. The note instructed her to go to a specific address, retrieve a red silk purse from the fifth floor, and deliver it to her father before eleven o'clock. The message was signed, "Sinbad the Sailor."

Although hesitant, Julie obeyed, seeking Emmanuel's counsel. Emmanuel accompanied her to the building but respected the instruction that she must go alone. Inside the apartment, Julie found the purse exactly as described. Inside it was a receipt for Morrel's debts and a magnificent diamond labeled "Julie's Dowry."

Racing home, Julie burst into her father's study just as the clock struck eleven. She handed him the purse, crying out that they were saved. Morrel, overwhelmed, held the purse in disbelief. The documents and diamond inside were undeniable proof that their debts had been miraculously cleared.

As the family celebrated their salvation, Cocles arrived with astonishing news: the *Pharaon*, thought lost at sea, was entering the harbor! Morrel and his family rushed to the docks, where they saw a ship identical to the one they had mourned. The ship even had its cargo intact. It was an almost divine restitution.

Amidst the jubilation, a mysterious figure observed the scene from the shadows. His face partially concealed by a beard, he smiled with quiet satisfaction before retreating to a waiting yacht. "Be happy, noble heart," he murmured. "The good you have done is repaid. Now, my task turns to those who are less deserving."

The Morrel family stood on the pier, their hearts filled with gratitude and awe. For them, the events of the Fifth of September would forever remain a testament to hope, resilience, and the kindness of an enigmatic benefactor.

Chapter 31: Italy & Sinbad the Sailor

At the start of 1838, two young men from Paris's elite society, Viscount Albert de Morcerf and Baron Franz d'Épinay, were traveling through Italy. They had planned to experience the Carnival in Rome, with Franz —an experienced traveler in Italy—acting as Albert's guide.

Knowing the demand for accommodations during Carnival, they had written ahead to reserve rooms at the Hôtel de Londres in Piazza di Spagna, Rome. The hotel manager, Signor Pastrini, offered them modest third-floor accommodations at a fair rate, which they accepted. However, with time to spare before the Carnival, Albert headed to Naples while Franz remained in Florence to explore its beauty and visit the Island of Elba, Napoleon's former exile.

While in Elba, Franz visited its historical sites and enjoyed brief hunts on neighboring islands. One day, his captain suggested visiting Monte Cristo, an isolated island rumored to be uninhabited but rich with wild goats. Intrigued, Franz agreed despite warnings that the island sometimes served as a haven for smugglers and pirates. The captain assured Franz that their visit would go unnoticed, steering the boat towards Monte Cristo as Franz marveled at the rugged beauty of the Mediterranean.

As night fell, the island loomed dark and mysterious. Franz noticed a fire on the shore—evidence of human presence. Despite initial hesitation, the captain decided to investigate. After silently approaching the shore, the crew confirmed the presence of smugglers and two Corsican bandits. Franz, curious and adventurous, decided to join their camp. He was assured that smugglers, though outside the law, posed no danger.

The smugglers extended an invitation to Franz, but with one peculiar condition: he must be blindfolded before being taken to their leader's residence. Intrigued by tales of the leader's wealth and mysterious nature, Franz agreed. After being blindfolded and led into a cave, Franz removed the covering at his host's command and found himself in a stunningly luxurious chamber. Crimson brocade walls, golden ornaments, and treasures that rivaled fairy tales surrounded him.

The host introduced himself as "Sinbad the Sailor," a man of enigmatic charm and power. His pale complexion and piercing eyes gave him an almost otherworldly presence. He apologized for the blindfold, explaining that it was necessary to protect the secrecy of his retreat. Franz, awestruck by his surroundings, assured him there was no offense.

The two men dined together, enjoying a lavish meal prepared with exotic ingredients and served on fine silver and Japanese china. Sinbad's servant, Ali, attended to them with remarkable skill, further impressing Franz. During the meal, Sinbad shared stories of his adventures and philosophy, hinting at a complex past filled with suffering, justice, and personal reinvention. He described himself as a philosopher and wanderer, free from societal constraints, yet deeply tied to a mysterious purpose.

After supper, Sinbad offered Franz a taste of hashish, describing its transformative effects on perception and imagination. Though skeptical, Franz tried it, succumbing to vivid and fantastical visions that blurred the line between reality and dream. In this altered state, he experienced a world of beauty and enchantment, feeling liberated from earthly concerns.

The evening ended with Franz retiring to a sumptuous chamber adorned with exotic animal skins and luxurious furnishings. As he drifted into a peaceful sleep, he marveled at the extraordinary encounter and the mysterious figure who had hosted him.

Little did Franz know, this meeting with Sinbad the Sailor was the beginning of an adventure that would intertwine their fates and challenge his understanding of identity, justice, and the power of a single, determined individual.

Chapter 32: The Waking

When Franz woke, he found himself caught between dream and reality. The ethereal visions of the previous night dissolved, replaced by the tangible coolness of stone beneath his hand. He was lying on a soft bed of dried heather, his long cloak serving as a blanket. Light filtered into the grotto, illuminating the scene with a golden glow.

Curiosity drew Franz toward the source of the light. As he stepped closer, he discovered an opening in the rock. Through this natural window, he saw the breathtaking expanse of a calm blue sea under an azure sky. The morning sun sparkled on the water, and a gentle breeze carried the fresh scent of salt air. Nearby, the sailors were chatting and laughing on the shore, while their boat bobbed gracefully in the tide.

For a while, Franz stood in peaceful contemplation, savoring the simple yet profound beauty of nature. Gradually, the tranquility brought clarity to his thoughts. Memories of the previous night—the grotto, the sumptuous feast, the enigmatic Sinbad, and the heady effects of hashish—came rushing back. The vividness of the experience had etched it deeply into his imagination, blurring the lines between fantasy and reality.

As Franz approached the sailors, their captain, Gaetano, greeted him with a smile. "Signor Sinbad left his regards for you," Gaetano said, "and apologizes for not bidding farewell in person. Urgent business required his immediate departure to Malaga."

"So, he's real?" Franz asked, half to himself. "Not a figment of my imagination?"

Gaetano gestured toward the horizon. "See for yourself. His yacht is still visible."

Franz looked towards the water, focusing on the sleek vessel gliding gracefully across the sea. There, at the stern, stood the enigmatic Sinbad, dressed as he had been the previous evening. Spotting Franz, Sinbad waved a handkerchief in farewell. Franz reciprocated the gesture before hearing the distant pop of a gunshot—a parting salute from Sinbad's crew. Smiling, Franz fired his carbine into the air in response, although he doubted the sound would carry over the waves.

Turning back to Gaetano, Franz announced, "I want to explore the grotto once more. Prepare a torch."

The captain raised an eyebrow but obliged. "Many have tried to uncover its secrets," he remarked as he handed Franz the torch. "None have succeeded."

Undeterred, Franz spent hours combing the grotto's granite walls, looking for hidden doors or secret mechanisms. He inspected every crack and crevice, pressing against projections and inserting his hunting sword into fissures. Despite his meticulous efforts, the grotto revealed no secrets. Finally, weary and frustrated, Franz gave up his search and returned to the shore.

Gaetano reminded Franz of the hunting trip they had planned, and Franz reluctantly agreed. With little enthusiasm, he wandered the island, shooting a goat and two kids—a meager haul that failed to lift his spirits. His thoughts remained anchored to the grotto and the mysterious Sinbad.

As the day wore on, Franz attempted another, equally fruitless search of the grotto before resigning himself to the reality that the grotto's mysteries were not his to uncover. When he returned to the camp, Gaetano had roasted one of the kids, and the sailors were preparing for their departure.

Seated on the shore, Franz watched the yacht vanish into the Gulf of Porto-Vecchio. "I thought he was heading to Malaga," Franz remarked.

"He's likely dropping off those Corsican bandits first," Gaetano replied with a knowing grin. "Sinbad fears neither man nor law and will go to great lengths to help those in need."

"But doesn't that put him at odds with the authorities?" Franz asked.

Gaetano chuckled. "Authorities? What do they matter to him? His yacht is faster than any frigate, and wherever he lands, he'll find allies. He's untouchable."

As they set sail for the mainland, Franz reflected on his extraordinary experience. The yacht, Sinbad, the grotto—all of it seemed like a fleeting dream, already fading with the distance. By the time they reached Florence, the enchantment of Monte Cristo had given way to the mundane concerns of daily life. Franz focused on reuniting with Albert in Rome, leaving behind the lingering allure of the mysterious island and its enigmatic host.

Yet he couldn't shake the feeling that this was not the end of his encounter with Sinbad the Sailor.

Chapter 33: Roman Bandits

The following morning, Franz awoke first and rang the bell. Before the sound faded, Signor Pastrini, the landlord, entered triumphantly.

"Excellency," he began, without waiting for Franz to speak, "I feared yesterday that you might be too late to secure a carriage. Unfortunately, I was right—there isn't a single one available for the next three days."

"The very days we need one most," Franz replied with a sigh. Just then, Albert entered the room.

"What's the problem?" Albert asked. "No carriages?"

"Exactly," Franz confirmed.

Albert scoffed. "What kind of Eternal City is this?"

Signor Pastrini, eager to defend his city, explained, "It's Carnival season. From Sunday to Tuesday evening, every carriage in Rome is booked. Until then, however, you can have fifty if you please."

"Ah, so there's hope!" Albert said. "Today is Thursday."

"Indeed," Franz interjected, "but in two days, ten or twelve thousand travelers will arrive, making it even more difficult."

Albert shrugged. "Let's enjoy the present and not dwell on future inconveniences. At least we can secure a window overlooking the Corso, right?"

"Not quite," Pastrini replied. "The last available window was rented by a Russian prince for twenty sequins a day."

Franz and Albert exchanged exasperated looks. "Venice would've been simpler," Franz mused.

"I came to Rome for the Carnival," Albert declared. "I'll see it—even if I have to do so on stilts!"

The landlord promised to try finding them a carriage, albeit at a high price. After some negotiation, Franz secured one for twelve piastres per day. An hour later, the modest vehicle arrived. Despite its humble appearance, the young men were relieved to have secured transport during Carnival.

Their first destination was Saint Peter's Basilica, a site so vast that it consumed their entire day. As dusk fell, Franz suggested they visit the Colosseum by moonlight. Albert readily agreed.

Over dinner, Pastrini interrupted their meal with a grim warning. "Excellencies," he began, "your planned route to the Colosseum—leaving through the Porta del Popolo and re-entering by the Porta San Giovanni—is extremely dangerous after dark."

"Dangerous? Why?" Franz inquired.

"Because of Luigi Vampa," Pastrini replied solemnly. "He's the most notorious bandit in the Roman countryside."

Albert laughed dismissively. "A bandit, you say? We've finally encountered one! Tell us, Signor Pastrini, what makes this Luigi Vampa so fearsome?"

Pastries sighed. "He's more ruthless and cunning than any bandit before him. Despite the authorities' best efforts, they've been unable to capture him. He's always one step ahead—whether hiding in the mountains, escaping to the coast, or vanishing into the islands. Travelers fear him, and for good reason. If you fail to pay his ransom, he executes you without hesitation."

Albert, unfazed, proposed an elaborate plan. "We'll arm ourselves with pistols and blunderbusses, capture this Vampa, and present him to the Pope. Our reward? A carriage and horses for Carnival."

Franz smiled at his friend's bravado but advised caution. "Signor Pastrini," he said, "tell us more about Luigi Vampa. Who is he?"

Pastrini nodded. "Vampa was once a shepherd on the San-Felice estate. Even as a boy, he displayed extraordinary intelligence and ambition. He learned to read and write from a kind priest and taught himself marksmanship with an old rifle. His skill with a gun became legendary."

The landlord recounted Vampa's rise from a humble shepherd to the leader of a feared bandit crew. He told tales of Vampa's cunning, his audacity, and his dangerous charm. Franz listened intently, while Albert remained skeptical.

As the clock struck nine, their carriage arrived. Pastrini's warnings still lingered in Franz's mind, but Albert was determined to proceed. "To the Colosseum!" he declared, lighting his third cigar of the evening.

"By the Porta del Popolo or through the streets?" the coachman asked.

"The streets, of course," Franz replied, choosing the safer route. Albert smirked but followed his friend into the carriage. Together, they set off into the Roman night, unaware of how close they were to the infamous Luigi Vampa's domain.

Chapter 34: The Colosseum

Franz carefully planned their route to the Colosseum, ensuring they avoided any of the ancient ruins along the way. He wanted the full, overwhelming effect of the iconic structure to strike them unmitigated. They traveled via the Via Sistina, bypassed Santa Maria Maggiore, and took the Via Urbana and San Pietro in Vincoli, eventually arriving directly opposite the colossal monument. This route had another advantage: it allowed Franz to dwell on Signor Pastrini's intriguing story from earlier.

But the Colosseum soon banished all thoughts of bandits. As the moonlight shown through its gaping arches, casting an eerie glow on the ruins, the magnitude of the structure struck them deeply. The carriage stopped near the Meta Sudans, and they stepped out to find a guide—one of many who seemed to materialize from the shadows, ready to lead tourists through the site.

As was customary in Rome, they ended up with not one but two guides: the hotel's own companion and a specialized guide for the Colosseum. Franz and Albert surrendered themselves to this inevitable arrangement, aware that torches and guides were necessary to explore the ruins by night. Albert, visiting the Colosseum for the first time, was captivated by its grandeur and history. Franz, on the other hand, had been here many times before and was content to let his companion marvel while he wandered off to absorb the atmosphere in solitude.

Franz climbed a half-crumbled staircase, seeking a quiet vantage point beneath the shadow of a massive column. From there, he could see Albert and their guides moving about with their torches, their flickering lights resembling ghostly figures. Lost in thought, Franz's attention was abruptly drawn to the sound of a stone dislodging on the opposite staircase. It seemed too deliberate to be accidental. He instinctively hid deeper in the shadows, watching as a cloaked figure cautiously emerged into the moonlight.

The figure was dressed in a large brown mantle, one fold of which covered the lower part of his face. His broad-brimmed hat further obscured his features, but his polished boots and tailored trousers suggested a person of refinement. Franz observed the stranger with growing curiosity, noting his hesitant movements and his apparent anticipation of someone's arrival.

Minutes later, a second figure appeared, descending nimbly from an opening in the roof with the aid of vines and plant growth. This newcomer, dressed in the traditional costume of the Trastevere district, greeted the cloaked man in the Roman dialect.

"I apologize for the delay, Your Excellency," he said. "Saint John Lateran just struck ten."

"No need for apologies," replied the cloaked man in polished Tuscan. "I'm early. What news?"

The man from Trastevere launched into a report: two executions were scheduled to be held in two days. One, a murderer, was to be bludgeoned, while the other, a shepherd named Peppino, was sentenced to decapitation for aiding Luigi Vampa's band.

"Peppino is no criminal," the cloaked man remarked. "He only brought provisions to the bandits. Yet the papal authorities seek to make an example of him."

The Trasteveran outlined his plan to storm the scaffold with twenty men and rescue Peppino. But the cloaked man dismissed this as reckless. "I will achieve more with two thousand piastres than you will with twenty stilettos. Leave it to me."

After further discussion, the men agreed on a signal: if the reprieve was secured, the middle window of the Café Rospoli would display a white tapestry with a red cross; if not, all three windows would show yellow drapery.

Franz, hidden in the shadows, absorbed every word. The cloaked man's voice, deep and resonant, was unmistakable. It was the same voice he had heard on the island of Monte Cristo. There could be no doubt: the cloaked man was "Sinbad the Sailor."

When the conversation ended, the Trasteveran disappeared, and the cloaked man descended by another staircase. Franz waited until they were both out of sight before returning to Albert, who was enthusiastically describing the Colosseum's architecture.

Franz kept his observations to himself but felt his curiosity deepen. The mysterious man's involvement in the impending execution and his efforts to secure Peppino's reprieve hinted at a complex, layered character. He resolved to unravel the secrets of this intriguing figure—but for now, he returned with Albert to their hotel, carrying the weight of yet another enigmatic encounter.

Back at the Hôtel de Londres, Franz and Albert were discussing the evening when a knock interrupted them. The innkeeper, Signor Pastrini, entered, his face bright with enthusiasm.

"Gentlemen," he said, "you are fortunate tonight. Your neighbor in the adjoining suite has expressed interest in meeting you."

"Our neighbor?" Albert asked, intrigued.

"Yes," Pastrini replied. "A most distinguished guest—the Count of Monte Cristo."

Franz and Albert exchanged glances. For Franz, the name struck like lightning. Before he could reply, Pastrini continued, "He is eager to make your acquaintance. Shall I send him in?"

Moments later, the Count entered, dressed in a dark coat that contrasted sharply with his piercing eyes. He greeted them with impeccable manners and a mysterious smile. "Gentlemen," he said, "it is a pleasure to meet fellow travelers who share a curiosity about this eternal city."

Albert was instantly charmed, engaging the Count in lively conversation about Rome's landmarks. Franz, however, remained guarded, his mind racing with questions about the man who had seemingly just stepped out of the shadows of the Colosseum and into their parlor.

Later that night, as Franz lay in bed, sleep eluded him. The events at the Colosseum replayed in his mind, confirming what he already suspected: the Count of Monte Cristo was far more than he appeared to be.

Chapter 35: La Mazzolata*

The morning sun bathed Rome in a golden glow, signaling the start of what promised to be a grim spectacle. Franz and Albert joined the Count of Monte Cristo for breakfast in his lavish apartment, where the conversation took a chilling turn.

"Gentlemen," the Count began, his tone calm but laced with intrigue, "you are about to witness a fascinating event: an execution at the Piazza del Popolo. It's a rare glimpse into the rituals of justice here in Rome."

Albert chuckled nervously, but Franz remained silent, his thoughts tangled with unease and curiosity. They quietly finished their meals and prepared to depart for the public execution.

Their carriage wound through the bustling streets, eventually reaching the city center, where crowds had already gathered. The Count's reserved window at the Rospoli Palace offered an unimpeded view of the scaffold—an ominous structure flanked by two upright beams and a gleaming blade suspended between them.

Franz, struggling to suppress his discomfort, asked, "Why is this event treated with such enthusiasm?"

---

*The Execution

The Count smiled faintly. "The spectacle of death fascinates humanity. It is both a reminder and a mystery. Here in Rome, the execution is woven into the carnival—a paradox of celebration and mortality."

Before long, a procession emerged from the nearby church of Santa Maria del Popolo. A line of penitents in gray sackcloth, holding lit candles, led the way. Behind them marched the executioner, a towering man with a sledgehammer resting on his shoulder. Following him were the condemned: Peppino, a young shepherd accused of aiding bandits, and Andrea, a murderer.

Peppino walked with quiet dignity, his head held high, while Andrea stumbled forward, his face twisted with terror. Two priests flanked each man, offering them crucifixes and murmuring prayers. The crowd's energy surged, a mixture of morbid curiosity and cruel anticipation.

Franz's gaze darted to the Count. Despite the macabre scene, Monte Cristo appeared unshaken, his dark eyes betraying neither sympathy nor disdain. Instead, there was an intensity—as though he were studying the depths of human nature.

When the procession reached the scaffold, a priest hurried forward, waving a document. The crowd fell silent as the proclamation was read aloud: "By the grace of His Holiness, Peppino, known as Rocca Priori, is hereby pardoned."

The square erupted into cheers, though some jeered in disappointment. Peppino's face lit with relief as he was led away. Andrea, however, screamed in rage.

"Why him?" Andrea bellowed. "We were supposed to die together! I won't die alone!" His cries grew frenzied as guards wrestled him onto the scaffold. The executioner's assistants pinned him down, ignoring his desperate thrashing.

Franz recoiled, but the Count placed a steadying hand on his shoulder. "Watch," he commanded softly. "This is a rare lesson in justice and vengeance."

The executioner raised his sledgehammer and brought it down with precise force, silencing Andrea's screams in an instant. The body crumpled, lifeless, as the crowd erupted into chaotic applause and chatter. Blood pooled beneath the scaffold, a stark reminder of mortality amid the festival atmosphere.

Franz sat back, pale and shaken. Albert, too, appeared disturbed, though he masked it with bravado, reaching for a cigar. The Count, meanwhile, remained composed, his demeanor almost triumphant.

As the crowd dispersed, Franz turned to the Count. "How can you remain so detached from such horror?"

The Count's lips curled into a faint smile. "Detachment, my dear Franz, is not indifference. It is understanding. Death is a certainty, but the path to it—whether through justice, vengeance, or fate—reveals the truth of human character. That is what fascinates me."

Albert exhaled a plume of smoke, his usual cheerfulness returning. "Well, Count, you've given us an experience to remember, though I can't say I'd repeat it willingly."

The Count chuckled. "Life is a tapestry, Viscount, woven with threads of joy and sorrow. Only by seeing it all can one truly understand its worth."

As they left the Piazza del Popolo, Franz couldn't shake the weight of what he'd witnessed. The Count's enigmatic perspective lingered in his mind, a puzzle he felt compelled to solve—even as its darker edges made him shudder.

Chapter 36: The Carnival at Rome

When Franz regained his senses, he found Albert sipping water, his face pale and his demeanor shaken. Across the room, the Count of Monte Cristo was calmly donning his masquerade costume. Franz's gaze shifted toward the piazza; the scene had transformed completely. The scaffold, the executioners, and the victims had all vanished. In their place, a throng of lively, masked revelers filled the square as the joyous peal of the Monte Citorio bell marked the opening of the Carnival.

"Well," Franz asked the Count, still trying to make sense of the abrupt change, "what just happened?"

"Nothing extraordinary," the Count replied with a faint smile. "The Carnival has begun. Now, make haste and dress yourself."

"That nightmare... It's over?"

"A dream, nothing more," the Count answered. "Only one of you has woken up. As for Peppino, he is safe among the crowd, enjoying his freedom, no doubt without a word of thanks. Man, as ever, is an ungrateful creature."

Albert, already halfway into his satin pants and varnished boots, interjected. "Franz, are you coming? The revelry is irresistible, and the Count's insights have certainly left an impression."

Resigned, Franz followed suit, masking his still-pale face with a hand-decorated mask. Together, the trio descended to a carriage laden with sweetmeats and bouquets, falling in line with the colorful chaos that had overtaken the Piazza del Popolo.

The stark transformation was almost surreal. Where grim silence had dominated, the square now pulsed with laughter and vibrant energy. Masks of every conceivable kind—clowns, knights, peasants, and harlequins—milled about, throwing flour-filled eggs, confetti, and jesting freely with strangers. It was a scene of uninhibited revelry, and Franz and Albert soon found themselves caught up in its infectious spirit.

A handful of confetti hurled from a neighboring carriage hit Albert squarely, prompting him to retaliate with equal vigor. Soon, he and Franz were fully immersed in the festive combat, their earlier unease fading with each toss of confetti and exchange of laughter.

Meanwhile, the Count observed the spectacle with his usual composed demeanor. His inscrutable expression gave little away, though his dark eyes seemed to absorb every detail. At the second turn of the square, he stopped the carriage.

"Gentlemen, if you grow weary of participating and prefer to observe, my window at the Rospoli Palace remains at your disposal. Enjoy yourselves," the Count said, stepping down gracefully. Moments later, he disappeared into the crowd.

Albert, distracted by a nearby carriage full of Roman peasants, seized the opportunity to flirt with the masked occupants, tossing bouquets with practiced charm. Franz, amused by his friend's antics, quipped, "Be careful, Albert. The Carnival may hold surprises even you can't anticipate."

By the end of the day, Albert had secured a small victory—a bunch of violets thrown from the carriage. He tucked it proudly into his buttonhole, declaring it the start of a promising adventure.

As night fell, the Carnival reached its zenith. The streets were ablaze with thousands of candles—moccoletti—each carried by revelers determined to protect their flame while extinguishing those of others. It was a wild and joyful chaos, a luminous dance of light and shadow accompanied by ceaseless laughter.

When the final bell tolled at midnight, all the lights were extinguished in a symbolic gesture. Darkness enveloped the city, and the revelers began to disperse. Franz, overcome by the day's events, returned to his hotel, where the Count had left a note inviting them to his box at the Argentina Theatre.

Albert, however, had other plans. The mysterious Roman peasant girl who had thrown him the violets had agreed to meet him the next day. As Franz observed his friend's growing infatuation, he couldn't help but feel both amused and apprehensive. For all the glittering allure of the Carnival, he sensed that its secrets were far from over.

Chapter 37: The Catacombs of Saint Sebastian

As Franz walked through the moonlit streets of Rome, a strange sense of unease enveloped him. The city, vibrant just hours earlier, now felt like a vast, silent tomb. The streets were dark, and the waning moon wouldn't rise until late, casting the city into a deep and almost unnatural darkness. The transformation from the festive gaiety of the Carnival to this eerie stillness was unsettling.

By the time Franz's carriage arrived at the Hôtel de Londres, the melancholy atmosphere had settled over him completely. Dinner was prepared, but Franz dined alone; Albert, his companion, had left earlier for a mysterious rendezvous. Despite Signor Pastrini's polite inquiries, Franz offered little explanation, saying only that Albert had accepted an invitation.

The sudden silence following the extinguishing of the street lanterns had left Franz in a pensive mood. He couldn't help but feel uneasy as he sat in the empty dining room, despite the landlord's attempts to offer comfort. Determined to stay awake until Albert returned, Franz ordered his carriage to be ready at eleven o'clock. But when the hour came, Albert was still absent.

Franz, now growing more anxious, decided to dress and step out into the night. He told Pastrini he intended to spend the evening at the

Duke of Bracciano's residence. The duke and duchess, famed for their hospitality, welcomed Franz warmly. Yet, even among the glittering guests and lively conversation, Franz's thoughts were with Albert. When asked about his companion's whereabouts, Franz admitted he hadn't seen Albert since their parting at the Carnival.

"He mentioned something about a rendezvous," Franz explained, trying to sound unconcerned. But the duke frowned.

"A night like this is no time for wandering the streets of Rome," the duke said gravely.

"Indeed," agreed his wife, overhearing the conversation. "Even in the Carnival season, the city has its dangers."

As Franz spoke with the guests, a servant approached with a message: a man had arrived at the hotel with a letter for Franz from Albert. Intrigued and a little relieved, Franz excused himself and hurried back to the Hôtel de Londres.

The messenger, cloaked and cautious, handed over the letter without stepping inside. Franz tore it open and read Albert's hurried handwriting:

My dear Franz,

I find myself in an extraordinary situation. Please take the letter of credit from my pocketbook and withdraw four thousand piastres from Torlonia's bank immediately. Give the money to the bearer of this note. My life depends on it. Trust me as I trust you.

Yours,

Albert de Morcerf

Below, in a different hand, were chilling words in Italian:

If the four thousand piastres are not delivered by six in the morning, the Viscount Albert will cease to live by seven.

Luigi Vampa

Franz's blood ran cold. Albert, who had dismissed bandit tales as fanciful, had fallen into the hands of Rome's most infamous outlaw.

Franz wasted no time. He retrieved the letter of credit but found it insufficient to cover the ransom. Desperate, he considered his options and recalled the Count of Monte Cristo—a man of considerable means and mysterious influence. Without hesitation, Franz requested an audience.

The Count received Franz in a richly appointed room, his demeanor as composed as ever. After reading the letter, he glanced at Franz.

"Do you have the money?" the Count asked.

"All but eight hundred piastres," Franz admitted.

The Count opened a drawer filled with gold. "Take what you need," he said. "But tell me, would you prefer another solution?"

Franz looked up. "What do you propose?"

"We'll visit Luigi Vampa ourselves," the Count replied calmly. "He owes me a favor."

Franz hesitated, then nodded. The Count summoned Peppino, the former bandit whose life he had saved the previous day. Within minutes, they were on their way, guided by Peppino through the moonlit ruins and along the ancient Appian Way.

At the entrance to the catacombs of Saint Sebastian, the Count's presence proved invaluable. A permit from the governor allowed them passage through the city gates, and Peppino's signals ensured safe passage past Vampa's sentries. As they descended into the catacombs, Franz couldn't help but marvel at the eerie beauty of the ancient tombs.

Deep within, they reached a chamber lit by a single flickering lamp. Vampa, seated and engrossed in a book, rose as they entered. His men, startled by the unexpected visitors, drew their weapons, but a single command from Vampa stilled them.

"Your Excellency," Vampa said, addressing the Count with evident respect, "I did not expect you."

The Count's tone was firm. "You've taken a friend of mine. Release him."

Vampa glanced at his men, then back at the Count. "Had I known he was under your protection, this wouldn't have happened."

Moments later, Albert was brought forth, groggy but unharmed. He was astonished to see Franz and the Count. After brief words of apology and assurance from Vampa, the group departed. Albert, regaining his usual humor, joked about the ordeal as they returned to the city.

By the time they reached the Duke of Bracciano's residence, it was nearly dawn. Albert, ever the charmer, joined the festivities as though nothing had happened. But for Franz, the night had revealed more about the Count of Monte Cristo than he could yet comprehend. The man's power and enigma loomed larger than ever, leaving Franz with more questions than answers.

Chapter 38: The Rendezvous

The morning after his dramatic rescue, Albert eagerly asked Franz to accompany him on a visit to the Count of Monte Cristo. Although Albert had already thanked the Count the previous evening, he felt that words could not fully convey his gratitude for the Count's intervention. Franz, sharing a mix of curiosity and unease toward the enigmatic Count, agreed to join Albert. He was reluctant to let his friend be further drawn into the Count's mysterious influence without his own presence.

Upon arriving at the Count's luxurious quarters, they were quickly ushered into the salon. After a short wait, the Count entered, his calm demeanor as imposing as ever.

"My dear Count," Albert began, rising to meet him. "Allow me to reiterate my deepest thanks for your timely assistance. I owe you my life and will never forget the debt I owe you."

The Count waved his hand dismissively. "You exaggerate, Monsieur de Morcerf. What I provided was a mere trifle—the cost of ensuring your safety is hardly worth mentioning. However, I must commend your composure under pressure. Few men can face such peril with such calm indifference."

Albert laughed lightly. "I suppose that's the French spirit—we meet every situation, even grim death, with a smile. But truly, Count, I am forever in your debt. Please, let me know if there is anything my family or I can do to repay your kindness. My father, the Count de Morcerf, has considerable influence in both Paris and Madrid. Anything within our power is yours."

The Count's lips curled into a subtle smile. "You honor me, Monsieur de Morcerf, and, as it happens, there is a favor I wish to ask."

"Name it," Albert said eagerly.

"I am a stranger to Paris," the Count explained. "Though I have long wished to visit, I know no one in its social circles. I wonder if you might help introduce me to the city's fashionable world?"

Albert's face lit up with enthusiasm. "It would be my pleasure! Paris is the finest city in the world, and it would be an honor to guide you through it. My family's home is at your disposal whenever you arrive."

"Then it is settled," the Count replied. "I shall arrive in Paris in three months' time. On May 21st, at precisely half-past ten in the morning, I shall visit you at 27 Rue du Helder."

Albert's smile widened. "Your precision is remarkable, Count. I shall ensure that breakfast is waiting."

The Count extended his hand, his cold touch startling Franz, who had silently observed the exchange. "Until then, gentlemen, I wish you safe travels."

As they left the salon, Albert turned to Franz, noting his friend's thoughtful expression. "What's on your mind?"

"Albert," Franz replied carefully, "I cannot shake the feeling that the Count is no ordinary man. There is something unsettling about him."

Albert dismissed the concern with a laugh. "You're overthinking it, Franz. The Count is a man of the world—wealthy, resourceful, and a bit eccentric, perhaps. But he's proven himself a true friend."

Franz hesitated but ultimately kept his deeper reservations to himself. That evening, as Albert prepared to return to Paris and Franz to continue his travels in Italy, the Viscount left a card for the Count, reiterating their agreement. Beneath his name, Albert wrote: *27 Rue du Helder, on the 21st of May, at half-past ten A.M.*

As Franz watched Albert depart, he couldn't help but feel that the events of the past days had only deepened the mystery surrounding the Count of Monte Cristo. What lay ahead, he wondered, for his friend and for himself in the shadow of such an enigmatic figure?

Chapter 39: The Guests

In the house on the Rue du Helder, Albert de Morcerf was busy preparing for his upcoming breakfast with the Count of Monte Cristo. The morning of May 21st dawned bright and clear, and Albert's staff moved briskly to ensure everything was perfect.

Albert's pavilion, a sleek structure at the edge of a large courtyard, offered both comfort and privacy. Its two street-facing windows allowed him to observe the bustling Parisian thoroughfare, while the rear windows overlooked a lush garden. The main family residence of the Count and Countess of Morcerf stood across the courtyard, a grand building in the imperial style. A high wall encircled the entire property, broken only by a gilded iron gate for carriages and a smaller entrance for pedestrians, which was watched over by a vigilant concierge.

Albert's pavilion was a masterpiece of modern luxury. His mother, the Countess, had selected the property with care, balancing her desire to keep her son close with the understanding that a young man needed his independence. Every detail of the home reflected Albert's tastes and whims, from the perfectly oiled secret side gate—his private escape into the city—to the eclectic collection of treasures scattered throughout his rooms.

The upper floors of the pavilion served as a sanctuary for Albert's many passions. There were hunting horns and musical instruments for his fleeting interest in music, easels and paintbrushes from his brief foray into painting, and racks of foils and gloves for his more enduring commitment to fencing and boxing. Persian rugs and Calcutta silks draped over ancient armchairs, creating a space where the aesthetic sensibilities of an artist mingled with the indulgent tendencies of a Parisian dandy.

By ten o'clock, Albert was settled in the small salon on the ground floor, ensuring the breakfast arrangements were to his satisfaction. A long table groaned under an assortment of tobaccos, from the dark leaves of Sinai to the golden blends of Porto Rico, each housed in earthenware jars. Next to these were rows of cigars, regalias, and narghiles, ready to cater to every preference.

Albert's valet, Germain, entered with a stack of papers and a bundle of letters. Albert sifted through them, selecting two in particular—delicate, perfumed envelopes bearing the handwriting of Madame Danglars and a certain Rosa. With a smirk, Albert dictated his replies: he accepted Madame Danglars' invitation to her opera box and promised to join Rosa for supper later that evening, instructing Germain to deliver a selection of fine wines and oysters to her as a prelude.

"By the way," Albert added, "borrow a liqueur chest from my mother's cabinet. Mine is missing a few essentials."

Germain nodded and left, just as the sound of carriage wheels on gravel announced the first guest.

"Monsieur Lucien Debray," the valet announced.

Debray, a polished young man with sandy hair and a sharp wit, entered with his usual air of controlled nonchalance. "Albert," he greeted, "your punctuality is unsettling. I arrived early expecting to be the first."

"Ah, my dear Debray," Albert replied, laughing. "The ministry must be in chaos if you've arrived early. Tell me, is Paris safe from revolution for another day?"

Debray rolled his eyes. "The government totters but never falls. It's a miracle, really. And don't get me started on Don Carlos—we've escorted him to Bourges as if he were a visiting dignitary."

Before Albert could reply, Beauchamp, a journalist with a cynical streak, was announced. "Am I late?" Beauchamp quipped, eyeing the room's decadent spread. "Or is this your idea of an early lunch?"

Albert welcomed him with a smile. "Relax, my friend. We're waiting for two more guests, and then we'll eat."

"Two more?" Beauchamp asked, raising an eyebrow.

"Yes," Albert said with a mischievous grin. "One of them is someone you'll find very interesting—the Count of Monte Cristo."

Beauchamp and Debray exchanged glances, intrigued by the mention of the enigmatic Count. As they settled in with glasses of sherry and cigars, the room buzzed with anticipation.

Chapter 40: The Breakfast

The guests were still settling into Albert's salon when Beauchamp, the sharp-tongued journalist, spoke up. "So, Albert, who exactly are we waiting to join us for this illustrious breakfast?"

"A gentleman and a diplomat," Albert replied with a grin.

"Then we'll wait two hours for the gentleman and three for the diplomat," Beauchamp quipped. "I may return for dessert—strawberries, coffee, and cigars—but for now, I'll grab a cutlet on the way to the Chamber."

Albert shook his head. "Stay put, Beauchamp. Even if the gentleman were a Montmorency and the diplomat a Metternich, we'll begin promptly at eleven. In the meantime, follow Debray's lead and enjoy a glass of sherry with a biscuit."

"Fair enough," Beauchamp conceded, pouring himself a drink. "I need something to distract me from the political melodrama of the day."

Their lively banter was interrupted by the arrival of Château-Renaud, a young nobleman whose dashing appearance and sharp wit preceded him. Trailing behind him was Maximilian Morrel, a captain of the *Spahis*, whose dignified bearing and sharp uniform marked him as a man of action and honor.

Albert greeted Château-Renaud warmly before turning to Morrel. "And this is…?"

"M. Maximilian Morrel," Château-Renaud announced, "a dear friend and my savior. Salute my hero, Albert."

Albert extended his hand to the captain. "Any friend of Château-Renaud's is welcome here."

"You honor me," Morrel replied with a polite bow.

"Saved your life?" Beauchamp asked, intrigued.

"Indeed," Château-Renaud confirmed, launching into the tale. "While retreating on foot during a campaign in Africa, my horse dead and my weapons spent, I was surrounded by six Arabs. Morrel charged in like a whirlwind, shooting one attacker and slicing another with his sabre. Thanks to him, I'm here to tell the tale."

Morrel waved off the praise. "Château-Renaud exaggerates. It was my duty as a soldier and a fellow man."

Albert clapped his hands. "Gentlemen, let us continue this conversation at breakfast. I believe another hero is about to join us."

Just as he spoke, Germain announced the arrival of the Count of Monte Cristo. All eyes turned to the doorway as the Count entered, his presence commanding immediate respect. Dressed impeccably in a tailored suit, he greeted the room with a slight smile and a nod.

"Gentlemen, thank you for your invitation. It's a pleasure to join such distinguished company."

Albert performed the introductions with an air of pride, highlighting each guest's unique achievements. The Count acknowledged each man with measured politeness, though his attention lingered briefly on Morrel. Something in his gaze suggested recognition, but the moment passed quickly.

Once seated, the breakfast commenced in earnest. Conversation flowed freely, from politics and society to art and philosophy. The Count contributed sparingly but with precision, each of his remarks hinting at a depth of experience that captivated his audience.

Debray leaned forward, his curiosity piqued. "Tell us, Count, you've traveled extensively. Do you have a secret to enduring the rigors of such a lifestyle?"

The Count smiled faintly. "Adaptation, Monsieur Debray. Whether dining on pilaf in Constantinople or swallows' nests in China, one must embrace the customs of each place. It's not about the fare but the spirit in which it's offered."

"And how do you rest?" Beauchamp pressed. "Surely such a schedule would exhaust anyone."

The Count reached into his pocket and produced a small emerald casket. Inside were tiny green pellets. "These," he said, "are a mixture of opium and hashish. One dissolves the worries of the day and grants the most peaceful sleep imaginable."

The casket passed around the table, eliciting awe at the craftsmanship of the emerald and curiosity about its contents.

Beauchamp laughed. "A man of many talents and secrets!"

"Secrets, perhaps," the Count replied with a knowing smile. "But talents? Only those borne of necessity."

As the meal concluded, Albert raised his glass. "Gentlemen, a toast: to the Count of Monte Cristo, a man who embodies the mystery and magnificence of the world beyond our own."

The guests echoed the toast, their glasses clinking. Yet, as they sipped their champagne, more than one guest wondered: who truly was this man who spoke with such authority and grace? For all his openness, the Count remained an enigma.

Chapter 41: The Presentation

When Albert found himself alone with Monte Cristo, he smiled warmly. "My dear Count," he said, "allow me to commence my duties as your guide by showing you a specimen of a bachelor's apartment. You, accustomed to the grand palaces of Italy, may find amusement in calculating how many square feet a young Parisian can call home. As we move from one room to another, I'll open the windows to let you breathe."

Monte Cristo had already glimpsed the breakfast room and salon on the ground floor, but Albert now led him to his favorite retreat—his workshop. Monte Cristo's discerning eye quickly took in the collection: antique cabinets, Japanese porcelain, Oriental fabrics, Venetian glass, and an array of arms from around the world. He recognized each artifact —its origin, craftsmanship, and era—with a familiarity that surprised Albert.

Morcerf had expected to play the role of guide, yet it was Monte Cristo who led the conversation, turning the tour into a lesson in archaeology, mineralogy, and natural history. Albert followed, amazed by the Count's erudition.

Descending to the first floor, Albert brought Monte Cristo to the salon, filled with modern art. Paintings by Dupré, Delacroix, Diaz, and

Boulanger adorned the walls, alongside sketches by Decamp and pastels by Giraud. The Count identified each work and its artist effortlessly, impressing Albert once again with his depth of knowledge.

From the salon, they entered Albert's bedroom, a space defined by tasteful simplicity. One item, however, captured Monte Cristo's full attention: a painting which depicted a young woman in the traditional Catalan fisherwoman's attire, her dark complexion and luminous eyes framed by the blue sea and sky. Monte Cristo's face paled slightly, his breathing quickened, and he stared at the portrait in silence. He recognized the striking features of Mercédès immediately.

"You have a most charming mistress, Viscount," Monte Cristo said at last, his voice composed but distant. "And this costume—a ball outfit, no doubt—suits her admirably."

Albert laughed. "Ah, Count, had you seen my mother, you wouldn't mistake this portrait for anyone else. This is her likeness, painted six or eight years ago during my father's absence. It's a treasured work, though it once caused some discord between my parents. My mother rarely visits this room without shedding a tear over it."

Monte Cristo listened intently, his gaze fixed on the portrait.

"Now that you've seen my modest treasures," Albert continued, "allow me to introduce you to my parents. My mother and father are eager to meet the man to whom we owe so much."

Monte Cristo bowed politely. "It will be my honor."

Albert summoned a servant to announce their visit. As they approached the salon, Monte Cristo's eyes lingered on a family crest above the doorway. "Your family arms?" he asked.

"Yes," Albert replied proudly. "On my father's side, we're French, while my mother's lineage is Spanish. Our history intertwines with the Crusades."

Monte Cristo nodded, his tone thoughtful. "Your arms are indeed beautiful, Viscount. They speak of a storied heritage."

They entered the salon, where another portrait caught Monte Cristo's attention: a man in the uniform of a general, adorned with the ribbons and stars of various orders. Monte Cristo examined it closely, his expression unreadable. Moments later, the Count of Morcerf himself entered the room. A man of fifty with white hair and a military bearing, he greeted Monte Cristo with warmth.

"Monsieur," Morcerf said, "welcome to our home. You have rendered my family a service that ensures our eternal gratitude."

Monte Cristo bowed deeply. "Your welcome honors me, Count. To preserve a life and spare a family grief is not a service but a duty."

The conversation flowed with ease as they awaited the Countess de Morcerf. When she entered, pale and composed, Monte Cristo rose. The Countess paused at the doorway, her hand resting on the frame. Her eyes met Monte Cristo's, and for a fleeting moment, an unspoken recognition passed between them.

"Monsieur," the Countess said, her voice trembling slightly, "I owe you my son's life. For this, you have my eternal gratitude."

Monte Cristo inclined his head. "Madame, the gratitude is unnecessary. To save a son, a mother's treasure, is a simple act of humanity."

The Countess smiled faintly but said no more. As the visit concluded, she invited Monte Cristo to return another day, an invitation he accepted with a silent nod.

As Albert escorted Monte Cristo to his carriage, he reflected on the remarkable impression the Count had made on his family. Watching the Count's departure, Albert mused, "This man is no ordinary guest. His presence stirs something profound in all who meet him."

Chapter 42: Monsieur Bertuccio

The Count of Monte Cristo arrived at his Parisian residence in just six minutes, though the journey was long enough to draw the attention of numerous young men. They admired his impressive carriage and fine horses, each costing 20,000 francs—a luxury they could only dream of affording.

The house, selected by Ali, stood prominently along the Champs-Élysées. Surrounded by a dense grove of trees and shrubs that partially obscured its grand façade, the property featured a double portico adorned with porcelain vases brimming with flowers. Two driveways curved around the shrubbery, leading to the main entrance. The property also boasted a secondary entrance on Rue de Ponthieu, enhancing its exclusivity. As Monte Cristo's coach approached, the gates swung open smoothly—a testament to the efficiency of his Parisian staff.

The carriage halted before the portico, and two figures emerged to greet him. One was Ali, whose joy at seeing the Count was evident in his radiant smile. The other was Bertuccio, the steward, who bowed respectfully and offered his arm to assist Monte Cristo from the carriage.

"Thank you, Monsieur Bertuccio," said the Count as he ascended the steps. "And the notary?"

"He awaits you in the small salon, Excellency," Bertuccio replied.

"And the engraved cards I ordered?"

"They are completed, Excellency. The first was delivered to Baron Danglars at 7 Rue de la Chaussée d'Antin. The remaining cards are on the mantlepiece in your bedroom."

Monte Cristo nodded approvingly. "What time is it?"

"Four o'clock, Excellency."

Handing his hat, cane, and gloves to a waiting footman, Monte Cristo proceeded to the small salon, where the notary awaited him. The steward accompanied him, ever ready to anticipate his needs.

Surveying the room's modest decor, Monte Cristo remarked, "These marbles are unremarkable. Ensure they're replaced soon."

Bertuccio bowed silently. The notary, a provincial scrivener elevated to this moment of importance, greeted Monte Cristo with deference.

"Are the sale documents prepared?" the Count asked.

"Yes, Count," the notary replied, producing the papers.

Monte Cristo glanced over the deed. "And this house I've purchased—where is it located?"

"In Auteuil, Excellency," the notary answered. At this, Bertuccio's complexion turned visibly pale.

"Auteuil?" Monte Cristo repeated. "That's quite near, isn't it? I had imagined something more rural. Why Auteuil, Bertuccio?"

The steward's voice wavered as he stammered, "Your Excellency… I… I didn't choose this property."

Monte Cristo's expression shifted subtly. "Ah, yes. Now I remember. This was my doing. I saw an advertisement and was enticed by its misleading description of a 'country house.' No matter—the transaction is already underway."

Bertuccio hesitated. "If it pleases your Excellency, I could find a better property elsewhere—perhaps in Enghien or Bellevue."

Monte Cristo dismissed the suggestion with a wave. "No, I'll keep this one. Let's not waste time."

The Count signed the deed swiftly, instructing Bertuccio to deliver 55,000 francs to the notary. Bertuccio complied, though his movements were stiff and hesitant. Once the transaction was complete, Monte Cristo dismissed the notary, who departed with heartfelt thanks for the Count's generosity.

Left alone, Monte Cristo retrieved a small locked book from his pocket, unlocking it with a key he wore around his neck. Flipping through its pages, he paused at an entry that confirmed his suspicions. "Auteuil, Rue de la Fontaine, No. 28," he murmured. "It's the same."

Striking a small gong, he summoned Bertuccio, who appeared promptly but with evident unease. "Monsieur Bertuccio," Monte Cristo began, "you've told me you've traveled in France. Have you ever visited Auteuil?"

Bertuccio's hands trembled slightly. "No, Excellency... never."

Monte Cristo observed him keenly. "That's unfortunate. I had hoped you might accompany me this evening to inspect my new property."

Bertuccio's reaction was immediate. "To Auteuil?" he blurted, his voice thick with panic. "Must I go to Auteuil?"

Monte Cristo's gaze hardened. "Of course. As my steward, it's your duty. Or must I summon the carriage myself?"

Bertuccio's shoulders slumped in resignation. "I'll prepare the horses at once, Excellency."

Moments later, the carriage was ready. As they departed, Monte Cristo's curiosity deepened. Whatever secrets Bertuccio harbored, they seemed intricately tied to Auteuil. By the end of the evening, Monte Cristo was determined to uncover them.

Chapter 43: The House at Auteuil

As they descended the staircase, Monte Cristo noticed Bertuccio make the Corsican sign of the cross in the air, muttering a hurried prayer under his breath. Anyone else might have felt pity for the steward, whose visible dread of this journey was almost pitiable. But the Count, driven by his insatiable curiosity, was determined not to let Bertuccio evade the trip to Auteuil. Within twenty minutes, they arrived at their destination, and Bertuccio's anxiety only seemed to intensify as they entered the village. Seated stiffly in the corner of the carriage, he scrutinized every passing house with a feverish intensity.

"Instruct the driver to stop at 28 Rue de la Fontaine," the Count commanded, fixing on Bertuccio with an unrelenting gaze.

The steward's forehead glistened with sweat, but he leaned out of the carriage window and relayed the instruction. The house, located at the village's edge, appeared amidst the twilight gloom, shrouded in an almost theatrical darkness that gave the surroundings an eerie, staged quality. As the carriage came to a halt, the footman opened the door.

"What's the matter, Monsieur Bertuccio?" Monte Cristo asked with a hint of irony. "Are you staying in the carriage tonight?"

Bertuccio flinched but quickly exited, offering his shoulder to assist the Count. Monte Cristo, this time, accepted the help, descending gracefully.

"Knock," the Count instructed, motioning toward the gate. "Announce my arrival."

The steward obeyed, his trembling hand knocking sharply on the door. A concierge appeared moments later, his expression curious but respectful.

"Who is it?" the concierge inquired.

"Your new master," Monte Cristo's footman declared, handing over the notary's letter.

"The house is sold, then?" the concierge asked. "And this gentleman will be living here?"

Monte Cristo stepped forward. "Indeed, my friend. I hope I'll give you no reason to regret your previous master's departure."

The concierge's face lit up. "Oh, monsieur, no regrets here. The old owner barely visited. It's been five years since he was last here. Honestly, it's a relief to see the house in new hands."

"And who was the previous owner?" Monte Cristo asked.

"The Marquis of Saint-Méran," the concierge replied. "An old Bourbon loyalist. His only daughter married Monsieur de Villefort, the former king's attorney."

Monte Cristo cast a subtle glance at Bertuccio, whose pallor had deepened, his hand gripping the gate for support.

"The Marquis of Saint-Méran," Monte Cristo murmured thoughtfully. "The name rings a bell. Is his daughter not deceased?"

"Yes, monsieur. She passed away years agos. Since then, we've barely seen the Marquis."

159

Monte Cristo nodded curtly. "Thank you for the information. Now, bring me a light."

The concierge scurried off but returned empty-handed. "I'm afraid we have no candles, monsieur."

Monte Cristo turned to Bertuccio. "Take one of the carriage lamps and show me through the house."

The steward complied, though his trembling hands betrayed his unease. Together, they toured the property. The ground floor revealed a spacious layout, while the first floor housed a salon, a bathroom, and two bedrooms. A winding staircase near one of the bedrooms led down to the garden.

Monte Cristo paused. "A private staircase—how convenient. Lead the way, Monsieur Bertuccio."

Bertuccio hesitated. "It… it should lead to the garden, Excellency."

Monte Cristo raised an eyebrow. "Should? Let's confirm."

The steward sighed and descended, the lantern casting flickering shadows on the walls. At the staircase's end, Bertuccio froze, his eyes darting wildly. Monte Cristo stepped past him and pushed open the door to the garden. The moonlight struggled to pierce the heavy clouds, casting a dim glow over the unkempt grounds.

Monte Cristo advanced, motioning for Bertuccio to follow. They reached a small clearing when the steward suddenly stopped, setting down the lantern and stepping back.

"No further," Bertuccio whispered, his voice quaking. "You're standing right where…"

"Where what?" Monte Cristo demanded, his patience thinning.

Bertuccio's breathing grew labored. "Where he fell."

Monte Cristo's expression shifted, his curiosity sharpening. "Explain yourself, Monsieur Bertuccio. What's this nonsense?"

"Excellency, I beg you to leave this place," Bertuccio pleaded, his voice breaking. "It's cursed… haunted by what happened here."

Monte Cristo's tone turned icy. "Enough melodrama. You'll tell me everything—now."

The steward clasped his hands, trembling before the Count's unyielding gaze. "Very well, Excellency. But I must warn you, the tale is grim."

Monte Cristo gestured for him to continue. "Speak. I have no tolerance for half-truths."

Bertuccio took a deep breath, his voice heavy with despair. "This house, Excellency… it's where I took my vengeance. Where I committed… murder."

Monte Cristo's eyes glinted with intrigue. "Go on."

And so, in the dim light of the garden, Bertuccio began his confession, the air thick with the weight of long-buried secrets.

Chapter 44: The Vendetta

Monte Cristo settled into a chair in the dimly lit garden, his calm and commanding demeanor urging Bertuccio to speak. The steward's trembling hands clasped together as he began his tale.

"At what point shall I begin my story, your Excellency?" Bertuccio asked hesitantly.

"Wherever you please," Monte Cristo replied evenly. "I know nothing at all of it."

"I thought the Abbé Busoni had told your Excellency some particulars."

Monte Cristo's lips twitched. "Perhaps, but that was years ago. Refresh my memory."

Bertuccio's voice steadied slightly. "Then I can speak without fear of tiring your Excellency."

"Go on," Monte Cristo urged. "You shall supply the want of the evening papers."

"The story begins in 1815," Bertuccio began.

Monte Cristo leaned back. "Ah, 1815. Not yesterday, but close enough."

"No, monsieur, and yet I remember everything as if it were yesterday."

Bertuccio recounted the tale of his older brother, a Corsican lieutenant who fought for the Emperor Napoleon and was wounded at Waterloo. In the turbulent months after Napoleon's defeat, Bertuccio's brother attempted to return home to Corsica, traveling through Nîmes.

"But as I entered Nîmes," Bertuccio said, his voice heavy with sorrow, "I found the streets drenched in blood. Bands of royalists were slaughtering Bonapartists. My brother, still in uniform, was murdered before reaching the inn where he sought refuge."

Monte Cristo's face remained unreadable. "And justice?" he inquired.

"I sought it," Bertuccio replied bitterly. "I went to the king's attorney in Nîmes, a man named Villefort. I begged him to find my brother's killers. His reply?" Bertuccio's eyes burned with anger. "He said my brother had been a soldier of the usurper and deserved his fate."

Monte Cristo's lips curled slightly. "And you vowed revenge?"

"Yes," Bertuccio said. "I declared the vendetta. I swore to kill Villefort, to repay blood with blood. From that moment, I followed him, waiting for my opportunity."

The steward's tale darkened as he described how Villefort relocated to Versailles, hoping to escape his shadow. Bertuccio pursued him relentlessly, finally discovering that Villefort often visited a secluded house in Auteuil.

"It was here," Bertuccio said, gesturing toward the house, "that I found him one night, burying a small box in the garden."

Monte Cristo leaned forward slightly. "A box?"

Bertuccio nodded. "My curiosity was as strong as my thirst for vengeance. As Villefort buried the box, I attacked him. My knife struck true, and he collapsed."

"And the box?" Monte Cristo pressed.

Bertuccio's voice dropped to a whisper. "I dug it up, expecting treasure. Instead, I found an infant inside, wrapped in fine linens and barely alive. The child had been buried alive, left to die."

Monte Cristo's eyes narrowed. "And what did you do?"

"I could not kill an innocent," Bertuccio said. "I revived the boy and left him at an orphanage in Paris. But the boy's life—his very survival—haunted me. Years later, he returned to Corsica, a corrupt and cruel young man named Benedetto. He brought nothing but ruin to those around him."

Monte Cristo stood, his silhouette casting a long shadow. "Yet Villefort still lives?"

"Yes," Bertuccio admitted. "I later learned he survived my attack. My vengeance was incomplete, and my conscience forever burdened by what followed."

Monte Cristo's gaze was inscrutable. "And now, Bertuccio, you are here again, standing where your past unfolded. Perhaps this time, you will find resolution."

The steward fell silent, overcome by the weight of his confession. Monte Cristo turned toward the house, his voice cutting through the darkness.

"The past has a way of returning, Monsieur Bertuccio. And when it does, we must be ready to face it."

Chapter 45: The Rain of Blood

The jeweler returned to the tavern, the storm outside has forced him to retreat back to the inn where he had just purchased a very expensive diamond. Caderousse still clutched the gold and banknotes from this recent sale, while his wife, La Carconte, greeted their guest with overly sweet smiles. Her sudden warmth would have seemed suspicious to anyone who knew her usual sour demeanor.

"Well, well," said the jeweler, his tone laced with irony, "it seems you were counting your fortune rather meticulously in my short absence."

"Oh no," Caderousse replied, feigning nonchalance. "We're just overwhelmed by this unexpected blessing. Seeing the money helps us believe it's not a dream."

The jeweler smiled skeptically. "Do you have other guests here?" he inquired casually.

"No one but us," Caderousse replied. "Our inn is too close to town; travelers rarely stop here."

"Then I hope I'm not imposing."

"Not at all, dear sir," La Carconte chimed in, her tone syrupy. "You're most welcome to stay."

"But where will I sleep?" asked the jeweler.

"Upstairs," La Carconte replied, avoiding her husband's puzzled stare. "We'll manage perfectly."

The jeweler hummed a cheerful tune as La Carconte kindled a fire to dry his wet clothes and prepared his supper. Meanwhile, Caderousse placed the banknotes and gold back into their hiding spot, locking them away with an air of reluctance. He then paced the room with restless energy, occasionally casting glances at his guest with eyes suggestive of a guilty nervousness .

The storm outside raged on, thunder shaking the house as rain lashed against the windows.

"You chose wisely to return," said La Carconte, as she set a modest supper before the jeweler.

The jeweler chuckled. "If the storm eases by the time I've eaten, I'll be on my way again."

"It's the mistral," said Caderousse with a heavy sigh. "It'll last till morning."

The jeweler ate in silence, La Carconte fawning over him while Caderousse avoided meeting his eyes. The uneasy atmosphere thickened with each passing minute.

When the jeweler finally retired to his room, the storm outside intensified, lightning illuminating the strained expressions of the innkeepers. Upstairs, the jeweler's footsteps creaked as he moved about, and soon the sound of the bed groaning under his weight signaled that he had settled in for the night.

Downstairs, La Carconte fixed her gaze on her husband, who sat slumped at the table. "Well?" she said in a low voice.

Caderousse did not reply, burying his head in his hands. The flickering firelight painted their tense silhouettes against the wall. As the night wore on, the storm's fury seemed to invade the very soul of the tavern.

A sudden gunshot shattered the stillness, followed by a bloodcurdling scream. The sound of quick moving footsteps echoed from above, then a loud thud as if a body had fallen. Immediately after, groans and the sounds of a struggle filled the air before a chilling silence descended.

Moments later, the staircase creaked. Caderousse emerged, his shirt soaked with blood. He carried a small shagreen case, which he opened to inspect its contents—the diamond—before tucking it into his red handkerchief. He retrieved the gold and banknotes, stuffed them into his pockets, and fled into the stormy night.

Left in the darkness, the tavern bore the scars of what had occurred. La Carconte was stone dead. The pistol heard had doubtless been fired at her. The shot had frightfully lacerated her throat, leaving two gaping wounds from which, as well as the mouth, the blood was pouring in floods.

The jeweler's lifeless body lay sprawled on the bedroom floor, his chest riddled with knife wounds. Next to him were his two pistols. The second pistol had not gone off, likely from the powder still being wet. Blood pooled beneath him, the scene one of chaos and violence.

When the authorities eventually arrived, they found the tavern in disarray, and all evidence pointed towards Caderousse.

Chapter 46: Unlimited Credit

At precisely two o'clock the next day, a grand calash pulled up to the residence of the Count of Monte Cristo. The carriage, drawn by two magnificent English horses, bore the armorial insignia of a baron and carried a man who appeared determined to make an impression. Dressed in a blue coat with matching buttons, a white waistcoat adorned with a heavy gold chain, and brown trousers, the visitor's appearance was as carefully curated as his air of superiority. His thick black hair, unnaturally glossy, seemed an odd contrast to the deep lines etched on his face, betraying his true age.

The man leaned out of the carriage, scrutinizing the house, the garden, and the livery of passing servants with a level of curiosity bordering on impertinence. His sharp eyes betrayed cunning more than intelligence, and his thin lips curled into a faint, dismissive smile. A glinting diamond on his chest and a red ribbon dangling from his buttonhole completed the image of opulence.

His groom[*] approached the porter's lodge. "Is the Count of Monte Cristo at home?" he inquired.

---

[*]Old French term for "servant"

"The Count resides here," the porter replied, glancing at Ali, who subtly shook his head. "But his Excellency does not receive visitors today."

"Here is my master's card," the groom insisted, presenting it. "Baron Danglars wishes the Count to know that, though pressed for time, he made the effort to pay his respects."

"The valet de chambre will deliver your message," the porter said coolly.

Returning to the carriage, the groom repeated the porter's response.

"How very grand," Danglars muttered, reclining in his seat. "A prince masquerading as a count, no doubt. But no matter—he has asked for a line of credit from me and my banking house. He'll come crawling soon enough when he needs funds." With that, Danglars signaled his coachman. "To the Chamber of Deputies."

Inside the house, Monte Cristo, having observed the exchange through a lorgnette, closed it with a click. "What a repellent face," he murmured, turning to Ali. "Summon Bertuccio."

Moments later, Bertuccio entered, bowing deeply. "Your Excellency wished to see me?"

"I did," Monte Cristo replied. "Did you notice the carriage outside a moment ago?"

"Yes, your Excellency," Bertuccio replied. "The horses were exceptional."

Monte Cristo's gaze hardened. "How is it that such fine horses are not in my stables? Did I not instruct you to procure the best in Paris?"

Bertuccio's face paled. "Your Excellency, those horses were not available when I purchased yours."

Monte Cristo's tone was icy. "Offer double the price."

"Sixteen thousand francs, your Excellency."

Monte Cristo's lips curled faintly. "A banker would never refuse to double his capital. Secure them by five o'clock. I have a visit to make."

Bertuccio bowed and exited, while Monte Cristo turned to his valet, Baptistin. "You've served me a year. Are you satisfied?"

Baptistin bowed low. "Entirely, your Excellency."

"Good. Your service pleases me, but let me be clear: discretion is paramount. Speak favorably or unfavorably of me, and you'll be dismissed. This is your first and last warning."

Monte Cristo's eyes gleamed coldly as Baptistin assured him of his loyalty. With a wave of his hand, the Count dismissed him, turning his attention to preparations for the evening.

By five o'clock, the newly acquired horses stood ready, their black coats gleaming in the fading sunlight. Monte Cristo descended the steps, his cape flowing as he entered the carriage. "To the residence of Baron Danglars," he commanded.

Arriving at the grand home, Monte Cristo's entrance caused a stir. Danglars, presiding over a meeting, excused himself to greet his visitor. As the Count was shown into the drawing room, Danglars' forced politeness barely masked his unease.

"Ah, the Count of Monte Cristo," Danglars began, gesturing grandly. "A pleasure, though I admit your letter of credit surprised me. In the letter—I think I have it here somewhere"—he patted his breast pocket—"ah, yes, here it is. This letter is asking for unlimited credit with our bank."

"Well, baron, what's difficult to understand about that?"

"Just the word 'unlimited'—nothing else, of course."

"Is that term unfamiliar in France? The writers are Anglo-German, you know."

"Oh, the letter's composition is fine; my concern is the validity of the document."

"Really?" asked the count, his tone a blend of innocence and candor. "Are you suggesting Thomson & French aren't considered reliable bankers? Please, baron, share your thoughts. I must admit I feel a bit uneasy, considering I've entrusted them with substantial assets."

"Thomson & French are absolutely solvent," Danglars replied, his smile teetering on mockery. "But the word 'unlimited' is so vague in financial terms."

"It is, quite literally, unlimited," Monte Cristo remarked.

"Exactly my point," Danglars exclaimed. "What's vague is doubtful. As a wise man once said, 'When in doubt, keep out.'"

"In other words," Monte Cristo replied, "Thomson & French may act recklessly, but Baron Danglars will not follow suit."

"Precisely."

"Very clear. Thomson & French impose no limits on their commitments, while M. Danglars wisely maintains his boundaries."

"Monsieur," Danglars retorted, drawing himself up haughtily, "no one has ever questioned the extent of my resources."

"Then it seems I'm the first," Monte Cristo said coolly.

"And by what right, sir?"

"By the right granted by your objections and inquiries, which must surely have a purpose."

Danglars bit his lip again. Defeated on his own ground, his forced politeness now bordered on insolence. Monte Cristo, however, remained effortlessly composed, his demeanor marked by an air of graceful simplicity that he could summon at will.

"Well, sir," Danglars said after a pause, "perhaps you could clarify the amount you intend to draw?"

"Why," Monte Cristo replied, not yielding an inch, "the reason I requested 'unlimited' credit is precisely because I don't know how much I'll need."

Danglars seized the opportunity to regain control. Leaning back in his chair, he said with a confident, almost pompous air, "Please, don't hesitate to name your amount. You'll see that, despite its 'limits,' the resources of the house of Danglars can meet any demand—even a million francs."

"Excuse me," Monte Cristo interrupted.

"I said a million," Danglars repeated, his tone brimming with self-assured ignorance.

"But what could I do with a mere million?" Monte Cristo retorted. "If such a trifling sum were sufficient, I wouldn't have bothered opening an account. A million? Forgive my amusement at the suggestion."

Monte Cristo pulled a small case from his pocket, retrieved two treasury orders for 500,000 francs each, and held them out. Danglars, a man impervious to subtle rebukes, froze. The sight of the documents left him pale and visibly shaken.

"Come now," Monte Cristo said. "Admit it—you don't fully trust Thomson & French. Anticipating this, I took precautions. Here are two additional letters of credit: one from Arstein & Eskeles of Vienna to Baron Rothschild, and another from Baring of London to M. Lafitte. If it eases your mind, I can present my credit elsewhere."

The words hit their mark. Trembling, Danglars inspected the documents with exaggerated scrutiny. Monte Cristo, holding them nonchalantly, might have found the banker's behavior offensive if it didn't serve his purpose.

"Ah, sir," Danglars finally said, his tone now reverential. "Three letters of unlimited credit! I can't doubt you any longer. Forgive my initial hesitations, Count."

Monte Cristo, with his characteristic grace, replied, "For sums as minor as these, your bank shouldn't be inconvenienced. So, can I assume I can draw upon you?"

"Of course, Count. At your service."

"Good. Then we understand each other?" Monte Cristo asked. Danglars nodded. "You're sure no suspicions remain?"

"None, Count. Never for a moment did I truly doubt you."

"No, you just needed reassurance. But now that we're aligned, let's set an initial annual amount—how about six million francs?"

"Six million?" Danglars choked. "Very well."

"If I need more," Monte Cristo added casually, "I'll draw upon you again. For now, please send 500,000 francs tomorrow. I'll be home until midday. If I'm not, I'll leave instructions with my steward."

Danglars, eager to comply, replied, "It will be done by ten o'clock, Count. You have my word."

"Thank you, Baron," Monte Cristo said, rising to leave. "And as for my wealth, it's only recently come into use after being held in trust for several generations. That explains why it may be unfamiliar to you. But in time, I'm sure you'll come to know me better."

Monte Cristo rose and prepared to leave when Danglars interjected, eager to shift the conversation toward more personal matters. "Before you go, Count, allow me the honor of introducing you to my wife. She's in the drawing room, entertaining some friends." Danglars' tone carried an air of pride. "She comes from an illustrious lineage, one of the oldest families in France, and her first husband was a marquis. I'm sure she would be delighted to meet a gentleman of your standing."

Monte Cristo nodded, his enigmatic smile returning. "I would be honored to make her acquaintance."

Danglars rang for a servant, who promptly confirmed that the baroness was at home and receiving visitors. With a theatrical gesture, Danglars extended his arm toward the doorway. "Shall we, Count?"

Monte Cristo followed him, his steps deliberate, as though preparing for a meeting that promised more revelations than simple pleasantries.

Chapter 47: The Dappled Grays

Baron Danglars, followed closely by the Count of Monte Cristo, led the way through a series of opulent apartments. The decor was ostentatious —heavy drapery, gilded furnishings, and a glaring display of wealth that lacked refinement. They finally arrived at Madame Danglars' boudoir, a charmingly distinct space compared to the rest of the mansion. The room's soft pink satin walls, adorned with white Indian muslin, and the delicate medallions of pastoral scenes were a striking departure from the baron's overwhelming taste. It was clear this sanctuary was the work of Madame Danglars herself.

Madame Danglars, though past her youth, remained a striking figure. She sat gracefully at an elaborately crafted piano, her fingers idly brushing the keys. Beside her, Lucien Debray—a frequent companion— was casually flipping through an album on a nearby table.

Lucien had already recounted the details of the Count's dramatic arrival in Paris and his enigmatic aura, heightening Madame Danglars' curiosity. She turned her keen gaze toward Monte Cristo as Danglars introduced him.

"Baroness," said Danglars with a flourish, "allow me to present the Count of Monte Cristo. He comes highly recommended by our associates in Rome, and I dare say he will be the talk of Paris. He plans to spend six million francs over the next year—an endeavor that promises balls, dinners, and entertainments galore. I trust we shall be frequent guests at his splendid affairs."

Madame Danglars' curiosity deepened. She studied the Count with a mixture of fascination and calculation. "When did you arrive in Paris, Count?" she asked.

"Yesterday morning, madame," Monte Cristo replied smoothly.

"And from where, if I may ask? Cadiz? Constantinople?"

Monte Cristo's lips curved slightly. "From Cadiz, this time."

The baroness offered a polite smile. "You've chosen a quiet season for your arrival. Summer in Paris offers little in the way of entertainment."

"I shall adapt," Monte Cristo assured her. "Perhaps you might guide me, madame, in discovering the amusements of your city?"

Their conversation was interrupted by Madame Danglars' maid, who whispered something in her mistress' ear. The baroness turned pale, her composure momentarily shaken.

"What is it?" Danglars asked, visibly uneasy.

"My horses," Madame Danglars exclaimed, her voice rising. "They're gone. My coachman says they were taken from the stables without his knowledge."

"Impossible," Danglars stammered. "Madame, please, calm yourself. Allow me to explain."

"Explain?" the baroness snapped. "Let me guess—you sold them! Those were my prized dappled grays, the finest in Paris. And you sold them to line your pockets."

Danglars attempted a placating tone. "They were too spirited for your safety. I found a buyer willing to pay an exceptional price—sixteen thousand francs. Surely, you'll agree it was a sound decision."

Madame Danglars glared at her husband with icy disdain. "Who bought them?" she demanded.

Before Danglars could reply, Lucien, who had moved to the window, exclaimed, "There they are! Your dappled grays, Baroness. They're harnessed to the Count's carriage."

Monte Cristo, feigning surprise, joined Lucien at the window. "Madame, these were your horses?" he asked. "I had no idea. My steward arranged the purchase this morning."

Madame Danglars' indignation shifted to confusion. "And what did you pay for them, Count?" she asked sharply.

Monte Cristo's expression was neutral. "Thirty thousand francs."

The room fell silent. Danglars' face flushed with humiliation, while Madame Danglars' expression softened into a calculating smile. "How generous of you, Count," she said. "I trust they're to your satisfaction?"

Monte Cristo inclined his head. "More than satisfactory, madame. Yet, if you wish, I would be honored to return them. A lady's preferences should never be compromised."

Danglars didn't respond; his mind was preoccupied with the looming confrontation with his wife. Her furrowed brow, stormy as an Olympian deity's, foretold an inevitable clash. Sensing the tension, Debray suddenly remembered an urgent appointment and made a hasty exit, eager to avoid the fallout of Madame Danglars' impending fury. Monte Cristo, recognizing the value of a strategic retreat, bowed politely and departed, leaving Danglars to face the full force of his wife's wrath alone.

As Monte Cristo left the Danglars residence, he allowed himself a rare smile. "The seeds are sown," he murmured. "Husband against wife, intrigue against intrigue. Paris will provide all the amusement I require."

As Monte Cristo returned home in his carriage, he reflected on the day's events. Later that afternoon, Madame Danglars received a courteous letter from the Count, returning her prized dappled gray horses. He claimed he could not bear the thought of owning them at the expense of a lady's regrets. To soften the gesture, the horses were returned adorned with diamonds on their harnesses. A similar letter was sent to Baron Danglars, playfully requesting forgiveness for the "whimsical gift" and the unconventional manner in which it was delivered. That evening, Monte Cristo departed for his estate in Auteuil with Ali.

The next day, as afternoon arrived, Monte Cristo summoned Ali. "Ali," he said, "I've heard you're exceptionally skilled with a lasso. Can you stop a pair of runaway horses?" Ali, confident as always, nodded in agreement. Monte Cristo tasked him to intercept a carriage with the dappled grays, should they bolt past his house.

Suddenly, the distant sound of wheels reached the Count's ears. A carriage came into view, careening down the street at a terrifying speed. The dappled gray horses were wild with panic, their driver struggling helplessly to regain control. Inside the carriage, a woman clutched a young boy tightly, her face frozen in terror as they hurtled through the street. The vehicle rattled and creaked, threatening to overturn with every bump. Ali jumped into action, running out of the estate and towards the commotion.

With practiced precision, Ali cast his lasso, catching one horse and bringing it down, snapping the carriage pole. He then restrained the second horse, calming the chaos in moments.

Monte Cristo rushed to the scene, carrying the fainted boy and his distraught mother into his home. "All danger is over," he assured her. He administered a single drop of a crimson elixir to the child, who soon opened his eyes, much to his mother's relief.

"My child and I owe you everything," the woman said tearfully.

"It was my privilege, madame," Monte Cristo replied. She introduced herself as Madame Héloïse de Villefort, wife of the prosecutor. Upon learning the horses belonged to Madame Danglars, Monte Cristo admitted he had returned them to the baroness that morning.

As she prepared to leave, Madame de Villefort expressed her gratitude to Ali, though Monte Cristo downplayed it, calling Ali's actions a mere duty. By evening, news of the dramatic rescue had spread across Paris, turning Monte Cristo into the talk of the city and solidifying his mystique.

VOLUME THREE

Chapter 48: Ideology

If the Count of Monte Cristo had been long familiar with the intricacies of Parisian society, he might have better appreciated the significance of the step M. de Villefort was about to take.

Villefort stood as a figure of prominence at court, regardless of the ruling monarch or political climate. Be it under a doctrinaire, liberal, or conservative government, Villefort managed to secure his position. While he was respected for his talent—as those who never suffer political defeat often are—he was hated by some, supported by others, and genuinely liked by no one.

Villefort's household, influenced by his young wife and a daughter from his first marriage, upheld the rigid traditions of the Parisian upper class. Politeness was formal and freezing, etiquette strictly maintained, and any deviation from conventional beliefs or customs was met with contempt. Villefort's personal philosophy was rooted in a profound distrust of idealism, leaving no room for sentimentality or abstract thought in either his private or public life.

As both a magistrate and something of a diplomat, Villefort cultivated an air of dignity and respectability. His connections to the former royal court bolstered his standing with the current regime, ensuring that his opinions were not only respected but occasionally sought. It wasn't mere talent that kept him in power but his position as the king's attorney, a role he manipulated with unparalleled skill. He would only abandon neutrality to take up opposition if it meant solidifying his fortress-like influence.

Villefort rarely made or returned visits himself; this responsibility fell to his wife. Society accepted his absence as the natural consequence of his numerous responsibilities. In reality, it was an expression of calculated pride and superiority—a living embodiment of the axiom, "Pretend to think well of yourself, and the world will think well of you."

For his allies, Villefort was a formidable protector; for his enemies, he was a relentless adversary. To those who neither loved nor hated him, he was a cold, impenetrable symbol of law and authority. His career had survived four political revolutions, each one strengthening the foundation of his professional life.

On this day, Villefort's carriage stopped before the Count of Monte Cristo's door. Announced by the valet de chambre, Villefort entered just as the Count was leaning over a large table, tracing a route on a map that spanned from St. Petersburg to China.

Villefort's entrance was deliberate, his measured steps reminiscent of his courtroom demeanor. Though time had altered his physique —transforming his slender frame into a more gaunt figure—his bearing remained imperious. Dressed in black, save for a white tie and a faint red ribbon in his buttonhole, he radiated solemnity.

Monte Cristo scrutinized Villefort, his curiosity barely concealed. Villefort, for his part, was suspicious of the Count. Accustomed to unmasking frauds and dissecting social phenomena, Villefort approached Monte Cristo not as a noble stranger but as a potential charlatan or fugitive.

"Sir," Villefort began in the clipped tone of a magistrate, "the service you rendered to my wife and son compels me to offer my thanks. I have come to discharge this duty and express my profound gratitude."

Monte Cristo replied coolly, "I am glad to have preserved a son for his mother, for maternal love is sacred. Yet I assure you, sir, the pleasure of fulfilling such a duty far outweighs any gratitude you might feel obligated to offer."

Villefort's astonishment was evident. Accustomed to deference, he was unprepared for such an aloof response. Searching for a new topic, his eyes fell on the map.

"You seem engaged in a study of geography," he remarked. "It must be fascinating for one who has traveled so extensively."

Monte Cristo's smile was faint. "Indeed, sir. I find the study of humanity, viewed collectively, a more illuminating pursuit than examining individuals in isolation. From the whole, one descends to the part, rather than ascending from the part to the whole. An algebraic approach, if you will."

Villefort raised an eyebrow. "Ah, you philosophize. Yet I confess, if I had your leisure, I might seek more entertaining pursuits."

"And yet, sir," Monte Cristo countered, "what you deem entertaining, I might consider trivial. You occupy yourself with human justice —a meticulous but slow-moving machine. I, on the other hand, compare it to natural justice, which often aligns more closely with divine will."

The conversation continued, shifting between philosophy, law, and morality. Villefort, though astonished by the Count's paradoxical views, could not help but be drawn into his enigmatic perspective. Monte Cristo's remarks, often tinged with irony, challenged Villefort's deeply held convictions.

Finally, Villefort's curiosity overcame his reserve. "Tell me, Count, have you no family ties? No nation you call home?"

"No," Monte Cristo replied. "I belong to no country, no family. My allegiance is to myself alone, for only by standing apart can one truly understand the mechanisms of this world."

Villefort studied the Count, his mind racing to comprehend the man before him. For the first time, he realized that Monte Cristo was not merely a man of wealth and mystery but a force unto himself—a being who operated beyond the constraints of society.

As Villefort took his leave, he could not shake the feeling that he had encountered not just a man, but a force of nature, one whose intentions and capabilities defied his understanding. Monte Cristo watched him depart, a faint smile on his lips.

"So it begins," he murmured.

Chapter 49: Haydée

The Count of Monte Cristo, after his meeting with Villefort, found his thoughts drifting to the more serene prospect of visiting his old acquaintances, Maximilian, Julie, and Emmanuel, who resided in the Rue Meslay. Their warmth and the simplicity of their company offered him a rare refuge from the intense emotions of his schemes. Yet, before indulging in that peaceful retreat, he set aside an hour for Haydée, a part of his life and heart that demanded its own sanctuary.

Haydée's apartments, separate from the rest of the Count's home, were a vivid embodiment of her origins and unique identity. Rich Oriental carpets covered the floors, and silk brocades adorned the walls, casting the rooms in luxurious hues. Divans surrounded by soft cushions were arranged for comfort, reflecting the Eastern aesthetic that Monte Cristo had meticulously recreated for her.

Haydée's beauty, both otherworldly and human, captivated all who saw her. Her attire that day—white satin trousers embroidered with delicate pink roses, a blue-and-white striped vest adorned with pearl buttons, and a bodice clasped with diamond fasteners—was as stunning as the young woman herself. Her black hair, tinged with a hint of blue in its intensity, was crowned by a cap embroidered with pearls, while a single purple rose nestled amidst her luxurious locks.

As she reclined in her boudoir, the room's rose-tinted glass ceiling bathed her in a warm glow. She drew leisurely from a Turkish hookah, the perfumed smoke trailing around her like an ethereal veil. The sight of her was an exquisite tableau of grace and serenity.

Monte Cristo's arrival was heralded by a servant who pulled back the tapestried curtain, revealing Haydée. With a smile that could disarm even the most impenetrable heart, she greeted him in her native tongue. "Why do you seek permission to enter? Are you not my master? Or have I ceased to be your slave?"

Monte Cristo returned her smile. "Haydée, you know well that you are free. Free to choose your life and your path."

"Free to leave you?" she asked, a shadow of sadness crossing her features. "Why would I do that? I have no desire to see anyone but you."

The Count's voice softened. "And should you one day find someone you prefer? I would not stop you."

Haydée's eyes glistened with emotion. "No one has ever been to me what you are. My love for you is different, deeper. If you were to leave me, I could not live."

Monte Cristo reached for her hand, but Haydée, with the innocence of a child and the affection of a devoted companion, instead offered her cheek. "Do you remember your father?" he asked gently.

"He is here," she said, touching her heart and her eyes. "And you? You are everywhere."

The Count's gaze softened further. "You must understand, Haydée, that in this house, you are your own mistress. You may live as you wish, go where you please. Yet, I ask only one thing: guard the secret of your heritage. Speak not of your illustrious father or the tragedies of your past."

Haydée nodded solemnly. "I have no need to speak to anyone but you."

Monte Cristo chuckled softly. "Even in Paris, such solitude may not always be possible. You must learn to adapt to this world, as you did in Rome, Florence, and Madrid. It may be of use to you someday, whether you choose to remain here or return to the East."

Her voice was filled with quiet determination. "Wherever we go, we shall go together."

The Count's expression grew thoughtful. "My dear child, one day, you will blossom further into youth and beauty, while I will grow old. It is the way of life."

"My father was old," Haydée replied, her voice unwavering. "Yet to me, he was the most handsome man I knew. And you, my lord, will always be the most beloved to me."

Monte Cristo's heart stirred at her words. As he prepared to leave, he took her hand once more, whispering, "Youth is a flower, and love its fruit. Happy is the one who, after nurturing it, is allowed to claim it as their own."

With those words, he departed, his thoughts lingering on the profound connection he shared with Haydée. As his carriage sped toward the Rue Meslay, he murmured to himself, "In a world of vengeance and justice, she is my peace."

Chapter 50: The Morrel Family

In a matter of minutes, the Count of Monte Cristo's carriage arrived at No. 7 Rue Meslay. The house, constructed of white stone, sat nestled within a small courtyard adorned with flower beds full of vibrant blooms. A modest fountain bubbled in a rocky basin at the courtyard's center, its gold and silver fish glinting in the light. The house's charming features had earned it the nickname "The Little Versailles" from its envious neighbors.

Cocles, the one-eyed concierge who opened the gate, failed to recognize the Count, but Monte Cristo's keen eye identified Cocles immediately. The Count's carriage turned carefully to avoid the fountain, a minor inconvenience for a home as uniquely elegant as this one. Behind the main house stood an expansive workshop and two pavilions, separated from the residence by a wall. Emmanuel, Julie's husband, had wisely purchased the property, using the workshops as a profitable rental venture while maintaining the house and half the garden as their private haven.

The interior reflected the couple's tastes: the breakfast room was paneled in oak, the salon boasted mahogany accents and blue velvet furnishings, and the bedrooms featured citronwood and green damask. Emmanuel had a study he rarely used, while Julie's music room sat idle but well-kept. The second floor mirrored these arrangements, with Maximilian's quarters offering a billiard room in place of a breakfast parlor.

When the Count's carriage stopped at the gate, Maximilian, cigar in hand, was grooming his horse in the garden. Hearing the commotion, he discarded his cigar and rushed to greet the visitor.

"The Count of Monte Cristo?" Maximilian exclaimed, his face lighting up. "Of course we'll see him! Thank you, Count, for remembering your promise."

Monte Cristo shook Maximilian's hand warmly, appreciating the young man's sincerity. "Come," said Maximilian, "I'll guide you myself. My sister's in the garden, tending to her roses, and her husband is nearby reading the papers. Wherever Julie is, Emmanuel is within a few steps—they're inseparable."

As they walked, Julie appeared, a graceful young woman in a silk morning gown. Her hands busily removed dead leaves from a rose bush, but at the sight of her brother and their guest, she paused, visibly surprised.

"Don't worry, Julie," Maximilian teased. "The Count is a man of taste. He'll appreciate the charms of a lady from the Marais."

Julie's smile broke through her initial shyness. "Maximilian, you always take me by surprise. Penelon!" she called.

An elderly man—weathered and strong, with a sailor's resolute demeanor—approached, removing his cap and attempting to hide the tobacco tucked in his cheek.

"Yes, Mademoiselle Julie?" he replied, maintaining the title he had used since her childhood.

"Penelon, please inform Emmanuel of our guest's arrival. Maximilian will escort the Count to the salon."

With a respectful nod, Penelon departed, and Julie excused herself to prepare for their distinguished visitor.

Monte Cristo turned to Maximilian as they entered the house. "I fear my visit has caused a stir."

Maximilian laughed. "You're a celebrated guest, Count. Look, there's Emmanuel now, trading his jacket for a more formal coat."

The house exuded warmth and tranquility. Emmanuel greeted the Count with genuine hospitality, showing him through the well-kept garden before returning to the salon. Inside, a vase of fragrant flowers filled the air with their scent, and the cheerful songs of birds in a nearby aviary added to the serene atmosphere. Julie soon joined them, her hair styled and attire elegant yet understated.

Monte Cristo absorbed the scene in silence, captivated by the familial harmony. At last, he spoke. "Madame, I must apologize for my reaction. Contentment is a rare sight for me. To witness it here, in your home, is profoundly moving."

Julie's smile softened. "We are happy, Count, but we have known great sorrow. Few families have faced trials as bitter as ours."

Maximilian nodded. "It's a simple story, Count, one that may not interest you. Yet it's the foundation of our lives."

Monte Cristo's curiosity was piqued. "And yet, your faith remains unshaken? Surely, the trials you speak of have strengthened you."

Julie's eyes glistened with emotion. "Yes, Count. In our darkest hours, God sent us an angel."

Monte Cristo's composure wavered. He coughed lightly, using his handkerchief to mask the sudden intensity of his feelings.

Emmanuel added, "We've learned to value life's true blessings. Those who endure storms at sea know the full beauty of calm waters."

Monte Cristo stood, his movements measured. "I admire your perspective. But tell me," he asked, pointing to a crystal case containing a silk purse and a large diamond, "what is the story behind this treasure?"

Maximilian's expression turned serious. "It's a relic of the angel Julie mentioned. A man saved us from despair, restored our family's honor, and provided this diamond as my sister's dowry."

Opening the case, Maximilian retrieved a letter and handed it to the Count, who read it with trembling hands. The signature, "Sinbad the Sailor," sent a surge of emotion through Monte Cristo.

Julie's voice broke the silence. "We've prayed to meet this man, to thank him, but he remains a mystery."

Monte Cristo's voice was steady but tinged with emotion. "If your benefactor is the man I think, he may be far away, perhaps never to return."

Julie's eyes filled with tears. "Even so, his kindness lives on in our hearts."

Monte Cristo pressed her hand gently. "If he knew the depth of your gratitude, it might reconcile him to the world."

As he prepared to leave, Monte Cristo's parting words lingered in the air. "Your family's joy is a beacon of hope. Thank you for allowing me to share in it."

Emmanuel and Maximilian watched him depart, their admiration evident. "A remarkable man," Emmanuel said.

Maximilian nodded. "And a kindred spirit. He understands more than he lets on."

Julie, her hand still warm from Monte Cristo's touch, whispered, "There's something familiar about his voice. Perhaps one day, we'll uncover the truth."

Chapter 51: Pyramus and Thisbe

About two-thirds of the way along the Rue du Faubourg Saint-Honoré, behind one of the most imposing mansions in this affluent neighborhood, stretched a vast garden. Towering chestnut trees lined its perimeter, their branches forming a natural barrier above the walls. Every spring, these trees would scatter their delicate pink and white blossoms into large stone vases perched on the two square pilasters of a wrought iron gate. The gate—an artifact from the time of Louis XIII—added an air of antiquity to the scene, though it had long fallen into disuse.

Despite the elegance of the entrance, it remained closed to visitors. Years ago, the mansion's owners chose to limit themselves to the courtyard and the inner garden, cutting off access to what was once a thriving kitchen garden. Over time, the demon of urban speculation had crept in. Plans for a new street at the far end of the property never materialized, leaving the land in limbo. Unable to sell, the owner resorted to leasing the space to market gardeners, but even that venture faltered. Now, only a sparse crop of lucern struggled for survival, the area neglected and forgotten.

The iron gate was boarded up to discourage prying eyes, though the planks' gaps offered narrow glimpses of the enclosed world. Within the garden, near a dense cluster of foliage that cast deep shadows even in summer, stood a stone bench surrounded by rustic seats. This secluded spot, shielded from the city's noise and the mansion's bustle, was a haven for those seeking peace and quiet.

On one warm spring evening, a book, parasol, and embroidery basket lay scattered on the stone bench. Nearby, a young woman stood by the iron gate, peering intently through its gaps. Her posture, rigid with focus, betrayed her heightened emotions.

The stillness was broken by the soft creak of a small side gate leading to the street. A tall, broad-shouldered man in a simple gray blouse and velvet cap slipped in, closing the gate behind him with deliberate care. Though his attire suggested humility, his well-groomed hair, beard, and mustache hinted at a more refined background.

The young woman startled at his sudden appearance, retreating instinctively. But the man's keen eyes caught the flutter of her blue sash through the wooden slats.

"Valentine, it's me," he called softly, his voice muffled by the barrier.

Reassured, Valentine stepped closer, her apprehension giving way to relief. "Maximilian! Why are you so late? It's nearly dinner time, and I barely managed to avoid my stepmother's suspicions. Why are you dressed like that? I hardly recognized you!"

Maximilian smiled, his dark eyes sparkling. "Dearest Valentine, forgive my lateness. The difference in our social stations weighs on me constantly. Yet, when I see you, I cannot help but tell you how much I love you. This disguise—it's part of my plan to stay close to you without arousing suspicion. I've become a gardener."

"A gardener?" Valentine repeated incredulously. "Maximilian, please be serious."

"I am," he said earnestly. "I've leased this patch of land. Now I have every right to be here, and no one will question it. I can even build a small hut close to this gate and tend my crops. For five hundred francs a year, I've bought the privilege of being near you."

Valentine laughed despite herself, though her tone quickly grew somber. "As much as I treasure these moments, Maximilian, we cannot deceive ourselves. My father is resolute, and my stepmother would do anything to ensure I marry Franz d'Épinay. Our meetings, however innocent, put us both in danger."

Maximilian's voice grew firm. "Danger does not scare me, Valentine. I've respected your boundaries, obeyed your every request. My love for you is unwavering, and I will endure anything for the chance to be near you. Tell me you love me, and I can face any obstacle."

Valentine hesitated before threading her fingers through a gap in the planks. Maximilian grasped her hand gently, pressing his lips to her fingertips. "You are my only solace," she whispered. "But my life feels like a prison. My father is indifferent, my stepmother despises me, and my only ally is my grandfather, who cannot even speak. If not for you, I'd be utterly alone."

"Valentine," Maximilian said tenderly, "I would sacrifice anything to bring you happiness. Franz is away for a year. In that time, let us hope for a miracle. Until then, I'll remain your devoted confidant."

Their moment was interrupted by a distant call. "Mademoiselle Valentine! Your stepmother is looking for you."

Valentine's heart sank. "I must go," she said hurriedly. "They'll grow suspicious."

"Who is it?" Maximilian asked.

"The Count of Monte Cristo," Valentine replied, her voice tinged with wonder.

Maximilian leaned on his spade, his expression thoughtful. "Monte Cristo? I wonder what connection he has to your family."

Chapter 52: Toxicology

It was indeed the Count of Monte Cristo who had just arrived at Madame de Villefort's residence to return the prosecutor's visit. At his name, the entire household was thrown into a flurry of activity.

Madame de Villefort, alone in her drawing-room when the Count was announced, immediately instructed that her son be brought to thank him once again. Edward, having heard about the illustrious visitor for two days, rushed in eagerly—not out of obedience or gratitude, but from sheer curiosity. The prospect of saying something mischievously clever made his eyes sparkle.

After exchanging pleasantries, the Count inquired about Monsieur de Villefort.

"My husband is dining with the chancellor," Madame de Villefort replied. "He left a short while ago and will regret not having had the pleasure of meeting you again."

Two visitors who had been present when the Count arrived quickly departed, their curiosity satiated after a polite interval. Once alone with the Count, Madame de Villefort addressed her son.

"What is your sister Valentine doing, Edward? Tell someone to bring her here so I may introduce her to the Count."

"You have a daughter?" the Count inquired. "She must be quite young."

"She is my husband's daughter from his first marriage," Madame de Villefort explained. "A beautiful young woman, though inclined to melancholy."

"Melancholy," Edward chimed in, as he tugged feathers from a parrot's tail to make a plume for his hat. "She's always sad. It's so boring."

"Edward, behave yourself!" Madame de Villefort scolded, though her tone betrayed indulgence. "He's a bright child, Count, but rather incorrigible."

Edward grinned mischievously, clearly enjoying the attention. "She's probably under the big chestnut tree," he announced when asked about Valentine's whereabouts. As if summoned by his words, Valentine entered, her graceful figure framed by the doorway. Her downcast eyes and faint traces of tears did not escape Monte Cristo's notice.

Madame de Villefort introduced her. "My stepdaughter, Valentine de Villefort."

The Count rose to greet her, his gaze lingering as if searching for a memory. "Have we met before?" he asked thoughtfully. "Your presence stirs a recollection, as though I've seen you somewhere… perhaps beneath a bright sky, amidst the scent of flowers."

Valentine shook her head gently. "I don't believe so, sir. I'm not fond of society and rarely venture out."

Monte Cristo smiled faintly. "Perhaps I'm mistaken. But the thought of meeting such grace twice in a lifetime is a pleasant one."

Their conversation turned to Italy when Valentine mentioned a trip to Naples two years prior for her health. Monte Cristo's expression lit up as he recalled, "Ah, Perugia on Corpus Christi Day. I remember now. Your mother sat beneath an arbor, your brother chased a peacock, and you held a bouquet of flowers. What a picturesque memory."

Madame de Villefort's face flushed with recognition. "Yes, I do recall a gentleman who spoke knowledgeably of art and science. Could it have been you?"

Monte Cristo inclined his head, his smile enigmatic. "Perhaps. Memory plays tricks, but coincidences often lead us back to the truth."

As the conversation deepened, Edward's antics continued. He interrupted with witty remarks about Mithridates, the king who immunized himself against poisons. His cheeky behavior earned both reprimands and indulgent laughter.

Monte Cristo's interest shifted as he addressed Madame de Villefort's knowledge of chemistry and poisons. Her fascination with the sciences mirrored his own, and they discussed toxicology with a disconcerting blend of academic detachment and morbid curiosity. Monte Cristo recounted the practices of Eastern alchemists and the historical use of poisons as both weapons and remedies.

"The Orientals excel in the art of subtlety," Monte Cristo explained. "Their poisons leave no trace, yet they act with precision. A mere drop can end life, while a gradual exposure can grant immunity. It's an art as much as a science."

Madame de Villefort listened intently, her eyes gleaming. "And you, Count? Have you studied these methods?"

"Extensively," he admitted. "In the East, survival often depends on one's ability to discern friend from foe. I've seen poisons turn from tools of death into instruments of salvation."

Their conversation was interrupted by the announcement of another guest. As Monte Cristo prepared to leave, Madame de Villefort extended her gratitude. "You've given me much to ponder, Count. Your insights are… enlightening."

Monte Cristo bowed. "It has been a pleasure, madame. Knowledge is best shared, even when it walks the fine line between light and shadow."

As he left, Monte Cristo's thoughts remained with Madame de Villefort. "A fertile mind," he mused, "and fertile minds often bear unexpected fruit."

Chapter 53: Robert le Diable

The evening of the opera *Robert le Diable* promised excitement at the Académie Royale. Levasseur, the renowned performer who had been absent due to illness, was making his grand return as Bertram, drawing an elite and fashionable crowd. As the most admired composer of the time, Meyerbeer ensured the opera was a magnet for Paris's high society.

Albert de Morcerf, like other young men of his status, held a prized orchestra seat. This privilege guaranteed not only a superb view but also easy access to a dozen private boxes occupied by acquaintances. His close friends, Château-Renaud and Beauchamp, had secured their usual spots, Château-Renaud beside Albert and Beauchamp roaming freely as a journalist with unrestricted access.

The minister's box had been offered to Lucien Debray, who, in turn, extended the invitation to the Morcerf family. When Mercédès declined, Albert passed it to the Danglars family, suggesting he might join them later. The baroness and her daughter Eugénie eagerly accepted the offer. For the wealthy Danglars, free opera tickets were irresistible, even while boasting fortunes that could rival royalty.

The performance began as usual with a nearly empty house, as Parisian fashion dictated arriving late. Early arrivals buzzed with chatter and observations of new arrivals, barely glancing at the stage.

Albert's attention was momentarily captured by the appearance of the Duke of Bracciano and his wife in their box.

"And who are they?" Château-Renaud asked.

"That would be the Duke of Bracciano," Albert replied. "Franz and I met him in Rome."

As their conversation continued, the audience's "Shut up!" drew their attention to the stage. Yet Albert and Château-Renaud carried on unabated, discussing the day's races at Champ-de-Mars and the unexpected victory of a horse named Vampa. Albert delighted in revealing his knowledge of the horse's owner: none other than the enigmatic Count of Monte Cristo.

Soon, the arrival of Madame Danglars and Eugénie, escorted by Lucien Debray, diverted Albert's focus. Château-Renaud commented on Eugénie's striking beauty, though Albert dismissed her as too formidable for his taste, comparing her to Diana the Huntress rather than a softer Venus.

As the curtain fell for intermission, the crowd surged into the lobbies and salons. Albert took the opportunity to visit the Duke, who welcomed him warmly. Their animated conversation covered the opera, the races, and the mysterious Count of Monte Cristo. Albert's tales about Monte Cristo's generosity and eccentricities fascinated the Duke.

Meanwhile, Madame Danglars, eager for more information about Monte Cristo, beckoned Albert to her box. There, she quizzed him relentlessly about the Count. Albert deflected many of her inquiries but shared anecdotes about Monte Cristo's wealth and unique habits, including his supposed slave, Haydée, whose beauty rivaled that of any princess. The baroness's fascination grew, and she mused about inviting Monte Cristo to a ball to satisfy her curiosity further.

Monte Cristo himself entered the theater with Haydée, her presence immediately capturing the audience's attention. Draped in an opulent gown and adorned with dazzling jewels, she embodied exotic elegance. Whispered speculations and stares followed her every move, as her origins and connection to Monte Cristo became the evening's hottest topic.

Albert's path crossed with Monte Cristo during the intermission. Their exchange, laced with wit and insight, revealed Monte Cristo's amusement at his growing fame.

"Paris is a peculiar city," Monte Cristo remarked. "Its fascination lies in its ability to turn the extraordinary into the mundane."

As the evening progressed, Monte Cristo's interactions with the audience deepened their intrigue. When introduced to Madame Danglars, he acknowledged her gratitude for his earlier acts of generosity and saved her the embarrassment of further effusive praise by shifting focus to Eugénie.

"Your ward is enchanting," Eugénie remarked, her artist's eye appraising Haydée's beauty.

"Haydée is a child of Greece," Monte Cristo explained. "Fate has placed her under my care."

The evening concluded with the rising of the curtain on the final act. Haydée, though initially captivated by the opera, seemed deeply unsettled after encountering a man from Monte Cristo's past. Her pale demeanor and whispered exchanges with Monte Cristo hinted at dark memories stirred by the encounter.

As the curtain fell, Paris buzzed with talk of the evening's events. Monte Cristo and Haydée departed quietly, leaving behind a theater filled with curiosity and speculation. For the Count, the night had been another calculated step in his intricate web of plans.

Chapter 54: A Flurry in Stocks

Several days after the opera, Albert de Morcerf visited the Count of Monte Cristo at his lavish residence on the Champs-Élysées. The mansion had already taken on the appearance of a small palace, reflecting the Count's immense wealth and impeccable taste. Albert's visit was prompted by his mother's gratitude for Monte Cristo's earlier generosity, expressed through a formal letter signed by "Baronne Danglars, née Hermine de Servieux."

Accompanying Albert was Lucien Debray, whose presence hinted at dual motives—one personal, the other likely driven by Madame Danglars' curiosity about the enigmatic Count. While Albert presented his thanks, Lucien wandered the room, discreetly inspecting the artwork, weapons, and luxurious furnishings with an air of nonchalance that barely masked his interest.

"You're in regular contact with the Danglars family, are you not?" Monte Cristo asked Albert casually.

"Yes, Count," Albert replied. "As I've mentioned, everything remains as expected on that front."

"More settled than ever," Lucien interjected, adjusting his monocle as he turned the pages of a finely bound album.

Monte Cristo's expression remained inscrutable. "I must admit, I didn't anticipate such swift progress."

Albert sighed. "Things tend to unfold on their own, don't they? My father and Danglars served together in Spain—my father in the army, Danglars in the commissariat. Both laid the foundations of their fortunes during those tumultuous times."

"Yes," Monte Cristo said thoughtfully. "Mademoiselle Eugénie—that's her name, I believe?"

"Indeed," Albert confirmed. "She's beautiful, no doubt, but not to my taste."

Monte Cristo's curiosity deepened. "You don't sound particularly enthusiastic about this marriage."

Albert hesitated before replying. "The wealth intimidates me, Count. It's overwhelming."

Monte Cristo chuckled softly. "Are you not wealthy yourself?"

"My father's income is fifty thousand francs a year. He might give me twelve thousand when I marry. Modest by Parisian standards."

Monte Cristo leaned back. "True, wealth isn't everything. But your name and station are of great value. A union with Mademoiselle Danglars could be quite advantageous. You would bring nobility; she would bring fortune. It seems a fair balance."

Albert frowned. "It's not that simple. My mother dislikes the idea of this marriage. Her reservations about the Danglars family are strong, though she hasn't explained why."

Monte Cristo's expression darkened briefly. "Perhaps her refined sensibilities object to their lack of aristocratic heritage."

"It's possible," Albert conceded. "But her disapproval is enough to make me reconsider. This entire situation is a source of great anxiety."

Monte Cristo's tone turned pragmatic. "Then why not refuse? Your father may be disappointed, but your mother's happiness should weigh just as heavily."

Albert appeared conflicted. "I'll think it over. Perhaps you could help me decide?"

Monte Cristo smiled faintly. "If my advice can aid you, I'll gladly offer it."

Their conversation was interrupted by Lucien, who had settled into a chair, pencil in hand, scribbling figures into a notebook.

"Are you sketching?" Monte Cristo asked, amused.

"Hardly," Lucien replied. "I'm calculating. Danglars recently made a fortune in Haitian bonds—they rose from 206 to 409 in three days. A prudent investment, yielding three hundred thousand francs."

Albert laughed. "That's not his largest profit. Last year, he earned a million in Spanish bonds."

"It's not Danglars," Lucien corrected, "it's Madame Danglars. She's the true gambler in the family. No one can influence her, not even her husband."

Monte Cristo's sharp gaze betrayed his growing interest. "A daring woman. But markets can be unforgiving. One poor gamble might teach her caution."

Lucien shrugged. "Even so, she thrives on risk. Changing her would be impossible."

The conversation drifted to lighter topics before Albert prepared to leave. "By the way, Count, my mother would be delighted if you visited us night for dinner. She admires you greatly."

Monte Cristo smiled politely. "I appreciate the invitation, but I must decline. I have a prior engagement."

Albert smirked. "Oh? You've been teaching me how to make excuses—now prove this engagement is real."

Monte Cristo rang the bell, and his valet Baptistin entered. "Tell the Viscount what I instructed you this morning," Monte Cristo said.

"To close the door at five and admit only Major Cavalcanti and his son," Baptistin replied.

"You see?" Monte Cristo said, smiling. "The Major is an Italian nobleman introducing his son, Andrea, to Parisian society. I promised to help them, and they'll dine with me tonight."

Albert laughed. "You're a true mentor, Count. I'll leave you to your guests, but give my regards to your illustrious Italians."

After Albert left, Monte Cristo summoned Bertuccio. "We'll host a dinner at Auteuil on Saturday. Replace the old furnishings but leave the red damask bedroom as it is. Make the yard unrecognizable, but leave the garden untouched."

"And the guest list?" Bertuccio asked.

Monte Cristo's smile was mysterious. "Even I don't know yet, but trust me—it'll be worth it."

His thoughts lingered on Albert's predicament and Madame Danglars' audacity. "Fate," he murmured, "has a way of unraveling even the best-laid plans."

Chapter 55: Major Cavalcanti

Both the Count and Baptistin were truthful in informing Morcerf about the impending visit of Major Cavalcanti, which had served as Monte Cristo's pretext for declining Albert's invitation. As the clock struck seven, Bertuccio, following the Count's orders, had left for Auteuil two hours earlier. Shortly after, a cab pulled up to the Count's residence. Its occupant stepped out, the cab quickly departing as if embarrassed by its passenger.

The visitor, a man of about fifty-two years, sported a green overcoat adorned with black frogs, blue trousers, and slightly worn boots. His buckskin gloves and a hat resembling those of the gendarmes gave him an eccentric yet formal appearance. A black cravat with white stripes encircled his neck, uncomfortably resembling a noose. This peculiar figure rang the gatebell and asked if he had arrived at No. 30 Avenue des Champs-Élysées, the residence of the Count of Monte Cristo. When the porter affirmed, he entered and ascended the steps with deliberate slowness.

Baptistin, having received a detailed description of the expected visitor, instantly recognized him. The man scarcely had time to state his name before the Count was informed of his arrival. Ushered into an elegant yet understated drawing room, the major was greeted by Monte Cristo with a welcoming smile.

"Ah, my dear sir, you are most welcome. I've been expecting you," the Count said warmly.

"You were aware of my visit, then?" the Italian asked with surprise.

"Certainly," Monte Cristo replied. "I was informed you'd arrive precisely at seven."

"Ah, excellent," said the visitor, his nervous demeanor easing slightly. "It seems no precaution was overlooked."

"Not at all," Monte Cristo assured him. "You must be the Marquis Bartolomeo Cavalcanti?"

"Indeed," the major replied, his face lighting up. "Formerly a major in the Austrian army."

"Precisely," Monte Cristo confirmed. "But your visit today was not entirely your idea, was it?"

"No," Cavalcanti admitted, "I was sent here by someone else."

"The excellent Abbé Busoni?" Monte Cristo suggested.

"Exactly!" the major exclaimed, producing a letter. Monte Cristo opened it and began reading aloud.

"'Major Cavalcanti, a distinguished patrician of Lucca, descendant of the Cavalcanti of Florence, possessing an income of half a million francs.' Magnificent!" Monte Cristo exclaimed, glancing up.

The major's eyes widened. "Half a million? I had no idea it was so much!"

"You've likely been misled by your steward," Monte Cristo suggested. "Perhaps it's time for a thorough audit."

Monte Cristo continued reading. "'He requires only one thing to complete his happiness—to recover a lost and adored son.'"

The major sighed dramatically. "Yes, my son, taken from me at five years old by gypsies or family enemies. I have searched for him for fifteen years."

"A tragic story," Monte Cristo said with sympathy. "And yet, you are in the right place. I can help restore your son to you."

The major's face brightened. "Then the letter speaks true?"

Monte Cristo nodded. "Without a doubt. The Abbé Busoni's reputation is impeccable. Here is a postscript: 'To spare Major Cavalcanti inconvenience, I enclose a draft for 2,000 francs for travel expenses and provide credit for an additional 48,000 francs.'"

The major's relief was evident. "You'll provide these funds?"

"Of course," Monte Cristo replied. "But first, let's ensure your comfort. Would you care for some wine and a biscuit?"

Monte Cristo rang for refreshments, which arrived promptly. As the major sipped his wine, Monte Cristo inquired further about his family, confirming the details with a series of leading questions. "Your marriage to the Marchesa Corsinari… was it not a remarkable event?"

"Indeed," Cavalcanti replied, visibly improvising. "We wed despite significant opposition."

Monte Cristo produced documents. "Here is your marriage certificate and your son Andrea's baptismal record. The Abbé Busoni was thorough."

The major marveled at the foresight. "You've saved me untold trouble already!"

Monte Cristo's expression turned serious. "But remember, in Paris, such stories of gypsies stealing noble children will not suffice. You must claim your son was sent to a provincial college for his education. People here value clear documentation."

The major nodded vigorously. "Of course, you're absolutely right."

Monte Cristo rose, signaling the conversation's conclusion. "Now, prepare yourself to meet your son. He's waiting in the adjoining room. I trust this reunion will bring you joy."

As Monte Cristo exited, the major's excitement was palpable. Alone, he muttered, "A fine young man, a fortune awaiting him… Paris will soon know the name Cavalcanti."

Chapter 56: Andrea Cavalcanti

The Count of Monte Cristo entered the adjoining room, a space Baptistin had prepared as the drawing room, and found a young man of striking elegance and charm reclining on a sofa. The visitor, who had arrived about half an hour earlier, had been immediately recognized by Baptistin as the tall young man with light hair, a red beard, and piercing black eyes whom the Count had so carefully described.

When Monte Cristo entered, the young man quickly rose, tapping his boot with a gold-headed cane as he greeted his host with a confident air.

"The Count of Monte Cristo, I presume?" he began.

"Indeed," replied Monte Cristo, "and I believe I have the honor of addressing Count Andrea Cavalcanti?"

The young man bowed elegantly. "Count Andrea Cavalcanti at your service."

Monte Cristo gestured toward a chair. "Please, make yourself comfortable. You bring with you a letter of introduction, do you not?"

Andrea hesitated slightly. "Yes, though I must admit the signature was most unusual."

"A letter from 'Sinbad the Sailor,' correct?" Monte Cristo inquired with a faint smile.

"Exactly. I confess I found it peculiar—I have only ever heard of Sinbad in the Thousand and One Nights."

Monte Cristo chuckled. "He is, indeed, a descendant of that famed adventurer—or so he claims. In reality, he is an eccentric Englishman named Lord Wilmore, a man of great wealth and peculiar habits."

"Ah, that explains much," Andrea said with a smile. "Well, monsieur, I am at your service."

Monte Cristo's eyes glinted with interest. "Then perhaps you could enlighten me with some details about your life and family?"

Andrea leaned back, his confidence evident. "Of course. I am Count Andrea Cavalcanti, son of Major Bartolomeo Cavalcanti. Our family, though still wealthy—my father's income exceeds half a million francs—has endured significant misfortunes. At the age of five, I was separated from my family under tragic circumstances. For fifteen years, I sought to reunite with my father, but only recently did I receive this letter directing me to Paris and to you."

Monte Cristo nodded thoughtfully, studying Andrea's face. "A most intriguing story. Your father is, indeed, in Paris and has been seeking you with great devotion. His account of your separation was profoundly moving."

Andrea's composure faltered momentarily. "My father is here? Truly?"

"Yes," Monte Cristo affirmed. "Major Bartolomeo Cavalcanti. I have spoken with him. He recounted how he received a letter promising your return in exchange for a ransom. Despite the cost, he acted without hesitation to bring you back."

Andrea's eyes narrowed as he processed this information, his mind clearly racing. "A remarkable tale," he murmured.

Monte Cristo's tone turned conversational. "Your father's primary concern is the life you've led during your separation—whether your captors treated you well, and whether you've retained the refinement befitting your noble heritage."

Andrea's smile returned. "I assure you, monsieur, my education and upbringing were exceptional. My captors sought to enhance my value, much like the scholars of antiquity trained slaves in medicine and philosophy to increase their worth."

Monte Cristo's expression revealed a mix of amusement and approval. "A clever analogy. But I must warn you—Parisian society is skeptical of such stories. Your tale is compelling, but I advise discretion. Too much detail may inspire suspicion rather than sympathy."

Andrea's confidence wavered slightly, but he quickly masked it. "You're quite right, Count. I'll heed your advice."

Monte Cristo stood, signaling the end of their discussion. "Your father awaits you in the adjoining room. I trust your reunion will be joyous."

Andrea bowed deeply. "Thank you, Count, for facilitating this moment. It means more to me than I can express."

After Andrea exited, Monte Cristo activated a concealed panel in the wall, revealing a small opening that allowed him to observe the adjoining room. Through the aperture, he watched as Andrea approached Major Cavalcanti. Their reunion, though outwardly heartfelt, bore the unmistakable marks of rehearsed theatrics.

"Ah, my dear father!" Andrea exclaimed with exaggerated warmth. "What a joy to see you after so many years!"

The major, equally performative, embraced him stiffly. "Indeed, my son. This is a moment I've long awaited."

Monte Cristo's lips curled into a faint smile. "Two actors in a most curious play," he murmured. "Paris shall soon bear witness to their performance."

Chapter 57: In the Lucern Patch

The narrative shifts back to the serene yet emotionally charged garden of M. de Villefort's residence. Behind the wrought iron gate, shaded by sprawling chestnut trees, Maximilian Morrel awaited the arrival of Valentine. He stood in the shadows, his heart beating in anticipation as he listened for her light footsteps on the gravel path.

When the sound he longed for finally reached his ears, it brought with it an unexpected surprise—two figures, not one, approached. Valentine was accompanied by Eugénie Danglars. The delay, it turned out, was caused by an extended visit from Madame Danglars and her daughter. Not wanting to seem neglectful of her promise to Maximilian, Valentine had suggested a walk in the garden to her guest. Maximilian's sharp instincts as a lover quickly grasped the situation, and he found comfort in the silent glances Valentine cast in his direction as she walked past.

Despite the physical distance and the presence of another, Valentine managed to convey her message through her expressive eyes. "Have patience," they seemed to say. "This is not my fault."

Maximilian obeyed, watching as Valentine and Eugénie passed. His thoughts wandered, comparing the two young women. Eugénie, with her commanding presence and sharp features, appeared every bit as confident as Valentine was gentle. The contrast between the two heightened Maximilian's admiration for his beloved.

After about half an hour, the garden finally belonged to Valentine and Maximilian alone. When Eugénie and Madame Danglars left, Valentine made her way back into the garden. She moved cautiously, ensuring no one observed her before joining Maximilian.

"Good evening, Valentine," Maximilian greeted her, his voice a mix of relief and affection.

"Good evening, Maximilian," Valentine replied softly. "I know I kept you waiting, but you saw the reason for my delay."

"Yes," he acknowledged, "I recognized Mademoiselle Danglars. I didn't realize you two were so close."

Valentine sighed lightly. "We're not. She confided her reluctance about marrying Albert de Morcerf, and I, in turn, shared my misery over my engagement to Franz d'Épinay."

Maximilian's face softened. "Dear Valentine, your candor means everything to me."

Their conversation turned to the stark differences between Valentine and Eugénie. Maximilian admired Valentine's sincerity and warmth, qualities he found lacking in Eugénie's aloof and independent demeanor. Valentine teased him gently about his observations, bringing lightness to their shared burdens.

The mood shifted when Valentine mentioned a summons from Madame de Villefort. "She asked to see me," Valentine explained, "regarding a matter tied to my fortune."

"Do you think it's about your marriage?" Maximilian inquired, concern lining his voice.

"I don't believe so," Valentine said, though her tone hinted at uncertainty. "Madame de Villefort has always seemed indifferent to the idea of my marrying M. d'Épinay."

Maximilian's face brightened momentarily. "If that's true, I might grow to admire her."

Valentine's laugh was tinged with sadness. "Don't be too quick to judge her favorably. Her true objection isn't to M. d'Épinay but to marriage itself. She once supported my wish to join a convent, though my grandfather's heartbreak dissuaded me."

Valentine's expression softened as she recounted her grandfather's silent yet profound love. "His tears stopped me," she said, her voice filled with emotion. "Whatever suffering I endure, his gratitude and love will always make it bearable."

Maximilian took her hand gently through the grating, his eyes full of devotion. "Your strength and compassion humble me, Valentine. I can't fathom what I've done to deserve you."

Their moment of intimacy was interrupted by the mention of Monte Cristo. "Do you know," Maximilian began hesitantly, "I've felt an inexplicable connection to the Count since the day we met."

Valentine's brow furrowed. "He's kind to you, then?"

Maximilian nodded. "More than kind. He has an uncanny ability to foresee events. I believe he's orchestrated our lives to align in ways we don't yet understand."

Valentine seemed skeptical but intrigued. "I wish I could share your faith in him. To me, he feels distant—powerful, yes, but disinterested in my pain."

Maximilian reassured her. "Perhaps you've misunderstood him. His actions often carry hidden kindness. Give him time, Valentine. He may yet surprise you."

As their time together dwindled, Maximilian held Valentine's hand one last time. "Promise me you'll hold on to hope. Whatever comes, we'll face it together."

Valentine smiled faintly, the weight of her circumstances momentarily lifted. "I promise, Maximilian. As long as you're with me, I'll endure anything."

With that, she withdrew, her figure disappearing into the shadows of the garden. Maximilian watched her go, his heart full of love and quiet determination.

Chapter 58: M. Noirtier de Villefort

The scene shifts to the solemn confines of M. Noirtier's room. Villefort, accompanied by his wife, enter to find the old man seated in his armchair, motionless but observant, his piercing eyes reflecting the only vitality left in his paralyzed body.

M. Noirtier was an extraordinary figure. Though confined to his chair, unable to speak or move, his eyes conveyed his thoughts with startling clarity. He communicated through an intricate system of signals understood only by three people: his granddaughter Valentine, his loyal servant Barrois, and Villefort himself. However, of these, only Valentine engaged him with genuine devotion, while Villefort's visits were infrequent and perfunctory.

Villefort addressed his father with formal gravity. "I trust you will not be displeased that Valentine is not with us and that I dismissed Barrois. Madame de Villefort and I have a matter of significance to discuss with you."

Noirtier's gaze remained inscrutable as Villefort continued. "We are planning Valentine's marriage. It is a union we are certain will meet your approval."

The old man's expression betrayed no reaction. Villefort, undeterred, pressed on. "Her betrothed is M. Franz de Quesnel, Baron d'Épinay. A man of wealth, rank, and impeccable character. Surely, you will find this match suitable."

At the mention of Franz's name, Noirtier's eyes flared with unmistakable anger. His pupils dilated, and his eyelids quivered with an intensity that signaled his vehement disapproval.

Madame de Villefort attempted to placate him. "We thought this news would please you, sir, given your affection for Valentine. Moreover, M. d'Épinay has agreed to allow you to live with them, ensuring you and Valentine will not be separated."

Noirtier's glare intensified, his silent defiance palpable. Villefort, interpreting the reaction, remarked coldly, "Your objections are clear, but this decision has been made with Valentine's best interests in mind. This union will secure her future."

Noirtier's fury was evident, yet he lacked the means to articulate his thoughts. Madame de Villefort, frustrated, asked, "Shall I send Edward to keep you company?"

Noirtier responded with a firm blink, his refusal unmistakable. "Then shall I send Valentine?" she asked.

At this, the old man's eyes brightened, and he signaled his eager consent. Villefort and his wife exited, instructing a servant to quickly summon Valentine.

Moments later, Valentine entered, her face flushed with concern. "Grandpapa, what's wrong? They've upset you, haven't they?"

Noirtier's eyes confirmed her suspicion.

"Was it my father?" she asked.

"No."

"Madame de Villefort?"

"No."

"Is it something I've done?" she pressed, alarmed.

Noirtier's eyes signaled again, this time affirming. "Have I hurt you, grandpapa?" Valentine asked, her voice trembling.

The old man's gaze softened, indicating that her actions had not directly caused his distress. Valentine's mind raced. "Is it about my marriage?" she ventured.

Noirtier's eyes blazed with anger and sorrow. Valentine knelt beside him. "Grandpapa, I don't want this marriage either. I don't love M. d'Épinay. If I could, I'd escape this fate."

Noirtier's expression shifted, a glimmer of hope replacing his earlier rage. He signaled for her to stay as he conveyed his next request. Valentine quickly interpreted his wishes through their established system. "You want a notary?" she asked.

His affirmative signal was immediate. She rang for Barrois and instructed him to fetch one. When Villefort returned, Valentine explained, "Grandpapa has requested a notary. It seems urgent."

Villefort regarded his father with suspicion but ultimately acquiesced. Barrois left to fulfill the task, leaving Noirtier triumphant, his resolute eyes promising that he still had a role to play in shaping Valentine's destiny.

Chapter 59: The Will

As soon as Barrois had left the room, Noirtier looked at Valentine with an expression that conveyed determination and a hint of mischief. Valentine understood him perfectly, as did Villefort, whose face darkened with irritation. Taking a seat, Villefort waited in silence for the notary to arrive, his demeanor calm but tinged with restrained frustration. Noirtier glanced at Valentine and then at Villefort, signaling that she was to remain present.

Three-quarters of an hour later, Barrois returned with the notary, who was greeted by Villefort with formal pleasantries.

"Sir," Villefort began, "M. Noirtier has summoned you, as you see. While his physical faculties are severely impaired, he is still capable of conveying his thoughts with some difficulty. My daughter will assist in interpreting his wishes."

Noirtier's gaze turned toward Valentine, his eyes filled with trust and urgency. She stepped forward. "Sir," she said to the notary, "I can easily communicate with my grandfather. His system of signs is precise, and I assure you that I understand him completely."

The notary hesitated, glancing at Villefort and then back at Valentine. "Forgive me, but such a situation requires the utmost caution. To proceed, I must be convinced that I fully understand M. Noirtier's intentions and that he is of sound mind."

Valentine's voice was steady. "I can demonstrate his mental clarity. My grandfather signals 'yes' by closing his eyes and 'no' by winking. Allow me to show you." She turned to Noirtier. "Grandpapa, do you understand me?"

Noirtier closed his eyes deliberately.

"And do you confirm that these are the signals you use to communicate?"

Again, he closed his eyes.

The notary nodded, impressed. "Very well. Let us proceed."

Villefort intervened, pulling the notary aside. "Sir, are you truly confident that a man in such a condition can fully comprehend legal matters? His faculties may be impaired."

The notary frowned. "His responses suggest otherwise. Still, I will test his understanding thoroughly before drafting any document."

Returning to his seat, the notary addressed Noirtier. "You summoned me to draft a will, correct?"

Noirtier closed his eyes in affirmation.

The process began, with Valentine serving as interpreter. She patiently named letters of the alphabet, pausing when Noirtier signaled the desired one. After much effort, the word "Will" emerged, confirmed by Noirtier's emphatic signals.

Villefort's wife entered the room, curiosity lighting her face as she observed the scene. The tension thickened as the notary asked, "To whom do you wish to leave your fortune?"

Madame de Villefort interjected, "Surely it will go to Valentine, who has cared for you so devotedly."

But Noirtier's vehement wink of dissent shocked everyone.

"Not to Mademoiselle de Villefort?" the notary asked, incredulous.

Noirtier's signal was clear: "No."

Valentine's face fell, confusion mingling with hurt. "Grandpapa, I never desired your fortune," she whispered. "Your love has always been enough."

Her grandfather's eyes softened, conveying reassurance. He looked toward the notary to continue.

Madame de Villefort, emboldened, suggested, "Perhaps the inheritance will go to Edward?"

Noirtier's eyes flashed with unmistakable anger, and his repeated winks left no doubt about his feelings.

The notary, intrigued, asked, "Do you intend to leave your fortune to charity?"

Noirtier closed his eyes in agreement.

Villefort's frustration boiled over. "Father, this is madness! You disinherit your family entirely?"

Noirtier's unyielding gaze silenced his son. The will was dictated, witnessed, and sealed. Its terms were irrevocable.

As the witnesses departed, Noirtier's triumphant eyes met Valentine's. Though she had been excluded from his fortune, the depth of his love for her remained evident. She understood that his decision was a declaration against the marriage she dreaded.

Villefort stormed out, muttering, "This old man's stubbornness knows no bounds." But as he left, Noirtier's gaze burned with quiet satisfaction. He had ensured that his will, both literal and metaphorical, would shape the future.

Chapter 60: The Telegraph

When M. and Madame de Villefort returned home, they found that the Count of Monte Cristo had visited during their absence and was still waiting in the drawing room. Madame de Villefort, still recovering from her earlier agitation, excused herself and retired to her bedroom. Villefort, more composed, entered the salon to meet the Count.

Though Villefort believed he had masked his inner turmoil, the Count's discerning gaze immediately detected the shadow clouding his host's demeanor. Monte Cristo's radiant smile only heightened the contrast.

"My dear Villefort," Monte Cristo said after the customary pleasantries, "you seem preoccupied. Have I arrived in the middle of some critical judicial matter?"

Villefort attempted a weak smile. "No, Count, you flatter me. It's nothing so dramatic. Merely a personal loss—a small matter of money."

Monte Cristo raised an eyebrow. "Ah, a financial setback. Even for a man of your means, such losses can sting."

"It's not just the money," Villefort admitted, his bitterness surfacing. "Nine hundred thousand francs is significant, but it's the principle.

To have one's hopes dashed by the whims of an old man lost in his second childhood… it's infuriating."

Monte Cristo feigned curiosity. "Nine hundred thousand francs? That is indeed a considerable sum. And may I ask who caused this unfortunate event?"

Villefort's face tightened. "My father, Noirtier."

"I thought you mentioned that his faculties were greatly diminished?" Monte Cristo asked, his tone carefully neutral.

"Physically, yes," Villefort replied. "But his mind remains sharp —sharp enough to dictate a will to notaries, entirely against my wishes."

Before Monte Cristo could respond, Madame de Villefort entered, her smile carefully composed. She greeted the Count warmly, but the tension between her and Villefort was evident.

"What is this talk of wills and misfortunes?" Monte Cristo asked, turning his attention to Madame de Villefort. "It seems I have stumbled into a family matter of great importance."

Madame de Villefort glanced at her husband before speaking. "It is indeed unfortunate, Count. My husband's father has made a decision that places our daughter Valentine at a significant disadvantage. But I trust my husband will find a way to rectify the situation."

Villefort frowned. "I have always respected my father, both as a parent and as a man of principle. But this… this is pure spite. To disinherit Valentine simply because of her marriage is unjust."

Monte Cristo's expression remained inscrutable, though his eyes sparkled with interest. "Surely there must be a deeper reason for such a drastic measure?"

Villefort hesitated, then spoke. "The issue lies with the family of her betrothed, Baron Franz d'Épinay. My father harbored animosity toward Franz's father due to political differences. He was a staunch Bonapartist, while General de Quesnel, Franz's father, aligned himself with the royalists."

Monte Cristo nodded thoughtfully. "Ah, politics. They have a way of sowing discord even within families."

Madame de Villefort, seizing the opportunity, added, "Still, the marriage is a matter of honor. We cannot allow an old feud to dictate our daughter's future."

"Indeed," Monte Cristo said. "Such unions often serve to heal old wounds."

Villefort's voice grew firm. "Regardless of my father's actions, the marriage will proceed. Valentine's happiness and our family's honor demand it."

Monte Cristo's faint smile betrayed nothing. "A noble sentiment. But tell me, have you considered informing the Baron of this situation? It might be best to address any concerns directly."

Villefort waved the suggestion away. "That would only complicate matters. No, the marriage must proceed as planned."

Monte Cristo rose, signaling his intent to leave. "A delicate situation indeed. I trust your wisdom will guide you to the best resolution. But now, I must take my leave. I have a peculiar appointment to keep."

"An appointment?" Madame de Villefort inquired.

"Yes," Monte Cristo replied with a glint of amusement. "I am visiting a telegraph station. I've always been fascinated by these devices, their black arms signaling messages across great distances."

"A telegraph?" Villefort repeated, surprised.

Monte Cristo nodded. "Indeed. There's a poetry to their movements, don't you think? But I fear my musings may bore you. Until Saturday, my friends."

With that, he departed, leaving Villefort and his wife to ponder the enigmatic Count's parting words. In his wake, the household buzzed with unresolved tension and a growing sense of unease.

Chapter 61: How a Gardener May Get Rid of the Dormice That Eat His Peaches

The following morning, the Count of Monte Cristo set out from Paris, heading through the Barrière d'Enfer and taking the road to Orléans. He passed the village of Linas without stopping, despite the telegraph's mechanical arms signaling above. Instead, his destination lay at the old tower of Montlhéry, perched on the highest point of the surrounding plain, and where another telegraph station was located.

Upon arriving, Monte Cristo dismounted at the base of the hill and began climbing a narrow, winding path. The ascent brought him to a quaint garden enclosed by a hedge bearing green fruit. He soon found a small wooden gate secured with a simple string and nail. Manipulating the mechanism, he stepped into the garden—a meticulously tended space adorned with flourishing plants and an old ivy-covered tower that seemed as though it held secrets from centuries past.

Monte Cristo scanned the grounds with an appreciative eye. The garden's paths formed intricate shapes, bordered by mature boxwood hedges. Rose bushes flourished without blemish, and even the air seemed to hum with the care lavished on this verdant retreat. A gardener's passion was evident in every corner.

Suddenly, his foot struck against something crouched behind a wheelbarrow. A man, startled, sprang up with an exclamation, clutching a handful of strawberries nestled on grape leaves.

"Gathering your crop, I see," Monte Cristo remarked with a smile.

The gardener, a man of about fifty with weathered features, tipped his cap in apology. "Excuse me, sir. I wasn't expecting visitors. You've caught me at my work."

Monte Cristo's benevolent smile reassured the man. "Don't let me disturb you. Please, continue."

The gardener hesitated, then returned to his task. "I've been keeping an eye on these strawberries for weeks. The season's been kind, but I suspect a few have gone missing—likely stolen by the boy from the village."

"A pity," Monte Cristo said, stooping to examine the vibrant plants. "But youth and temptation often go hand in hand."

The gardener nodded solemnly. "True enough, but it's still vexing." His gaze flicked to Monte Cristo's fine attire. "Forgive me, sir. You're not an inspector, are you?"

Monte Cristo chuckled. "Far from it. I'm merely a traveler with a curiosity about this place."

Relieved, the gardener invited Monte Cristo to explore further. They spoke of gardening, the telegraph's workings, and the gardener's humble life. "I earn a thousand francs a year," the gardener explained. "Not much, but it's enough to get by."

Monte Cristo's interest sharpened. "And do you ever understand the messages you relay?"

"Rarely," the gardener admitted. "Most are gibberish to me. That's the beauty of it—I'm just a machine, a cog in the system."

Monte Cristo's gaze grew contemplative. "Fascinating. And if you were distracted… if you missed a signal, what would happen?"

"A fine," the gardener said grimly. "A hundred francs—a tenth of my annual income."

Monte Cristo's tone turned casual. "But suppose, for a moment, you were offered fifteen thousand francs to alter a signal. What would you say to that?"

The gardener froze. "Fifteen thousand?"

Monte Cristo drew a packet of banknotes from his pocket. "Imagine: a small house, two acres of land, and financial security. All you need do is repeat three simple signals from this paper."

The gardener's hands trembled as Monte Cristo pressed the money into them. His protests were weak. "But… the consequences…"

Monte Cristo's voice turned firm. "You'll harm no one. Trust me. This act will serve the greater good."

Under Monte Cristo's calm yet commanding presence, the gardener complied. Together they walked into the telegraph station. With shaking hands, he manipulated the telegraph's levers to transmit the signals Monte Cristo provided. Nearby operators, confused but duty-bound, repeated the signals faithfully.

As the final message was sent, Monte Cristo smiled. "Congratulations. You've just improved your life. And remember, you've wronged no one."

The gardener stared at the banknotes, disbelief and relief mingling on his face. "Thank you, sir. I'll… I'll make good use of this."

Monte Cristo left the tower, his expression inscrutable.

Back in Paris, the erroneous telegraph message reached key figures. Among them was Danglars, who, misled by false news of political upheaval in Spain, rushed to sell his Spanish bonds at a loss. By the next morning, the correction in the press revealed the truth: the crisis had been fabricated. The bonds soared, and Danglars had lost a fortune.

At breakfast, Monte Cristo shared the news with Maximilian Morrel, his tone light but purposeful. "I've learned something valuable, my friend. With enough care, even the smallest gardener can rid himself of the dormice that threaten his harvest."

Chapter 62: Ghosts

From the outside, the house at Auteuil appeared modest, its exterior bearing no trace of the opulence associated with the Count of Monte Cristo. This simplicity was deliberate, adhering to the Count's explicit instructions to maintain the understated facade. The true grandeur lay within, meticulously crafted to reflect its master's taste.

Bertuccio, ever efficient, had transformed the interior with remarkable speed and precision. Where the courtyard had once been bare, he had planted sycamores and poplars, following the Count's detailed plans. The paved stones were replaced with a lush lawn, still glistening with morning dew. Inside, every detail was a reflection of Monte Cristo's refined preferences. The house, which had seemed lifeless just a day earlier, now exuded vitality, imbued with the Count's favorite fragrances and adorned with his beloved books, art, and treasures.

By the time Monte Cristo arrived, the residence felt as though it had always been his. His dogs greeted him enthusiastically, and birds sang from their perches. The entire house, like an awakened memory, seemed to breathe and flourish under his presence. Servants moved through the corridors with practiced ease, as though they had served there for years. Even the stables were alive with activity, the horses responding to their grooms with familiar neighs.

Yet, one room remained untouched. This chamber, hidden and mysterious, was avoided by all—even Bertuccio passed it with a visible shudder. The room's closed door seemed to guard secrets known only to its master.

Monte Cristo's expression unreadable as he surveyed the house. He walked through the rooms without comment until he reached his bedroom, where a rosewood cabinet caught his attention.

"A glove holder, I presume?" he said with a trace of amusement.

Bertuccio, standing nearby, beamed. "Would your Excellency care to open it? You'll find gloves within."

Monte Cristo's brief nod of approval left Bertuccio elated. The steward's unease dissipated, replaced by pride in having met his master's expectations.

At six o'clock, the sound of approaching hooves signaled the arrival of Maximilian Morrel. He dismounted gracefully and greeted the Count with unrestrained enthusiasm. "I've arrived early, Count. I wanted a moment with you before the others came. My sister and Emmanuel have much to share with you as well."

Monte Cristo smiled. "Your horse will be well cared for, Maximilian. And I trust your ride was enjoyable?"

Maximilian's laughter was infectious. "Médéah is magnificent. I've never ridden a finer horse. She's worth every franc."

Soon, the guests began to arrive. Among them were Madame Danglars, accompanied by Lucien Debray, and her husband, whose pallor betrayed his inner turmoil. Monte Cristo's sharp eyes noticed every nuance, including the subtle exchange of a note between Madame Danglars and Debray—a gesture so practiced it escaped everyone's attention but his.

Madame Danglars complimented Maximilian's horse, expressing a playful desire to buy it. Monte Cristo intervened smoothly, weaving a tale of a wager Maximilian had made to tame the horse, ensuring he couldn't part with it without losing face. The baroness accepted this explanation with a smile, though her husband's curt remark about already owning enough horses was met with uncharacteristic silence.

Monte Cristo led the guests through the house, showcasing its treasures with a storyteller's flair. He recounted the history of immense porcelain jars, supposedly baked in an emperor's oven and submerged in the sea for centuries. His tales captivated the guests, save for Danglars, who absentmindedly plucked flowers and leaves from a nearby orange tree.

The arrival of Major Cavalcanti and his son, Andrea, added to the intrigue. The younger Cavalcanti, newly polished and eager to impress, became the focus of quiet scrutiny among the other guests. Monte Cristo introduced them to Danglars, hinting at the son's intention to find a Parisian bride—a statement that seemed to pique Madame Danglars' interest.

The evening's tension peaked when Villefort and his wife arrived. Though Villefort's exterior remained composed, Monte Cristo felt the tremor in his handshake. Madame de Villefort's carefully constructed smile masked the unease she shared with her husband. Observing them, Monte Cristo reflected silently, "Women alone know the art of true dissimulation."

As the dinner hour approached, Bertuccio appeared, his face pale and strained. He whispered urgently to Monte Cristo, his gaze fixed on Madame Danglars. "That woman... she's the one. The woman from the garden."

Monte Cristo's expression did not change, though his voice carried a quiet command. "Compose yourself, Bertuccio. We have guests."

Bertuccio's trembling finger pointed toward Villefort. "And him... the one I failed to kill."

Monte Cristo's voice remained calm. "Your imagination runs wild. Lawyers, you see, are tenacious creatures."

Bertuccio's agitation grew, but Monte Cristo silenced him with a glance. "The dinner waits," Bertuccio finally announced, steadying himself against the wall.

Monte Cristo offered his arm to Madame de Villefort. "Shall we?" he said, his tone as smooth as ever. As Villefort escorted Madame Danglars, the guests moved to the dining room, each harboring their own secrets, while the Count watched, his mind a labyrinth of plans and revelations yet to come.

Chapter 63: The Dinner

As the guests entered the dining room, a shared curiosity filled the air. Each person seemed to question what strange force had brought them to this enigmatic house, and yet, despite their unease, none would have preferred to be absent. Monte Cristo's reputation, his extraordinary wealth, and the mystery surrounding him had proven more compelling than his decorum.

The seating arrangement itself heightened the intrigue. Villefort sat between Madame Danglars and Maximilian Morrel, while Monte Cristo was flanked by Madame de Villefort and Danglars. Debray found himself placed between the two Cavalcantis, and Château-Renaud sat between Madame de Villefort and Morrel.

The feast was unlike anything the Parisian guests had ever experienced. Monte Cristo had curated an Oriental banquet fit for Arabian tales. Exotic fruits from every corner of the globe were piled high in ornate vases, while rare birds and colossal fish were served on gleaming silver platters. The wines, sourced from the Archipelago, Asia Minor, and the Cape, sparkled in bottles so uniquely crafted they seemed to enhance the flavors within.

As the guests marveled, Monte Cristo's humor broke the tension. "Ladies and gentlemen, when one reaches a certain level of fortune, the pursuit of the extraordinary becomes the only goal. The marvelous, after all, is simply that which we do not understand."

He gestured toward two magnificent fish on the table. "For example, one of these comes from fifty leagues beyond St. Petersburg, the other from five leagues outside Naples. Isn't it amusing to see them both here, side by side?"

"Impossible!" exclaimed the guests.

Monte Cristo chuckled. "Impossible? Nothing is impossible. Each fish was transported alive, one in river herbs, the other in lake rushes, across many miles. And yet here they are, ready to grace our table."

Danglars, who was skeptical, smirked. "You're a man of fables, Count."

Monte Cristo snapped his fingers, summoning servants carrying casks. Inside were live specimens of the same fish. The room erupted in applause and laughter.

As the dinner progressed, the conversation shifted to the rapid transformation of the house. Château-Renaud commented, "I was here a week ago. The entrance was entirely different, and the courtyard was barren. Today, it's a lush paradise."

Monte Cristo smiled enigmatically. "Why not? I enjoy grass and shade."

Madame de Villefort remarked, "This was once the residence of M. de Saint-Méran, wasn't it?"

"Yes," Monte Cristo confirmed. "But it was my steward who finalized the purchase."

Château-Renaud's voice lowered. "It's said that uninhabited houses often conceal dark secrets. This one always seemed… haunted."

Monte Cristo's gaze turned distant. "There is something about this house. Certain rooms seem to breathe sadness, as though they carry the weight of the past."

After dinner, the guests followed Monte Cristo to one such room. Its faded red damask drapery and ancient furnishings created an atmosphere of foreboding. Madame de Villefort shivered. "It's unsettling."

Monte Cristo gestured toward a concealed staircase. "Imagine, if you will, someone descending these stairs on a stormy night, carrying a burden they wish to hide from man and God."

Madame Danglars, visibly distressed, leaned heavily on Villefort's arm. Debray approached, concerned. "Madame, are you unwell?"

"Just the air," she murmured. "I need air."

Monte Cristo's smile softened. "Ah, but imagination can be cruel. Let us return to the garden for coffee."

As the group dispersed, Monte Cristo lingered with Villefort and Madame Danglars under the shade of a large tree. "It was here," he said, stamping the ground, "that we unearthed a box containing the skeleton of a newborn."

Madame Danglars stiffened, her face ashen. Villefort's hand trembled.

"A newborn?" Debray asked, his voice sharp with interest.

"Yes," Monte Cristo replied. "Why bury a child here unless to hide a crime?"

Villefort's voice cracked. "Who said it was alive when buried?"

Monte Cristo's gaze was piercing. "Why bury it at all if it were not?"

The guests fell silent. Monte Cristo, sensing the tension, waved it away. "Enough of grim tales. Let us enjoy our coffee."

As they returned to the garden, Villefort whispered urgently to Madame Danglars. "We must speak. Tomorrow, at my office."

Monte Cristo observed them, his serene smile betraying nothing.

Chapter 64: The Beggar

The evening unfolded with an air of subdued tension. Madame de Villefort was the first to express a desire to return to Paris, a sentiment Madame Danglars secretly shared but had not dared to voice. Taking the lead from his wife, Villefort signaled the departure. He offered Madame Danglars a seat in his landau to ensure she was under the care of his wife. Meanwhile, Danglars, deeply engaged in an animated conversation with Major Cavalcanti, appeared entirely indifferent to the arrangements.

Monte Cristo, ever the observer, had discreetly noted Villefort's low-toned exchange with Madame Danglars earlier in the evening. Though their words had been inaudible, their body language betrayed a conversation of significant gravity. Allowing events to unfold without interference, the Count permitted Morrel, Château-Renaud, and Debray to leave on horseback, while the ladies were escorted in Villefort's carriage. Danglars extended a seat in his own carriage to Major Cavalcanti, while Andrea prepared to depart in his tilbury[*], the groom waiting patiently beside the vehicle with exaggerated poise.

Andrea, for his part, had been unusually reserved during dinner. His sharp mind had kept him cautious, fearful of saying something that

---

[*]A two-wheeled carriage, without a top or cover

might betray his ignorance or background in the company of such distinguished figures, particularly Villefort. His silence had earned him a favorable impression, reinforcing Danglars' belief that the young man was the scion of a noble family whose wealth and manners reflected untold refinement.

As Andrea approached his tilbury, a sudden hand on his shoulder startled him. Expecting Danglars or Monte Cristo, he turned to find instead a face from his past: a man with a sunburnt complexion, sharp teeth glinting beneath a wolfish smile, and eyes that gleamed with unsettling intensity. A red handkerchief bound his gray hair, and his threadbare clothing barely concealed his gaunt frame. This apparition's presence sent a shiver down Andrea's spine. It was someone from his past he would have rather forgotten: a man named Caderousse.

"What do you want?" Andrea demanded, his voice strained.

"Pardon me," Caderousse replied, his voice a sinister blend of mockery and familiarity. "I need to speak with you."

Andrea's groom attempted to intervene, but the stranger's biting retort and menacing grin drove him away. Andrea steeled himself. "Speak quickly, then," he said, masking his unease.

The man leaned closer, his voice dropping to a whisper. "Spare me the walk back to Paris. I'm tired, and unlike you, I didn't dine on fine fare tonight."

Andrea recoiled at the audacity. "What do you mean?"

"Take me with you," the man insisted, his tone dangerously casual. "Your carriage is fine enough for two, isn't it? Or should I address you by your real name, Benedetto?"

At this name, Andrea's composure faltered. After a brief internal struggle, he waved his groom away, instructing him to walk back to the barrier and find a cab. Left alone with the intruder, Andrea gestured toward the tilbury. "Get in," he said coldly.

The man clambered in without hesitation, his ragged form an odd contrast to Andrea's polished appearance. They drove past the last house in the village in tense silence before Andrea stopped the horse and faced his unwanted passenger.

"Now," Andrea demanded, "why have you come to disrupt my life?"

The man's grin widened. "Why did you deceive me?"

"Deceive you? How?"

"When we parted ways at the Pont du Var, you said you were heading to Piedmont and Tuscany. Yet here you are in Paris, living like a prince."

Andrea's patience wore thin. "What does it matter to you where I go?"

The man's voice turned venomous. "It matters because I helped you once. And now, it's time you returned the favor."

"You want money?" Andrea guessed.

"Smart boy," the man sneered. "Let's say a hundred francs a month to keep me quiet."

Andrea produced a pouch of coins and handed over two hundred francs. "Here," he said. "This will last you a while. Take it and disappear."

The man's eyes gleamed with greed, but he shook his head. "I'll take your money, but I'm not going anywhere. You'll hear from me again, Benedetto. Count on it."

Andrea's hand drifted toward his pocket, where a pistol rested, but the man's sharp eyes caught the movement. He reached behind his back, producing a long knife, its blade glinting in the moonlight.

"Let's not make this unpleasant," the man said with mock civility. "We understand each other, don't we?"

Andrea withdrew his hand, his expression hardening. "Fine. But this is the last time."

The man laughed darkly. "Oh, Benedetto, you're too clever for that. I'll see you soon."

With that, he leapt from the tilbury and disappeared into the shadows, leaving Andrea alone with his thoughts. As he resumed his journey, Andrea muttered bitterly, "One can never be truly free of the past."

Chapter 65: A Conjugal Scene

The Villefort household was unusually tense that morning. Villefort had risen earlier than usual and left for the Palais de Justice without sharing his plans with his wife. Madame de Villefort, however, had a sharp intuition for detecting trouble, and her husband's demeanor only heightened her suspicions.

It was close to noon when Villefort finally returned. Madame de Villefort had spent the morning pacing in the salon, her fingers drumming against the armrest of her chair. When her husband entered, she stood, her composure intact, though her eyes betrayed her concern.

"You've been gone since dawn," she said evenly. "Did something urgent arise?"

Villefort removed his gloves with deliberate slowness. "The court always demands urgency," he replied, avoiding her gaze.

Madame de Villefort's lips tightened. "And yet your expression suggests this morning was no ordinary affair."

Villefort sighed, sinking into a chair. "You're as perceptive as ever. Indeed, it was not. I've had a meeting with the Baron Danglars."

At the mention of Danglars, Madame de Villefort's curiosity deepened. "And?"

"The discussion concerned Valentine's future," Villefort said, his tone measured. "Specifically, her marriage to Franz d'Épinay. Danglars has hinted at second thoughts regarding the arrangement."

Madame de Villefort's eyebrows rose. "Second thoughts? But why? He's been unwavering in his support until now."

Villefort hesitated before answering. "It seems he has been approached by another suitor. A young man of considerable fortune—Andrea Cavalcanti."

Madame de Villefort's lips curved into a faint smile. "Wasn't he only recently introduced to Parisian society by the Count of Monte Cristo?"

Villefort nodded. "Precisely. And that connection alone has made Danglars reconsider. The Count's reputation carries weight."

Madame de Villefort's smile lingered. "How fascinating. And what do you think of this Cavalcanti?"

Villefort's expression darkened. "I think little of him. His sudden appearance and mysterious fortune are suspicious. But Danglars sees only the promise of wealth and influence."

Madame de Villefort's voice took on a soothing tone. "And what of Valentine? Have you considered how she feels?"

Villefort's frustration flared. "Feelings? What role do feelings play in matters of marriage? Valentine's duty is to secure the family's position, not indulge in sentiment."

"And yet," Madame de Villefort countered, "it's clear she harbors no affection for Franz. Perhaps this Cavalcanti presents an alternative worth considering."

Villefort's voice hardened. "Enough. The decision has already been made. Valentine will marry Franz, and that is final."

Before Madame de Villefort could respond, a servant entered with a note. Villefort opened it, his face tightening as he read. "I must leave again," he announced, standing abruptly. "This matter requires immediate attention."

Madame de Villefort watched him go, her thoughts racing. Left alone, she considered the implications of her husband's words and the potential opportunities they presented. Though Villefort's mind was fixed on duty and tradition, hers was ever calculating, seeking the advantage in every situation.

As the door closed behind Villefort, Madame de Villefort allowed herself a rare moment of satisfaction. Change was in the air, and she intended to ensure it worked in her favor.

Chapter 66: Matrimonial Projects

The day after Madame Danglars' tense conversation with her husband, Debray failed to make his usual visit on his way to the office. By half-past twelve, instead of waiting idly, Madame Danglars summoned her carriage and departed. Danglars, concealed behind a curtain, watched her leave with a calculating gaze. He had instructed the servants to notify him upon her return, but as the clock struck two, she had not yet arrived.

Growing restless, Danglars ordered his horses and departed for the Chamber, where he registered his name to speak against the budget. He had remained in his study, surrounded by correspondence, becoming increasingly agitated as he unraveled the financial disasters plaguing him. Among the many unwelcome visitors that morning was Major Cavalcanti, who arrived punctually, as agreed the previous night, to finalize his business with the banker.

Leaving the Chamber after an unusually heated session, Danglars—whose demeanor betrayed mounting frustration—directed his coachman to the Avenue des Champs-Élysées, No. 30. Monte Cristo received him but asked him to wait in the drawing room, as he was engaged with another guest.

As Danglars waited, the door opened, and a man in clerical attire entered. Without pause, the man bowed politely and disappeared into an adjacent room. A moment later, Monte Cristo emerged, his expression apologetic yet composed.

"Forgive me, Baron," he said. "That was Abbé Busoni, an old friend who has just arrived in Paris. I hadn't seen him in years, and our conversation took longer than I anticipated. I hope I haven't inconvenienced you."

Danglars forced a smile. "Not at all. I regret choosing an inopportune time and can return later."

Monte Cristo waved away the suggestion. "Nonsense. Please, have a seat. But I must admit, you appear troubled. Is something amiss?"

Danglars sighed heavily, sinking into a chair. "I've had a streak of bad luck, Count. This month alone, I've suffered one financial setback after another. It's as if fate conspires against me."

Monte Cristo's tone carried both concern and curiosity. "I'm sorry to hear that. May I ask what troubles you?"

Danglars recounted his misfortunes, beginning with a bankrupt associate in Trieste. "Jacopo Manfredi—a man who has never failed me—suspended payments while owing me nearly a million francs. Then, there was the debacle in Spain, where I lost 700,000 francs due to false reports of Don Carlos' return. All told, I've lost nearly 1.7 million francs this month."

Monte Cristo's eyebrows lifted in mock surprise. "An unfortunate series of events, indeed. But tell me, do you attribute all these losses to mere chance?"

Danglars frowned. "What else could it be?"

Monte Cristo's smile was enigmatic. "In my experience, Baron, the threads of fate are often manipulated by unseen hands. But enough of such grim topics. Perhaps I can be of assistance. Do you require funds?"

Danglars stiffened, his pride wounded. "I assure you, Count, my situation is not so dire. I have other investments yielding returns. This is merely a temporary setback."

Monte Cristo's expression softened. "I'm relieved to hear it. And what of Major Cavalcanti? Has he proven a reliable client?"

"Thus far, yes," Danglars replied. "He presented a bond for 40,000 francs this morning, signed by Abbé Busoni and endorsed by you. I've also opened an account for his son, Andrea, who receives a monthly allowance of 5,000 francs."

Monte Cristo chuckled. "A modest sum for a young man of his standing, wouldn't you agree?"

"Indeed," Danglars said. "But should Andrea require additional funds, I've been instructed to deny them unless specifically authorized by his father."

Monte Cristo nodded approvingly. "A prudent measure. And what do you think of young Cavalcanti?"

Danglars hesitated. "He's polished but somewhat reserved. I understand he's new to Paris and unfamiliar with its ways."

"A natural trait for one raised under a strict tutor," Monte Cristo remarked. "But tell me, Baron, have you considered introducing him to your daughter? It seems a match worth contemplating."

Danglars' smile grew calculating. "An intriguing suggestion, Count. Andrea's fortune and lineage would certainly complement Eugénie's standing."

Monte Cristo's eyes gleamed. "Then let us toast to new beginnings. But a word of caution: delve deeper into the Cavalcanti family's history before committing. Appearances, as you well know, can be deceiving."

As Danglars left, his mind churned with possibilities. Meanwhile, Monte Cristo watched from the window, his expression inscrutable. The pieces of his intricate plan were aligning, and the game was far from over.

Chapter 67: The Office of the King's Attorney

After departing in her carriage that morning, Madame Danglars directed her driver to the Faubourg Saint-Germain, weaving through the narrow streets until they arrived at the Passage du Pont-Neuf. Once there, she alighted and discreetly entered the passage on foot. Dressed plainly and with a thick black veil concealing most of her face, she blended easily into the crowd, her steps purposeful as she hailed a cab.

She instructed the cabdriver to take her to the Rue de Harlay. As the cab crossed the Pont-Neuf and entered the bustling district near the Palais de Justice, Madame Danglars adjusted her veil, using a small mirror to ensure her disguise was intact. Only her pale complexion and striking eyes were visible beneath the fabric.

When the cab came to a halt, she paid the driver and stepped lightly up the stairs of the courthouse. The Palais was alive with activity that morning; attorneys, clerks, and petitioners filled the Salle des Pas-Perdus. Few paid attention to the veiled woman making her way toward the antechamber of the King's Attorney, where her presence caused an immediate stir.

The door-keeper approached her respectfully. "Madame, you are expected," he said, ushering her through a private passage into the office of M. de Villefort.

Villefort was seated at his desk, his back to the door, absorbed in writing. He did not look up as the door closed behind her. Only when he heard the sound of her footsteps did he rise, bolt the door, and draw the curtains. Satisfied they were alone, he turned to greet her.

"Thank you for your punctuality, Madame," he said, gesturing toward a chair.

Madame Danglars accepted the seat, though her hands trembled as she adjusted her veil. Her heart pounded, the oppressive atmosphere of the room making her feel as though she were on trial.

"It has been a long time since we last spoke alone," Villefort began, his voice tinged with both regret and reproach. "I'm afraid our conversation today will be a painful one."

Madame Danglars' voice wavered. "I'm here because you insisted, though I suspect this discussion will be far more difficult for me than for you."

Villefort's lips curled into a bitter smile. "You are wrong. Today, I feel more like a prisoner than a judge."

His words startled her, but Villefort continued before she could respond. "Madame, you know I am not prone to deception without cause. What I have to share concerns both of us deeply. It is a shadow from the past, one I fear will soon resurface in a most troubling way."

Madame Danglars' composure faltered. "What do you mean?"

Villefort leaned closer, his voice dropping to a near whisper. "It's about the child we thought lost. The one we… buried."

Her breath caught. "Thought we lost?" she echoed, the word trembling on her lips.

Villefort nodded grimly. "Yes. I've reason to believe the child may have survived."

Madame Danglars' gasp was audible. "Survived? But how? You told me… you said it was motionless… lifeless."

Villefort's tone was sharp. "That's what I believed. But recent events have cast doubt. The Count of Monte Cristo—he knows something. He mentioned the disinterment of a child beneath the flowers, a child I could not find when I later returned to the garden so many years ago."

Madame Danglars clutched the arms of her chair, her knuckles white. "You returned! You searched?"

Villefort's expression hardened. "Yes. I dug where I had buried the child, but the chest was gone. At first, I thought it had been stolen. Later, I feared the child had been taken alive."

The baroness' eyes filled with tears. "Alive?"

"Yes," Villefort said grimly. "Someone may have taken the child to the foundling hospital. I traced records, found evidence of a child matching the description. But the trail went cold when a woman claiming to be the mother came to claim it, presenting the other half of a torn napkin bearing your monogram."

Madame Danglars' voice broke. "And you… stopped searching?"

Villefort's frustration was evident. "I searched for years! Agents, spies, endless inquiries—all led nowhere. Now, the Count's knowledge has rekindled old fears. Someone knows the truth, and that truth could destroy us both."

Madame Danglars rose shakily to her feet. "What do we do?"

Villefort's gaze was steely. "We must discover what the Count knows and why he has chosen this moment to reveal it. Until then, trust no one. Speak of this to no one. Our survival depends on our silence."

As she departed, Madame Danglars felt the weight of her past pressing down on her. The carriage ride back to her home was silent, save for the pounding of her heart and the whispers of fear echoing in her mind.

Chapter 68: A Summer Ball

The same day Madame Danglars met with Villefort, a traveling carriage pulled into the courtyard of No. 27 Rue du Helder. Moments later, the door opened, and Madame de Morcerf stepped out, leaning on her son Albert's arm. Albert soon left his mother's side, instructing the servants to prepare his horses. After dressing meticulously, he rode to the Champs-Élysées to visit the Count of Monte Cristo.

Monte Cristo received Albert with his characteristic enigmatic smile. While his demeanor appeared welcoming, there remained an unyielding barrier, as though no one could truly breach his defenses. Albert, eager and animated, approached the Count warmly, but Monte Cristo extended only a cool handshake in return.

"Here I am, dear Count," Albert began.

"Welcome home," Monte Cristo replied.

"I arrived just an hour ago," Albert continued. "From Tréport, not Dieppe."

"Indeed? And what brings you here so quickly?" Monte Cristo asked, feigning indifference.

"I came directly to see you," Albert admitted. "And to ask if you've done anything for me while I was away."

Monte Cristo's expression remained neutral. "Had you commissioned me for something?"

Albert laughed. "Come now, Count. Don't pretend to be so detached. Surely you've thought of me."

Monte Cristo inclined his head slightly. "Perhaps. But if I have done anything, it has been without conscious intent."

Albert raised an eyebrow. "How intriguing. Please, enlighten me."

"Very well," Monte Cristo said. "M. Danglars dined with me recently, as did your Italian friend, Andrea Cavalcanti."

"Your so-called prince?" Albert teased.

Monte Cristo's tone turned playful. "He calls himself count. But who am I to question titles? Everyone addresses him as such."

Albert chuckled. "You're a strange man, Count. But tell me, did they speak of me?"

"Not a word," Monte Cristo replied. "Though I suspect you'd prefer they forgot you altogether."

Albert shook his head. "If they didn't mention me, I'm sure they thought of me, and that's even worse."

Monte Cristo raised an eyebrow. "Why should it matter? Especially if Mademoiselle Danglars wasn't present."

Albert sighed dramatically. "I'm not concerned about her thoughts. Frankly, I'd be delighted if she forgot me entirely. Marriage to her would be a nightmare."

Monte Cristo's curiosity was piqued. "You're so resolute. Why?"

"She'd make a fine mistress, perhaps," Albert admitted, "but as a wife? Perish the thought. Marriage to Mademoiselle Danglars would mean enduring her songs, her poetry, her constant presence. It's unbearable even to imagine."

Monte Cristo's lips twitched. "You're difficult to please, my friend."

Albert shrugged. "I often wish for the impossible. A wife like my mother, for instance."

Monte Cristo's face grew thoughtful as Albert continued. "My mother is extraordinary. Beautiful, witty, and captivating. Spending time with her at Tréport was a delight. Few sons can say the same about their mothers."

The Count smiled faintly. "Such praise could make others envious."

Their conversation shifted as Albert broached another topic. "By the way, my parents are hosting a summer ball this Saturday. My mother insists you attend. Will you?"

Monte Cristo's tone was noncommittal. "If the Countess de Morcerf invites me, how can I refuse?"

Albert's grin widened. "Excellent. And might I extend an invitation to M. Cavalcanti as well?"

Monte Cristo hesitated. "Invite him if you wish. But don't expect me to vouch for him. I hardly know the man."

As Albert departed, Monte Cristo watched from the window, his enigmatic smile lingering. Moments later, Bertuccio entered the room.

"Well?" the Count asked.

"She went to the Palais de Justice," Bertuccio reported. "She stayed for an hour and a half."

Monte Cristo nodded. "Good. Prepare for our trip to Normandy. It's time to set the next stage of our plan into motion."

Chapter 69: The Inquiry

True to his word to Madame Danglars, M. de Villefort began investigating how the Count of Monte Cristo had uncovered the history of the house at Auteuil. On the same day, he wrote to M. de Boville, a former inspector of prisons now serving in a high-ranking police role, requesting pertinent information. M. de Boville responded promptly, asking for two days to gather details.

At the end of the second day, Villefort received a note:

The person known as the Count of Monte Cristo is an intimate acquaintance of Lord Wilmore, a wealthy foreigner currently in Paris. He is also closely associated with Abbé Busoni, a Sicilian priest renowned for his charitable works in the East.

Intrigued, Villefort ordered thorough investigations into both individuals. The next evening, a detailed report arrived:

The Abbé Busoni resides in a modest two-story house behind Saint-Sulpice. The lower level comprises a dining room and a sparsely furnished parlor, while the upper level serves as a library and bedroom.

The abbé's library is filled with theological books and ancient manuscripts. His only servant screens visitors through a wicket, often claiming the abbé is away. Despite this, the abbé is known for his generosity, leaving alms for distribution even in his absence.

Lord Wilmore resides at Rue Fontaine-Saint-Georges. He is a typical English traveler who rents furnished apartments, spends little time there, and rarely sleeps in the city. Although he avoids speaking French, he writes it fluently.

Armed with this information, Villefort decided to visit the Abbé Busoni first. Arriving at the abbé's olive-green door in the Rue Férou, he was initially informed that the priest was out. However, after leaving his card and a sealed letter, he arranged to return at eight o'clock that evening.

When Villefort returned, he was ushered into the abbé's dimly lit study. The room's only source of light was a shaded lamp on the desk where the abbé, dressed in a monk's robe with a cowl, awaited him.

"Have I the honor of addressing the Abbé Busoni?" Villefort asked.

"Yes, sir," the abbé replied in a soft, Italian-accented voice. "And you are the emissary from the police?"

Villefort nodded. "I come on behalf of a magistrate seeking information regarding public safety. Your reputation for integrity led us to you."

The abbé gestured for Villefort to sit. "Ask your questions, sir. I will answer to the best of my conscience."

Villefort hesitated. "Do you know the Count of Monte Cristo?"

"Ah, you mean Monsieur Zaccone," the abbé said with a faint smile. "Yes, I know him well."

"Who is he?" Villefort pressed.

"The son of a wealthy shipbuilder from Malta," the abbé replied.

"And his immense fortune? Where does it come from?"

The abbé's smile widened. "He derives an income of 200,000 livres annually, which, when capitalized, amounts to about four million."

Villefort frowned. "I have heard his wealth estimated much higher."

"Exaggeration is common when discussing the rich," the abbé said. "As for his title, he purchased it. Such things are quite common in Italy."

Villefort's questioning continued, delving into Monte Cristo's youth, his supposed adventures, and his purchase of the Auteuil house. The abbé remained composed, deflecting suspicion with calm and credible explanations.

Finally, Villefort asked, "Do you know why he bought the house at Auteuil?"

The abbé's expression remained serene. "To establish a charitable institution, similar to the one founded by the Count of Pisani in Palermo."

Satisfied, Villefort rose to leave. "You are a generous man, Abbé Busoni. If I may, I would like to contribute to your charitable efforts."

The abbé shook his head. "I thank you, sir, but my rule is to give only from my own resources. Seek out the needy yourself, and you will find no shortage of opportunities for benevolence."

Villefort departed, his mind uneasy despite the abbé's reassurances. His next visit was to Lord Wilmore, whose blunt demeanor contrasted sharply with the abbé's refinement. Wilmore, claiming enmity with Monte Cristo, provided a vastly different account, painting the Count as a reckless speculator and adventurer.

By the end of the day, Villefort's investigations yielded little clarity but heightened his unease. Returning home, he resolved to remain vigilant, aware that the Count of Monte Cristo was no ordinary adversary.

Chapter 70: The Ball

It was one of the warmest nights of July, the kind where the air itself felt alive. The long-awaited Saturday had arrived, and the Morcerf residence buzzed with activity for the grand ball hosted by the Count and Countess. By ten o'clock, the garden's towering trees stood silhouetted against a starlit sky, where faint traces of an earlier storm lingered as wisps of cloud.

Inside, music spilled from the ground-floor apartments, punctuated by the lively rhythms of waltzes and gallops. Streams of light escaped through the Venetian blinds, and the soft glow illuminated the garden, where colored lanterns and lavish floral arrangements transformed the space into an ethereal wonderland. The supper—originally planned for the dining room—had been moved under a grand tent on the lawn, thanks to the clear weather. Wax candles and fragrant blooms adorned the tables, creating a scene worthy of an Italian midsummer night.

By the time the Countess of Morcerf returned indoors, having given her final instructions for the supper, the guests had begun to arrive. Among the first was Madame Danglars, who—despite recent anxieties—radiated splendor. Her earlier hesitation about attending had been dispelled by an encounter that morning with Villefort.

"You're going to Madame de Morcerf's tonight?" Villefort had asked when their carriages met by chance.

"No, I'm feeling unwell," Madame Danglars had replied.

Villefort had leaned closer, his tone firm. "You must go. It is important."

"Important?"

"Yes, for appearances," Villefort had insisted. "Trust me."

Thus convinced, Madame Danglars arrived at the ball, where she was greeted by Albert, who complimented her on her elegance and escorted her to a seat. As they walked, Albert glanced around.

"You're looking for Eugénie?" Madame Danglars teased.

"I confess, I am," Albert replied. "Could you really have been so cruel as to leave her behind?"

Madame Danglars laughed lightly. "Fear not. She's here, with Mademoiselle de Villefort. Look, they're over there—one with white roses, the other with blue."

As they reached her seat, Madame Danglars asked, "Will the Count of Monte Cristo attend tonight?"

Albert smiled. "You're the seventeenth person to ask me that. Yes, he's coming. The Count is quite the sensation these days."

Meanwhile, the conversations among the guests carried on in a similar vein, many speculating about Monte Cristo's mysterious origins. One whispered to another, "He's Maltese—the son of a shipowner. Discovered mines in Thessaly and now plans to open a mineral water spa at Auteuil."

Albert, hearing the chatter, chuckled and approached Madame de Villefort, who had been attempting to catch his attention.

"I wager I know what you were about to ask me," Albert said.

"Oh?" Madame de Villefort replied, raising an eyebrow.

"You were about to ask if the Count of Monte Cristo had arrived."

Madame de Villefort laughed. "Not at all. I was going to ask if you'd heard from M. Franz."

"He left earlier," Albert replied. "But don't worry; the Count will be here."

Just then, the man of the hour arrived. As Monte Cristo entered, conversations quieted, and heads turned toward him. His appearance—an elegant yet unadorned black coat, a pale complexion, and an aura of serene mystery—commanded attention. Madame de Morcerf, standing by a mirror, watched his entrance and greeted him with a smile.

The Count exchanged a few polite words with her before moving through the crowd. He caught Albert's eye and approached.

"Have you seen my father?" Albert asked.

"He's over there," Monte Cristo replied, nodding toward a group discussing politics.

Albert grinned. "And what do you think of our Parisian intellectuals?"

Monte Cristo's tone was wry. "A fascinating species. That gentleman, for instance… what's his claim to fame?"

"He discovered a lizard with an extra vertebra," Albert said, chuckling. "The discovery made quite a splash in the academic world."

Monte Cristo raised an eyebrow. "And earned him a medal, no doubt?"

"Naturally," Albert replied. "Our city loves rewarding such groundbreaking work."

Their banter continued until Danglars approached Monte Cristo, pale and agitated. "Have you heard about Franck & Poulmann of Frankfurt?" Danglars asked.

"Yes," Monte Cristo said. "They've gone bankrupt. Luckily, I withdrew my investments a month ago."

Danglars' face fell. "They drew on me for 200,000 francs… and I honored their drafts."

Monte Cristo's expression remained impassive. "Then you've lost it."

As Danglars drifted off, Albert approached his mother. "Did you notice the Count hasn't eaten or drunk anything?" Mercédès asked softly.

Albert shrugged. "Perhaps he isn't hungry."

Mercédès' expression grew solemn. "Or perhaps there's a deeper reason."

Later, as the evening cooled, the blinds were opened to reveal the garden, adorned with lanterns and filled with guests enjoying the night air. Mercedes approached Monte Cristo and asked, "Count, will you escort me to the garden?"

Monte Cristo hesitated briefly before offering his arm. Together, they stepped into the illuminated garden, their silence conveying more than words could express.

Chapter 71: Bread and Salt

Madame de Morcerf guided Monte Cristo through a shaded archway of linden trees, the soft rustle of leaves accompanying their steps. The pathway led to a conservatory that glowed faintly in the moonlight.

"It was stifling in the ballroom, wasn't it?" she asked, glancing at him.

"Indeed, madame," Monte Cristo replied. "Opening the doors and blinds was an inspired idea."

As he spoke, he noticed her hand trembling slightly on his arm. "But you, with only that gauzy scarf to cover your shoulders, must be feeling cold."

Instead of answering, she said, "Do you know where I'm taking you?"

"No, madame," Monte Cristo admitted. "But you see I make no resistance."

"To the greenhouse," she explained, gesturing ahead.

Monte Cristo studied her carefully but refrained from questioning further. They walked in silence until they reached the conservatory, its glass walls glistening with condensation. Inside, the air was heavy with the sweet aroma of ripened fruit nurtured by artificial warmth.

Mercédès released his arm and plucked a cluster of golden Muscatel grapes. "Our French grapes cannot rival those of Sicily or Cyprus, but I hope you'll make allowances for our northern sun." Her smile was wistful, her eyes glistening with unshed tears.

Monte Cristo bowed but took a step back. "I must decline, madame. I never eat Muscatel grapes."

Her hand faltered, and the grapes fell to the ground. She turned to a peach ripening against the warm wall and plucked it instead. "Then take this peach," she offered.

Again, he refused. Her voice trembled. "You pain me deeply."

A long silence followed, her sigh mingling with the soft rustle of leaves. "Count," she said at last, her tone beseeching, "there is a beautiful custom in Arabia: sharing bread and salt under the same roof creates an unbreakable bond of friendship."

Monte Cristo inclined his head. "I'm familiar with the tradition, madame. But we are in France, where eternal friendships are as rare as the custom you describe."

She gripped his arm, her gaze intense. "But we are friends, are we not?"

Monte Cristo's face paled, his composure momentarily slipping. Blood surged to his cheeks, then ebbed, leaving him ashen. "Of course," he said quietly. "Why wouldn't we be?"

Her shoulders sagged, and she turned away, her sigh heavier than words. They resumed their walk, the silence stretching between them.

"Tell me, Count," Mercédès asked suddenly. "Is it true that you've traveled so far, seen so much, and endured such suffering?"

Monte Cristo's voice was steady. "Yes, madame, I have suffered deeply."

"And now? Are you happy?"

His response was measured. "Happiness is relative. I do not complain, and in silence, one might find a semblance of contentment."

She hesitated, her voice softening. "Are you married?"

Monte Cristo recoiled slightly, his tone sharpened. "Married? No. Who told you such a thing?"

"No one," she said. "But you've often been seen at the opera with a young woman."

"A slave I purchased in Constantinople," he explained. "The daughter of a prince. I have adopted her as my own, for I have no one else to care for."

"No one?" she repeated. "No family? No siblings? No children?"

"None," he said simply.

"How do you go on without anyone to anchor you?"

"It's not by choice," he replied. "Once, at Malta, I loved a young woman and was on the verge of marriage. But war intervened, separating us. I believed her love strong enough to endure my absence. When I returned, she was married."

Mercédès faltered, clutching at her chest. "And did you ever see her again?"

"Never," he said. "I never returned to her country."

She lowered her gaze. "And have you forgiven her?"

Monte Cristo's expression softened. "Yes. I harbor no resentment toward her."

Her voice cracked. "But do you still hate those who separated you?"

Monte Cristo's gaze was steady. "Hate them? Not at all. Why would I?"

She stepped closer, holding the grapes again. "Please, take some."

Monte Cristo's tone was unchanged. "Madame, I do not eat Muscatel grapes."

She threw the grapes into the shadows, her frustration breaking through. "Inflexible man!" she murmured.

Albert burst into the conservatory, his face pale. "Mother, a terrible misfortune!"

Mercédès turned to him, her composure faltering. "What is it?"

"M. de Villefort is here," Albert explained. "He's come to take his wife and daughter away. Madame de Saint-Méran has arrived in Paris with news of her husband's death. Mademoiselle Valentine collapsed upon hearing it."

Mercédès placed a hand on Albert's arm, her voice trembling. "The father of Villefort's first wife?"

"Yes," Albert said. "He was coming to expedite her marriage to Franz. But now…"

Monte Cristo observed silently as Mercédès stepped forward, grasping his hand and Albert's, joining them. "We are friends, are we not?"

Monte Cristo's voice was soft. "Madame, I would not presume. But I am always your most devoted servant."

Mercédès turned away, tears glistening as she walked into the night. Albert, watching her, asked, "Don't you and my mother get along?"

Monte Cristo smiled faintly. "On the contrary, didn't you hear her call us friends?"

Chapter 72: Madame de Saint-Méran

The atmosphere at the Villefort residence was somber as news of Monsieur de Saint-Méran's death cast a shadow over the household. Valentine, overwhelmed by the suddenness of the loss, had fallen into a near-catatonic state, requiring constant care. Her grief-stricken demeanor was heightened by Madame de Saint-Méran's arrival, her grandmother's presence amplifying the oppressive air of mourning.

Madame de Saint-Méran, a woman of advanced age, entered the house with a mixture of sorrow and purpose. Dressed in deep black, her stern features betrayed not only the pain of her husband's passing but also a determination to fulfill her familial duties. Upon entering the drawing room, she immediately summoned Villefort.

"Monsieur," she began, her voice trembling but firm, "my husband's dying wish was for Valentine's marriage to Franz d'Épinay to proceed without delay. It is my duty to honor that wish."

Villefort bowed solemnly. "Madame, your resolve is admirable. However, given the circumstances, perhaps we should allow Valentine time to recover from this loss."

Madame de Saint-Méran's eyes flashed. "Time? There is no time to waste, Monsieur. My health is failing, and I must see Valentine's future secured before it is too late. The formalities must be arranged at once."

Villefort hesitated, glancing toward Valentine's room. "Valentine's state…"

"She will do as she is told," Madame de Saint-Méran interrupted sharply. "Her duty to her family outweighs her personal grief."

Their conversation was interrupted by the arrival of Valentine herself. Pale and fragile, she entered the room supported by a maid. Her presence immediately softened Madame de Saint-Méran's tone.

"My child," the older woman said, reaching out to her. "You must find strength in these difficult times. Your grandfather's wish was clear; he wanted to see you settled and protected. You understand the importance of this marriage, don't you?"

Valentine's eyes welled with tears, but she nodded faintly. "Yes, Grandmother. I understand."

Madame de Saint-Méran's stern demeanor softened as she embraced her granddaughter. "Good. Then let us honor his memory by fulfilling his wishes."

As the preparations for the engagement progressed, Villefort's wife, Madame de Villefort, observed the unfolding events with a detached interest. Her sharp gaze missed nothing, though she offered little commentary. When she did speak, it was with a veneer of sympathy that concealed her true thoughts about the sudden loss of her father.

"Poor Valentine," she remarked to Villefort one evening. "To endure so much loss and still face the prospect of marriage. She must possess extraordinary fortitude."

Villefort, weary from the weight of his own responsibilities, merely nodded. "She is her mother's daughter," he replied. "Strong and dutiful."

Meanwhile, Valentine found solace in her clandestine meetings with Maximilian Morrel. In the quiet of the garden, away from the watchful eyes of her family, she poured out her heart to him.

"I feel as though I'm being suffocated," she confessed one evening, her voice breaking. "Every decision is made for me, every step dictated. My life is not my own."

Maximilian took her hands in his, his voice steady and reassuring. "You are not alone, Valentine. Whatever happens, I will be here for you. We will find a way to be together."

Their moments of stolen intimacy provided Valentine with a glimmer of hope amid the oppressive demands of her family. Yet, as the days passed, the weight of expectation grew heavier. Madame de Saint-Méran's health visibly declined, her frailty adding urgency to the preparations for the engagement.

One evening, as the family gathered in the drawing room, a sudden commotion startled them. A servant rushed in, his face pale.

"Madame de Saint-Méran!" he cried. "She has collapsed!"

The family hurried to her room, where the elderly woman lay unconscious. A doctor was summoned, but his prognosis was grim. By dawn, Madame de Saint-Méran had passed away, leaving the household in renewed mourning.

Valentine, overwhelmed by the loss of both grandparents in such quick succession, retreated further into herself. Her engagement to Franz, once imminent, was now uncertain, delayed by the endless rituals of grief.

In the shadows, Madame de Villefort observed the unfolding drama with a calculating expression. To her, every tragedy was an opportunity, every disruption a chance to exert influence. And as the household mourned, she began to lay the groundwork for her own ambitions, quietly weaving her plans into the fabric of their sorrow.

Chapter 73: The Promise

It was indeed Maximilian Morrel who had endured a wretched existence since the previous day. With the instinct peculiar to lovers, he had anticipated that something significant would occur at the Villefort residence, following the return of Madame de Saint-Méran and the death of the marquis. His uneasy forebodings drove him, pale and trembling, to the gate beneath the chestnut trees.

Valentine, unaware of the cause of his sorrow and anxiety, went to the garden gate by what seemed like accident—or perhaps through some unspoken connection. Hearing Morrel call, she ran to him.

"You here at this hour?" she asked, startled.

"Yes, my poor Valentine," replied Morrel. "I come to bring and to hear bad news."

Valentine's face fell. "This house is already a place of mourning," she said softly. "Speak, Maximilian, though the cup of sorrow already overflows."

"Dearest Valentine," Morrel began, struggling to conceal his emotion. "When are you to be married?"

Valentine sighed deeply. "I will tell you everything. This morning, the topic was raised. My grandmother, whom I relied on as my only ally, not only supported the idea but insisted the marriage proceed as soon as M. d'Épinay arrives. The contract is to be signed tomorrow."

A deep sigh escaped Morrel, his gaze lingering mournfully on Valentine.

"Alas," he said, "I hear my own sentence from your lips. It seems everything is decided. But since you say nothing remains but M. d'Épinay's arrival, you should know… he is already in Paris. He came this morning."

Valentine gasped. "No!"

Morrel nodded. "I was at the Count of Monte Cristo's an hour ago. We were discussing your grief when a carriage arrived. At first, I thought it might be someone else, but then Albert de Morcerf entered, followed by a young man. The Count introduced him as Baron Franz d'Épinay."

Valentine's eyes brimmed with tears. "My poor Maximilian," she murmured.

"Valentine," he said urgently, "the moment of decision has come. What do you intend to do?"

Valentine trembled, overwhelmed. "What can I do, Maximilian? To oppose my father, to defy my deceased grandmother's wishes… it would be sacrilege. I cannot."

Morrel's tone turned solemn. "You are noble and selfless, Valentine. But tell me, do you resign yourself to this fate without even attempting to fight?"

"To fight?" she repeated, incredulous. "Against my father, my family? Impossible!"

Morrel's expression hardened. "Then you choose to let fate decide? To surrender your happiness?"

Valentine's tears fell freely. "What choice do I have? My father is resolute. My grandmother's final wish was clear. To oppose them would only cause more pain."

Morrel sighed. "If you will not fight for us, Valentine, then I must act alone. I have nothing left to lose. I will challenge Franz d'Épinay to a duel. If he refuses to release you from this engagement, then either he will die… or I will."

Valentine clutched his arm, horrified. "No, Maximilian! You must not! There must be another way."

Morrel's gaze softened. "Then tell me what to do, Valentine. Give me hope."

She hesitated, her voice trembling. "If… if I can delay the marriage… will you wait?"

"Yes," he vowed, "as long as you promise me that you will not marry him."

"I swear it," she said fervently. "By all that I hold sacred, I will never be his."

Morrel clasped her hands, his resolve steadying. "Then I will wait. But if they force you to the altar, come to me. We will escape together."

Valentine nodded, her tears glistening in the moonlight. "I promise. But until then, we must not tempt fate. We cannot meet like this again."

"You are right," he said reluctantly. "But remember, Valentine, I will be here for you. Always."

As they parted, Valentine whispered, "Adieu, my love."

Morrel watched her disappear into the shadows of the garden, his heart heavy yet hopeful. The promise she had made was his only solace, a fragile thread binding their shared fate.

VOLUME FOUR

Chapter 74: The Villefort Family Vault

Two days later, a significant crowd gathered around the entrance to M. de Villefort's residence. By ten in the morning, a long line of mourning coaches and private carriages stretched along the Faubourg Saint-Honoré and Rue de la Pépinière. Among them was an unusual black-painted wagon, which seemed to have traveled some distance. Upon inquiry, it was discovered that the wagon which carried the body of the Marquis de Saint-Méran, also included his wife. Strangely, those who had come to attend one funeral found themselves witnessing two.

The Marquis de Saint-Méran, a steadfast supporter of Louis XVIII and King Charles X, had many friends who joined the funeral procession. Combined with those compelled by societal conventions to attend on behalf of Villefort, the turnout was immense. The authorities had approved holding both funerals simultaneously, and a second hearse was brought to Villefort's door to transfer the Marquis's coffin. The two caskets would be laid to rest in the cemetery of Père-Lachaise, in a tomb Villefort had prepared for his family. Renée's remains were already interred there, and now, ten years later, her parents would join her.

Parisians, ever curious and affected by public mourning, watched in respectful silence as the grand procession escorted two figures of the old aristocracy to their final rest. Among the coaches, Beauchamp, Debray, and Château-Renaud discussed the sudden death of the Marchioness.

"I saw Madame de Saint-Méran last year in Marseilles," said Château-Renaud. "She seemed destined to live to a hundred. How old was she?"

"Franz told me she was sixty-six," Albert replied. "But it wasn't age that killed her; it was grief. She never recovered from the Marquis's death."

"What exactly did she die of?" Debray asked.

"They say it was a stroke or apoplexy*," said Albert.

Beauchamp shook his head. "Unlikely. Madame de Saint-Méran was slight and nervous—not the type for apoplexy."

"Well, whatever the cause," Albert mused, "Villefort inherits a fortune of 80,000 livres annually, which will double when Noirtier passes."

"That old Jacobin is resilient," Beauchamp remarked. "It's as if he's bargaining with death."

The conversation moved on as they arrived at the cemetery. The dull, overcast sky matched the solemn occasion. Among the mourners, Château-Renaud noticed Morrel, who had arrived alone and walked silently among the yew trees.

"Maximilian Morrel! What brings you here?" Château-Renaud asked, linking arms with him. "I've never seen you at Villefort's."

"I'm no acquaintance of his," Morrel replied. "But I knew Madame de Saint-Méran."

---

*In the late 14th to the late 19th century, the diagnosis *apoplexy* referred to any sudden death that began with abrupt loss of consciousness; sometimes proceeded by extreme anger.

Albert joined them with Franz. "Gentlemen, allow me to introduce Franz d'Épinay, a fellow traveler and good friend."

Morrel hesitated, but remembering his oath, greeted Franz politely. Meanwhile, Debray and Beauchamp speculated about the strange timing of the deaths.

When the procession arrived at the Villefort family vault, the two coffins were placed in the Saint-Méran crypt. Inside the bronze gates was a somber chamber, free from the bustle of cemetery visitors. Villefort, Franz, and a few close relatives entered to perform the final rites. Outside, Albert, Château-Renaud, and Morrel discussed the proceedings.

After the ceremony, Villefort took Franz aside. "M. d'Épinay, Madame de Saint-Méran's dying wish was for Valentine's wedding to proceed without delay. The notary has all the documents prepared. Can I count on your cooperation?"

"Sir, given Mademoiselle Valentine's grief, it seems inappropriate to proceed so quickly," Franz replied.

Villefort dismissed the concern. "Valentine's greatest comfort will be fulfilling her grandmother's wish. We can finalize the contract today."

Franz reluctantly agreed, requesting that Albert and Château-Renaud act as witnesses. Preparations were made for the signing that evening.

Valentine was shocked by the news. Seeking solace, she tried to visit Noirtier, but Villefort intercepted her. Meanwhile, Madame de Villefort, pale and weary, sat quietly with young Edward. As the guests arrived, Valentine's pallor betrayed her distress, while Franz appeared equally uneasy.

Before the contract could be signed, Barrois entered, announcing firmly, "M. Noirtier wishes to speak with M. Franz d'Épinay immediately."

Villefort objected, but Barrois insisted. "If denied, M. Noirtier will have himself brought here."

Valentine's face lit with hope. She moved toward the door, but Villefort stopped her. Franz, however, intervened. "Let me go," he said. "I'd be honored to meet M. Noirtier."

Villefort, visibly unsettled, followed as Franz and Valentine descended the stairs. Albert and Château-Renaud exchanged puzzled glances, sensing the tension but remaining in the dark about its source.

Chapter 75: A Signed Statement

Noirtier awaited them, dressed in black and seated in his armchair with a composed yet determined expression. When Villefort, Valentine, and Franz entered the room, he gestured for the valet to close the door.

"Listen," Villefort whispered harshly to Valentine, whose joy at seeing her grandfather was evident. "If my father attempts to delay your marriage, I forbid you to understand him."

Valentine blushed but said nothing. Villefort stepped forward. "Here is M. Franz d'Épinay," he said. "You requested this meeting. I hope it will resolve your objections to Valentine's marriage."

Noirtier responded with a piercing look that chilled Villefort. He motioned for Valentine to approach. Used to his communication style, Valentine quickly understood. He wanted a key from a drawer in a chest between the windows. Retrieving it, she followed his gaze to an old secretaire long considered obsolete.

"Should I open it?" Valentine asked.

Noirtier's eyes signaled "yes." She opened the middle drawer and began removing papers under his direction. Finally, she held up a bundle, but Noirtier's gaze dismissed it. Then his eyes settled on a dictionary.

"The dictionary?" Valentine asked, realizing his intent. "Is there a secret compartment?"

"Yes," his gaze confirmed. He signaled for Barrois, the old servant. Barrois entered, following Noirtier's directions to activate a hidden spring in the secretaire. A false bottom slid out, revealing a bundle of documents tied with a black ribbon.

"Shall I give these to M. de Villefort?" Barrois asked.

Noirtier's gaze said no. "To Valentine?" Again, no. "To M. Franz d'Épinay?" At last, an emphatic yes.

Franz, puzzled, stepped forward. "To me, sir?" he asked.

Noirtier's gaze affirmed it. Franz untied the ribbon, revealing a document. The room's tension was palpable as he read aloud:

"Extract from the Minutes of the Bonapartist Club meeting, February 5, 1815."

Franz froze. "February 5, 1815—the day my father was murdered."

Villefort, Valentine, and Franz were silent, while Noirtier's gaze urged him to continue:

"The undersigned declare that on February 4, a letter from the Island of Elba recommended General Flavien de Quesnel to the Bonapartist Club. The general, a supposed supporter of the Emperor, was invited to a meeting the following evening. Blindfolded, he was escorted to the venue and questioned. Despite initial courtesy, General de Quesnel refused to support the Emperor, declaring allegiance to King Louis XVIII."

Franz paused, visibly shaken. "Yes, my father was a royalist. His stance was clear."

Noirtier's gaze remained steady, urging him on. Franz resumed:

"The general's refusal incited murmurs among the members. The president warned him of the consequences, emphasizing their distrust of Louis XVIII. The general stood firm, calling their actions dishonorable. Ultimately, the president declared, 'You must die.'"

Franz's voice cracked. Valentine clasped her hands, trembling. Villefort paced, his face pale. Noirtier's expression exuded quiet authority.

"The meeting ended with General de Quesnel escorted away. At the Quai des Ormes*, the president challenged him to a duel. Despite his skill, the general fell. After verifying his death, the witnesses disposed of his body in the river, ensuring secrecy."

The room fell silent as Franz finished reading. "Who was the president?" he demanded, turning to Noirtier. "Who killed my father?"

"Hold, sir," said Villefort, "do not prolong this dreadful scene. The names have been purposely concealed; my father himself does not know who this president was, and if he knows, he cannot tell you; proper names are not in the dictionary."

Noirtier's eyes locked on his son, unwavering. Valentine, understanding his answer before he conveyed it, stepped back in shock. Villefort, now also understanding, fumbled for the door handle, his face a mask of fear.

Noirtier looked at the dictionary. Franz took it with a nervous trembling, and repeated the letters of the alphabet successively, until he came to M. At that letter the old man signified "Yes."

"M," repeated Franz. The young man's finger, glided over the words, but at each one Noirtier answered by a negative sign. Valentine hid her head between her hands. At length, Franz arrived at the word MYSELF.

"You?" Franz whispered, horrified. "You killed my father?"

---

*Now called the "Pont Marie Bridge" in English.

Noirtier's gaze confirmed it. Franz collapsed into a chair, overwhelmed. Villefort fled the room, consumed by terror, while Noirtier sat, unyielding, his dignity intact despite the storm of emotions around him.

Chapter 76: Progress of Cavalcanti the Younger

While Marquis Cavalcanti Sr. returned to his usual habits in the gaming halls of Lucca, Andrea Cavalcanti thrived in Parisian society. The elder Cavalcanti, having exhausted his funds, retreated, satisfied with the role he had played in establishing his son's fabricated lineage. Meanwhile, Andrea inherited documents proving his supposed noble heritage as the son of the Marquis Bartolomeo and Marchioness Oliva Corsinari, a tale that Paris embraced with open arms.

Andrea quickly ascended in Parisian circles, earning the title of count and the reputation of possessing a fortune worth 50,000 livres annually. Rumors of immense family wealth hidden in Saravezza quarries only bolstered his mystique. With a fair command of the French language, a polished demeanor, and cash for his indulgences, Andrea became a sought-after figure among Paris's elite. Such was his standing when Monte Cristo visited the Danglars household one evening.

Upon his arrival, Monte Cristo was informed that Baron Danglars was out, but the baroness would receive him. Since the infamous dinner at Auteuil, Madame Danglars had grown wary of the Count's name. Yet his charm and impeccable manners consistently disarmed her, dissolving her initial unease.

Monte Cristo entered the boudoir, where Madame Danglars lounged on a sofa, examining sketches handed to her by Eugénie and Andrea. Andrea, dressed impeccably in black, exuded the romantic air of a Goethe protagonist. With every wave of his hand through his golden locks, he flashed a diamond on his little finger, a brazen display Monte Cristo had advised against. His attentions—glances and sighs alike—were directed unabashedly at Eugénie. But Eugénie, ever cold and sardonic, returned his advances with indifference.

Eager to escape the tension, Eugénie excused herself to practice music with her friend Louise d'Armilly. From the adjoining study came the sound of cheerful voices and piano notes, contrasting sharply with the stilted atmosphere left behind. Andrea hovered at the door, reluctant to intrude but desperate to linger.

Soon after, Danglars returned. His initial greeting was reserved for Monte Cristo, but his second glance landed on Andrea, his approval evident. Danglars commented on Andrea's absence from the piano, prompting the young man's melodramatic lament about not being invited to join. Opening the door to the study, Danglars revealed Eugénie and Louise seated together at the piano, sharing a single chair and playing a duet, their harmony captivating.

Monte Cristo observed the scene with quiet amusement. Danglars, however, seemed preoccupied, hinting at financial losses in Milan that morning. The baroness praised her husband's resilience, noting how adeptly he concealed such setbacks. Monte Cristo, ever the instigator, remarked, "Perhaps he no longer finds losses worth boasting about. A shift in priorities, perhaps?"

Their conversation turned to recent tragedies in the Villefort family, culminating in Franz d'Épinay's abrupt withdrawal from his engagement to Valentine. While Danglars mused on these developments with philosophical detachment, Albert de Morcerf's sudden arrival added an unexpected twist.

Albert's composure remained unshaken despite learning that Andrea was inside, accompanying Eugénie. Danglars' efforts to provoke jealousy fell flat, as Albert praised the duet without betraying any discomfort. His indifference unsettled Danglars, who retreated to confer privately with Monte Cristo.

"What do you think of our so-called prince?" Danglars asked, gesturing toward Andrea.

Monte Cristo's response was measured. "He is an intriguing young man, but appearances can be deceiving."

Danglars sighed. "I cannot decide whether to proceed with the engagement. Albert's demeanor is cold, distant… hardly the attitude of a devoted fiancé. Yet, Andrea lacks the stature of the Morcerf name."

Monte Cristo's expression turned sly. "Perhaps you should resolve this tension directly with the Morcerfs. Clarify their intentions. As for Andrea, one cannot overlook his charm, though it is wise to investigate further."

As Danglars mulled over the advice, Albert and Monte Cristo prepared to leave. Albert's farewell to Eugénie was cordial yet indifferent, leaving no trace of romantic attachment. Meanwhile, Andrea remained in the room, basking in the attention he received from both Danglars and Eugénie's parents.

Outside, Albert remarked to Monte Cristo, "Andrea Cavalcanti—or whatever his name truly is—has an unsettling air. Yet, one must admit, he plays his part to perfection."

Monte Cristo chuckled. "Ah, my dear Albert, Paris thrives on such performances. Let us see how long his charade can endure."

Chapter 77: Haydée

As Monte Cristo's carriage turned the corner of the boulevard, Albert burst into laughter—loud and perhaps too forced to be genuine.

"Well," Albert began, "I will ask you the same question which Charles IX. put to Catherine de' Medici, after the massacre of Saint Bartholomew: 'How have I played my little part?'"

Monte Cristo raised an eyebrow. "To what are you referring?"

"To the grand debut of my rival at the Danglars residence," Albert replied.

"Your rival?"

"Indeed, your protégé, Andrea Cavalcanti!"

Monte Cristo's face remained impassive. "Ah, the young Cavalcanti. But I assure you, I've no hand in his dealings with M. Danglars."

Albert sighed. "Whether aided by you or not, it's evident that he is courting Mademoiselle Eugénie with all the airs of a romantic hero."

"And does that trouble you, my dear viscount?" Monte Cristo's tone was calm, almost amused.

"Let's just say I'm losing ground. Eugénie scarcely acknowledges me, and her confidante, Mademoiselle d'Armilly, ignores me altogether."

Monte Cristo observed him thoughtfully. "Do you truly care for Mademoiselle Danglars?"

Albert's reply was interrupted by their arrival at Monte Cristo's home. As they stepped inside, the count summoned Baptistin, who appeared almost instantly with a tray of tea prepared as if by magic. Albert marveled at the efficiency.

"Your household could run a kingdom," Albert said, lighting a tobacco pipe offered by Ali. "And yet, I hear music. Is that a guitar?"

Monte Cristo smiled. "That, my friend, is Haydée playing her guzla. A far cry from Mademoiselle Danglars's piano, don't you agree?"

Albert's curiosity piqued. "Haydée. An enchanting name. Is she as unique as it suggests?"

Monte Cristo nodded. "Indeed, she is. But tread lightly. Haydée has seen much in her young life."

Albert, always intrigued by the exotic, pressed further. "Might I meet her?"

Monte Cristo agreed, with two conditions: Albert must keep the meeting a secret and refrain from mentioning his father. Albert agreed, swearing on his honor.

Ali soon led them to Haydée's chambers, where she awaited. Draped in luxurious silks, she sat cross-legged in Eastern fashion. Her gaze met Monte Cristo's with warmth, but when she turned to Albert, her expression was curious yet reserved.

Monte Cristo introduced them, and Haydée addressed Albert in flawless Italian, her voice melodic and dignified. Her presence, regal and composed, left Albert spellbound. She spoke of her homeland, evoking vivid images of lush landscapes and her father's palace by a shimmering lake.

As their conversation deepened, Albert's fascination grew. Haydée's narrative shifted to the night her life changed forever—a violent betrayal that led to her father's death and her enslavement. Her words painted a picture of courage amidst despair, her voice steady but tinged with sorrow. Monte Cristo watched her closely, his expression unreadable.

Albert, moved by her tale, struggled to reconcile her tragic past with the poised woman before him. "How is it possible," he asked gently, "that one who has suffered so much remains so composed?"

Haydée's gaze softened. "Because I am grateful to my lord and master. He saved me from despair and restored my dignity."

Monte Cristo placed a hand on her shoulder. "Your courage inspires us all, Haydée."

Albert left Monte Cristo's home that evening, his mind awhirl with admiration and intrigue. As their carriage rolled into the Paris night, he murmured, "The Count of Monte Cristo never ceases to astonish. And Haydée… she is like a vision from another world."

Monte Cristo, his gaze distant, replied softly, "Sometimes, Albert, the most extraordinary stories are hidden in plain sight."

Chapter 78: We hear From Yanina

If Valentine could have witnessed the trembling steps and pale face of Franz as he left Monsieur Noirtier's room, even she might have pitied him. Villefort, on the other hand, retreated to his study, barely managing a few incoherent words before receiving a letter two hours later:

Given the revelations made this morning, Monsieur Noirtier de Villefort must surely see the impossibility of an alliance between our families. Monsieur d'Épinay is shocked that Villefort, who seemed aware of these facts, did not preemptively address this matter.

Villefort's pride was deeply wounded by this curt and uncharacteristic letter from Franz, a man known for his respect and politeness. The magistrate had believed his father's duel with General de Quesnel to be an assassination, not a fair fight. Noirtier had never shared the truth, leaving Villefort wholly unprepared for the devastating disclosure.

Madame de Villefort, finding herself left with the notary and witnesses after Franz's abrupt departure, excused herself under the pretense of investigating the situation. Upon confronting her husband, Villefort coldly explained that the engagement between Valentine and Franz was broken. To avoid further embarrassment, she returned to the others and fabricated a story about Noirtier suffering a sudden apoplectic fit, postponing the matter for several days. The guests departed, perplexed but silent.

Meanwhile, Valentine, elated and terrified, thanked her grandfather for dismantling the engagement she thought unbreakable. She sought permission to retire, but instead of heading to her room, she slipped into the garden where Maximilian Morrel was waiting.

Maximilian, already suspecting the outcome after observing Franz's agitated behavior, was relieved when Valentine emerged. Ignoring her usual caution, she approached him directly.

"We're saved!" Valentine exclaimed, her voice trembling with joy.

"Saved?" Maximilian repeated, scarcely daring to believe it. "By whom?"

"My grandfather," she said. "You must love him for his kindness to us."

"I swear I will," Maximilian replied, his admiration for Noirtier swelling to near reverence.

Valentine began to recount the events but hesitated, realizing she would reveal a secret that could endanger others. "I'll tell you everything," she promised, "but only when I'm your wife."

Though impatient, Maximilian couldn't argue with the good news. They arranged to meet again the following evening, both feeling more hopeful about their future together. As the drama unfolded in the Villefort household, another storm brewed in Paris.

Early the next morning, Danglars, seated at his desk, gestured for his usual stack of newspapers. He flipped through them with practiced indifference, setting several aside with a flick of his wrist. Then, his hand paused. His eyes caught sight of a bold headline in *L'Impartial*, a paper edited by Beauchamp. The words demanded attention:

News from Yanina

A correspondent from Yanina reveals a long-buried secret: the fortress protecting the town was betrayed to the Turks by a French officer named Fernand, who had been trusted implicitly by the grand vizier, Ali Pasha.

Danglars leaned back, a smirk spreading across his face as he absorbed the weight of the revelation. The implications were as clear as they were damning.

"This," he muttered to himself, folding the paper with deliberate precision, "should make explaining myself to the Count of Morcerf entirely unnecessary."

Satisfied, Danglars placed the paper neatly on his desk, his mind already calculating the fallout this revelation would cause. He smirked, sensing an opportunity to discredit Morcerf without direct confrontation.

That same morning, Albert, dressed in black, sought out Monte Cristo. Upon learning the count was out, he ventured to Gosset's shooting gallery, where he found Monte Cristo practicing. Albert explained his predicament: the article's insinuations threatened his father's honor, and he intended to demand a retraction from Beauchamp, the journalist responsible.

"Well," said Monte Cristo with a calm smile, "what about that article has you so upset?"

"What about it?" Albert shot back. "It implicates my father—Count Fernand de Morcerf."

Monte Cristo raised an eyebrow. "Your father served under Ali Pasha?"

"Yes. He fought in the war for Greek independence. This accusation is a blatant attempt to smear his name."

Monte Cristo leaned forward. "Albert, think about it. How would anyone in France connect an officer named Fernand to the Count of Morcerf? And who still cares about events from Yanina nearly twenty years ago?"

"That's the point!" Albert said, his frustration mounting. "Someone deliberately dredged up this ancient history just to disgrace him—and by extension, me. I'm going to Beauchamp, and I'll demand a retraction in front of witnesses."

Monte Cristo sighed. "Beauchamp won't retract. He'll argue there were dozens of officers named Fernand in the Greek army."

"Then we'll duel," Albert declared. "I won't stand by while my father's honor is attacked. My father, a hero with a brilliant career—"

Monte Cristo interrupted. "Even if Beauchamp retracts, it won't erase the insinuation. And suppose the claim is true?"

Albert stood abruptly. "Impossible! I refuse to even consider such a thing."

Monte Cristo's expression softened. "Listen to me, Albert. Confront Beauchamp privately. Don't bring witnesses—it will only escalate matters unnecessarily. Give him a chance to explain or correct the article voluntarily. Trust me, wounding a man's pride in public only makes him dig in his heels."

Albert hesitated, his temper cooling slightly. "Fine. I'll go alone, but if he refuses, I'll demand satisfaction."

Monte Cristo's gaze hardened. "I cannot be your second, Albert."

Albert blinked. "Why not? You're my friend!"

Monte Cristo stood, his tone firm. "There are reasons you don't yet understand. But know this—I'm always at your side, just not for this."

Albert stared at him for a long moment before nodding curtly. "Then I'll ask Franz and Château-Renaud. And if it comes to a duel, perhaps you'll at least give me a lesson or two in fencing or shooting?"

Monte Cristo smiled faintly. "That, too, is out of the question."

"Why do you refuse to get involved in anything?" Albert muttered, throwing up his hands.

Monte Cristo's voice was calm but unyielding. "Because I refuse to play into the foolish games of others. You'll understand one day."

Albert left in a storm of frustration, going off to find Beauchamp in his office.

The journalist's workspace was dusty and cluttered, with newspapers scattered everywhere.

"Albert!" Beauchamp exclaimed, rising to greet him. "What's the matter? Come to have breakfast or pick a fight?"

Albert ignored the jest. "It's about the article in *L'Impartial*."

Beauchamp frowned. "What about it?"

Albert tossed the paper onto the desk. "This article insults my father. I demand a retraction."

Beauchamp picked up the paper, reading the paragraph again. "Albert, it mentions a 'Fernand'—but nowhere does it link him to your father."

"People will connect the dots," Albert snapped. "Retract it, or I'll consider this a personal insult."

Beauchamp leaned back, studying him. "I didn't write this piece, Albert. I didn't even notice it until now."

Albert's voice rose. "You printed it, and that makes you responsible!"

Beauchamp sighed. "I'll investigate the claim. If it's false, I'll retract it. But if it's true, I won't publish a lie for anyone, not even a friend."

Albert's anger boiled over. "If you won't retract it, I'll send my seconds. We'll settle this with a duel."

Beauchamp met his gaze evenly. "If it comes to that, Albert, I won't shy away. But give me three weeks to verify the facts. If I find the article to be false, you'll have your retraction. If it's true—then we'll talk about your next steps."

"Three weeks?" Albert spat. "That's a lifetime when my family's honor is at stake!"

"Patience," Beauchamp replied coolly. "Let me do my work, and we'll revisit this."

Albert stormed out, fuming. As he climbed into his carriage, he caught sight of Maximilian Morrel walking along the street, his step light and his demeanor calm. Albert muttered bitterly, "There goes a happy man. I wish I could say the same for myself."

Chapter 79: The Lemonade

Maximilian Morrel was in an uncontainable rush of happiness. M. Noirtier had summoned him, and his eagerness to discover the reason had him skipping the convenience of a cab, trusting his own two legs more than a horse's four. So, he dashed from the Rue Meslay toward the Faubourg Saint-Honoré at a vigorous pace.

Barrois, the elderly servant, trailed behind him as best he could. Morrel, young and driven by love, sped ahead effortlessly, while Barrois, at sixty, struggled under the summer's oppressive heat. Despite their differences in age and energy, they were bound by their shared connection to Noirtier.

Upon arriving, Barrois, out of breath, ushered Morrel in through a private entrance. Soon, the rustle of a dress announced Valentine's arrival. In her black mourning dress, she looked radiant, a vision that momentarily rendered Morrel speechless with delight.

Moments later, the sound of Noirtier's wheelchair rolling across the floor brought their attention back. The elderly man entered, his eyes radiating kindness as he acknowledged Morrel's gratitude for his intervention in Valentine's engagement.

Valentine, seated a little apart, hesitated before speaking. At Noirtier's prompting gaze, she began, "Monsieur Morrel, my grandfather has many things he wished to say and has asked me to relay them. I will convey his intentions exactly."

Morrel leaned forward eagerly. "I am listening with all my heart."

Valentine's eyes dropped briefly, her voice softening. "My grandfather plans to leave this house. Barrois is seeking new accommodations for him."

"But you, Mademoiselle de Villefort?" Morrel asked anxiously. "Surely you are not leaving him?"

"No," Valentine assured him. "I will stay by his side. Either my father will agree to this arrangement, or I will wait until I come of age in ten months. Then, I will fulfill the promise I made to you—with my grandfather's blessing."

Her words, spoken with a mix of resolve and shyness, filled Morrel with joy. "I swear to be patient and wait as long as you need," he declared.

Valentine smiled faintly. "Until then, we must act with discretion. Let us not jeopardize the happiness we hope to share."

Noirtier watched the exchange with quiet satisfaction, while Barrois, smiling through his exhaustion, wiped his brow.

"Barrois, you look overheated," Valentine said kindly. "Take a glass of lemonade."

Valentine poured him a full glass from a pitcher waiting nearby Noirtier. Gratefully, Barrois took the glass and drank it in one long gulp, visibly refreshed. Valentine and Morrel exchanged a few more words before a doorbell interrupted them.

"It must be Doctor d'Avrigny," Valentine guessed. "Morrel, you must leave now."

As Barrois returned, he stumbled, his face pale and twisted in pain. "What is wrong?" Valentine exclaimed.

Barrois clutched at furniture, his voice barely audible. "My head... my chest... burning..." His legs stiffened, and he collapsed, convulsing violently.

Valentine cried out, "Doctor! Help, someone, please!"

Villefort appeared at the commotion, his face a mask of shock. As the doctor entered, Barrois's condition worsened. With each moment, his symptoms—rigid limbs, foaming mouth, and labored breathing—grew more severe. Noirtier's gaze bore into the scene, his expression both anguished and knowing.

Dr. D'Avrigny acted swiftly. "Bring water and ether," he commanded. But Barrois, gasping, whispered hoarsely, "The lemonade... it was bitter."

The doctor seized the decanter, smelled its contents, and turned to Villefort. "Fetch the syrup of violets immediately."

When the syrup arrived, D'Avrigny performed a chemical test, pouring drops of the lemonade into the syrup. Before their eyes, the liquid turned a sinister green. The room fell silent, the result undeniable.

"This man has been poisoned," D'Avrigny declared grimly.

Villefort paled, his voice trembling. "Poisoned? Here, in my home?"

D'Avrigny's gaze darkened. "Yes, and I believe it is not the first time. Too many sudden deaths have occurred here. I fear a sinister hand is at work."

As Villefort fainted into a chair, overwhelmed by the accusation, Noirtier's expression remained sharp, as though he alone understood the full scope of the tragedy unfolding in their midst.

Chapter 80: The Accusation

Doctor d'Avrigny swiftly brought Villefort back to consciousness. The magistrate, pale and disoriented, resembled a second corpse in the room already shrouded in death.

"Death has invaded my house!" Villefort exclaimed, his voice shaking.

"No, not death." the doctor replied firmly. "Say instead—crime."

Villefort clasped his hands together, trembling. "Doctor, I feel consumed by terror, grief, and madness. What is happening here?"

D'Avrigny's tone remained calm but forceful. "It's time to act. We cannot allow this stream of death to continue unchecked. As a doctor, I cannot bear to know the truth without hope of justice for the victims."

Villefort lowered his gaze, his voice barely audible. "In my house," he murmured. "In my house..."

"You are a magistrate, sir," the doctor said, his words cutting through Villefort's despair. "Show your integrity. Rise above personal concerns and honor your profession. You must act."

Villefort's face contorted in agony. "Do you mean... sacrifice?"

"Yes," D'Avrigny replied. "A sacrifice of your complacency."

"Do you suspect someone?" Villefort's voice faltered, his question trembling with dread.

The doctor's gaze was unrelenting. "I do not suspect; I observe. Death moves deliberately in this house, targeting not at random but with purpose. Consider its victims: M. de Saint-Méran, Madame de Saint-Méran, and now Barrois. And let us not ignore the most chilling truth of all—the poison in the lemonade was meant for Noirtier."

Villefort staggered back, horror dawning on his face. "Noirtier?"

"Yes," D'Avrigny continued. "The poison intended for Noirtier was mistaken by Barrois. His death was a tragic accident, but make no mistake—the target was clear."

"Why?" Villefort whispered, his voice cracking. "Why Noirtier?"

"Because he changed his will," the doctor said. "He had once disinherited you and your family, but his new will likely disrupted someone's plans. These deaths are calculated—deliberate and vile."

Villefort's head fell into his hands, his breath ragged. "This is too much."

"No," D'Avrigny snapped. "You must confront it. Follow the path of the crime. M. de Saint-Méran died, then Madame de Saint-Méran. Barrois followed. And still, Noirtier lives, by sheer luck."

Villefort's voice rose in desperation. "You accuse… Valentine?"

"I accuse no one," D'Avrigny replied. "But the evidence points clearly to the same hand in each case. Valentine prepared the medicines for Madame de Saint-Méran. She gave the lemonade to Barrois. These connections demand investigation."

Villefort dropped to his knees, his voice breaking. "Spare her! She is innocent! Her heart is pure as a diamond, her soul untainted. Doctor, you must be mistaken."

The doctor's face hardened. "If Valentine has committed these crimes, it is my duty to bring her to justice. But even if she has not, someone within this house is responsible. Ignoring this will only invite further tragedy."

Villefort grasped at D'Avrigny's arm, pleading. "I cannot… I will not see my daughter condemned. I will handle this privately. But I beg you, do not abandon us."

D'Avrigny stared at him, his expression unreadable. Finally, he relented. "Very well. I will wait. But if another life is taken, do not call for me. I will not assist in a house that allows crime to fester."

Villefort nodded, defeated. "Thank you. I will protect her. I will protect my family."

Without another word, Doctor D'Avrigny left the room. The servants, already unsettled by Barrois's sudden death, quickly spread rumors of the poison. By evening, many had given notice, unwilling to remain in a household shrouded in fear.

Valentine sat quietly, tears streaming down her face as she watched the staff leave. Villefort glanced between her and his wife, whose thin lips curled into a faint, inscrutable smile. The magistrate's heart sank further as the storm within his house intensified, and the shadow of death loomed ever closer.

Chapter 81: The Room of the Retired Baker

Andrea Cavalcanti arrived at the Danglars' residence in the evening. Impeccably dressed, his hair curled and his gloves fitting perfectly, Andrea exuded confidence. He wasted no time and soon pulled Danglars aside into a secluded corner of the drawing room.

"Baron," Andrea began smoothly, "I must express my gratitude for the kindness your family has shown me. I have found a most charming focus for my affections in your daughter, Mademoiselle Eugénie."

Danglars's eyes gleamed, though he feigned hesitation. "But are you not rather young to consider marriage?"

"In Italy," Andrea replied confidently, "it is customary for noblemen to marry young. Life's uncertainties compel us to secure happiness while we can."

The banker nodded thoughtfully. "If my wife and daughter approve, we could proceed. But such negotiations traditionally involve the fathers."

Andrea smiled, anticipating this. "My father, the Marquis, foresaw my intentions. He has authorized an annual allowance of 150,000 livres upon my marriage. This is but a fraction of our family's wealth."

Danglars's interest deepened. "I plan to settle 500,000 francs on my daughter, and she will inherit my estate. Together, your family's and mine could achieve great prosperity."

Andrea's smile widened. "Indeed, sir, such a union would be most advantageous."

By the next morning, Danglars had arranged for Andrea to receive a substantial advance of 80,000 francs, solidifying his confidence in the young man's potential as a son-in-law. Andrea, flush with his newfound wealth, planned to keep Caderousse—his dangerous acquaintance—pacified with a small portion of the funds.

Later that evening, Andrea returned to his quarters only to find the porter holding a letter. "Sir, a man left this for you," the porter said. Andrea's face darkened when he saw the familiar seal of Caderousse.

The letter read:

You know where to find me. Come tomorrow morning at nine.

Andrea burned the letter immediately, his mind racing. The next morning, disguised in a servant's livery, Andrea arrived at a shabby apartment in Rue Ménilmontant. There, Caderousse greeted him with exaggerated cheerfulness.

"Ah, my dear Andrea! Or should I call you Benedetto?" Caderousse's grin was a mixture of mischief and menace.

Andrea scowled but composed himself. "Why did you summon me?"

"To share breakfast, of course," Caderousse replied, gesturing to a table laden with food. "We must talk, old friend."

Andrea's instincts screamed danger, but he sat reluctantly. As they ate, Caderousse's true intentions surfaced.

"Andrea," he said, leaning in, "you're living quite the life now—fine clothes, rich acquaintances. But where's my share? I've kept your secrets, after all."

Andrea's smile was tight. "I've given you money, haven't I? What more do you want?"

Caderousse's tone turned sharp. "I want enough to live comfortably—say, thirty thousand francs. And don't act like you can't afford it. Your new father-in-law is a banker, after all."

Andrea's patience wore thin. "Do you want me to ruin myself?"

Caderousse's eyes gleamed with malice. "Better you ruin yourself than I expose you. Imagine what Danglars would think if he knew the truth about his future son-in-law."

Andrea's heart raced, but he forced a laugh. "Fine. You'll have your money. But after this, we're done."

Caderousse's grin returned. "Of course, my boy. I'm nothing if not reasonable."

After leaving Caderousse, Andrea resolved to take drastic measures to eliminate his growing liabilities. Meanwhile, Caderousse, left alone, studied the details of Andrea's life he had gleaned, plotting his next move. Both men, consumed by greed and desperation, continued their dangerous game, unaware of how close they were to their ultimate reckoning.

Chapter 82: The Burglary

The day after the events of the last chapter, the Count of Monte Cristo set off for Auteuil, accompanied by Ali and a small entourage. He also brought along a few horses to test their capabilities. This trip, which had been unplanned the day before, was prompted by Bertuccio's return from Normandy with news about the house and the sloop. The house was ready, and the sloop, which had arrived a week prior, was anchored in a small cove. Its six-man crew had complied with all regulations and was prepared to sail again.

The Count praised Bertuccio for his efficiency and ordered him to prepare for an imminent departure, as he planned to leave France in a month.

"I might need to get from Paris to Tréport overnight," the Count said. "Make sure there are eight fresh horses stationed along the way. I want to cover fifty leagues in ten hours."

"That's already arranged, sir," Bertuccio replied. "I personally acquired the horses and placed them in quiet villages where they wouldn't attract attention."

"Good," Monte Cristo nodded. "I'll stay here for a day or two. Adjust the plans accordingly."

As Bertuccio left to carry out the orders, Baptistin entered with a letter on a silver tray.

"What brings you here, Baptistin? I don't recall summoning you," Monte Cristo said, noticing the dust on his valet's clothes.

Without a word, Baptistin handed over the letter. "It's urgent," he said.

Monte Cristo opened the envelope and read:

Count of Monte Cristo,

Tonight, someone will break into your house on the Champs-Élysées to steal documents believed to be in the secretaire in your dressing room. Your courage makes involving the police unnecessary, and their presence might compromise the one sending this warning. If you remain discreet and vigilant, you can handle this matter personally and possibly identify an enemy. You may not receive another warning if this attempt fails. Take care.

Monte Cristo's initial thought was that this could be a ploy—a distraction to lure him into a trap. He almost forwarded the letter to the police, despite the sender's advice, but then reconsidered. Perhaps it was a personal enemy, someone he alone could recognize and confront. This was a challenge he couldn't resist.

"Baptistin," Monte Cristo called, "return to Paris and gather the staff still at the house. I want everyone moved to Auteuil, except the porter."

"But, sir," Baptistin hesitated, "the porter's lodge is far from the main house. If something happens—"

"If thieves want my belongings, they can take them. What matters is that my orders are followed." Monte Cristo's tone left no room for argument.

That evening, Monte Cristo dined alone, attended only by Ali. After dinner, the Count slipped out with Ali and quietly made his way back to his Parisian home.

By twilight, he stood across the street from the house. The only light came from the porter's lodge, about forty paces away. Everything seemed still.

Monte Cristo entered through a side door with Ali, using a servant's staircase to reach his bedroom undetected. Inside, he inspected the dressing room and double-locked the secretaire, pocketing the key. Ali brought him a short carbine and a pair of pistols. Armed and ready, Monte Cristo settled in to wait.

Hours passed. The house remained silent, the darkness unbroken. At a quarter to midnight, Monte Cristo heard a faint sound in the dressing room. A soft scrape, then another—someone was cutting the glass with a diamond. His heartbeat quickened, though his demeanor remained calm.

Through the dressing-room window, a shadow moved. A pane of glass cracked, and a man's arm reached through to unlatch the window. Moments later, the intruder climbed inside.

"That's bold," Monte Cristo murmured to himself.

Ali gestured toward the street. Another man lingered outside, keeping watch.

Monte Cristo nodded. "There are two of them. One works; the other guards."

Inside, the thief bolted the doors and moved toward the secretaire. He fumbled with a set of skeleton keys, trying to unlock it.

"Just a thief," Monte Cristo whispered, slightly disappointed.

The thief lit a small lantern, revealing his face. Monte Cristo froze in recognition. "It's him," he muttered.

Monte Cristo signaled Ali to stay hidden. Disguising himself as the Abbé Busoni, he waited for the right moment. As the thief worked on the lock, Monte Cristo opened the door silently, holding a taper to illuminate the room.

"Good evening, Caderousse," he said, his voice calm but firm. "What brings you here at this hour?"

The thief dropped his tools in shock. "The Abbé Busoni!"

Monte Cristo blocked the thief's escape. "I see you haven't changed."

"Reverend," Caderousse stammered, "I swear, it's not what it looks like."

"A pane of glass, a dark lantern, skeleton keys... Spare me your excuses."

Caderousse's desperation grew. "You saved me once. Save me again!"

Monte Cristo's expression hardened. "You've squandered every chance you've been given. Write a confession. Now."

Terrified, Caderousse complied. He confessed everything, from his crimes to the involvement of Andrea Cavalcanti—Monte Cristo's target.

When the confession was complete, Monte Cristo dismissed Caderousse. "Leave, and don't come back. If you make it home safely, perhaps God will forgive you."

Caderousse fled, but his escape was short-lived. Outside, his accomplice suddenly turned on him, delivering rapid blows with a blade. As Caderousse lay dying, he cried out for help. Monte Cristo and Ali, hearing and responding to his pleas, arrive just in time to hear his final words.

Chapter 83: The Hand of God

Caderousse's frantic cries filled the air. "Help, reverend sir! Help!"

Monte Cristo stepped closer, his expression calm but curious. "What's the matter?"

"I've been attacked! Murdered!" Caderousse gasped, clutching his side as crimson seeped through his fingers. "It's over. Too late. You've come just in time to see me die."

He went unconscious. Monte Cristo signaled to Ali, who swiftly carried the wounded man into a nearby room. Inside, the count inspected the wounds with precision, his face a mask of grim resolve.

"God," he murmured, "your justice may be slow, but it is inescapable."

Monte Cristo turned to Ali. "Fetch the prosecutor, M. de Villefort, from the Faubourg Saint-Honoré. And alert the porter to summon a surgeon."

Ali nodded and left without hesitation, leaving Monte Cristo alone with the unconscious Caderousse.

When Caderousse stirred, his eyes fluttered open to meet Monte Cristo's somber gaze.

"A surgeon... I need a surgeon," he croaked.

"He's on his way," Monte Cristo replied.

"It's too late for that. I'm dying. But I can still name my killer."

"Who was it?"

"Benedetto," Caderousse spat, his voice laced with venom. "The Corsican. My so-called comrade."

Monte Cristo's eyes narrowed. "The one you once called a friend?"

"Yes. He gave me the plan to rob this house, hoping the count would kill me, or that I'd kill him and clear the way for Benedetto to inherit everything. But instead, he betrayed me."

"I've sent for the authorities," Monte Cristo assured him.

"They'll be too late," Caderousse rasped, his breaths growing shallower. "Write down my statement. Quickly."

Monte Cristo retrieved a pen and paper. "Dictate."

Caderousse's voice trembled but held firm. "I die, murdered by Benedetto, my cellmate at Toulon. Prisoner number 59."

Monte Cristo handed him the pen. With trembling hands, Caderousse signed the statement before collapsing back onto the bed.

"Promise me," he pleaded, "that he'll pay. That he'll face justice."

Monte Cristo's voice was steady. "He will."

As Caderousse's life ebbed away, he turned his gaze to Monte Cristo, suspicion mingling with desperation. "You knew this would happen. You could have stopped it."

Monte Cristo's expression didn't falter. "I saw divine justice at work and dared not intervene."

"Justice?" Caderousse sneered. "If God were just, so many would suffer who walk free."

Monte Cristo leaned closer, his tone unwavering. "God is patient. Merciful, even. He gave you countless chances, and you squandered them all."

"I don't believe in God," Caderousse spat weakly.

Monte Cristo's gaze hardened. "Then why do you curse him now? Denial in the face of death doesn't make him any less real."

Caderousse shivered. "Who are you?"

Monte Cristo stepped into the light, his dark hair gleaming as he removed his wig. Caderousse's eyes widened in recognition.

"You… you're not the abbé," he whispered. "You're…"

Monte Cristo's voice dropped to a whisper. "Look closely."

As realization dawned, Caderousse's face twisted in terror. "God forgive me!" he cried. "You are his hand on earth."

His strength gave out, and he slumped lifelessly. Monte Cristo straightened, his gaze fixed on the still body.

"One," he said softly, a note of finality in his voice.

Moments later, the surgeon and prosecutor arrived, finding Monte Cristo—once again the Abbé Busoni—calmly praying beside the corpse.

Chapter 84: Beauchamp

The attempted robbery at the count's residence dominated Parisian gossip for weeks. Caderousse's dying declaration identified Benedetto as the killer, prompting an intense manhunt. The evidence—a knife, a dark lantern, a set of keys, and Caderousse's bloodied clothes—was secured at the registry. Meanwhile, his body was unceremoniously taken to the morgue. Monte Cristo, ever the enigma, claimed to know only what Abbé Busoni had relayed—a convenient story that kept suspicion at bay. No one had heard of the name Benedetto before, and they certainly didn't suspect that he and Andrea Cavalcanti were one in the same. Only the Count knew the truth.

Bertuccio's face betrayed his unease whenever Benedetto's name surfaced, though no one thought to question it. Villefort, tasked with prosecuting the case, prepared his arguments with his usual fervor, but weeks passed without progress. As Paris's fascination with the crime waned, attention shifted to an impending societal event—the wedding of Mademoiselle Danglars to Count Andrea Cavalcanti.

Though Andrea basked in the baron's adoration, Mademoiselle Danglars barely concealed her disdain. Her aversion to matrimony was well known, and Andrea's persistent courtship did little to endear him. The baron dismissed her resistance as a mere whim, oblivious to the depth of her dissatisfaction. Letters from Andrea's supposed father in Parma arrived, laden with promises of a generous wedding gift and glowing approval, further solidifying the union in the baron's eyes.

Elsewhere, Albert de Morcerf wrestled with a storm of emotions. Beauchamp's damning article, implicating his father in treachery at Yanina, remained an open wound. Though he heeded Monte Cristo's advice to let the matter fade, Albert's pride demanded satisfaction. Beauchamp, the source of his ire, had vanished on a mysterious journey, leaving Albert to stew in uncertainty.

One morning, Albert's valet announced Beauchamp's arrival. Albert dressed quickly and met his friend in the smoking room, where Beauchamp paced nervously.

"You didn't wait for me to call on you," Albert began coldly. "Shall I offer you forgiveness, or do we settle this with a duel?"

"Albert," Beauchamp replied gravely, "let us sit and talk first."

"No. Answer me now. Will you retract your accusation, or must we fight?"

Beauchamp sighed. "This is not a question of yes or no, Albert. Your father's honor… your family's future… these are matters too grave for simple answers."

"Then explain," Albert demanded impatiently.

"I've just returned from Yanina," Beauchamp said, producing his passport as proof.

Albert's skepticism turned to astonishment. "Yanina?"

"Yes. I went to verify the claims myself."

Albert's face paled as Beauchamp laid out the evidence: sworn testimonies from Yanina's residents, incriminating documents bearing Fernand Mondego's name, and irrefutable proof of his betrayal for personal gain. Albert staggered under the weight of the revelation.

"Beauchamp," he whispered, his voice breaking, "this can't be true."

"I hoped it wasn't," Beauchamp said softly. "But the truth is undeniable."

Albert collapsed into a chair, his grief overwhelming. "What am I to do? My father's a disgrace… my mother…"

Beauchamp placed a comforting hand on Albert's shoulder. "The sins of the father need not tarnish the son. If you wish, I will destroy this evidence. The secret will die with me."

Albert's eyes filled with gratitude. "Thank you, my friend."

Beauchamp handed him the documents. Albert shredded them with trembling hands before burning the pieces. "Let it all be forgotten," he murmured.

Though Beauchamp's gesture offered temporary solace, Albert's anguish lingered. "How can I face him now? My father… my family's name… everything is ruined."

"You must find strength," Beauchamp urged. "The world has yet to learn this secret. You can still protect your family. But be prepared. The storm may still come."

Albert nodded, his resolve hardening. "You're right. I must be ready."

"And what of Mademoiselle Danglars?" Beauchamp asked carefully.

Albert's expression darkened. "The engagement is off."

"Then let us walk," Beauchamp suggested, eager to lift his friend's spirits. "Perhaps we should visit Monte Cristo. He has a way of reviving hope."

Albert managed a faint smile. "Yes, let's. I could use his wisdom now more than ever."

Chapter 85: The Journey

Monte Cristo greeted the young men with a broad smile. "Ah, excellent! Everything has been resolved, I take it?"

"Yes," Beauchamp replied. "The ridiculous rumors have died down, and if they resurface, I'll be the first to squash them. Let's not waste another moment discussing it."

"That's exactly what I told Albert," Monte Cristo said, gesturing toward the papers in front of him. "Now look at this tedious chore I've been stuck with."

"What are you working on?" Albert asked. "It looks like paperwork."

"Thankfully, no. I don't have any papers of my own. These belong to Monsieur Cavalcanti."

"Monsieur Cavalcanti?" Beauchamp raised an eyebrow.

"Yes, haven't you heard?" Albert smirked. "The Count here has been introducing him around town."

Monte Cristo shook his head. "Let's not get carried away. I've done no such thing, and I certainly haven't introduced him."

Albert's smile turned bitter. "Ah, but he is the one who's now set to marry Mademoiselle Danglars, taking my place—a fact that wounds me deeply."

"What?" Beauchamp exclaimed. "Cavalcanti is marrying Mademoiselle Danglars?"

"Yes, it's all over Paris," Monte Cristo said. "You, a journalist, must be out of the loop!"

"And you, Count, are responsible for arranging this match?" Beauchamp asked.

"Absolutely not. Don't pin this on me. If anything, I've tried to prevent it."

Beauchamp turned to Albert. "I suppose he did this to spare your feelings?"

"Hardly," Albert said. "I've been urging him to break off my engagement for months. If anything, I should be thanking him for my freedom."

Monte Cristo sighed. "To be clear, I opposed this union for my own reasons. Monsieur Danglars is enamored with Cavalcanti's wealth and title, and no amount of warning could deter him. So here I am, writing letters to secure Cavalcanti's paperwork, while metaphorically washing my hands of the whole affair."

Albert chuckled despite himself. "You're too generous, Count."

Monte Cristo noticed Albert rubbing his temples. "What's wrong? You don't seem like yourself."

"I've got a splitting headache."

"Ah, I have just the cure: a change of scenery. Why don't you join me? I'm planning to leave Paris for a bit."

"You, leaving Paris?" Beauchamp asked. "Why?"

"Let's just say I need to get away from the constant stream of problems. For example, Villefort is preparing a case against some criminal named Benedetto, which means every thief in Paris has suddenly taken an interest in my house."

Albert's curiosity piqued. "Where are you planning to go?"

"Someplace peaceful, where the air is clean, the ocean humbles even the proudest, and the quiet restores the soul. You could use the change too, Albert."

Albert smiled. "A trip to the sea? Count me in."

That evening, Albert and Monte Cristo set off in a luxurious carriage drawn by four powerful horses. The Count's pace was unrelenting, with fresh horses waiting at each post station along their route. The journey was swift and exhilarating, with the wind rushing past them as Ali expertly commanded the reins.

"This speed is incredible!" Albert exclaimed. "Where do you find such magnificent horses?"

"They're bred from a Hungarian mare I purchased years ago," Monte Cristo explained. "Her descendants are trained for speed and endurance."

Albert laughed. "You've thought of everything."

As they traveled, the conversation waned, and Albert reflected on how effortlessly the Count seemed to live, always surrounded by luxury and control. It was a stark contrast to Albert's own life, which now felt uncertain.

By midnight, they reached their destination: a grand estate by the sea. Albert was shown to a beautifully appointed room where a bath and supper awaited. Exhausted, he fell asleep to the soothing sound of waves crashing against the shore.

The next morning, Albert stood on a terrace overlooking the ocean. Below, a sleek sloop bearing Monte Cristo's crest was moored among local fishing boats. As always, the Count's presence brought an air of elegance and authority to even the humblest of settings.

Albert spent the next few days immersed in the activities Monte Cristo excelled at—hunting pheasants, fishing for trout, and exploring the estate. The days passed in a blur of exertion and relaxation.

On the evening of the third day, Albert was startled by the arrival of his valet, Florentin, who had ridden hard to deliver a sealed letter and newspaper. Albert tore open the letter, his face growing pale as he read the first lines. His hands trembled, and he nearly collapsed.

"Florentin," he gasped, "is my mother all right?"

"She's fine, sir," Florentin assured him. "But she was in tears when I left. Monsieur Beauchamp sent me here with urgent news."

Albert continued reading, his expression darkening with fury. "This is a grave insult to my family's honor. I must return to Paris at once."

He rushed to Monte Cristo. "Count, I'm sorry, but I have to leave immediately."

Monte Cristo frowned. "What's happened?"

"I can't explain. Just lend me a horse."

"Of course, but wouldn't a carriage be safer?"

"No," Albert insisted. "I need the strain of riding."

Monte Cristo reluctantly summoned Ali to prepare a horse. As Albert mounted, he handed the Count the newspaper. "Read this after I'm gone. It will explain everything."

Albert spurred his horse and disappeared into the night. Monte Cristo unfolded the newspaper and read the damning article exposing Albert's father's betrayal in Yanina. A deep sadness settled over him as he whispered, "The sins of the father are visited upon the son."

Chapter 86: The Trial

At eight in the morning, Albert arrived at Beauchamp's door. The valet, following prior instructions, ushered him in immediately. Beauchamp was in the bath.

"Here I am," Albert announced as he entered.

"Well, my friend," Beauchamp replied, "I was expecting you."

"I don't need to say how much I trust you. Your decision to send for me only reinforces your loyalty. So please, tell me—do you have any idea where this devastating attack came from?"

"I believe I do, but first, let me explain everything."

Beauchamp began recounting the details of the scandal while Albert listened in stunned silence. Two days earlier, the article had re-appeared not only in *l'Impartial* but also in a prominent government paper. Beauchamp had been having breakfast when he first read it. Alarmed, he rushed to the publisher's office. The editor, despite holding opposing political views, was an old friend. Beauchamp found him reviewing his latest editorial with evident pride.

"Ah, Beauchamp," the editor greeted, holding up the paper. "I suppose you've come about that piece."

"Yes, and I hope you realize the risk of publishing such inflammatory claims," Beauchamp said, trying to keep his composure.

"Not at all," the editor replied calmly. "We've verified the sources thoroughly. Morcerf won't dare challenge us. Exposing dishonor, especially from someone of his rank, is a service to the nation."

Beauchamp left the office in shock, realizing nothing could be done to suppress the story. Worse still, events escalated quickly. That same day, the House of Peers was abuzz with speculation. Members discussed the damning accusations against Morcerf, piecing together corroborating details. The Count of Morcerf, oblivious to the storm brewing around him, spent his morning riding and writing letters. By the time he arrived at the House, tension filled the air.

As Morcerf walked through the corridors, colleagues avoided his gaze. The business of the day had already begun when a member of the House, one of Morcerf's long-standing adversaries, took the floor. With measured solemnity, he announced that a matter of grave importance demanded their attention. At the mention of "Yanina" and "Colonel Fernand," Morcerf visibly paled.

The speaker had detailed the charges, proposing an official inquiry. Morcerf managed to rise and, though shaken, insisted he was ready to address the allegations immediately. His defiance earned him some sympathy, even from those predisposed against him. The House approved an investigation, set to begin that evening.

Beauchamp relayed these events to Albert, whose emotions swung from hope to rage and then to despair. When Beauchamp hesitated to continue, Albert pressed him.

"What happened next?"

"My friend, what comes next will be hard to hear. Are you certain you want me to continue?"

"Completely. I'd rather hear it from you than anyone else."

Beauchamp complied with his friend's request and continued relaying the events that unfolded while Albert was away.

That evening, the House was packed. Paris held its breath as rumors swirled—some claimed Morcerf would prove his innocence, while others speculated he had fled. Beauchamp, using his connections, secured a spot in the gallery to witness the proceedings.

At eight, Morcerf entered, his military uniform immaculate, his demeanor composed. He carried documents he claimed would exonerate him. Beginning his defense, he described his role in Yanina, producing letters from Ali Pasha and a ring symbolizing trust. He explained that he had tried to protect Ali's family after the Vizier's death but had lost track of them.

Albert flinched at the mention of Ali's family. Haydée's story resurfaced in his mind.

At that moment, a letter was delivered to the president of the committee. As the president read its contents, his expression darkened.

"Count," the president said, "you claim to have lost contact with Ali Pasha's family. But this letter states otherwise. The writer, an eyewitness to Ali's final moments, claims to know the fate of everyone involved. Shall we hear this witness?"

The room held its breath as the decision was made to admit the witness. Minutes later, a veiled woman entered, accompanied by a servant. Removing her veil, she revealed a striking figure in Grecian attire. It was Haydée.

"Madame," the president addressed her, "you claim to be an eyewitness to the events in Yanina. Please state your identity."

"I am Haydée, daughter of Ali Tepelini, Pasha of Yanina, and his wife, Vasiliki," she declared.

The assembly was stunned. Morcerf, visibly shaken, could barely look at her. Haydée recounted the betrayal in vivid detail, her voice unwavering. She accused Morcerf, then known as Fernand Mondego, of selling her and her mother into slavery after murdering her father's loyal servant.

When asked for evidence, Haydée presented documents proving her lineage and the record of her sale. The papers bore the imperial seal, leaving no room for doubt.

Morcerf's silence condemned him further. When pressed by the president, he stammered denials but offered no proof. His colleagues, once willing to give him the benefit of the doubt, now regarded him with contempt.

As Haydée concluded her testimony, she cast a final, piercing look at Morcerf. "Do you deny it, Fernand Mondego?" she asked. "Do you not recognize me, or the blood on your hands?"

Morcerf, overwhelmed, fled the chamber without a word. The House unanimously declared him guilty of treason and conduct unbecoming of a peer.

Haydée remained composed until the end. Bowing gracefully to the assembly, she departed with the dignity of a queen avenging her family.

Chapter 87: The Challenge

Beauchamp continued, "I took advantage of the darkness and silence to leave the House unnoticed. The usher who had introduced me earlier led me to a private exit onto Rue de Vaugirard. I left with mixed emotions—grief for you, Albert, and admiration for that courageous girl, seeking justice for her father. Whatever the source of this scandal may be, whether friend or foe, they are merely the instrument of Providence[*]."

Albert held his head in his hands. Raising his tear-streaked face, flushed with shame, he gripped Beauchamp's arm.

"My friend," Albert said, his voice breaking, "my life is over. I can't simply accept that 'Providence struck the blow,' as you suggest. I must uncover who is behind this hatred, and when I find them, either they'll kill me, or I'll kill them. I need your help, Beauchamp. Please tell me contempt hasn't replaced your friendship."

"Contempt? Albert, how could this misfortune tarnish you? Thankfully, we no longer hold the son responsible for the father's sins. Look at your life—it's only just begun, and its start was as bright and untarnished as a summer's day. My advice? Leave Paris. All scandals are quickly forgotten here amidst the ever-changing frenzy of the city.

---

[*]Used in place of "God"; or to describe the expression of God's will or plan.

Come back in a few years with a Russian princess for a bride, and no one will remember this happened."

Albert shook his head. "Thank you, Beauchamp, for your kind words, but that's not possible. I've made up my mind. I don't see this as divine justice but as the work of a human hand. I will find whoever struck this blow, and I will make them pay for what my family has endured. I need your help, Beauchamp, as my friend."

"Very well," Beauchamp said. "If you insist on seeking your enemy, I'll help you. My honor is nearly as entangled in this as yours."

"Good. Then let's begin immediately. Every moment wasted feels unbearable. The person behind this still thinks they're safe, but I'll make them regret it."

"Albert, listen carefully. I may have a lead—something I hesitated to mention before. It's not definitive, but it might guide us."

"Tell me everything."

"When I returned from Yanina, I made inquiries with the chief banker in the town. Before I could say much, he interrupted me.

'Ah,' he said. 'I know why you're here.'

'Why?' I asked.

'Because someone else wrote me and asked about the same thing a fortnight ago.'

'Who was it?'

'A Parisian banker—Danglars.'"

Albert's face darkened. "Him! Of course. Danglars has hated my father for years. His envy knows no bounds. The broken engagement, his bitterness about my father becoming a peer—it all fits."

"Don't jump to conclusions," Beauchamp cautioned. "Investigate first. If it's true, then act."

"Oh, it's true," Albert growled. "And if it is, he'll pay dearly."

"Be careful, Albert. Danglars is older, and—"

"I'll respect his age as much as he respected my family's honor. If he had an issue with my father, he should have confronted him directly, not slandered him behind his back."

"Albert, I understand your anger, but don't act recklessly. Let's approach this together."

"Absolutely. You'll be my second, Beauchamp. This will be settled before the day is out—either Danglars dies, or I do."

"When you're determined like this, action must be swift," Beauchamp said. "Shall we go to Danglars now?"

Albert nodded, and they summoned a carriage.

Arriving at the banker's mansion, they noticed Andrea Cavalcanti's carriage parked outside.

"Perfect," Albert muttered grimly. "If Danglars refuses to face me, I'll challenge his son-in-law instead. Cavalcanti will fight."

Albert forced his way past the footman who tried to block his entry. Danglars, startled by Albert's sudden appearance, stood up from his desk.

"Sir," Danglars snapped, "do you think you can barge into my home uninvited?"

"Certain situations demand exceptions," Albert replied coldly.

"And what situation would that be?"

"I'm here to demand a duel," Albert said, stepping closer. "Ten minutes in a secluded spot will suffice for one of us to remain standing."

Danglars turned pale, while Cavalcanti shifted uncomfortably by the fireplace. Albert turned to him.

"You, Cavalcanti—if Danglars won't fight, perhaps you will. Consider it a privilege as almost-family."

Danglars, realizing the situation was spiraling out of control, stepped between Albert and Cavalcanti. "Albert," he said, his voice trembling with a mix of anger and fear, "if you think I have wronged you, take your grievances elsewhere. Your father's disgrace has nothing to do with me."

Albert's voice thundered. "Everything to do with you! You set this in motion."

"Are you mad?" Danglars sputtered. "How could I be involved in something that happened in Greece?"

"You wrote to Yanina," Albert accused.

"Yes, I wrote," Danglars admitted, "but only because someone advised me to."

"Who?"

"The Count of Monte Cristo," Danglars said. "He suggested I write for details about your father's history. I'll show you the correspondence if you wish."

Albert froze. Beauchamp stepped forward. "Danglars, do you realize you're accusing someone who isn't here to defend himself?"

"I'm merely telling the truth," Danglars insisted. "Monte Cristo knew your father's full name and background. When I received the reply from Yanina, he saw it. That's all."

Albert, overwhelmed with rage and betrayal, whispered to Beauchamp. "It's clear now. Monte Cristo orchestrated this. Danglars is just a pawn."

"You may be right," Beauchamp replied. "You need answers from Monte Cristo."

Albert turned to Danglars. "This isn't over. I'm going to Monte Cristo for an explanation. Don't think for a moment that I forgive you."

He left with Beauchamp, ignoring Danglars' feeble protests of innocence.

Chapter 88: The Insult

As they stood outside the banker's door, Beauchamp stopped Albert.

"Listen," he said. "Earlier, I told you that you needed to demand an explanation from Monte Cristo."

"Yes, and that's exactly where we're heading," Albert replied.

"Think carefully, Albert. Reflect for a moment before taking this step."

"What should I reflect on?"

"The gravity of what you're about to do. This is far more serious than confronting Danglars."

"How so?"

"Danglars is just a money-obsessed coward. Men like him calculate risks and avoid duels. But Monte Cristo… he's a different kind of man. Do you not fear he might be more dangerous than you expect?"

Albert shook his head. "The only thing I fear is finding someone who refuses to fight."

"That won't be a problem," Beauchamp said grimly. "My concern is that he might be too strong for you."

Albert gave a bittersweet smile. "That would be for the best. If I die in my father's place, at least some honor might be restored."

"And your mother? What about her?"

Albert's expression darkened, and he brushed his hand over his face. "She would grieve herself to death, I know. But better grief than the shame she faces now."

"Are you fully decided?"

"Yes. Let's go."

"Do you think we'll find him at home?"

"He returned a few hours after I did, so I'm sure he's there now."

The driver was instructed to take them to 30 Champs-Élysées. Beauchamp suggested going in alone, but Albert insisted that the circumstances justified breaking etiquette. Beauchamp relented and followed him.

Albert strode up the steps and was met by Baptistin.

"The Count has just returned but is in his bath," the servant said, "and he's not accepting visitors."

"What about after his bath?" Albert asked.

"He'll have dinner."

"And after dinner?"

"He'll take a nap."

"And then?"

"He's going to the Opera."

Albert nodded. "That's all I needed to know."

Turning to Beauchamp, Albert said, "If you have anything to do, take care of it now. If you've made any plans for tonight, cancel them. I'll need you at the Opera, and bring Château-Renaud with you if possible."

Beauchamp agreed and left. Meanwhile, Albert went home to prepare for the evening. He sent word to Franz, Debray, and Morrel, inviting them to join him at the Opera. Before leaving, he visited his mother, who had confined herself to her room since the humiliation of the previous day.

He found his mother, Mercédès, lying in bed with her face pale and swollen from tears. The sight of Albert brought fresh sobs, though her tears seemed to bring her some relief. Albert stood silently by her side, his pale face betraying his inner turmoil.

"Mother," he finally said, "do you know if Fernand has any enemies?"

Mercédès flinched at his words, noticing he didn't refer to the Count of Morcerf as "my father."

"My son," she said, "in a position like his, enemies are inevitable. But it's often the ones you don't see who are the most dangerous."

"Your instincts are sharp, Mother. Tell me, why did Monte Cristo refuse to eat or drink at our house during the ball?"

Mercédès sat up abruptly. "Monte Cristo? What does he have to do with this?"

"You know he's almost an Oriental, Mother. Among them, it's a custom to refuse food in the house of someone they intend to harm, so they won't be bound by hospitality."

Mercédès turned even paler. "Are you saying Monte Cristo is our enemy? Albert, that's absurd! Monte Cristo saved your life, and you introduced him to us as a friend. Please, my son, if you've harbored such a thought, abandon it. Keep him as an ally."

"You have a specific reason for saying that," Albert said, watching her closely.

"I?" Mercédès blushed, then grew paler than before.

"Yes, to keep him from harming us further."

Mercédès trembled under her son's intense gaze. "Albert, just three days ago, you considered him a friend. What changed?"

Albert didn't answer, and Mercédès, sensing his determination, said, "Stay with me tonight. Don't leave me alone."

"I can't, Mother. There's something urgent I must do."

With a sigh, Mercédès whispered, "Go then, Albert. I won't stop you."

Albert bowed and left. Once he was gone, Mercédès summoned a servant and instructed him to follow her son and report back. Then, despite her weakness, she began to dress, preparing for whatever might come.

At ten minutes to eight, Beauchamp arrived. Château-Renaud had agreed to join them at the Opera. The two men climbed into Albert's carriage and headed to the theatre, where Château-Renaud was already waiting.

Albert entered the Opera, his eyes scanning the crowd for Monte Cristo. He watched anxiously as the first act began and ended without the Count appearing. Finally, at the start of the second act, the door to Monte Cristo's box opened. The Count, dressed in black, leaned forward, surveying the crowd. Albert's pale face and burning eyes caught his attention, but Monte Cristo feigned indifference and turned away.

When the curtain fell at the end of the second act, Albert left his seat and made his way to Monte Cristo's box. Bursting in, he found the Count chatting casually with Maximilian Morrel.

"Well, young man," Monte Cristo greeted him with his usual composed demeanor, "it seems you've achieved your goal. Good evening, Monsieur de Morcerf."

Albert's trembling voice barely rose above a whisper. "I didn't come for pleasantries. I came for an explanation."

"An explanation? At the Opera?" Monte Cristo asked with a raised brow. "I didn't think this was the place for such matters."

"You leave me no choice," Albert retorted. "You hide behind your meals, your baths, your naps. You're unreachable. So yes, here and now."

Monte Cristo's expression remained cold. "You're not yourself, Monsieur. Whatever this is about, lower your voice or leave."

Albert's fury boiled over. "I'll make you leave," he snarled, gripping his glove.

Monte Cristo's eyes sharpened. Without rising, he extended his hand and plucked the glove from Albert's grasp. "Consider your challenge accepted," he said. "You'll have it back wrapped around a bullet. Now, leave before I summon my servants."

Albert stormed out, his friends following closely.

Turning to Morrel, Monte Cristo said calmly, "He'll have his duel tomorrow morning. And I'll kill him."

Chapter 89: The Night

Monte Cristo waited until Duprez finished singing his famous "*Suivez-moi!*" before rising and leaving the opera. At the door, he bade farewell to Morrel, who reiterated his promise to join him the next morning at seven with Emmanuel. Monte Cristo, calm and composed, returned home within minutes.

The moment he entered, his demeanor shifted. "Ali," he called, "bring me my pistols with the ivory cross."

Ali promptly delivered the box. Monte Cristo carefully examined the pistols, as one might when entrusting their life to something so fragile as powder and shot. These weapons, specially designed for him, were often used for target practice in his private quarters. With their soft caps, they made no sound beyond the adjoining room, keeping his activities discreet.

As he tested the aim against an iron plate in his study, the door opened unexpectedly. Baptistin appeared, and behind him was a veiled woman who, upon seeing Monte Cristo armed, rushed into the room. Baptistin, at a gesture from his master, quietly withdrew, closing the door.

"Who are you, madame?" Monte Cristo demanded.

The woman surveyed the room to ensure they were alone. Then, as if overwhelmed by emotion, she bent forward as though to kneel, clasping her hands together.

"*Edmond*, you will not kill my son!"

Monte Cristo staggered back, letting the pistol fall from his hand.

"What name did you just use, Madame de Morcerf?" he asked, his voice sharp.

"Yours," she cried, throwing back her veil. "Yours, which I alone remember. Edmond, I am not here as Madame de Morcerf. It is Mercédès who stands before you."

Monte Cristo stiffened. "Mercédès is dead, madame. That name has no meaning for me."

"Mercédès lives," she replied firmly. "I recognized you the moment I saw you—no, even before that, from your voice. I have watched you, feared you, followed you. It was not hard to see whose hand dealt this recent blow against Fernand."

"Fernand, you say?" Monte Cristo retorted bitterly. "If we are naming names, let us use them all." His tone, dripping with hatred, sent a shiver through Mercédès.

"Edmond, please," she pleaded, "spare my son!"

"And what makes you think I intend to harm him?"

"A mother knows," she replied. "I saw you tonight at the Opera. I was hidden, but I saw it all."

"Then you saw your son publicly insult me," Monte Cristo replied, his voice icy. "You saw him almost throw his glove in my face."

"My son has guessed who you are," she said. "He blames you for his father's downfall."

Monte Cristo's gaze hardened. "Madame, you are mistaken. I am not the one punishing Fernand. This is Providence at work."

"And who appointed you as its agent?" Mercédès asked. "What does Fernand's betrayal of Ali Tepelini matter to you?"

"It matters little to me," he admitted. "This is not about the French captain or the Count of Morcerf. It is about the soldier Fernand—the man who betrayed me, Edmond Dantès."

Mercédès sobbed. "If you seek vengeance, Edmond, direct it at me. I am the one who failed you. My weakness allowed me to marry him."

Monte Cristo's voice cracked as he demanded, "And why did you marry him? Why was I not there to stop it?"

"Because you were arrested!" she cried. "You were taken from me!"

"And why was I arrested?" he pressed.

"I don't know," she whispered, trembling.

"I'll tell you," he said coldly. "Danglars wrote a letter accusing me of treason. And Fernand delivered it."

He retrieved the infamous letter from his desk and handed it to her. Mercédès read it, her face pale with horror.

"This letter," Monte Cristo continued, "cost me fourteen years in the Château d'If. Fourteen years of despair. Fourteen years during which I lost everything. And while I suffered, you married Fernand. My father died of hunger."

Mercédès gasped, her hands trembling. "I didn't know," she whispered.

"Now you do," he said. "For the sake of my father and the Mercédès I loved, I swore revenge. And I have taken it."

"But not on my son," she begged. "Edmond, he is innocent!"

Monte Cristo looked at her, his face a mask of anguish. "It is written that the sins of the father shall fall upon the children. Why should I make myself better than God?"

"Because I love you, Edmond," Mercédès cried. "I have loved you all my life. Don't destroy that love by killing my son."

Monte Cristo clenched his fists, his resolve wavering. "Very well," he said at last. "Your son shall live."

Mercédès collapsed to her knees, her tears falling freely. "Thank you, Edmond. You are the man I always believed you to be."

Monte Cristo turned away, his face shadowed with pain. "This is the end, Mercédès. After tomorrow, I will cease to exist."

"Don't say that," she implored. "You have forgiven him. There's no need to fight."

"There is," Monte Cristo replied solemnly. "The duel will happen. But instead of his blood, it will be mine."

Mercédès stared at him, stunned. "Edmond, no! I trust you will keep your word. My son's life is enough. I don't ask for more."

Monte Cristo gazed at her, the weight of his sacrifice evident in his eyes. "Then go, Mercédès. Live your life. I have nothing left to give."

Mercédès left silently, her heart heavy with gratitude and sorrow. As her carriage rolled away into the night, the clock struck one. Monte Cristo stood alone, his whispered words echoing in the empty room:

"What a fool I was not to tear my heart out when I first resolved to seek revenge."

Chapter 90: The Meeting

After Mercédès left, Monte Cristo was overcome by a profound gloom. It was as though his thoughts, so sharp and vivid, had suddenly ground to a halt. His mind, usually teeming with energy, now felt as drained as a body after enduring great physical strain.

"What is this?" he murmured to himself, his voice breaking the silence of his dimly lit room. The lamp and candles around him were nearly burned out, and his servants waited impatiently in the anteroom for any instructions. "What is this? This grand edifice that I've labored over for so long, built with such care and toil, is about to crumble from a single word, a single gesture? This self, which I once despised in the dungeons of Château d'If but later built into something mighty, will be reduced to nothing but dust tomorrow.

"It's not death itself that I fear," he continued, his voice low but resolute. "Death is merely rest—something I've yearned for in my darkest moments, back when starvation seemed my only escape before Faria appeared. No, it isn't existence that I regret losing. It's the collapse of my plans, those years of meticulous design and relentless effort. Providence seemed to support me until now, only to abandon me at the end."

Monte Cristo pressed his head into his hands, grappling with his torment. "Have I become a fatalist again?" he wondered. "Fourteen years of despair and ten years of hope made me believe in Providence. But now… now I wonder if it's all a cruel joke."

His thoughts turned to Mercédès, her voice echoing in his mind. "This heart," he admitted, his tone bitter, "which I thought had turned to stone, has only been dormant, waiting for the right moment to betray me. A single woman's voice woke it, and now my strength falters."

For a fleeting moment, he envisioned a scene. "She'll come tomorrow," he speculated, "throw herself between us, and plead with tears in her eyes. What she imagines as noble will appear ridiculous to all who witness it. No, I won't let that happen. I would rather die than endure that humiliation."

Determined, he reached for a pen and drew out a paper from his desk. It was his will. Beneath the original text, he added a codicil, explaining the nature of his death.

"I do this," he whispered, glancing heavenward, "for the sake of God's honor as much as my own. In the ten years since my escape from prison, I believed myself to be an agent of divine vengeance. Morcerf, Danglars, Villefort—they must know their reprieve is not by chance but by my choice. They may escape my justice here, but they cannot escape it forever. Eternity will hold them accountable."

As he wrote, the first rays of dawn crept through the windows, casting a faint light over his desk. At that moment, a soft sigh reached his ears. He froze, listening intently. The sound came again, unmistakably real.

Monte Cristo rose and walked to the door of the adjoining room. There, he saw Haydée, slumped in a chair, her arms limp and her head tilted back. She had been waiting for him, standing guard at the door until exhaustion claimed her.

"She remembered she had a son," Monte Cristo murmured, his expression softening. "And I forgot I had a daughter."

Shaking his head in regret, he whispered, "Poor Haydée. She must have suspected something."

He returned to his desk and wrote another clause into his will. This time, it was for her. "I leave twenty million francs to Maximilian Morrel," he wrote, "If his heart is free, he will marry Haydée. and by doing so will thus accomplish my last wish. She has been like a daughter to me, and this will has already constituted her the rest of my fortune which is estimated at sixty million francs."

He went across the room to grab a wax seal for his document when a sudden cry startled him. Turning quickly, he saw Haydée standing before the will, her face pale and stricken.

"Did you read it?" he asked gently.

"Yes," she replied, her voice trembling. "Why are you writing these things? Why are you leaving everything to me? Are you planning to leave me, my lord?"

Monte Cristo smiled sadly. "I'm preparing for a journey, my dear child. And if something should happen to me…"

"No!" she interrupted, her voice firm. "If you die, I want nothing. Your wealth means nothing to me without you."

With that, she grabbed the document and tore it into pieces. The effort drained her, and she collapsed onto the floor.

Monte Cristo rushed to her side, lifting her in his arms. For the first time, he saw her not as a daughter but as a woman. A wave of realization struck him. "Could she… does she love me in a way I never imagined?"

A pang of regret pierced his heart. "I could have been happy," he murmured, his voice thick with sorrow. "Perhaps happiness was still within my grasp."

He carried Haydée to her room and left her in the care of her attendants. Returning to his study, he rewrote the will, sealing it just as he heard a carriage arrive. Looking out the window, he saw Maximilian and Emmanuel step out.

"Good," he said to himself. "It's time."

Minutes later, Morrel entered the study. "I'm early," he admitted, "but I couldn't sleep. None of us could."

Monte Cristo clasped Morrel's hand. "Your loyalty means everything to me, my friend. Let's go."

The three men departed for the dueling grounds. Monte Cristo carried an air of calm resolve, his mind made up.

By eight o'clock, they arrived. Albert soon followed, his face pale and weary but resolute. As the parties gathered, Albert stepped forward.

"I have something to say," he announced, his voice trembling but growing steady. "I was wrong to accuse the Count of Monte Cristo. He had every right to seek justice against my father. I thank him for his restraint."

The crowd was stunned. Monte Cristo extended his hand, and Albert clasped it, bowing his head.

As Albert departed, Monte Cristo stood motionless, overwhelmed. "Providence," he whispered, "you have spoken once more."

Chapter 91: Mother and Son

The Count of Monte Cristo bowed to the five young men with a solemn yet dignified smile, then climbed into his carriage alongside Maximilian and Emmanuel. Left behind, Albert, Beauchamp, and Château-Renaud exchanged looks. Albert's gaze lingered on his two friends, not with timidity, but as if to gauge their reactions to his actions.

"My dear friend," Beauchamp said first, his voice carrying a note of genuine emotion, "allow me to congratulate you. This is an unexpected yet admirable conclusion to such an unpleasant affair."

Albert remained silent, his mind clearly preoccupied. Château-Renaud tapped his polished boot with his cane in a gesture of detached amusement.

"Are we leaving?" he asked after a tense pause.

"Whenever you wish," Beauchamp replied. "But first, let me commend M. de Morcerf on his remarkable display of chivalry."

"Oh yes," Château-Renaud added coolly.

"It's extraordinary," Beauchamp continued. "Such composure under pressure! Truly inspiring."

Château-Renaud shrugged. "I can't imagine showing that level of restraint."

Albert finally spoke, his tone calm but firm. "Gentlemen, I don't think you fully understand the significance of what just transpired between Monte Cristo and me."

"Perhaps not," Beauchamp admitted, "but others will be even less likely to grasp it. Sooner or later, you'll have to explain your actions, perhaps in ways that will threaten your safety. Let me offer some advice: leave Paris. Go to Naples, St. Petersburg, or anywhere calmer than here. Live quietly for a while, and then return to France when tempers have cooled. Isn't that wise, M. de Château-Renaud?"

"Indeed," Château-Renaud agreed. "Nothing incites more trouble than a duel avoided."

Albert smiled faintly. "Thank you for your concern, gentlemen, but my decision was made long before today. I've already planned to leave France. Still, I appreciate your support as my seconds—it's a kindness I'll always remember."

The finality in Albert's tone left Beauchamp and Château-Renaud at a loss. After an awkward pause, Beauchamp extended his hand. "Goodbye, Albert," he said lightly. Albert barely seemed to notice, his distant expression betraying his inner turmoil.

Château-Renaud followed suit, offering a curt "Goodbye" before stepping into the waiting carriage with Beauchamp.

Albert stood motionless as his friends departed. After a moment, he untied his horse, mounted, and galloped toward Paris.

Within fifteen minutes, he reached his home on Rue du Helder. As he dismounted, he thought he glimpsed his father's pale face at the window. Albert quickly looked away and entered the house.

Reaching his apartment, he paused to take in the familiar surroundings. The luxurious comforts of his privileged life—paintings, sculptures, fine weapons, and priceless ornaments—suddenly seemed hollow. Slowly, he began to dismantle it all.

He removed his mother's portrait from its gilded frame, leaving it bare and stark. Carefully, he cataloged every possession: Turkish sabers, English firearms, delicate china, and bronze sculptures. He locked the cupboards and left the keys on the desk, along with a detailed inventory. Everything was in order, except for the loose bundle of cash and trinkets he tossed into a drawer.

As Albert worked, his valet entered, despite strict instructions not to disturb him.

"What is it?" Albert asked, more resigned than annoyed.

"Forgive me, sir," the valet replied. "The Count of Morcerf summoned me."

"Why come to me first?"

"Because the count likely knows I accompanied you this morning and might question me about what happened."

"Then tell him the truth."

"The truth, sir?"

"Yes. Tell him the duel didn't take place, and that I apologized to the Count of Monte Cristo. Now go."

The valet bowed and left, leaving Albert to resume his task.

Moments later, the sound of hooves in the courtyard drew his attention. He watched as his father entered a carriage and drove away. Without hesitation, Albert went to his mother's room.

To his surprise, Mercédès was engaged in a task eerily similar to his own. Dresses, jewelry, and keepsakes were neatly arranged. She was carefully collecting the keys to her belongings when Albert rushed forward.

"Mother!" he cried, embracing her tightly.

Mercédès returned his embrace, her face a mixture of love and sorrow. "What are you doing, my son?" she asked softly.

"What are you doing, Mother?" Albert countered, his voice trembling.

"Ah, my dear child," Mercédès said, "I see we share the same resolve. I was hoping you would join me."

"I can't," Albert replied, his voice steady. "I've chosen a life of humility and labor. I'll leave this house, this name, and all its trappings behind. I'll rebuild my life from the ground up, starting with nothing. Please don't follow me into poverty."

Mercédès placed a gentle hand on his cheek. "You're braver than I could ever have imagined, Albert. But let me share your burden. I, too, am ready to leave."

Albert's resolve wavered, but he quickly recovered. "Then let's act now. Father is gone, and this is the perfect time to leave without confrontation."

Mercédès nodded. Albert fetched a carriage and prepared to escort her to a modest lodging he had arranged on Rue des Saints-Pères. As the carriage arrived, a man approached Albert and handed him a letter. Recognizing Bertuccio, Albert opened it immediately, but when he looked up, the messenger was already gone.

Albert read the letter and returned to his mother with tears in his eyes. Silently, he handed it to her.

Mercédès read the note, her expression softening as she finished. "Albert," she said, her voice trembling, "he's given us a way forward. I accept his offer. It's not charity—it's justice."

She folded the letter and tucked it into her dress. Taking Albert's arm, she whispered, "Let's go."

With surprising strength, she walked down the stairs, ready to face the future.

Chapter 92: The Suicide

Monte Cristo returned to Paris with Emmanuel and Maximilian. The mood in their carriage was light, with Emmanuel openly expressing his joy at the peaceful resolution of the duel. Maximilian, though equally relieved, was quieter, his happiness evident only in the relaxed expression on his face.

As they reached the Barrière du Trône, Bertuccio was waiting, standing motionless like a sentinel. Monte Cristo leaned out of the window and exchanged a few quiet words with him. Without a word, Bertuccio vanished into the city.

"Count," said Emmanuel as they approached the Place Royale, "drop me off at my home so I can reassure my wife that everything is fine."

"If it wouldn't seem like a boastful display of triumph," said Maximilian, "I'd invite the Count to join us. But I imagine you have other matters to attend to."

Monte Cristo smiled. "Don't make me lose both of you. Emmanuel, go to your charming wife and give her my regards. Morrel, why not accompany me to the Champs-Élysées?"

"With pleasure," Maximilian replied. "I have business in that part of town anyway."

After dropping Emmanuel off, Monte Cristo and Maximilian continued their journey.

"See what good fortune I bring you," Maximilian said with a grin.

Monte Cristo nodded. "Indeed, and that's precisely why I want to keep you close."

"It's truly miraculous," Maximilian continued, as if answering his own thoughts.

"What is?" Monte Cristo asked.

"The way Albert handled himself this morning. It was... unexpected."

"Yes," Monte Cristo agreed. "Albert is brave. I've seen him face danger without flinching."

"But how do you reconcile that with his actions today? Apologizing, withdrawing... It's unlike him."

"It's your influence," Monte Cristo said with a small smile.

Maximilian shook his head. "It's fortunate Albert isn't in the army. Such an apology on the dueling ground would ruin him."

Monte Cristo's expression softened. "Don't judge too harshly. His actions were not cowardly—they were principled. A different kind of courage."

Maximilian smiled faintly. "Perhaps you're right. Still, he wasn't as brave today as he was yesterday."

Monte Cristo chuckled lightly. "You'll join me for breakfast, won't you?"

"No, I have to leave by ten."

"Surely you'll eat something before you go?"

"Not if I'm not hungry," Maximilian replied.

Monte Cristo leaned back, his tone playful. "Ah, there are only two things that can suppress an appetite: grief and love. Since you're clearly not grieving, I can only assume..."

Maximilian laughed. "Well, you might be onto something, Count."

Monte Cristo's eyes twinkled with curiosity. "Will you share your secret with me?"

Maximilian shook his head. "Let's just say my heart has found its home, and I must go to it."

Monte Cristo nodded, his voice warm. "Go, then. But remember, if you face any obstacle, come to me. I have some influence in this world, and I'll gladly use it for you."

Maximilian smiled. "I'll remember that. Goodbye for now."

They arrived at the Champs-Élysées. Maximilian stepped out, disappearing down the Avenue de Marigny, while Bertuccio greeted Monte Cristo at the steps.

"She's leaving her house," Bertuccio reported.

"And her son?"

"Florentin says he's planning to leave as well."

Monte Cristo gestured for Bertuccio to follow him into the study. There, he quickly wrote a letter and handed it to his steward. "Deliver this immediately," he instructed. "But first, let Haydée know I've returned."

As if summoned by his thoughts, Haydée appeared, her face radiant with relief. "You're safe," she murmured, her voice filled with joy.

Monte Cristo smiled, his heart momentarily lightened by her presence. "Yes, my child. Everything is fine now."

Their reunion was interrupted when Baptistin entered. "The Count of Morcerf is here to see you."

Monte Cristo's eyes narrowed. "Which one? The father or the son?"

"The father."

Monte Cristo's face darkened slightly. "Show him to the drawing room."

Haydée clutched his arm. "Is it not over yet?"

"It is," Monte Cristo reassured her. "You have nothing to fear."

Baptistin led Fernand to the drawing room, where the disgraced general paced anxiously. When Monte Cristo entered, his calm demeanor contrasted sharply with Fernand's agitated state.

"Ah, the Count of Morcerf," Monte Cristo said coolly. "I wasn't expecting you."

"I came to ask about my son," Fernand began, his voice strained.

Monte Cristo's expression didn't waver. "Albert apologized to me this morning. He acted honorably."

Fernand's face contorted with anger. "He disgraced me by refusing to fight."

Monte Cristo's voice remained calm but firm. "Albert is no coward. He made his choice based on truths he's come to understand."

"And you," Fernand growled, his rage bubbling over, "you've been the architect of my ruin."

Monte Cristo stepped closer, his voice dropping to a dangerous tone. "Your ruin began long before I returned to France."

Fernand's fury turned to desperation. "Who are you? You call yourself Monte Cristo, Sinbad the Sailor, and more. But what is your real name?"

Monte Cristo's face hardened. "You know it already. It's the name that haunts your dreams: *Edmond Dantès*."

Fernand stumbled back, his face ashen. "It's not possible..."

Monte Cristo's cold gaze bore into him. "You destroyed my life, my future, my love. But now, justice has found you."

Fernand fled, his composure shattered. He barely made it to his carriage before collapsing into his seat, gasping for air.

When he arrived home, the sight of Mercédès and Albert leaving the house with their belongings broke what little resolve he had left. Retreating to his room, Fernand locked the door. Moments later, a gunshot echoed through the mansion, signaling the end of the Count of Morcerf.

Chapter 93: Valentine

Maximilian Morrel's destination after leaving Monte Cristo's home was clear. He headed toward Villefort's house, walking slowly, even though the distance was only a few hundred steps. He wanted time to collect his thoughts before seeing Valentine. She had given him permission to visit twice a week, and he cherished these moments. This morning, he knew she would be with her grandfather, Noirtier, giving him his breakfast—an hour when she was certain to be undisturbed.

When Maximilian arrived, Valentine was waiting for him. She seized his hand with an anxious urgency and led him to her grandfather. Her worry stemmed from the rumors surrounding the incident at the Opera and the anticipated duel. She feared Maximilian's involvement as Monte Cristo's second and the risks he might face due to his courage and loyalty to the Count.

The relief in Valentine's eyes was unmistakable as Maximilian recounted the peaceful resolution of the affair.

"Now," Valentine said, motioning for him to sit beside her grandfather while she took her place on the footstool at Noirtier's feet, "let's talk about our own matters. You know, Maximilian, Grandpapa once thought of leaving this house and finding an apartment elsewhere."

"Yes," Maximilian replied. "I remember, and I thought it was a good idea."

"Well, he's thinking of it again," Valentine said with a smile.

"That's wonderful news!" Maximilian exclaimed.

"Do you know why?" she asked, her expression playful.

Before Maximilian could answer, Noirtier looked sharply at Valentine, as if to warn her, but she ignored him, her attention focused entirely on Maximilian.

"Whatever his reason, I'm sure it's a good one," Maximilian said.

Valentine grinned. "He claims the air here in the Faubourg Saint-Honoré isn't good for me."

Maximilian looked at her with concern. "You haven't seemed well lately. Perhaps he's right."

"It's nothing serious," Valentine assured him. "Just a general uneasiness. I've lost my appetite, and my stomach feels unsettled. Grandpapa has become my doctor, and I trust him completely."

"Are you really unwell?" Maximilian asked, his concern deepening.

"It's hardly worth mentioning," she said. "I've been taking a spoonful of the mixture Grandpapa uses every morning. I started with one spoonful, but now I take four. He calls it a cure-all."

Maximilian studied her closely. She was as beautiful as ever, but her pallor was more pronounced, her eyes unusually bright, and her hands had lost their healthy glow, now resembling wax with a faint yellow hue.

"Isn't that mixture prepared for your grandfather?" he asked.

"Yes," Valentine admitted, "and it's very bitter. It makes everything else I drink taste bitter too."

Noirtier watched her intently, his expression filled with concern.

"Yes, Grandpapa," Valentine said, noticing his gaze. "I drank some sugared water earlier, and even that tasted bitter."

Noirtier's face grew pale, and he signaled that he wanted to speak. Valentine fetched the dictionary to help him communicate, but as she stood, she suddenly swayed.

"Oh," she said with a faint laugh, "I can't see. Is the sun in my eyes?" She leaned against the window for support.

Maximilian rushed to her side, alarmed by Noirtier's distressed expression.

"Don't worry," Valentine said weakly. "It's nothing. I feel better already. Isn't that a carriage I hear in the courtyard?"

She hurried to the window and glanced outside. "It's Madame Danglars and Eugénie," she announced. "I must go greet them." She turned to Maximilian. "Stay here with Grandpapa. I'll come back soon."

As she left, Maximilian noticed Noirtier signaling urgently. He retrieved the dictionary and began translating the old man's message. After several minutes, he pieced together the meaning: "Fetch the glass of water and the decanter from Valentine's room."

Maximilian rang for a servant, who returned with both items—but they were empty. Noirtier's expression grew darker as he signaled for an explanation.

"Mademoiselle Valentine drank the remaining water before going to Madame de Villefort's room," the servant explained. "As for the decanter, young Master Edward emptied it to make a pond for his ducks."

Noirtier's eyes filled with despair, his gaze fixed on the door as if willing Valentine to return.

Meanwhile, Madame Danglars and Eugénie were in the drawing room with Madame de Villefort, delivering the news of Eugénie's impending marriage to Prince Cavalcanti. Eugénie's blunt honesty about her lack of enthusiasm for the match left Valentine feeling uneasy. When the topic shifted to Albert's apology at the duel, Valentine grew distracted, her thoughts turning to Maximilian.

As the conversation continued, Valentine began to feel faint. Her pale complexion alarmed the other women, and Madame de Villefort insisted she leave to rest.

Valentine made her way back toward Noirtier's room, but as she descended the small staircase, her vision blurred, and she stumbled. Maximilian, hearing the commotion, rushed to her side and caught her just as she collapsed.

"Valentine!" he cried, gently placing her in a chair.

She opened her eyes, trying to smile. "I'm fine," she insisted, though her voice was weak. "I just missed a step."

"You're not fine," Maximilian said, his voice filled with worry.

"It's nothing, Maximilian," she assured him. "Let's talk about something happier. Did you know Eugénie's wedding is next week? There's to be a grand celebration in three days."

"When will it be our turn to celebrate, Valentine?" Maximilian asked softly.

She smiled faintly. "Soon, Maximilian. Soon."

But as she spoke, her strength failed her. Her body went rigid, her head fell back, and she slumped lifelessly in the chair.

"Help!" Maximilian shouted, ringing the bell frantically. Servants rushed in, and the house was thrown into chaos as they carried Valentine to her room.

In the drawing room, Madame Danglars and Eugénie, on their way out, overheard the commotion.

"I told you so," Madame de Villefort said grimly. "Poor child."

Chapter 94: Maximilian's Avowal

At the same moment, Villefort's voice was heard from his study, demanding, "What's the matter?"

Morrel turned to Noirtier, who had regained his composure, and with a glance, the old man indicated the closet where Maximilian had once taken refuge during a similar situation. Without hesitation, Morrel grabbed his hat and darted into the closet, barely making it before Villefort's footsteps echoed in the passage.

Villefort burst into the room, his eyes wide with panic. He ran to Valentine and gathered her limp body in his arms.

"A doctor! Fetch Dr. d'Avrigny immediately!" Villefort shouted. "No—I'll go myself!"

He dashed out, and at the same time, Morrel slipped quietly through another door, his mind racing. A horrifying memory surfaced—the conversation he had overheard between Villefort and Dr. d'Avrigny on the night of Madame de Saint-Méran's death. The symptoms Valentine exhibited now mirrored those he had seen in Barrois. Adding to his unease, Monte Cristo's earlier words rang in his ears: "Whatever you need, Morrel, come to me. I have great power."

Acting on impulse, Maximilian sprinted down the Rue Matignon and onto the Avenue des Champs-Élysées, heading straight for the Count's residence.

Meanwhile, Villefort reached Doctor d'Avrigny's home in a hired carriage, pounding on the door with such force that the porter answered in alarm. Without explanation, Villefort rushed upstairs.

"In his study, Monsieur Procureur," the porter called out as Villefort shoved past him.

Villefort flung open the door to find the doctor, who looked up with a mix of calm and apprehension.

"It's you?" d'Avrigny asked.

"Yes, it's me," Villefort replied, his voice shaking as he slammed the door shut. "My house is cursed, Doctor! Do you hear me? Cursed!"

D'Avrigny's face darkened. "Another victim?" he asked, his voice calm but heavy with emotion.

"Yes," Villefort admitted, clutching his head in despair. "It's Valentine. My daughter!"

The doctor's expression hardened. "So, the truth has caught up to you."

"Come with me," Villefort pleaded. "See for yourself that you were wrong to doubt her!"

"Each time you've summoned me," d'Avrigny said grimly, "it has been too late. But I'll go—though we must act swiftly. With the kind of enemy you face, there's no time to lose."

"I'll find the culprit," Villefort vowed, his voice trembling with rage.

"Let's save the victim first," d'Avrigny replied as they left together.

At the same time, Morrel arrived at Monte Cristo's home. Baptistin announced him, and the Count, who had been reading a document brought hastily by Bertuccio, rose immediately to meet him.

"What's wrong, Maximilian?" Monte Cristo asked, noting his pale face and trembling frame.

Morrel sank into a chair, his breath labored. "I've just come from a house where death has entered."

"De Morcerf's?" Monte Cristo asked.

"No," Morrel replied. "Wait—has something happened there?"

"The general has just taken his own life," Monte Cristo said coolly.

Morrel was stunned. "What a tragedy!"

"For the countess and Albert, perhaps," Monte Cristo replied. "But for Morcerf, death is better than dishonor. Blood can wash away shame."

Monte Cristo's calmness unsettled Maximilian, but he quickly pressed on. "It's Valentine," he said, his voice breaking. "She's dying—or already dead."

The Count's expression changed. "Explain," he demanded.

"I overheard Villefort and Dr. d'Avrigny once," Morrel began, "discussing the two mysterious deaths in the house. The doctor suspected poison, but nothing was done. Now, it's happening again. Valentine... she's the next victim."

Monte Cristo's face hardened. "You love her."

"More than life itself," Maximilian admitted. "I came to you because you promised to help me if I ever needed it. Save her, Count—save Valentine!"

Monte Cristo's composure cracked for a moment, his eyes flashing with an intensity Maximilian had never seen. "You love Valentine," he repeated, his voice a mix of pain and fury. "The daughter of that cursed family."

Maximilian recoiled, startled by the Count's outburst. But Monte Cristo quickly regained control, his expression softening. "You're right to come to me," he said, his voice now calm. "Go home, Maximilian. Do nothing. Say nothing. Trust me."

"Can you save her?" Morrel asked, his voice trembling with hope.

Monte Cristo looked at him, his expression resolute. "If Valentine isn't dead by now, she won't die. I promise you that."

Morrel hesitated, overwhelmed by the Count's confidence. "Are you human, Count? Or something more?"

Monte Cristo smiled faintly. "I am whatever you need me to be. Go now—I need to act quickly."

Subdued, Maximilian obeyed, leaving the Count to his thoughts.

Meanwhile, Villefort and d'Avrigny arrived at Valentine's room. The doctor examined her with meticulous care, his expression grim but focused. After a tense silence, he finally spoke.

"She's still alive."

Villefort's relief was palpable, though his voice trembled. "Will she survive?"

"She has a chance," d'Avrigny replied.

Noirtier's eyes glistened with triumph, and he motioned for d'Avrigny to stay. The doctor dismissed everyone else, including Villefort.

Once alone with Noirtier, d'Avrigny questioned him. "Did you know this would happen?"

Noirtier signaled yes.

"Did you prepare for it?"

Again, Noirtier's eyes confirmed it.

Realization dawned on d'Avrigny. "You've been giving her small doses of your medicine to build her resistance, haven't you?"

Noirtier's expression showed relief and satisfaction.

"You've saved her," d'Avrigny said. "The poison was strong, but not strong enough to overcome her newly built immunity."

At that moment, Villefort returned with the prescribed medicine. D'Avrigny took the bottle and administered the first dose himself, ensuring nothing had been tampered with.

As they worked to stabilize Valentine, a new tenant moved into the house next door—a serious-looking Italian priest named Abbé Busoni. By nightfall, workers were already making repairs to the building.

Chapter 95: Father and Daughter

As recounted earlier, Madame Danglars had visited Madame de Villefort to formally announce the impending marriage of her daughter, Eugénie Danglars, to Andrea Cavalcanti. This public announcement, signifying mutual agreement among the parties involved, was preceded by a private conversation to which we now turn. Let us step back to that eventful morning, in the opulent, gilded salon of Baron Danglars' residence, a room he took great pride in.

At around ten o'clock, Danglars paced the room with evident impatience, glancing repeatedly at both doors and straining to catch every sound. Finally, when his patience ran thin, he called for his valet.

"Étienne, go see why Mademoiselle Eugénie has asked me to meet her here and why she's keeping me waiting so long," he said irritably.

The valet departed, and Danglars calmed himself. Eugénie had requested the meeting that morning and specifically chosen the drawing room for it—a formality that both puzzled and intrigued her father. Danglars' curiosity only grew as he waited. Soon, Étienne returned.

"Mademoiselle's maid says she is finishing her toilette and will be here shortly," the valet reported.

Danglars nodded, masking his irritation with a facade of patience. To his household and the world, he cultivated the image of a genial, indulgent father. Privately, however, his true nature often surfaced—a domineering, self-centered man with little tolerance for defiance.

"Why on earth couldn't she summon me to my study if she wanted to speak?" Danglars muttered under his breath. "What's this about, anyway?"

Before he could puzzle further, the door opened, and Eugénie entered. She was dressed elegantly in a black satin gown, her hair styled impeccably, and her gloved hands exuding an air of sophistication, as if she were headed to the opera.

"Well, Eugénie," Danglars began, his tone gruff but curious, "what is it you want? And why drag me to the drawing room instead of speaking in the study?"

Eugénie motioned for him to sit. "I understand your questions, Father, and they relate directly to why I called you here. I chose this room deliberately. The study, with its ledgers, locked drawers, and mountains of correspondence from across the globe, is not conducive to the kind of conversation we need to have. Here, surrounded by our portraits and pastoral scenes, we can focus on what truly matters—family."

Danglars frowned, unsure where this preamble was leading, but he let her continue.

"Let's address your first question," Eugénie said, her tone calm but resolute. "I've asked to meet with you because I need to tell you something important: I will not marry Andrea Cavalcanti."

Danglars sprang from his chair, his face a mixture of shock and anger.

"Yes," Eugénie continued, unfazed by his reaction. "I realize this announcement surprises you. I've remained silent until now because I wanted to respect your wishes. But the time has come to make my stance clear—I refuse this marriage."

"But why?" Danglars demanded, his voice rising. "What's wrong with Cavalcanti? He's wealthy, well-connected—"

Eugénie raised a hand to silence him. "It's not about his wealth or his connections. And it's certainly not because I have feelings for someone else—I don't. The simple truth is that I don't want to marry at all. I value my independence too much to tie my life to another's out of convenience or expectation."

Her confidence only angered him further, but Danglars knew better than to argue with her in this mood. After a pause, he spoke.

"Very well. You've explained yourself. Now let me explain why I insist on this marriage. It's not for your sake—it's for mine. This marriage would secure my financial future. Andrea Cavalcanti is worth three million francs, money I desperately need to rebuild my fortune."

Eugénie looked at him sharply. "So that's it," she said. "You want me to marry him for the money."

"Yes," Danglars admitted. "With those funds, I can repair my credit and stabilize my business. Without them, I'm facing financial ruin."

Eugénie's expression remained unreadable. "And if I refuse?"

"If you refuse," Danglars said grimly, "you condemn me to disgrace and bankruptcy."

Eugénie stood silently for a moment, considering his words. Then she nodded. "Fine. I'll agree to the marriage—but on one condition."

"What condition?" Danglars asked, surprised.

"That you restore your fortune without touching a single franc of Cavalcanti's money," Eugénie said firmly. "I will not be complicit in ruining others."

Danglars hesitated, but he could see she was resolute. Finally, he sighed. "Very well. Do we have a deal?"

"We do," Eugénie replied, extending her hand.

Danglars shook it, but there was no warmth between them. The tension in the room was palpable. Eugénie stood, her posture unyielding. As she left the room, Danglars watched her go, his anger giving way to a grudging respect for her resolve.

VOLUME FIVE

Chapter 96: The Contract

Three days after the events previously described, toward five o'clock in the afternoon—the time set for the signing of the marriage contract between Mademoiselle Eugénie Danglars and Andrea Cavalcanti—a fresh breeze stirred the leaves in the small garden in front of the Count of Monte Cristo's house. The Count himself was preparing to go out. His horses, already harnessed to his carriage, pawed impatiently at the ground, while the coachman sat ready on the box.

Suddenly, the elegant phaeton[*] belonging to Andrea Cavalcanti turned sharply into the entrance gate, stopping just in front of the steps. Andrea, dressed as if for a royal wedding, descended, his confident smile radiating excitement. Bounding up the stairs, he met Monte Cristo at the top.

"Good afternoon, my dear Count," Andrea exclaimed with his usual familiarity.

Monte Cristo, his tone dry, replied, "Ah, Monsieur Andrea. What brings you here?"

"I came to discuss a thousand things," Andrea said cheerfully. "But first, tell me—are you heading out or just returning?"

---

[*]A small, sporty carriage

"I was about to leave," Monte Cristo replied.

"Perfect! Then I'll join you in your carriage, if you don't mind. Tom can follow with my phaeton."

Monte Cristo gave an almost imperceptible smile of contempt. "No, I think we'd better speak here," he said. "Conversations are always better indoors, without coachmen overhearing."

He led Andrea into a small drawing room on the first floor, motioning for him to sit. Andrea, unbothered by the Count's coolness, settled in with his characteristic ease.

"You know, my dear Count," Andrea began, "the ceremony is tonight at nine o'clock. The contract will be signed at my future father-in-law's house."

"Yes, I'm aware," Monte Cristo replied.

"Didn't Monsieur Danglars inform you?" Andrea asked, feigning surprise.

"Oh, he sent a letter," Monte Cristo said nonchalantly. "But it didn't specify the hour."

"Well, I suppose he assumed everyone would know. After all, this marriage is the talk of Paris!"

Monte Cristo's expression didn't change. "You're very fortunate, Monsieur Cavalcanti. Mademoiselle Danglars is a charming young woman."

"She is," Andrea agreed, his tone almost modest.

"And very wealthy, I believe," Monte Cristo added.

Andrea's eyes sparkled at the mention of wealth. "Do you think so?"

"It's said that Monsieur Danglars conceals half his fortune. He openly acknowledges having fifteen or twenty million francs."

"And there's talk of him earning another ten million from a railway project," Andrea added, his voice brimming with excitement.

Monte Cristo nodded. "And as Mademoiselle Danglars' only heir, her fortune will one day be yours. Quite the accomplishment for someone so young."

Andrea grinned. "I was born to negotiate, Count. It's in my nature."

"Diplomacy is indeed an innate skill," Monte Cristo said with a hint of irony. "Tell me, have you lost your heart in this alliance?"

Andrea laughed lightly. "I fear I have. After all, she accepted me!"

Monte Cristo raised an eyebrow. "You've certainly been... fortunate in your endeavors."

"I owe much of that fortune to you," Andrea said, his tone shifting to one of flattery.

Monte Cristo's expression hardened slightly. "I assure you, sir, any influence I may have had was incidental. Your father's wealth and reputation are what truly paved the way for your success."

Andrea tried to mask his unease, realizing the Count saw through his manipulations. "Well, Count," Andrea said after a pause, "I came to ask a favor."

"What sort of favor?"

"My father cannot attend tonight's ceremony. He's old, injured, and unable to travel. I hoped you might take his place."

Monte Cristo's face remained impassive. "You ask too much, Monsieur Cavalcanti. I would sooner lend you a fortune than stand as your father at the altar."

Andrea's face fell. "Then will you at least attend the ceremony?"

"I see no reason not to," Monte Cristo replied.

"And sign the contract?"

Monte Cristo's voice softened. "If that will suffice, I'll sign it. But don't ask for more."

Andrea forced a smile. "Then I'll be content with your presence."

After a brief exchange of courtesies, Andrea left, climbing back into his phaeton and disappearing down the street.

As the hours passed, the Danglars mansion filled with Parisian society's elite. The grand salon and adjoining galleries sparkled with light and opulence. Mademoiselle Danglars, dressed in an understated white silk gown, moved through the crowd with grace and composure, her dark hair adorned with a single white rose. Madame Danglars, meanwhile, mingled with her guests, exuding her usual air of shallow sophistication.

At nine o'clock precisely, the arrival of the Count of Monte Cristo caused a ripple through the crowd. Dressed simply in black, his pale face and commanding presence drew the attention of everyone in the room. He greeted Madame Danglars with measured politeness, exchanged brief words with Eugénie, and then approached Monsieur Danglars, who was flanked by deputies and financiers.

The notary began reading the marriage contract, listing the enormous sums involved in the union. Whispers of envy and admiration filled the room as Andrea basked in the attention of his peers.

Just as the contract was to be signed, Monte Cristo stepped forward. "Before we proceed," he said, his voice cutting through the noise, "I must share a discovery made earlier today on my property. It concerns a certain waistcoat—stained with blood and pierced over the heart."

Andrea turned pale, his confidence faltering.

Monte Cristo continued, addressing the room. "The waistcoat belonged to a man named Caderousse, who was recently murdered. In its pocket was a letter addressed to none other than Baron Danglars."

Gasps filled the air as the revelation sunk in. Andrea, seeing no escape, slipped away toward the anteroom.

At that moment, officers entered the salon, demanding the whereabouts of Andrea Cavalcanti. The guests recoiled in shock as the commissary announced: "Andrea Cavalcanti is a fugitive—a galley-slave accused of murder!"

As panic spread, Monte Cristo stood calmly, watching as the carefully constructed facade of Andrea's life crumbled.

Chapter 97: The Departure for Belgium

Minutes after the chaos erupted in the grand salon of Monsieur Danglars' mansion, following the sudden arrival of the brigade and the shocking revelations about Andrea Cavalcanti, the house was deserted with startling speed. It was as if the guests believed they were fleeing an outbreak of plague or cholera.

People poured out through every door, down every staircase, and out every exit, not even bothering with the usual empty condolences reserved for such catastrophes. The mansion, once vibrant with music and laughter, was left hollow and silent, save for a few occupants.

In his study, Danglars sat with an officer of the gendarmes, giving his statement with a mix of fear and humiliation. Madame Danglars, pale and trembling, had retreated to her boudoir, where she tried to compose herself. Meanwhile, Eugénie Danglars, with her signature poise and defiant air, had locked herself in her room with her closest confidante, Louise d'Armilly.

The numerous servants, more abundant than usual that evening thanks to extra staff brought in from the Café de Paris, gathered in clusters throughout the house. Their murmurs of anger and frustration at what they called the "insult" to their employers echoed through the hallways and kitchens. None of them paid much attention to their duties, which had been thoroughly disrupted by the scandal.

Among all these individuals, only Eugénie and Louise deserve our full attention.

Once inside her room, Eugénie locked the door behind them, her movements deliberate and firm. Louise, however, sank into a chair, visibly shaken.

"What a dreadful thing!" Louise exclaimed. "Who could have imagined? Monsieur Andrea Cavalcanti—a murderer, a fraud, an escaped convict!"

An ironic smile curled Eugénie's lips. "It seems I was destined for this," she said coolly. "I escaped Morcerf only to fall into the hands of Cavalcanti."

"Oh, don't lump the two together, Eugénie!" Louise pleaded.

"Why not? Men are all the same—infamous and unworthy. At least now, I have the luxury of despising them, not merely detesting them."

"What should we do?" Louise asked, her voice trembling.

"Do? Exactly what we planned to do three days ago—leave."

"Even though the wedding won't happen now?"

"Of course," Eugénie replied with conviction. "This changes nothing. I hate this hollow, artificial life dictated by society's rules and expectations. I want the freedom of an artist, a life accountable to no one but myself. Staying here would only mean another attempt at marriage in a month or two. Perhaps they'd pair me with Monsieur Debray next. No, Louise. Tonight's events are the perfect excuse to leave. I didn't ask for this scandal, but it's a gift from the heavens, and I'll seize it gladly!"

Louise looked at her friend with admiration. "You're so strong and courageous."

"Have you only just realized that?" Eugénie replied, her tone light but resolute. "Now, let's focus on practical matters. The post-chaise?"

"Ready and waiting," Louise confirmed.

"The passports?"

Louise retrieved a document from her bag. "Here."

Eugénie unfolded the paper and read aloud: "Monsieur Léon d'Armilly, twenty years old; profession, artist; hair black, eyes black; traveling with his sister."

"Perfect," Eugénie said, her tone cheerful. "Monte Cristo's advice was invaluable. When I told him I feared traveling as a woman, he arranged this passport for me. I added the part about 'traveling with his sister.' Now, let's pack our things. We're leaving tonight."

"But think it through, Eugénie!" Louise protested.

"I've done enough thinking," Eugénie replied sharply. "No more market reports, no more stock fluctuations, no more Haitian bonds! Instead, we'll have freedom, fresh air, music, and the beauty of the world —Lombardy's plains, Venice's canals, Naples' bay. How much money do we have, Louise?"

Louise opened a small, locked portfolio and counted the notes. "Twenty-three thousand francs."

"And as much again in jewels," Eugénie added. "That's forty-five thousand francs. We'll live like queens for two years and then comfortably for four. But within six months, your music and my voice will double our fortune. Now, pack quickly!"

The two women worked efficiently, stowing their belongings into a single portmanteau. Once packed, Eugénie changed into a man's suit —boots, trousers, waistcoat, and coat—transforming herself with practiced ease.

"You look incredible!" Louise exclaimed. "But what about your hair? It won't fit under a man's hat."

Eugénie smirked and, without hesitation, cut her long, luxurious hair, letting it fall to the floor. Her short, dark curls framed her face, giving her an even more striking appearance.

"Now," Eugénie declared, "we're ready."

They extinguished the lights and crept downstairs. Eugénie boldly called for the gate to be opened, her deep contralto voice convincing the porter she was a man. The two women slipped into the night, their suitcase carried by a hired porter, and made their way to a safe house.

An hour later, their carriage was ready, loaded with their belongings. Eugénie gave the driver instructions.

"To Fontainebleau," she said confidently, then whispered to Louise, "We'll change direction soon to avoid any betrayal."

As the carriage rolled through the Barrière Saint-Martin, leaving Paris behind, Louise sighed with relief.

"We did it," she said.

"Yes," Eugénie replied, her voice filled with triumph. "The escape is complete."

Chapter 98: The Bell and Bottle Tavern

Let us now leave Mademoiselle Danglars and her friend on their way to Brussels and return to the unfortunate Andrea Cavalcanti, whose rise to fortune was so abruptly interrupted. Despite his youth, Andrea was exceptionally cunning and resourceful. As soon as he heard the first whispers of trouble in the salon, he had edged toward the door, crossed several rooms, and disappeared.

In his hurried escape, he passed through a room where Mademoiselle Danglars' lavish trousseau was on display—diamonds, cashmere shawls, lace, veils, and other treasures designed to make a bride's heart flutter. Andrea, ever opportunistic, helped himself to the most valuable items before leaping out of a window to escape.

Fueled by adrenaline and clutching his stolen goods, Andrea roamed the streets like a fugitive gladiator. Guided by instinct, he headed toward the outskirts of Paris, eventually finding himself near the Rue La Fayette. Breathing heavily, he paused to consider his next move.

"Am I going to be caught?" he muttered to himself. "Not if I can outrun them. My survival depends entirely on my speed now."

Just then, he spotted a cab at the top of the Faubourg Poissonnière. The driver, lazily puffing on his pipe, was heading toward the Faubourg Saint-Denis.

"Hey, there!" Andrea called out.

"What do you need, sir?" the driver asked, eyeing him suspiciously.

"Is your horse tired?"

"Tired? He's barely done any work today. Four measly fares and just seven francs earned. I should have made ten by now!"

Andrea grinned, pulling out a handful of coins. "How about I double your day's earnings? Take me toward Louvres as fast as your horse can go."

"Done!" the driver exclaimed.

Andrea climbed into the cab, urging the driver to hurry. As they sped through the city, Andrea fabricated a story about meeting a friend who had likely grown tired of waiting and left without him. The driver, happy for the extra fare, pushed his horse hard, stopping only to ask passersby if they had seen a green cabriolet with a bay horse. Each inquiry brought false hope, and as they reached Louvres, Andrea decided to end the farce.

"Here are your thirty francs," Andrea said, hopping out. "I'll spend the night at the Cheval Rouge and catch the first coach in the morning."

The driver pocketed the coins with a grin and turned back toward Paris, while Andrea slipped into the shadows, heading toward Chapelle-en-Serval.

By now, Andrea realized he couldn't rely on public transport. He needed to avoid detection at all costs. He concocted a plan: find a peasant's house, adopt a disguise, and travel under the pretense of being a wandering artist or woodcutter. With this new identity, he would cross the border into safety.

He reached an inn in Chapelle-en-Serval and convinced the innkeeper to lend him a horse by claiming his own had thrown him during a ride. After paying handsomely, Andrea set off toward Compiègne, riding through the night and arriving at the Bell and Bottle Tavern just before dawn.

The tavern was familiar to Andrea from past escapades. Exhausted, he ordered a cold fowl, a bottle of Bordeaux, and a room with a view of the courtyard. Though his circumstances were dire, Andrea ate with surprising gusto, the stolen diamonds in his pocket a small comfort. He then retired to his room, leaving the shutters open and a knife on the table within arm's reach.

The next morning, Andrea awoke to the sunlight streaming through his window. His first thought was still that of escaping the law. Peering outside, he spotted a gendarme in the courtyard. His heart raced. Moments later, two more gendarmes appeared, blocking all exits.

"They're here for me," he thought, panic surging through him.

Andrea quickly drafted a note, leaving a valuable pin as payment for his room. Then, improvising like a seasoned thief, he climbed into the chimney, hoping to escape onto the roof.

Meanwhile, the gendarmes, led by a brigadier, entered the inn. The sight of the ajar door and the abandoned pin confirmed their suspicions. When they found no trace of Andrea inside, they set the chimney alight, hoping to smoke him out.

Andrea, anticipating their move, had already climbed onto the roof. Crouching low, he watched as the gendarmes declared the room empty and regrouped in the courtyard.

But his relief was short-lived. From a window in the Hôtel de Ville next door, a gendarme's head appeared, scanning the rooftops. Andrea froze, then scrambled to another chimney, descending into an adjacent room.

Unfortunately, this room was occupied—by none other than Eugénie Danglars and her companion, Louise d'Armilly.

Eugénie screamed, and Louise rang the bell furiously. Andrea begged for their silence, but it was too late.

"Save me!" he pleaded. "I'm being hunted like an animal!"

Eugénie's voice was cold. "You deserve no mercy."

The gendarmes burst in moments later, finding Andrea cornered and holding his knife. With no other option, Andrea surrendered.

As he was led away in shackles, Andrea turned to Eugénie with a mocking grin. "Have you any message for your father, Mademoiselle Danglars? I'll be seeing him soon enough."

Eugénie recoiled, covering her face in shame.

An hour later, Eugénie and Louise left the inn, dressed once again in feminine attire. As they climbed into their carriage, the sneers and whispers of onlookers followed them. Eugénie closed her eyes, wishing she could escape not only the crowd but the entire world.

By evening, Andrea was securely imprisoned in the Conciergerie, awaiting his fate.

Chapter 99: The Law

Danglars brooded over the massive debts dragging him toward bankruptcy, Madame Danglars sought solace in her confidant, Lucien Debray. The baroness had pinned her hopes on Eugénie's marriage to free her from the burdensome role of guardian to a daughter whose intelligence and independence she both feared and resented.

Eugénie's disdain for Debray further complicated the baroness's ambitions. Madame Danglars saw her daughter's contempt as a direct challenge to her own authority, especially since Eugénie seemed to understand the nature of her mother's intimate—and scandalous—relationship with Debray.

When Andrea's scandal shattered her plans, Madame Danglars instinctively turned to Debray for advice. Yet, when she arrived at his apartment, she found only his absence. Debray, like the rest of Paris, had fled the fallout of the disastrous wedding contract scene and sought refuge at his club, where he debated whether marrying Eugénie—along with her substantial dowry—might not be the worst idea after all.

Meanwhile, Madame Danglars returned home to her darkened mansion, slipping upstairs unnoticed. She hesitated outside Eugénie's locked door, unaware that her daughter and Louise d'Armilly had already fled. Reassured by the maid that the young women were inside, Madame Danglars retired to her room to reflect on the night's events.

The more she thought about it, the clearer the truth became. What she had dismissed as a minor embarrassment was, in fact, a devastating disgrace. Worse still, she had once judged Mercédès harshly for enduring a similar public humiliation. Now, she realized, her own family was similarly ruined.

Her thoughts turned to Villefort, the public prosecutor. While his exposure of Andrea had disrupted her family's plans, she concluded that he hadn't acted maliciously. Instead, he had sought to sever their family from an association with Andrea, the criminal. Deciding that Villefort might still help her, she resolved to appeal to him.

The next morning, dressed simply and veiled, she left her mansion and made her way to Villefort's house. The building was a grim sight, its shutters mostly closed, and its air one of mourning. Neighbors whispered about the string of tragedies that had plagued the Villefort family, speculating whether another death might soon follow.

When Madame Danglars rang the bell, the concierge opened the door just wide enough to inquire who she was.

"I'm the baroness Danglars," she announced.

The concierge hesitated. "We require verification, madame. I must take your card to Monsieur de Villefort."

She handed him her card, muttering complaints about the overly strict security measures. After some time, the door creaked open, and she was escorted inside, her guide explaining apologetically that the magistrate's household had become consumed by fear and suspicion.

Once in Villefort's study, Madame Danglars began to protest her treatment but stopped when she saw the prosecutor's pale, grief-stricken face.

"Forgive my servants," Villefort said, his voice heavy with sorrow. "They are merely following orders. Our house has known too much tragedy."

"You too are suffering?" the baroness asked.

"Yes," Villefort replied simply. "And what brings you here, madame?"

"I need your help," she said. "This scandal with Andrea Cavalcanti—it threatens to destroy my family."

Villefort's face hardened. "Andrea Cavalcanti? Let's call him by his true name—Benedetto. He's not just an impostor, madame. He's a murderer and a thief."

"Surely, sir, there's a way to handle this quietly?" she pleaded.

Villefort shook his head. "Justice cannot be silenced. The wheels are already in motion."

"What if he escapes?"

"He won't," Villefort replied grimly. "The orders for his capture are in place."

Madame Danglars tried a new tactic, appealing to his compassion. "Surely you understand, Monsieur de Villefort, how deeply this affects me. Delay the trial—give us time to recover."

Villefort's expression remained stern. "No, madame. Justice will proceed swiftly. Even I am subject to its demands."

Desperation filled the baroness's voice. "He's an orphan, abandoned by everyone. Doesn't that earn him any mercy?"

Villefort's reply was cold and unyielding. "If anything, his isolation proves the inevitability of his fate. No one will mourn him, just as no one mourned the victims of his crimes."

At that moment, a valet entered, handing Villefort a sealed message. Breaking the seal, Villefort's face lit up with grim satisfaction.

"He's been arrested," he announced. "Taken at Compiègne. It's over."

Madame Danglars stood, her face pale and her heart heavy. "Goodbye, sir," she said quietly, turning to leave.

Villefort escorted her to the door, his mood almost buoyant. Once alone, he returned to his desk, striking the message with the back of his hand.

"A forgery, three robberies, two arsons—and now a murder. This will make for a spectacular court session!"

Chapter 100: The Apparition

Valentine was still far from recovered. Exhausted and frail, she remained confined to her bed. It was in her own room, through Madame de Villefort's account, that she learned about the startling events that had unfolded—the flight of Eugénie Danglars, the arrest of Andrea Cavalcanti (or rather Benedetto), and the accusations of murder against him. Yet, in her weakened state, the weight of these revelations barely registered. Her fevered mind was a fog of vague ideas and fleeting impressions, blending reality with imagination.

By day, Valentine's thoughts were clearer, thanks in part to the steady presence of Noirtier. Her grandfather spent hours by her side, his silent, watchful tenderness a source of comfort. Villefort, too, often joined them after returning from the courts, offering what solace he could.

Every evening at six, Villefort would retreat to his study, and at eight, Dr. d'Avrigny would arrive with the nightly draught prepared for Valentine. Once the doctor departed and Noirtier was carried away, a nurse—chosen by d'Avrigny himself—would take over, staying with Valentine until she fell asleep around ten or eleven. The nurse would then hand the keys to Villefort, ensuring no one could enter Valentine's room without passing through that of Madame de Villefort and young Edward.

Each morning, Maximilian Morrel called on Noirtier for updates. Though Valentine's condition remained fragile, her survival offered him hope. Monte Cristo's words echoed in his mind: "If she survives the next two hours, she will live." Four days had now passed, and Valentine still lived.

However, her nights were far from restful. Fevered dreams haunted her, blurring the line between reality and delusion. In the dim glow of her alabaster lamp, shadows seemed to dance and figures appeared at her bedside. Sometimes she thought she saw her stepmother looming over her menacingly; other times, Morrel stretched out his arms to her, or even the Count of Monte Cristo stood silently watching. Furniture seemed to move, and the room itself appeared alive. These visions persisted until around three in the morning, when sheer exhaustion would finally grant her a deep sleep.

On the evening she learned of Eugénie's escape and Benedetto's arrest, Valentine lay lost in thought. Villefort, Noirtier, and Dr. d'Avrigny had all retired, leaving her alone with her nurse. By eleven, the nurse had locked the door and left, heading downstairs to join the servants, who entertained themselves with macabre tales of the house's recent tragedies.

But something unexpected unfolded in Valentine's room, now locked and seemingly secure.

Ten minutes after the nurse's departure, Valentine, gripped by the nightly fever, found herself caught in a loop of anxious thoughts and vivid hallucinations. The flickering light of her lamp cast strange shapes across the room, feeding her imagination. Then, to her astonishment, the door to her library—a door she knew had been firmly shut—opened silently.

At another time, Valentine might have pulled the silken bell-pull to summon help. But her current state made her dismiss the sight as another illusion. After all, by morning, her nocturnal phantoms always vanished without a trace.

Through the door stepped a figure—a man, moving so quietly that even the creak of the hinges was absent. Valentine stared, half-expecting the figure to morph into someone she recognized. Her pulse quickened as the man approached the bed, stopping to listen attentively. A ray of light briefly illuminated his face, and Valentine's heart sank.

"It's not Morrel," she murmured, convinced she was still dreaming. She reached for the glass of medicine on her bedside table, hoping it would calm her nerves. But as her trembling hand extended, the figure moved swiftly, placing a firm but gentle grip on her arm to stop her.

This time, the sensation was too real to dismiss. Her eyes widened in terror as the man took the glass, walked to the lamp, and inspected its contents. He poured a small amount into another glass, tasted it, and then returned.

"Now you may drink," he said softly, his voice filled with urgency.

Valentine froze. Never before had her visions spoken. Her fear deepened as she whispered, "The Count of Monte Cristo!"

"Yes, Valentine," Monte Cristo replied, his voice calm yet commanding. "You are not dreaming. I am here—not as a phantom, but as a friend."

Her initial terror gave way to confusion. "Why are you here?" her eyes seemed to ask.

Monte Cristo read her unspoken question. "I've been watching over you for days," he said. "Maximilian entrusted me with your life, and I vowed to protect you."

"Maximilian?" she repeated, her cheeks flushing at the sound of his name.

"Yes," Monte Cristo confirmed. "He told me that his life is yours, and I promised him that you would live."

"But how?" she asked. "Are you a doctor?"

Monte Cristo nodded. "The best one you could have right now."

Valentine's unease deepened. "But you say you've been watching me. How? From where?"

Monte Cristo gestured toward the library door. "From the room beyond that door, which connects to the house I've rented next door."

Valentine turned away, a mix of modesty and indignation flashing across her face. "Your presence feels less like protection and more like an intrusion."

Monte Cristo's expression softened. "Valentine, my only concern has been your safety. I've watched what you eat and drink. When I saw poison poured into your glass, I acted—replacing it with something harmless. That's why you're alive."

"Poison?" Valentine whispered, horrified. "Who would do such a thing?"

"You'll know soon enough," Monte Cristo said grimly. "But for now, you must trust me. Drink this."

He poured a few drops of a red liquid into her glass, drank from it himself, and handed it to her. Reluctantly, she drank.

"It's the same taste," she said, her voice trembling. "The same drink that's eased my pain these past nights. Thank you."

Monte Cristo's voice was heavy with emotion. "For four nights, I've watched over you, terrified that I might be too late. I fear they may turn to the blade once they realize the poison was not effective. Tonight, we'll discover who's behind this."

At that moment, the clock struck midnight. Monte Cristo turned to leave, but before stepping through the library door, he whispered, "Pretend to be asleep. Don't move or speak. Your life depends on it."

With that, he vanished into the shadows, leaving Valentine alone to face the darkness—and the truth.

Chapter 101: Locusta*

Valentine lay alone in her room. Outside, two slower clocks joined the chime of Saint-Philippe-du-Roule, marking the hour of midnight. Save for the distant rumbling of carriages, silence enveloped the house. Valentine's attention turned to the clock in her room, its ticking magnified in the stillness. She began counting the seconds, realizing they were much slower than the frantic beat of her heart.

It seemed unimaginable to Valentine that anyone would wish her harm. Why would they? What could she have done to warrant such malice? Yet, Monte Cristo's warning haunted her: someone had tried to poison her and now might escalate to a blade. What if the Count failed to intervene in time? What if her final moments approached, and she never saw Maximilian again?

Terrified, Valentine fought the urge to ring the bell and summon help. But through the door to the library, she imagined she saw Monte Cristo's piercing gaze. The thought of his vigilance brought both shame and comfort. Could she ever repay his daring loyalty?

---

*A notorious maker of poisons in the 1st-century Roman Empire; she was a favorite of Emperor Nero. She supposedly took part in the assassinations of Claudius and Britannicus.

Twenty long minutes dragged by, then another ten. At last, the clock struck half past twelve.

A faint sound broke the silence—fingernails scraping against the library door. The noise assured Valentine that Monte Cristo was still watching. Then, from the direction of Edward's room, she heard the floor creak. She held her breath, straining to listen as the lock turned and the door to her room opened slowly.

Heart pounding, Valentine barely managed to lie back down, shading her eyes with her arm and feigning sleep. Someone approached her bed, drawing back the curtains. Summoning all her willpower, Valentine breathed evenly, mimicking the tranquil rhythm of slumber.

"Valentine," a low voice whispered.

She stiffened but did not respond.

"Valentine," the voice repeated.

Still, she remained silent, recalling her promise to Monte Cristo.

The room grew still again, except for the faint sound of liquid being poured into her glass. Daring to peek through her lashes, Valentine saw a figure in a white dressing gown holding a vial. It was Madame de Villefort!

Valentine's heart sank. Her stepmother leaned closer, seemingly to confirm whether Valentine was truly asleep. Reassured by Valentine's stillness, Madame de Villefort poured the remaining contents of the vial into the glass. Valentine caught her breath, horrified by the sight. When her stepmother finally left the room, her retreat was so silent that Valentine barely noticed her absence—except for the arm that disappeared behind the curtains, an arm that seemed so delicate and youthful, yet capable of spreading death.

The faint scraping at the library door brought Valentine out of her stunned state. Moments later, Monte Cristo appeared, his face grave and resolute.

"Well," he asked, "do you still doubt?"

Valentine, her voice trembling, whispered, "Oh!"

"Have you seen?"

"Yes," she replied weakly.

"Do you recognize her?"

A sob escaped Valentine's lips. "Yes. But I cannot believe it."

Monte Cristo's eyes softened. "Would you rather die, Valentine? And in doing so, bring Maximilian to despair?"

Tears welled in Valentine's eyes. "Can I not leave this house? Can I not escape?"

Monte Cristo shook his head. "The hand that seeks your life will follow you wherever you go. Servants can be bribed, and poison can take many forms. You'd find death in the water you drink, the fruit you eat."

"But the doctor said my grandfather's precaution had neutralized the poison," Valentine protested.

"True," Monte Cristo replied. "But now the poison has changed. Tonight, your stepmother used a different substance—a narcotic dissolved in alcohol. If you had drunk it, Valentine, you would be doomed."

"Why is this happening to me?" she cried.

Monte Cristo's voice was steady but heavy with meaning. "Because you are rich, Valentine. You stand between your stepmother and the fortune she desires for her son. Each death in this house has served to bring that inheritance closer to him."

"Edward?" Valentine gasped. "Poor child! Are all these crimes committed for his sake?"

Monte Cristo nodded. "Now you understand. This is why M. and Madame de Saint-Méran were killed, why your grandfather was targeted, and why you are next. Your death would leave your father as the heir, and Edward, as his only son, would inherit everything."

"But why spare my grandfather?"

"His death would serve no purpose. The inheritance would revert to Edward regardless, so killing Noirtier now would only draw further suspicion."

Valentine shuddered. "Could a woman truly devise such a monstrous plan?"

"Do you recall the harbor in Perugia," Monte Cristo asked, "where your stepmother inquired about aqua tofana? Her schemes began there."

A wave of despair swept over Valentine. "Then I am doomed."

"No," Monte Cristo said firmly. "Your enemy is defeated. I know her plans, and I will protect you. You must trust me."

"What must I do?" Valentine asked.

"Take what I give you, and trust in me completely."

"For myself, I would rather die," she murmured.

Monte Cristo gently touched her arm. "You must not die, Valentine. You must live—for Maximilian, for your grandfather, and for the happiness that awaits you. Whatever happens, do not fear. Even if you lose consciousness, awaken in a coffin, or find yourself in a strange place, trust that I am watching over you."

Valentine clasped her hands together, praying for strength. Monte Cristo reached into his pocket, retrieving a small emerald box. From it, he took a pill the size of a pea and placed it in her hand.

"Take this," he instructed.

Valentine hesitated but saw the unwavering determination in his eyes. She swallowed the pill.

"You're safe now," Monte Cristo said. "Rest, my child."

As the narcotic took effect, Valentine drifted into a deep, peaceful sleep. Monte Cristo emptied most of the poisoned glass into the fireplace, ensuring it would appear untouched, then cast a final, protective glance at Valentine before disappearing into the shadows.

Chapter 102: Valentine

The night-light flickered on the mantelpiece, its last drops of oil struggling to sustain the dim flame. The reddish glow it emitted cast eerie shadows across the room, resembling the final, convulsive moments of a dying creature. The faint, dismal light fell on the bed and curtains that surrounded Valentine. Silence pervaded the streets outside, heightening the sense of desolation in the chamber.

It was then that the door to Edward's room opened, and a shadowy figure emerged—Madame de Villefort. She moved cautiously, her steps inaudible against the silence. She paused by the door, her gaze fixed on the room, before advancing to the bedside table.

Valentine's glass sat there, its contents still a quarter full. Madame de Villefort hesitated, then poured the liquid into the ashes of the fireplace, stirring them with her handkerchief to absorb the liquid completely. She rinsed the glass carefully and replaced it, her movements precise and deliberate.

If anyone had witnessed her actions, they would have noticed the hesitation with which she approached Valentine's bed. Leaning over the young girl, Madame de Villefort observed her intently. The dim light, oppressive silence, and weight of her own conscience filled her with dread.

Finally, she drew back the curtain and leaned closer to Valentine's still form. The girl's lips were white, her eyes closed beneath long lashes, and her cheeks pale as wax. Madame de Villefort pressed her hand against Valentine's chest, feeling no warmth, no heartbeat—only the pulse in her own trembling fingers.

The arm that hung over the edge of the bed was perfectly sculpted but stiffened in a position of unnatural rigidity. Madame de Villefort shuddered and drew back. There was no doubt—Valentine appeared lifeless. Her work was done.

Madame de Villefort stepped back but couldn't tear her gaze from the motionless figure. She lingered, the curtains draped in her hand like a funeral shroud. The image of her crime held her transfixed, a mix of fascination and horror. Minutes passed before she finally dropped the curtain.

As she retreated, the lamp gave one last flicker, startling her. She dropped the curtain hastily, extinguishing the faint light. The room plunged into darkness, and the clock struck half-past four. Overcome with fear, she groped her way to the door and fled to her own quarters.

At dawn, faint light crept through the blinds, gradually illuminating the room. The nurse arrived with Valentine's morning draught, coughing as she entered. Approaching the table, she noticed the glass was mostly empty.

"Good," she murmured, assuming Valentine had taken the medicine. She lit the fire and, unable to resist the quiet of the room, sat down for a moment of rest. She dozed off until the clock struck eight, waking with a start.

The nurse approached Valentine and noticed the unnatural rigidity of her arm. When she tried to reposition it, the stiff movement filled her with dread. She leaned closer, finally noticing Valentine's white lips and lifeless expression. Screaming, she ran for help.

"What's the matter?" Dr. d'Avrigny called from the stairs as he arrived for his morning visit.

"Help! Help!" the nurse cried.

Villefort rushed from his room, his voice trembling. "Doctor, do you hear her?"

"Yes. Let's go!"

The two men hurried to Valentine's room. Servants, alerted by the commotion, arrived first, but they froze at the sight of Valentine's still form. They fled in terror, leaving d'Avrigny and Villefort alone.

D'Avrigny approached Valentine, lifting her gently. "This one too?" he muttered, his voice heavy with anguish.

Villefort entered the room, his face pale. "What are you saying, doctor?"

D'Avrigny turned to him solemnly. "I'm saying Valentine is dead."

Villefort staggered, burying his head in the bedclothes as the weight of the declaration consumed him.

At that moment, Madame de Villefort entered the room, hastily dressed. Her eyes darted between the occupants, her expression wavering between disbelief and calculated innocence. But her composure faltered when she saw d'Avrigny examining Valentine's glass, now filled to a third of its capacity.

"How is that possible?" she whispered to herself.

D'Avrigny, oblivious to her turmoil, conducted a chemical analysis. Dropping nitric acid into the remaining liquid, he watched it turn blood-red.

"It's no longer brucine," he murmured. "She used a different poison."

Madame de Villefort staggered backward, her face pale, before disappearing into the adjoining room. A loud thud echoed moments later, but no one paid attention—except d'Avrigny, who found her lifeless on the floor.

"Help Madame de Villefort," he instructed the nurse. "She is ill."

"But Mademoiselle Valentine—"

"Mademoiselle Valentine no longer needs help," d'Avrigny replied grimly. "She is dead."

"Dead?" Villefort groaned, his grief breaking through his stoic facade.

"Who said Valentine is dead?" a voice demanded.

They turned to see Maximilian Morrel standing in the doorway, his face pale with terror.

Chapter 103: Maximilian

Villefort stood, half-ashamed of being caught in the throes of such profound grief. His twenty-five years as a prosecutor had hardened him, making him more a creature of duty than a man of emotion. His wandering gaze settled on Maximilian Morrel.

"Who are you, sir," he asked sternly, "to forget the decorum required in a house struck by death? Leave at once!"

But Maximilian stood rooted, unable to tear his eyes away from the disheveled bed and Valentine's lifeless form.

"Go!" Villefort insisted, while Dr. d'Avrigny moved to escort Morrel out.

Morrel stared at the scene for a moment longer, his eyes darting from Valentine to the two men. He opened his mouth to speak, but his emotions choked the words. He staggered out, clutching his hair, leaving Villefort and d'Avrigny to exchange a glance that seemed to say, 'He's mad'.

Less than five minutes later, the staircase groaned under a heavy weight. To their astonishment, Morrel returned, carrying Noirtier's wheelchair with superhuman strength. Once on the landing, he rolled it into Valentine's room. His extraordinary energy seemed fueled by desperation, while Noirtier's expression—intense, sorrowful, and angry—spoke volumes. His bloodshot eyes and strained features were those of a man silently screaming.

"Look what they've done!" cried Maximilian, one hand gripping the chair and the other gesturing toward Valentine. "See for yourself, my father—look!"

Villefort recoiled, stunned by the young man's audacity in addressing Noirtier as his father. The old man's chest heaved with labored breaths, his veins bulging as though he might burst. Tears glistened in his eyes, breaking free where words could not.

"Tell them!" Maximilian pleaded, grasping Noirtier's hand. "Tell them who I am, why I belong here. Speak for me! I loved her—I was her betrothed. She was my only blessing in this world, my entire future. That body—that corpse—belongs to me!"

Overcome, Maximilian fell to his knees beside Valentine's bed, gripping the sheets with convulsive hands and pressing his face into them. His muffled sobs filled the room, his anguish palpable. Even d'Avrigny, hardened by years of medical practice, turned away, unable to bear the sight.

Villefort, his own grief momentarily softened by Maximilian's raw pain, extended a hand toward him. But Maximilian, blind to all else, had grasped Valentine's cold hand in his own, venting his despair in groans that echoed through the chamber.

Finally, Villefort spoke, his tone steady but sorrowful. "Sir, you claim to have loved Valentine, to have been betrothed to her. I knew nothing of this, yet I see your grief is genuine. I forgive you for entering my home this way. But the angel you loved is no longer of this world. Take her hand one last time and bid her farewell. Then leave her to the ministrations of the priest."

"You are wrong, sir," Maximilian said, rising to one knee, his voice cutting through the room like a blade. "Valentine does not need a priest; she needs an avenger. You, Monsieur de Villefort, summon the priest. I will find the assassin!"

Villefort flinched. "What do you mean?" he demanded, his voice trembling.

"I mean," Maximilian replied, his voice gaining strength, "that Valentine was murdered!"

Villefort paled, d'Avrigny stepped closer, and Noirtier's eyes burned with a terrible intensity.

"In today's world," Maximilian continued, "no one can die under such circumstances without an investigation. I denounce this crime. As procureur, it is your duty to uncover the murderer!"

Villefort glanced nervously at d'Avrigny, whose grim expression offered no solace. Noirtier's unwavering stare left no room for doubt.

"You're mistaken," Villefort stammered, struggling to maintain control. "No one here commits murder. We are victims of fate."

"No," Maximilian retorted. "Four deaths in four months. Valentine's life was saved once by her grandfather's precautions, but the poison was doubled, the method changed. This time, it succeeded. You cannot deny it!"

Villefort's feeble protests crumbled under Maximilian's relentless accusations. D'Avrigny, unable to remain silent any longer, stepped forward. "I, too, demand justice," he said. "I ignored the signs before. I will not do so again."

Morrel turned to Noirtier. "Do you know who did this?"

"Yes," Noirtier answered with his eyes.

"Will you tell us?"

Noirtier indicated for everyone but Villefort to leave. Reluctantly, Maximilian obeyed, d'Avrigny guiding him out.

Fifteen minutes later, Villefort emerged from the room, his face ashen, his hands trembling. "The murderer has been named," he said hoarsely. "I swear to you, justice will be done. Within three days, I will deliver vengeance so terrible it will shake even the boldest soul."

Chapter 104: Danglars' Signature

The morning dawned dull and cloudy, casting a somber light over Paris. During the night, undertakers had performed their grim duties, wrapping Valentine's body in a shroud—her final garment. Ironically, the fine cambric she had purchased only a fortnight earlier now symbolized the fleeting luxury of life.

Earlier in the evening, two attendants had carefully moved Noirtier from Valentine's room to his own. Surprisingly, the old man did not resist the separation from his beloved granddaughter. Meanwhile, the Abbé Busoni—who had kept vigil through the night—departed before dawn without alerting anyone.

By eight o'clock, Dr. d'Avrigny returned to check on Noirtier. He met Villefort on his way to the old man's room, and they entered together to find Noirtier resting in his armchair. Contrary to expectations, he appeared calm, even smiling faintly in his sleep.

"Nature has its ways of soothing even the deepest grief," d'Avrigny observed. "No one can doubt how much M. Noirtier loved his granddaughter, and yet he sleeps."

Villefort, surprised, nodded. "Yes, it's remarkable. The slightest agitation would normally keep him awake all night, yet now he sleeps so peacefully."

"Grief can sometimes stun the mind," d'Avrigny suggested, and the two men returned to Villefort's study in thoughtful silence.

Once there, Villefort gestured toward his undisturbed bed. "See? I haven't slept at all. Grief doesn't stun me. For two nights, I've been wide awake, but look at my desk—look at what I've written!" He motioned to stacks of papers. "I've spent these hours drafting the charges against Benedetto. Work—my solace, my escape—it's the only thing that can quiet my mind!"

Villefort gripped d'Avrigny's hand tightly.

"Do you need me for anything now?" the doctor asked.

"No, not until eleven," Villefort replied. "At noon, the—" He choked on his words, overcome by emotion. "Oh, my poor child!"

"Will you attend the reception room?"

"No," Villefort said flatly. "I've asked a cousin to manage that. I'll stay here and work. When I work, I can forget."

The doctor left him, descending the steps where he encountered the cousin—a man of little importance but punctual and dressed in mourning attire. His face wore a practiced solemnity, ready to mirror the tone of the occasion.

By eleven o'clock, mourning coaches began to arrive, filling the courtyard with a sense of grim ceremony. The Rue du Faubourg Saint-Honoré buzzed with onlookers, drawn as much by morbid curiosity as by the spectacle of wealth and status on display.

In the reception room, familiar faces appeared—Debray, Château-Renaud, and Beauchamp among them. They gathered in small groups, murmuring their condolences.

"Poor girl," Debray said quietly. "So young, so beautiful, and so rich. Who could have imagined this, Château-Renaud? Just three weeks ago, she was preparing to sign her marriage contract."

"Indeed," Château-Renaud agreed.

"Did you know her?" Beauchamp asked.

"I met her a few times at Madame de Morcerf's," Château-Renaud replied. "She seemed charming but melancholy."

"What about her stepmother? Is she here?"

"She's staying with the wife of the man hosting us today," Debray said.

"And who is he?"

"Oh, just some cousin of Villefort's—a nobody, really," Beauchamp replied.

The conversation shifted to the absence of the Count of Monte Cristo.

"I saw him on the boulevard," Beauchamp said. "He was heading to Danglars' bank. Perhaps he's leaving Paris."

At the same time, Monte Cristo entered the banker's mansion. Danglars greeted him with an air of forced politeness.

"Ah, Count," Danglars began, extending his hand, "come to sympathize with me? Misfortune seems to have taken over my house. First, the disgrace of the Morcerfs, and now the humiliation of Benedetto's betrayal. And to top it all off, my daughter has left us!"

Monte Cristo raised an eyebrow. "Eugénie has left?"

"Yes," Danglars replied bitterly. "She couldn't bear the shame. She's gone abroad with a relative. I doubt she'll ever return."

Monte Cristo raised an eyebrow. "And Madame Danglars?"

"She remains, though I doubt she'll stay long." Danglars shrugged. "But tell me, Count, to what do I owe the honor of this visit?"

Monte Cristo smiled faintly. "I came to settle accounts. I believe I still hold a credit of six million francs with you."

Danglars stiffened. "You're withdrawing the entire amount?"

"Yes," Monte Cristo replied calmly. "But I'll make it easy for you. I'll take five million in bank drafts now and consider the remaining balance settled."

Danglars hesitated but couldn't refuse. He handed over the drafts, though his hand trembled slightly.

"Thank you," Monte Cristo said, slipping the papers into his pocket. "Your efficiency is admirable. These notes are quite impressive."

"They're bonds on the Bank of France, payable to bearer," Danglars explained proudly. "Surely you don't mean to cash them now?"

Monte Cristo smiled faintly. "Why not? I'm curious to see how quickly the Bank of France honors such a sum."

Danglars hesitated, then laughed nervously. "Very well, Count. Take the bonds. They're as good as gold."

Monte Cristo pocketed the notes, his expression inscrutable. "Thank you, Baron. I'll send someone to the bank immediately."

As Monte Cristo left, he encountered M. de Boville, the Receiver-General of Charities, who was arriving to collect a promised donation from Danglars. Monte Cristo's faint smile deepened as he passed him.

Moments later, Danglars realized the full implications of what had just happened. He bolted the doors, gathered his remaining cash, and prepared a hastily written letter addressed to his wife.

By the time Boville returned to demand the promised funds, Danglars was already planning his escape.

Chapter 105: The Cemetery of Père-Lachaise

The funeral procession carrying Valentine Villefort to her final resting place moved solemnly through Paris. The weather was gloomy, with storm clouds gathering and a cold wind scattering the last yellow leaves of the season. M. de Villefort, ever mindful of appearances, had selected Père-Lachaise Cemetery as the resting place for his family—a choice that reflected his belief in the cemetery's prestige. He had purchased a vault, now bearing the inscription: "The Families of Saint-Méran and Villefort," fulfilling the last wish of Renée, Valentine's late mother.

The mourners set out from the Faubourg Saint-Honoré, crossing Paris to reach the cemetery. The procession was grand, with twenty mourning coaches followed by more than fifty private carriages and a crowd of over five hundred people on foot. Among them were young friends and admirers of Valentine, who braved the biting cold to pay their respects to the kind, beautiful girl whose life had been cut tragically short.

As the procession wound its way through the city, a carriage drawn by four horses approached at high speed. It stopped abruptly, and the Count of Monte Cristo stepped out, blending into the crowd following the hearse on foot. Château-Renaud spotted him and joined him immediately, followed by Beauchamp.

Monte Cristo scanned the crowd intently, clearly searching for someone.

"Where is Morrel?" he asked. "Have either of you seen him?"

"We've been asking the same question," Château-Renaud replied. "No one has seen him."

Monte Cristo said nothing but continued to scan the faces around him. When the procession arrived at the cemetery, his sharp eyes finally caught sight of a shadow moving among the yew trees. It was Maximilian Morrel, standing apart from the crowd, his face pale and his coat tightly buttoned.

The burial proceeded as expected, with mourners dressed in black scattered across the cemetery's white avenues. The occasional snap of a twig or crunch of leaves broke the heavy silence, accompanied by the priests' solemn chants and the occasional sob from a hidden mourner.

Morrel stood apart from the others, leaning against a tree with an unobstructed view of the mausoleum. His expression of calm concealed the storm of emotions within him, a stillness that was deeply unsettling to those who knew his pain.

Monte Cristo, keeping a watchful eye on Morrel, withdrew from the crowd and concealed himself behind a large tomb. As the mourners dispersed, Maximilian approached the grave, waiting until the last of the workers had left.

Monte Cristo stepped closer, his movements silent as he approached the young man. Morrel knelt at the grave, clutching the iron grating as he murmured, "Oh, Valentine!"

The Count's heart ached at those two words. He placed a hand on Morrel's shoulder and said gently, "I was looking for you, my friend."

Morrel turned, his voice steady despite his turmoil. "You see, I am praying."

Monte Cristo studied him carefully before offering, "Shall I take you back to Paris?"

"No, thank you," Morrel replied, his tone distant.

"Is there anything you need?"

"Leave me to pray."

Monte Cristo nodded and withdrew but did not leave. Instead, he followed Morrel at a distance as the young man walked back to Paris, crossing the canal and entering the Rue Meslay.

When Maximilian entered his home, Monte Cristo waited only five minutes before following. Julie greeted him warmly in the garden, where she was supervising Penelon, now busy grafting roses.

"Has Maximilian returned?" Monte Cristo asked.

"I think I saw him pass by," Julie replied. "But please, call Emmanuel. He'll want to see you."

"Forgive me, madame," Monte Cristo said with urgency, "but I must speak with Maximilian immediately."

Julie smiled understandingly and stepped aside. Monte Cristo ascended the stairs to Maximilian's room, his heart heavy with foreboding. Finding the door locked and a red curtain drawn over the glass panel, he hesitated. Finally, driven by a terrible conviction, he smashed the glass with his elbow and entered the room.

Maximilian sprang up from his desk, startled by the sound.

"Forgive me," Monte Cristo said. "I slipped and broke the glass. Since it's open, I'll let myself in."

Morrel's discomposure was evident. He tried to intercept the Count, but Monte Cristo advanced, his sharp eyes taking in every detail of the room. His gaze fell on the pistols lying on the desk.

"My friend," Monte Cristo said softly, "do not act rashly. I beg you."

"I'm merely preparing for a journey," Morrel said with forced nonchalance.

Monte Cristo's voice grew firm. "Maximilian, let us stop pretending. I can see through your mask of calm just as you can see through my feigned indifference. You are planning to take your own life."

Morrel's composure shattered. "And why not?" he cried. "What reason is there to live when everything I loved is gone? Let me go, Count! Even you cannot prevent this."

"But I can," Monte Cristo said, his tone unwavering. "I am the only one in the world who has the right to tell you this: Maximilian Morrel, your father's son shall not die today."

Stunned, Maximilian staggered back as Monte Cristo revealed his true identity. "I am Edmond Dantès, the man who saved your father from despair and ruin. I sent the purse to your sister, the *Pharaon* to your family. And I will not let you throw your life away."

Overwhelmed, Maximilian fell to his knees, sobbing. The Count embraced him, his own eyes filling with tears.

"You must trust me," Monte Cristo said gently. "Give me one month, Maximilian. If I cannot restore your will to live, I will personally place the means of death in your hands. But until then, you must promise me to live."

With trembling hands, Maximilian swore his promise.

Monte Cristo smiled faintly. "Come now. You will live with me. Together, we will leave Paris and find healing elsewhere. Hope, Maximilian. Hope."

Chapter 106: Dividing the Proceeds

In a modest first-floor apartment in the Rue Saint-Germain-des-Prés, Albert de Morcerf had secured a new home for his mother, Mercédès. This apartment was located in the same building that housed a mysterious tenant whose identity was the subject of much speculation. Known only as "Lucien" by the discreet concierge, this enigmatic man kept to an unusual routine, arriving punctually at four o'clock in the afternoon, winter or summer, but never spending the night.

The day after Monte Cristo's dramatic encounter with Baron Danglars, the mysterious Lucien deviated from his usual schedule. He arrived at ten in the morning, his face hidden as always by a scarf or handkerchief. Shortly afterward, a cab arrived, and a veiled woman hurried up the stairs. She knocked lightly on Lucien's door, and when it opened, she exclaimed, "Oh, Lucien—oh, my friend!"

Her voice carried enough to reveal to the concierge that the tenant's name was indeed Lucien. True to his reputation for discretion, the concierge resolved to keep this revelation to himself.

"What's the matter, my dear?" Lucien asked, his tone calm despite the woman's evident agitation.

"Oh, Lucien, everything has gone wrong!" she cried. "Danglars has left—he's abandoned me!"

"Left? Where has he gone?"

"I don't know!"

"What do you mean? Surely, he plans to return?"

"No," she said. "He left last night with his valet and took a post-chaise to Fontainebleau, leaving behind only this letter."

She handed Lucien a note from Danglars. He hesitated briefly, then unfolded the letter and read aloud:

Madame,

When you read this, I will be far from Paris. I owe you an explanation, and as you are no stranger to my affairs, you will understand. This morning, I received a request by a creditor for five million francs, which I promptly paid out. Shortly afterward, another demand for the same amount arrived. Rather than face my creditors, I've chosen to leave.

You, madame, have enriched yourself at my expense, and I trust you'll continue to prosper. As for me, I have decided to start afresh. I leave you as I found you: wealthy, but with little respect to your name. Farewell.

Yours,

Baron Danglars.

Lucien finished reading and looked at the baroness with carefully masked indifference.

"Well?" she asked, her voice trembling.

"Well, madame, it seems clear. Danglars has abandoned you to save himself."

"What should I do?" she implored.

"Travel," Lucien said coldly. "Leave Paris. Claim destitution and tell your friends that you are starting over. Sell your possessions, surrender your jointure, and the world will praise your humility."

The baroness was visibly shaken, her proud demeanor breaking under the weight of his dispassionate advice. "And what about us?" she asked softly.

Lucien shrugged. "We've shared our gains, madame. Here are your accounts." He produced papers showing her investments and profits.

"You furnished a principal of 100,000 francs," he explained. "In six months, your share has grown to 1,200,000 francs, plus interest. I've already withdrawn the funds—here they are."

He opened a chest, revealing a stack of banknotes, a certificate for government bonds, and a check for the remaining balance. The baroness accepted them without a word.

"And now, madame," Lucien continued, "you also have nearly 60,000 francs in annual income. Use it wisely. If you ever need assistance, I'm willing to lend you more."

"Thank you," she murmured, her voice devoid of emotion. She rose abruptly, descending the stairs without a backward glance.

Lucien watched her go, his expression unreadable. "She'll gamble away her fortune at cards soon enough," he muttered, returning to his accounts.

Upstairs, in another apartment, Mercédès and Albert de Morcerf were also discussing their future. Mercédès had changed visibly, her once-radiant smile replaced by a quiet sadness. Their humble surroundings reflected their new reality: bare walls, simple furniture, and the absence of the luxurious touches they had once taken for granted.

"Mother," Albert began, "we need to plan. We have 3,000 francs buried in the garden of our old house in Marseilles. With that, I can send you to live comfortably there."

"And what about you?" she asked.

"I've joined the army," he replied. "I sold myself as a substitute for another man and received 2,000 francs. I'll serve in Algeria and earn a name we can both be proud of."

Mercédès wept quietly but did not protest. Together, they calculated the cost of her journey, carefully budgeting every franc. Albert reassured her with his unwavering determination.

"We'll survive, Mother," he said. "You'll see. I'll make us proud again."

The next day, Mercédès boarded the diligence bound for Marseilles. As she left, a figure hidden behind the window of a nearby banking house watched her depart. It was Monte Cristo, his face clouded with doubt and sorrow.

"God help me," he whispered. "How can I restore the happiness I've taken from them?"

Chapter 107: The Lions' Den

In one of the most secure sections of La Force prison lies the Saint-Bernard courtyard, nicknamed the "Lions' Den" by its inhabitants. This part of the prison is reserved for the most dangerous and desperate criminals, and its foreboding nickname reflects the ferocity of those confined within. The thick walls, fortified bars, and relentless scrutiny of hulking, cold-eyed guards underscore the reputation of this grim enclosure.

The courtyard itself, bordered by massive stone walls, sees little sunlight. When the sun does manage to penetrate its depths, it falls obliquely, casting fleeting rays over the paved yard. Here, prisoners pace restlessly, their pale faces and hollow eyes betraying their despair. They cling to the walls where the sun's warmth lingers, talking in hushed tones or standing alone, their eyes fixed on the door—waiting for it to open, either to release a fellow captive or to usher in another outcast from society.

The visitors' area of the Lions' Den is as unwelcoming as the prison itself. A long room divided by two layers of thick grating prevents any physical contact between visitors and prisoners. This damp, oppressive space has borne witness to countless agonizing farewells and desperate conversations, yet the prisoners regard it as a rare privilege—a brief escape from the unrelenting monotony of their confinement.

On this particular day, the yard held a figure who attracted significant attention from the other prisoners. This young man stood apart, his hands in his pockets, and an air of defiance in his demeanor. His clothes, though torn, hinted at refinement; their fine fabric retained a faint sheen despite their state of disrepair. His shirt, though discolored, still showed traces of its original elegance, and his boots, polished with the edge of a monogrammed handkerchief, glistened in the dim light.

The other inmates watched him with a mix of admiration and mockery.

"Look at the prince, grooming himself," one sneered.

"He's a fine-looking fellow," another added. "If only he had a comb and some pomade, he'd outshine the gentlemen in white gloves."

"Pity about the gendarmes tearing up his clothes," said another.

Andrea Cavalcanti—or Benedetto, as he was known in truth—ignored their taunts as he approached one of the guards.

"Come now," he said in a tone that mingled arrogance with pleading. "Lend me twenty francs. You'll get it back soon enough; I've relatives worth millions."

The guard merely shrugged, unfazed by Andrea's attempts at charm.

"Heartless brute," Andrea muttered. "I'll see to it you're replaced."

This drew laughter from the surrounding prisoners, who jeered at Andrea with growing malice. Their taunts escalated, some calling for brutal games of punishment while others prepared makeshift weapons.

But Andrea, well-versed in the language of the underworld, gave a series of subtle gestures—a signal Caderousse had once taught him. Instantly, the mood shifted. Recognizing him as one of their own, the prisoners backed off, their hostility replaced with begrudging acceptance.

Just then, a guard called out from the gate, "Benedetto! You're wanted in the visitors' room!"

Andrea straightened, his confidence restored. "Ah, at last," he muttered, brushing past the stunned prisoners and guards. "Now you'll see how a Cavalcanti is treated."

He was escorted to the visitors' area, where, behind the iron grating, he saw a familiar face: Bertuccio.

"Ah," Andrea said, his voice faltering as he recognized the Count's steward.

"Good morning, Benedetto," Bertuccio replied, his deep voice steady.

"You," Andrea whispered, suddenly cautious. "Why are you here?"

"Do you not recognize me?" Bertuccio asked, his tone heavy with meaning.

"Lower your voice!" Andrea hissed, glancing nervously at the guards.

Bertuccio produced a signed order, arranging for their conversation to continue in a private room. Once inside the sparse, whitewashed chamber, Andrea threw himself onto the bed, while Bertuccio took the chair.

"Well?" Bertuccio asked. "What do you have to tell me?"

"I should ask you the same," Andrea countered. "Who sent you?"

"No one," Bertuccio replied.

Andrea's eyes narrowed. "Then why are you here? What do you want from me?"

"I came to see what you've become," Bertuccio said coldly. "You've robbed, you've killed, and now you're paying the price."

Andrea smirked. "Save your sermons. Tell me about my father."

"That name," Bertuccio said gravely, "is not yours to utter. The man you speak of is no father to you."

Andrea's confidence wavered. "Who is he, then?"

"Someone beyond your reach," Bertuccio replied. "Someone too favored by Heaven to have fathered the likes of you."

Before Andrea could press further, a guard interrupted. "The magistrate is waiting for the prisoner."

As Andrea was led away, he glanced back at Bertuccio. "Tomorrow, then," he said.

"Tomorrow," Bertuccio replied, his expression unreadable.

Chapter 108: The Judge

The Abbé Busoni remained with Noirtier in the chamber of death, where only the priest and the grieving grandfather kept vigil over Valentine's lifeless body. Something in the Abbé's kind words, gentle prayers, or quiet presence seemed to soothe Noirtier's despair. The old man's violent grief transformed into a calm resignation that surprised everyone familiar with the intensity of his love for Valentine.

M. de Villefort had avoided his father since the day after Valentine's death. The entire household had been reorganized—new servants were hired for Villefort, Noirtier, and Madame de Villefort. Everywhere, from the concierge to the coachmen, unfamiliar faces replaced the old, deepening the divisions within the family. Meanwhile, Villefort threw himself into his work, obsessively preparing the case against Benedetto for the upcoming assizes[*]. The crime had captivated Paris, and Villefort hoped the trial would showcase his prosecutorial skill and restore his sense of self-worth.

The night before the trial, Villefort, overwhelmed by grief and fatigue, wandered the garden. His cane tapped against the withered rose bushes lining the path, knocking away their brittle branches. His restless

---

[*]A criminal trial court involving defendants accused of felonies. It is the only French court that uses a jury trial.

steps brought him to the boarded gate overlooking the deserted enclosure, but his eyes were drawn to a different scene. Through an open window, he saw Noirtier sitting in the sunlight, his sharp gaze fixed on the garden below.

Following Noirtier's line of sight, Villefort's heart froze. Beneath the nearly bare linden trees, Madame de Villefort sat with a book in her hand, smiling at Edward, who was tossing a ball from the drawing room into the garden. Noirtier's expression was one of ferocious hatred, his intense stare burning with reproach. Villefort understood immediately what his father's gaze meant.

The old man's eyes shifted from his daughter-in-law to Villefort himself, and the look of condemnation deepened. Villefort turned away, unable to bear it, but Noirtier raised his eyes to heaven, silently reminding his son of a forgotten oath.

"Have patience but one day longer," Villefort murmured to his father. "What I promised, I will do."

Reassured, Noirtier turned his gaze elsewhere, while Villefort stormed into his study, his thoughts in turmoil.

That night, while the rest of the household slept, Villefort worked feverishly. He reviewed interrogatories, compiled witness depositions, and finalized the indictment against Benedetto. By five in the morning, he was exhausted. He opened the window, letting the crisp air revive him as dawn's pale light crept across the horizon.

"Today," he whispered to himself, "justice must strike wherever guilt is found."

His eyes wandered to Noirtier's window, but the curtain was drawn. Still, Villefort felt his father's silent presence.

"Yes," he said aloud, "be satisfied."

After pacing the room, Villefort collapsed onto a sofa, too restless to sleep but needing to rest his limbs. As the household stirred to life, the familiar sounds of doors opening, bells ringing, and Edward's laughter reached his ears. A valet entered with a cup of chocolate.

"Who sent this?" Villefort demanded.

"Madame de Villefort, sir. She thought it would strengthen you for the trial."

Villefort stared at the cup before swallowing its contents in a single gulp. For a moment, he seemed to hope it was poisoned, an escape from the duty he dreaded. But when no ill effects followed, he resumed pacing, a bitter smile on his lips.

At eleven, the valet returned. "Madame de Villefort wishes to know if you'd like her to accompany you to the Palais."

Villefort froze. "She wishes to attend the trial?"

"Yes, sir."

Villefort's voice hardened. "Tell her I will see her in her room."

After dressing in black, Villefort entered his wife's quarters. She sat elegantly dressed, her bonnet on the chair beside her. Edward played nearby, tearing apart newspapers as his mother turned the pages.

"Ah, here you are," she said lightly. "But how pale you look! Shall I come with you, or take Edward instead?"

Villefort ignored her questions, his expression cold. "Edward, go to the drawing room. I must speak with your mother."

The boy hesitated until Villefort barked, "Go!" Startled, Edward obeyed, leaving his parents alone.

"Madame," Villefort said, his voice like ice, "where do you keep the poison you use?"

Madame de Villefort froze, her face draining of color. "I—I don't understand," she stammered, her voice barely audible.

Villefort's gaze was unrelenting. "Do not deny it. You poisoned my father-in-law, my mother-in-law, Barrois, and my daughter Valentine."

"Sir, please," she pleaded, falling to her knees.

"You may beg," Villefort said, his voice rising with anger. "But your crimes are known. You've killed with precision, patience, and cold calculation. Did you not save a final dose for yourself? Or are you too cowardly to face your own justice?"

Tears streamed down her face as she begged for mercy. "For the sake of our son, spare me!"

Villefort's expression hardened further. "One day, if you live, you might kill him too."

Madame de Villefort screamed, collapsing into sobs. Villefort stepped back, his voice calm but unyielding. "When I return, justice must be done. If you're still alive, I'll have you arrested."

He locked the door behind him, leaving her alone with her despair.

Chapter 109: The Assizes

The trial of Benedetto, also known as the "Benedetto Affair," had captivated all of Paris. From the Café de Paris to the Bois de Boulogne, whispers of the false Cavalcanti's spectacular fall from grace spread like wildfire. The man who once dazzled high society with his charm, wealth, and fabricated nobility was now the centerpiece of a courtroom drama. Those who had once rubbed shoulders with "Prince Andrea Cavalcanti" were eager to witness his downfall, and the Palais de Justice overflowed with spectators, from the curious public to the most seasoned journalists.

The spectacle was not just about the man but the myth he represented. To some, Benedetto was a victim of legal overreach, while others saw him as the embodiment of society's fascination with deception. Rumors circulated that his father, the elusive "Count Cavalcanti," might reappear to defend his son. Despite the scandal surrounding him, many still recalled Benedetto as charming, generous, and amiable, leading some to suspect a conspiracy against him.

The trial hall, on this bright September day, buzzed like a drawing room during a grand soirée. By seven in the morning, crowds gathered at the iron gates, jostling for the best positions. By eight, the privileged seats were filled, and an hour later, the hall was bursting with people exchanging whispers, nodding to acquaintances, or gesturing across rows of seated lawyers.

Among the attendees were familiar faces from Parisian high society. Beauchamp, the celebrated journalist, adjusted his monocle as he scanned the room. Beside him were Château-Renaud and Debray, who had persuaded a sergeant-at-arms to grant them better positions. The trio discussed the affair with a mixture of detachment and intrigue.

"Well," Beauchamp said, his tone sardonic, "our 'prince' certainly had an illustrious rise—and what a fall."

"He played the part convincingly enough," Debray replied. "But no amount of borrowed nobility can outshine the truth."

"I hear he'll be condemned swiftly," Château-Renaud added.

"Most likely," Beauchamp agreed. "But the real drama lies elsewhere. Did you hear what Villefort said last night?"

"No, enlighten us," Château-Renaud urged.

"The president[*] called Benedetto 'a silly rascal.' Can you imagine? A man so cunning, reduced to such an insult."

As they exchanged theories, Beauchamp's gaze caught a veiled woman entering the courtroom.

"Wait," he murmured. "Is that Madame Danglars?"

Château-Renaud and Debray followed his line of sight.

"Impossible," Château-Renaud scoffed. "She wouldn't dare show her face here so soon after her husband's disgrace and her daughter's flight."

"It may not be her," Debray said hastily, his color rising. "She's likely abroad. Let's not jump to conclusions."

---

[*]The court official who oversees the proceedings within the legal system, essentially acting as the "president" of the court in the context of the narrative.

Their conversation shifted to the tragedy at Villefort's household. "How is it that Madame de Villefort is not here?" Beauchamp asked.

"Perhaps tending to her charity work," Debray suggested lightly. "Or perfecting some new cosmetic."

Château-Renaud snorted. "I find her detestable. She has an air that grates on the nerves."

Their discussion ended abruptly as the sergeant called the court to order. A hush fell over the room as the judges entered, taking their seats beneath the imposing seal of the French Republic. The hall buzzed again as Benedetto was led in, his once-proud bearing replaced with defiance.

Among the exhibits was a blood-stained waistcoat, a key piece of evidence connecting Benedetto to the murder of Caderousse. The spectators leaned forward as the item was placed on the desk, its significance clear to everyone present.

The trial began, a mixture of testimony, legal arguments, and dramatic revelations. As the case unfolded, it became evident that Benedetto's charade was unraveling completely. Every lie he had told, every false identity he had assumed, was laid bare before the court.

The day's proceedings ended with murmurs of anticipation for the sentencing. As the crowd dispersed, the trio of Beauchamp, Château-Renaud, and Debray lingered briefly, discussing the implications of the trial.

"Do you think the Count of Monte Cristo will appear tomorrow?" Château-Renaud asked.

Beauchamp shook his head. "I doubt it. He's too closely tied to the drama, from the Cavalcanti affair to Caderousse's murder."

"Still," Debray mused, "he always seems to have a hand in events, whether we see it or not."

As they exited, the setting sun cast long shadows over the courthouse steps, a fitting end to a day filled with revelations and portents of justice yet to be served.

Chapter 110: The Indictment

The judges took their seats amidst profound silence, and the jury followed, settling into their places with solemn gravity. Villefort, the focus of unusual attention, sat in his armchair, exuding an aura of tranquility that contrasted sharply with the storm of emotions surrounding him. His severe, impassive demeanor—a man seemingly untouched by human frailties—provoked both admiration and unease.

"Gendarmes," the president ordered, "bring in the accused."

All eyes turned toward the door as Benedetto was led into the courtroom. His entrance drew gasps of astonishment. Far from displaying the fear or remorse expected of someone in his position, Benedetto's demeanor was calm, almost arrogant. One hand rested casually on his hat, the other tucked into the opening of his white waistcoat. His gaze swept the courtroom, lingering on the president before fixing intently on Villefort, whose usually composed expression faltered for the briefest moment.

Beside Benedetto stood the court-appointed defense attorney, a young man whose pale complexion and nervous energy contrasted sharply with his client's unsettling composure. Benedetto's indifference toward the proceedings was palpable, as if the trial were a mere formality.

The president called for the indictment to be read. This document, crafted with Villefort's characteristic eloquence and precision, painted a vivid and damning picture of Benedetto's crimes. It detailed his fraudulent past, his transformation into a conman and murderer, and his relentless descent into depravity. Villefort's mastery of rhetoric ensured that the jury—and the public—condemned Benedetto long before the law rendered its verdict.

Yet Benedetto seemed unaffected. He listened to the accusations with the indifference of a spectator at someone else's trial. Villefort, however, watched him closely, his piercing gaze failing to unsettle the accused.

When the reading concluded, the president began his interrogation.

"Accused," he said, "state your name and surname."

Benedetto rose gracefully. "Mr. President," he replied in a clear voice, "I must apologize in advance. I intend to answer your questions, but not in the usual order. I believe I can provide more valuable information if permitted to speak freely."

The courtroom buzzed with astonishment. The president exchanged glances with the jury, then with Villefort, whose pale face betrayed a growing unease.

"Your age?" the president persisted.

"I will answer that in due time," Benedetto said smoothly, "but let's not rush."

"Your age," the president repeated sternly.

"I am twenty-one," Benedetto said, his tone casual, "or rather, I will be in a few days. I was born on the night of September 27, 1817."

Villefort, who had been jotting notes, froze at the mention of this date. He glanced up sharply, his face ashen.

"And where were you born?" the president continued.

"At Auteuil, near Paris," Benedetto replied.

Villefort's expression hardened, his features contorted as if staring at a ghost. Benedetto dabbed his lips with a fine handkerchief, his composure unshaken.

"What is your profession?"

Benedetto's answer was chilling in its candor. "I started as a forger, became a thief, and more recently, an assassin."

The courtroom erupted in outrage. Gasps, murmurs, and even cries of disgust echoed throughout the hall. Judges exchanged incredulous looks, and the jury recoiled at the accused's brazen cynicism. Villefort pressed his hands to his temples, his pale complexion turning crimson with suppressed rage.

"Are you looking for something, Mr. Procureur?" Benedetto asked, his voice laced with mockery.

Villefort did not respond, his trembling hands betraying his inner turmoil.

The president, regaining control, asked, "Will you now tell us your name?"

Benedetto's reply sent a chill through the room. "I cannot tell you my name, as I do not know it. But I can tell you my father's name."

An audible silence gripped the courtroom. Villefort sat frozen, beads of sweat rolling down his face.

"My father," Benedetto continued calmly, "is the king's attorney."

The president's confusion mirrored that of the audience. "The king's attorney?" he repeated.

"Yes," Benedetto said, his voice unwavering. "My father is M. de Villefort."

The courtroom exploded. Cries of outrage, insults, and gasps filled the air. Guards struggled to maintain order as the crowd surged forward. In the midst of the chaos, Villefort staggered to his feet, his disheveled appearance shocking those who had admired his composure just moments earlier.

"Father," Benedetto said, his voice cutting through the noise, "shall I continue?"

"No," Villefort choked out, his voice hoarse and broken. "It's true—all of it is true."

The president pounded his gavel, demanding order, but the courtroom remained in chaos. Villefort's confession stunned even the most cynical observers.

"I yield," Villefort murmured. "I am in the hands of an avenging God."

He stumbled toward the door, which a guard hastily opened. The courtroom watched in stunned silence as he disappeared, leaving behind a legacy shattered by his own sins.

Chapter 111: Expiation

Amidst the dense crowd outside the Palais de Justice, M. de Villefort found the throng parting before him as if by instinct. There is a solemnity to great misfortunes that can elicit even a crowd's sympathy for the most disgraced individuals. Though Villefort had confessed his guilt, the weight of his suffering shielded him from reproach. There are moments when raw anguish transcends reason, moving people with its sheer authenticity.

Villefort staggered out of the Palais in a state of stupor. His body seemed to rebel against itself, every nerve stretched taut, every muscle aching. Without conscious thought, he navigated the corridors, shedding his magistrate's robe like a tormenting shroud. He reached his carriage, roused the coachman himself, and collapsed onto the cushions, muttering directions to the Faubourg Saint-Honoré.

As the carriage sped through Paris, Villefort's mind churned. He had faced his crimes, but the repercussions loomed vast and unknowable. He gripped the edge of his seat, murmuring, "God... God..." The word escaped him without purpose or plea, a reflex born of desperation.

His restless movements dislodged something—a fan belonging to Madame de Villefort. The sight of it struck him like a bolt of lightning.

"Oh!" he gasped, clutching his chest.

For the past hour, his mind had been consumed by his own guilt, but now another, equally terrible realization surged forward. His wife—he had condemned her to death. Overcome with remorse, he imagined her in her final moments, reliving her crimes, begging for forgiveness, perhaps even composing a last letter.

"She must not die!" he shouted. "She will live. I'll save her."

Villefort ordered the coachman to drive faster, his voice electrified with urgency. "Faster!" he cried, the horses galloping as though sensing their master's despair.

He rehearsed his pleas as the carriage neared his home. "I'll confess everything to her," he resolved. "We'll flee together. She loves Edward—she acted for his sake. No mother can be beyond redemption when her child is her motive."

When the carriage finally stopped, Villefort leaped out and stormed into the house. He ascended the stairs two at a time, ignoring the servants' startled glances. Reaching his wife's room, he found Edward's adjoining chamber empty. His heart sank as he noticed her bedroom door bolted from within.

"Héloïse!" he called, pounding on the door.

A faint sound of furniture scraping against the floor was her only reply.

"Héloïse!" he shouted again.

Finally, her trembling voice answered. "Who is it?"

"It's me," he cried. "Open the door!"

The door remained closed. Panic rising, Villefort hurled himself against it, splintering the lock. He burst into the room to find Madame de Villefort standing pale and rigid, a crystal bottle clutched in her hands.

"It's done," she rasped, her voice hollow and her eyes wide with terror. "What more do you want from me?"

She collapsed onto the floor. Villefort rushed to her side, prying the bottle from her clenched fingers. But it was too late—she was dead.

"My son!" Villefort exclaimed, a new terror gripping him. "Where is Edward?"

The servants gathered at the sound of his frantic cries.

"Master Edward is not downstairs," one reported.

"He must be playing in the garden," suggested another.

"No," the valet corrected. "Madame de Villefort sent for him earlier. He hasn't been seen since."

Villefort stumbled back into his wife's room, his mind reeling. The adjoining boudoir's door stood ajar, revealing Edward lying still on the satin couch.

"Edward!" Villefort cried, rushing to his son's side. He lifted the boy into his arms, only to find his body cold and lifeless.

A folded letter fell from Edward's chest. Trembling, Villefort opened it and read his wife's final words:

You know I was a good mother. For my son's sake, I became a criminal. A good mother cannot leave this world without her child.

Villefort collapsed to his knees, his cries of anguish reverberating through the house. "Still the hand of God," he murmured.

Overwhelmed, Villefort staggered out of the room, desperate for solace. He found himself in Noirtier's chamber, where the Abbé Busoni stood solemnly by the old man's side.

"You here?" Villefort asked, his voice breaking. "Do you only appear to escort death?"

"I came to pray over your daughter," the Abbé replied.

"Why are you here now?" Villefort demanded.

"To tell you that your debt is repaid and to ask God to forgive you, as I have," Busoni said. At those words, the Abbé removed his wig, revealing his true identity.

"Monte Cristo!" Villefort gasped.

"No," the Count replied. "Think further back—to Marseilles, twenty-three years ago. *I am Edmond Dantès,* whom you condemned to a living death."

Villefort's face contorted in realization. Grasping Monte Cristo's arm, he dragged him upstairs to the bodies of Héloïse and Edward.

"Are you satisfied?" he demanded, his voice a mix of rage and despair. "See what your vengeance has wrought!"

Monte Cristo became pale at this horrible sight. Kneeling beside Edward, he whispered, "Have I gone too far?"

He left Villefort to his madness, descending the stairs with the boy's lifeless body cradled in his arms. Placing Edward gently beside his mother, he left the house, his heart heavy with the weight of his revenge.

Outside, Villefort was frantically digging in the garden, his hands blistered and bleeding. "I'll find it!" he screamed. "You can't hide it from me!"

Monte Cristo turned away, horrified. "He's lost his mind," he murmured.

For the first time, he questioned his mission. "Have I gone beyond God's will?" he wondered aloud. He felt he had passed beyond the bounds of vengeance, and that he could no longer say, "God is for and with me."

"Enough. I must save what remains."

Returning to his house, he found Maximilian Morrel waiting like a shadow.

"We leave Paris tomorrow," Monte Cristo told him. "There's nothing more for us here."

"Is your work complete?" Maximilian asked.

Monte Cristo's answer was solemn. "God grant I haven't done too much."

Chapter 112: The Departure

Paris buzzed with the recent downfall of Morcerf, Danglars, and Villefort. These rapid, catastrophic events dominated conversation in every salon and café. In the modest apartment on the Rue Meslay, Emmanuel and Julie discussed these tragedies with awe, their astonishment mingled with sympathy. Maximilian, who was visiting, listened silently, lost in his usual melancholic reverie.

"Emmanuel," Julie said, "is it not as though those once prosperous and powerful figures were visited by some vengeful spirit? Like the wicked fairies in Perrault's tales, who curse the uninvited at a celebration, this spirit appeared to exact retribution for their arrogance."

"What terrible misfortunes," Emmanuel agreed, only thinking of Morcerf and Danglars.

"And such dreadful suffering," Julie added, her thoughts turning to Valentine, though she refrained from mentioning her name out of sensitivity to her brother.

"If these tragedies were ordained by the Supreme Being," Emmanuel said gravely, "then perhaps these individuals' past lives offered no redemption to lessen their punishment."

"Don't judge so harshly, Emmanuel," Julie replied. "Remember my father. When he was on the verge of taking his life, would it have been fair to say he deserved his suffering?"

"But your father was spared," Emmanuel reminded her. "Someone intervened to stay the hand of death."

Just then, the doorbell rang, announcing a visitor. Moments later, the Count of Monte Cristo appeared in the doorway. Julie and Emmanuel greeted him joyfully, while Maximilian merely lifted his head before letting it fall back in despair.

"Maximilian," the Count said, ignoring the varied reactions to his arrival, "I have come for you."

"For me?" Maximilian echoed, as if waking from a dream.

"Yes," Monte Cristo replied. "Did we not agree that you would accompany me? I told you yesterday to prepare for departure."

"I am ready," Maximilian said quietly. "I came to bid my family farewell."

"Where are you going, Count?" Julie asked.

"To Marseilles, madame," Monte Cristo replied.

"To Marseilles?" the couple exclaimed in unison.

"Yes, and I am taking your brother with me."

"Oh, Count," Julie implored, "will you bring him back to us, free of this sadness?"

Monte Cristo turned to her with a soft smile. "You believe him unhappy?"

"Yes," Julie admitted. "I fear he finds our home rather dull."

"I shall take care of him," the Count assured her.

Maximilian interjected, "I am ready to leave. Goodbye, my kind friends. Farewell, Emmanuel—Julie."

Julie looked at him, heartbroken. "Must you leave so suddenly? Without any preparation?"

"Delays only worsen the pain of parting," Monte Cristo said gently. "Maximilian has everything he needs, as I advised him to prepare."

"I have my passport and packed belongings," Maximilian confirmed.

Julie clung to her brother, her voice trembling. "Oh, Maximilian, you are hiding something from us. Your indifference is breaking my heart."

Monte Cristo intervened, his tone soothing. "Fear not, madame. He will return to you brighter and more joyous than before."

Julie watched them leave with tears in her eyes. "Please, Count," she whispered, "restore my brother to happiness."

Monte Cristo pressed her hand, offering the same silent reassurance he had given her eleven years earlier. "Trust Sinbad the Sailor," he said with a smile.

Julie nodded. "I do."

The Count and Maximilian departed, their carriage waiting with four restless horses. Ali stood by, sweating from a recent errand.

"Did you deliver the letter?" Monte Cristo asked in Arabic.

Ali nodded.

"And his response?"

Ali mimicked Noirtier's gesture of closing his eyes, signaling "Yes."

"Good," Monte Cristo murmured. "Let's go."

As the carriage raced through the night, Monte Cristo ordered a stop atop Villejuif Hill. Standing alone under the starlit sky, he gazed at Paris, its countless lights resembling phosphorescent waves.

"Great city," he murmured, "I entered your gates. I came guided by Providence, and now I leave, my mission complete. I have neither pride nor hatred, only regret."

He re-entered the carriage, and they continued toward Marseilles.

By morning, they arrived at Châlons, where Monte Cristo's steamboat awaited. The journey resumed with breathtaking speed, and the fresh air seemed to momentarily lift the shadows from Maximilian's face.

Finally, Marseilles came into view—its vibrant port, sunlit streets, and ancient towers awakening memories in both travelers.

"This," Maximilian said, leaning on the Count's arm, "is where my father greeted me when the *Pharaon* returned. I can still feel his tears on my cheek."

Monte Cristo smiled. "I was over there," he said, pointing to a street corner.

A loud cry drew their attention away fom the corner. A veiled woman waved tearfully to a passenger aboard a departing ship.

"That ship's officer," Maximilian exclaimed, "it's Albert de Morcerf!"

"Yes," Monte Cristo confirmed.

"What brings him here?"

The count smiled, as he was in the habit of doing when he did not want to make any reply, and he again turned towards the veiled woman, who soon disappeared at the corner of the street. The Count turned to his friend.

"Dear Maximilian," said the count, "have you nothing to do in this land?"

"I have to weep over the grave of my father," replied Morrel in a broken voice.

"Well, then, go,—wait for me there, and I will soon join you. First, I also have a pious visit to pay."

Near the port, he turned down a familiar street to a house he had known long ago. The dwelling, now occupied by Mercédès, bore the marks of time and hardship but stood resilient—much like the woman within.

Monte Cristo entered unannounced, his presence met with a sob that cut through the still air. Under an arbor of Virginia jessamine, Mercédès sat weeping, her grief unmasked for the first time since her son, Albert, had departed.

"Madame," Monte Cristo said softly, "I cannot restore your happiness, but I offer you the solace of a friend. Will you accept it?"

Mercédès raised her head, her tear-streaked face a portrait of anguish. "What comfort is there left for me? My son is gone. My life is empty."

Monte Cristo's tone was both gentle and resolute. "Albert carries a noble heart. He will find strength and honor in his journey. You must believe in his future."

Her sorrow deepened, but there was no anger in her gaze—only a haunting self-reproach. "I have been weak, Edmond. When you returned, I saw you as an avenging angel, and yet I could not bring myself to hate you. My choices brought me here; my cowardice sealed my fate. Now, I live in the shadow of what could have been."

Monte Cristo knelt before her, his voice tinged with regret. "You have every reason to despise me, Mercédès, yet you show only grace. Do not let the weight of the past consume you."

Her reply was both sorrowful and resolute. "I cannot change what has been, Edmond. My love for you remains a cherished memory, but it belongs to a time long gone. Now, I must find peace in the quiet corners of this house and in the prayers I offer for my son."

As the Count prepared to leave, he made one final offer. "Is there nothing you wish for yourself, Mercédès?"

She shook her head. "My only wish is for Albert's happiness. Beyond that, I need nothing. The little you left for me years ago is more than enough. I will spend my remaining days here, in quiet reflection."

Monte Cristo hesitated, the weight of their shared past pressing heavily upon him. Finally, he said, "If ever you need anything, Mercédès, you need only ask."

Her parting words were spoken with quiet conviction. "We will meet again, Edmond. If not in this life, then in the next."

Monte Cristo departed, his steps heavy with unspoken sorrow. As Mercédès watched him go from the window, her voice trembled with the echo of a name she could never forget. "*Edmond, Edmond, Edmond.*"

Chapter 113: The Past

The Count of Monte Cristo departed Mercédès' home with a heavy heart, knowing it was likely the last time he would ever see her. Little Edward's death had profoundly changed him. After achieving his long-sought vengeance, the satisfaction he anticipated was replaced by an abyss of doubt. His recent conversation with Mercédès had stirred countless memories, forcing him to confront his choices. A man of Monte Cristo's intensity could not linger long in despair—it was not in his nature. Yet he found himself questioning whether his path, so meticulously plotted, had been a grave mistake.

"Could I have deceived myself?" he murmured. "Did I pursue a false end? Could a single moment destroy the foundation of all my hopes? No. This must be a trick of my mind, a false perspective on the past."

He walked along the Rue de la Caisserie, revisiting familiar streets. Twenty-four years earlier, he had been dragged through these same streets by silent guards, en route to imprisonment. Then, the houses had been dark and lifeless. Now, under the sun's bright rays, they were lively and welcoming.

"They are the same," Monte Cristo muttered. "The difference is the light of day, not the streets themselves."

He made his way to the quay where he had once embarked for the Château d'If. A small pleasure boat with a striped awning caught his eye, and he hired it to take him out to sea. The water sparkled in the sunlight, fish leapt from the surface, and the horizon shimmered with distant fishing boats and merchant vessels. Yet, Monte Cristo's thoughts remained dark, replaying the terrible journey to the Château d'If.

Every detail returned vividly: the solitary light of the Catalans village, the looming silhouette of the Château d'If, his desperate struggle against the gendarmes, and the cold muzzle of a carbine pressed against his forehead. The idyllic scene around him faded, replaced by the black sky and shadowy walls of the fortress that had once imprisoned him.

When the boat reached the shore, the oarsman's cheerful call broke through his reverie: "Sir, we're here."

Monte Cristo stepped ashore, his mind racing. He recalled being dragged up this very slope by armed guards, bayonets prodding him forward. Now, every stroke of the oar had awakened memories of his despair and the resolve he forged amidst it.

The Château d'If had not held prisoners since the July Revolution. A concierge now gave tours of its dark cells, a grim curiosity for visitors. Monte Cristo asked if any of the old jailers remained. They had all retired, the concierge explained, leaving him, a newcomer, to guide visitors through the prison.

Monte Cristo insisted on seeing his former cell. The light struggled to penetrate the narrow opening, and the marks of the Abbé Faria's secret passage were still visible. Sitting on a log of wood, Monte Cristo trembled as he took in the place that had once consumed fourteen years of his life.

"Do any stories of this prison survive?" he asked.

"Yes," the concierge replied. "There's a tale about this very dungeon, involving a clever young prisoner and a mad priest."

Monte Cristo's pulse quickened. "Mad?"

"He claimed to possess great wealth and offered millions for his freedom. The guards thought him delusional."

Monte Cristo listened intently as the concierge described how the prisoners communicated secretly, dug a tunnel, and exchanged ideas. When the priest died, the young prisoner hatched a daring escape plan, hiding in the corpse's sack, only to be thrown into the sea with a cannonball tied to his feet.

"Poor soul," the concierge concluded. "The fall must have killed him instantly, or the weight dragged him to the bottom."

Monte Cristo, overwhelmed, whispered, "And the prisoner? Was he ever heard of again?"

"Never. He became a legend, known only as Number 34."

"Great is truth," Monte Cristo murmured. "Fire cannot burn it, nor water drown it."

He insisted on seeing the Abbé Faria's cell next. There, he saw the meridian Faria had drawn to mark time and the remains of the bed where the priest had died. Instead of pain, Monte Cristo felt a deep gratitude. Kneeling by the bed, he prayed, "Oh, noble heart, if you can still hear me, grant me a sign. Free me from doubt, or my remorse will consume me."

The concierge interrupted, holding a bundle of cloth. "I found this hidden beneath the stones," he said.

It was Faria's manuscript, written on strips of cloth. Monte Cristo's eyes fell on the opening epigraph: *Thou shalt tear out the dragons' teeth and trample the lions underfoot, saith the Lord.*

"Here is my answer," Monte Cristo whispered, clutching the manuscript as though it were a divine revelation. He handed the concierge a pocketbook containing ten thousand francs. "Take this," he said, "but do not open it until I leave."

The Count departed, glancing back at the Château d'If one last time. "Woe to those who imprisoned me," he vowed. "And woe to those who forgot me."

As he passed the Catalans, he buried his face in his cloak, murmuring a name that brought him both pain and solace: Haydée.

Monte Cristo returned to Marseilles and found Maximilian at the cemetery, gazing at his family's graves.

"Do not look there," Monte Cristo said gently, pointing to the sky. "The dead are everywhere, but their souls belong above."

Maximilian nodded, his grief palpable.

"Will you meet me on October 5th at the Isle of Monte Cristo?" the Count asked.

"I will," Maximilian replied, though his voice was heavy with despair.

Monte Cristo placed a hand on his shoulder. "Then trust me, as I trusted Providence. We are not yet finished."

Chapter 114: Peppino

As the steamer disappeared behind Cape Morgiou, a man traveling swiftly along the road from Florence to Rome passed the small town of Aquapendente. Despite the speed of his journey, the man remained inconspicuous, his worn greatcoat marked by the ribbon of the Legion of Honor pinned on his chest. His French accent and limited knowledge of Italian—restricted to musical terms like allegro and moderato—betrayed his origins.

As his carriage approached La Storta, where the dome of Saint Peter's often draws the awe of travelers, the man paid it no mind. Instead, he drew a folded paper from his pocket, examined it reverently, and muttered, "Good, I still have it."

Arriving in Rome, his carriage entered through the Porta del Popolo and stopped at the Hôtel d'Espagne. Old Pastrini greeted the traveler with practiced politeness. After ordering a hearty dinner, the traveler inquired about Thomson & French, the renowned banking house in the Via dei Banchi near St. Peter's.

The arrival of a post-chaise always drew attention in Rome. Street urchins and idle spectators swarmed to gawk at the horses, the carriage, and its occupant. Among them, a shadowy figure silently detached himself from the crowd and followed the Frenchman as he left for Thomson & French on foot.

The banker, introduced as Baron Danglars, entered the building while his mysterious pursuer loitered inconspicuously. Danglars was led into a private office where he finalized business involving a letter of credit for five million francs—money fraudulently drawn on the account of the Count of Monte Cristo. The clerk, satisfied, exited the room, leaving Danglars glowing with satisfaction as he exited the building.

Unbeknownst to him, the man who had shadowed him since his arrival, Peppino, was now firmly on his trail. Peppino communicated briefly with another shadowy figure, and the two melted into the Roman streets, waiting for their next move.

That evening, Danglars dined and retired early to bed, placing his precious pocketbook under his pillow for safekeeping. Meanwhile, Peppino gambled with the locals, drank a bottle of wine, and stationed himself outside Danglars' door.

The next morning, Danglars awoke refreshed, though his sleep had been restless for days. Eager to leave Rome, he ordered post-horses for noon, only to face delays. The horses arrived at two, and his passport was only cleared by three. By this time, a crowd of idlers had gathered outside the hotel, eager to profit from the baron's generosity. Flattered by their cries of "Your Excellency," Danglars distributed coins liberally before stepping into his carriage.

"Which road?" asked the postilion.

"The Ancona road," Danglars replied. The carriage sped off, its occupant dreaming of the wealth awaiting him in Venice and Vienna.

After three leagues, the day faded into night. Danglars, confident in his plans, settled into his seat, stretching luxuriously as his carriage rolled on. Occasionally, he glanced out the window, observing the aqueducts silhouetted against the moonlight.

Suddenly, the carriage jolted to a halt. Expecting to find himself at a posting station, Danglars leaned out the window, but the sight before him sent a chill through his spine. He saw shadowy figures moving amidst ruins, and a strong hand shoved him back inside before the carriage resumed its journey.

An hour passed, and the aqueducts appeared on the opposite side of the road, indicating the carriage had doubled back toward Rome. Panic set in.

"Mon Dieu," Danglars muttered, "what if this isn't the law pursuing me, but bandits?"

His fears deepened as the carriage turned onto the Appian Way. Danglars recognized landmarks described by Albert de Morcerf during his ill-fated trip to Rome—Caracalla's circus and the dark ruins of ancient monuments.

At last, the carriage stopped. A commanding voice ordered, "Scendi!"

Danglars descended, more dead than alive, surrounded by armed men. He was led through a winding path, deeper into the countryside. After ten minutes, the group reached a thicket of weeds concealing a rocky passage. Danglars was forced through the narrow opening, stumbling into a dark, cavernous network lit only by the flickering torch held by Peppino.

They descended into the catacombs of St. Sebastian, where hollowed tombs stared like the empty eyes of the dead. A sentinel challenged their approach, but Peppino's declaration of "A friend!" allowed them to pass. Finally, they entered a crypt illuminated by torches, where Luigi Vampa, seated with a book in hand, awaited.

"Is this the man?" Vampa asked without looking up.

"Yes," Peppino replied.

Vampa studied Danglars' pale, terrified face. "He's tired. Show him to his bed."

Danglars groaned but followed obediently. He was led to a small cell carved from the rock, its bare furnishings consisting of dried grass and goat skins.

Relieved to see a real bed, Danglars muttered, "God be praised." For the first time in years, he invoked the divine.

The door slammed shut, the bolt clicked into place, and Danglars was left alone in the darkness, a prisoner in the clutches of Luigi Vampa and his bandits.

Chapter 115: Luigi Vampa's Bill of Fare

The dreaded sleep from which Danglars feared he might never awaken finally released him. Opening his eyes, he was greeted by the cold, whitewashed walls of his cell—a stark contrast to the opulence he once enjoyed. Accustomed to velvet drapes, soft perfumes, and the comforts of Parisian luxury, Danglars felt as though he were trapped in a never-ending nightmare.

"Yes," he muttered, reality sinking in, "I am in the hands of the bandits Albert de Morcerf spoke of."

His first instinct was to check his body for injuries—a habit he had borrowed from *Don Quixote*, the only book he had ever read and faintly remembered. "No wounds," he said aloud, relieved. "But perhaps they've robbed me!"

He plunged his hands into his pockets, only to find them untouched. The hundred louis he had reserved for his journey from Rome to Venice remained in his trousers, and his letter of credit for 5,000,000 francs was still in his greatcoat.

"Strange bandits!" he exclaimed. "They left me my purse and pocketbook. They must want a ransom. Ah, here's my watch." He checked the time—half-past five in the morning. Without it, he would have been lost, as no daylight penetrated his cell.

Unsure whether to demand answers or wait for the bandits to propose terms, he decided patience was the safer route. Hours passed. At noon, the sentinel at his door was replaced by another—a towering, red-haired brute who devoured black bread, cheese, and onions with ferocious appetite.

"An ogre," Danglars muttered, retreating from the smell of brandy wafting through the cracks in the door.

As hunger gnawed at his stomach, Danglars tried to negotiate. Knocking on the door, he called, "It's time for something to eat!"

The giant merely grunted, indifferent to Danglars' pleas. Insulted, Danglars threw himself back onto his goat-skin bed, resolving to wait for a more cooperative guard.

Four hours later, his patience was rewarded. The new guard was Peppino, whom Danglars recognized as the man who had escorted him the night before. Peppino sat outside the door with a bowl of chickpeas stewed with bacon, a basket of Villetri grapes, and a flask of Orvieto wine.

Danglars' mouth watered. "Perhaps this one will listen," he thought, tapping on the door.

"On y va—coming!" Peppino replied in perfect French, his tone cheerful.

"Good evening," Danglars said, trying to be pleasant. "Might I have some dinner?"

Peppino raised an eyebrow. "Are you hungry, excellency?"

"Famished!" Danglars exclaimed. "I haven't eaten in twenty-four hours."

"No problem," Peppino said with a smile. "We can provide anything you desire—at a price."

"Of course," Danglars replied, though privately fuming. "After all, even bandits should feed their prisoners."

Peppino shrugged. "Not our custom. What would you like?"

"A fowl, perhaps. Yes, bring me a fowl."

Peppino shouted into the shadows, and a young bandit appeared moments later, carrying a roasted chicken on a silver dish. Danglars stared, momentarily transported back to the Café de Paris.

"Here's your dinner," Peppino said, placing the dish on a table.

Danglars asked for a knife and fork, which Peppino provided—a dull knife and a boxwood fork. Danglars was about to dig in when Peppino stopped him.

"Excellency," he said, "we require payment in advance."

"How much for a fowl?" Danglars asked, pulling a louis from his pocket.

"A hundred thousand francs," Peppino replied matter-of-factly.

Danglars laughed nervously. "A hundred thousand francs for a chicken? Surely you jest!"

"We never joke," Peppino said solemnly.

Reluctantly, Danglars handed over a louis, but Peppino shook his head. "That's just a down payment. You owe 4,999 louis more."

Fuming, Danglars threw himself back onto his bed. Peppino removed the chicken, resumed eating his peas, and ignored the banker's grumbles.

Hours passed, and hunger drove Danglars back to the door. "Fine," he said. "Bring me bread instead. Surely that's cheaper."

Peppino shouted for bread, which was brought promptly.

"How much?" Danglars asked warily.

"Another hundred thousand francs," Peppino replied.

"What? That's the same price as the fowl!" Danglars protested.

"Fixed prices," Peppino explained. "Bread or banquet, it's all the same."

Realizing he had no choice, Danglars reached for his letter of credit. "If I pay, will you let me eat in peace?"

"Certainly," Peppino said.

Danglars wrote a draft for the amount, his hands trembling with rage. Peppino examined it carefully, pocketed it, and returned the chicken. Danglars carved the fowl, muttering, "Thin as it is, it's the most expensive meal I've ever had."

Chapter 116: The Pardon

The following day, Danglars awoke to hunger gnawing at him again. Despite his attempts to economize, his stash of bread and leftover fowl had run out. Though he hoped to survive the day without further expense, his thirst soon overwhelmed him. Danglars endured until his tongue felt glued to the roof of his mouth. Unable to bear it any longer, he called out for help.

The door opened, revealing a new sentinel. Danglars hesitated but decided to request Peppino, the familiar bandit who had attended him previously.

"Here I am, your excellency," Peppino said with eager cheerfulness that Danglars found promising. "What do you need?"

"Something to drink," Danglars replied, his voice cracking.

"Ah, your excellency knows wine is beyond all price near Rome," Peppino said with a grin.

"Then give me water," Danglars snapped, attempting to sidestep the trap.

"Water?" Peppino exclaimed. "It's even rarer than wine. The drought has made it scarce."

Danglars forced a smile to mask his irritation but felt perspiration bead on his temples. "Come, my friend," he said, attempting diplomacy. "Surely, you won't refuse me a glass of wine?"

"I've already told you, we don't sell at retail," Peppino said.

"Then bring me a bottle of the least expensive wine."

"They're all the same price," Peppino replied.

"And what is that?"

"Twenty-five thousand francs a bottle," Peppino declared.

Danglars groaned in frustration. "You're robbing me in pieces," he grumbled. "Why not take everything at once?"

Peppino shrugged. "Perhaps that's the master's intention."

"The master?" Danglars asked. "Who is he?"

"The man you met yesterday," Peppino replied, stepping aside to reveal Luigi Vampa.

"You want to see me?" Vampa asked, stepping forward.

"Yes," Danglars said. "Are you the leader of these men?"

"I am," Vampa replied.

"Then tell me, what ransom do you demand for my freedom?"

"Five million francs," Vampa said bluntly.

Danglars clutched his chest as though stabbed. "That's all I have left in the world," he gasped. "Take it if you must, but spare my life!"

"We are forbidden to shed your blood," Vampa said coldly.

"Forbidden? By whom?"

"The one we serve."

"And who is that?"

Vampa's eyes glinted. "The one above me."

Danglars' desperation deepened. "Will you take less? A million? Two? Four? Please, take four million and let me go!"

"No," Vampa said. "I will not accept less than the full amount."

"Then kill me!" Danglars shouted, his voice hoarse with rage. "Torture me, but I won't sign again!"

"As you wish," Vampa said, turning on his heel.

For two days, Danglars resisted, clutching his resolve. On the third day, hunger broke him. He offered a million francs for food, which Vampa accepted. After a lavish meal, Danglars resolved to suffer no longer. Over the next twelve days, he surrendered nearly four million francs to satisfy his ravenous hunger.

When he realized he had only 50,000 francs left, his desperation took a new form. He prayed fervently, asking for deliverance. His prayers, though frequent, were often broken by delirium. He imagined himself as an old man dying of hunger and began to see visions of his past sins.

On the fifteenth day, Danglars crawled to the door of his cell, weak and trembling. "Are you not a Christian?" he begged Peppino. "Would you let a brother starve to death?"

Peppino did not reply.

Danglars fell to the ground. Rising again in despair, he cried out, "The chief! Let me speak to the chief!"

"What do you want?" Luigi Vampa asked coolly.

Danglars offered his remaining gold. "Take it! Just let me live. I ask nothing more."

Vampa's reply was piercing. "There are those who have suffered far more than you."

A deep voice interrupted, its solemnity freezing Danglars in place. "Do you repent?"

Danglars' head snapped toward the figure emerging from the shadows, his feeble eyes struggling to focus. "Of what must I repent?" he stammered.

The figure stepped closer, the light revealing a face that was as familiar as it was haunting. "Of the evil you have done," the voice answered, and with that, the figure dropped his cloak.

"The Count of Monte Cristo!" Danglars gasped, his pallor deepening.

The man shook his head. "No. I am he whom you sold and dishonored. I am he whose fiancée you betrayed. I am he whom you condemned to the darkness of a prison cell. I am the son of the man you left to die of hunger. *I am Edmond Dantès.*"

Danglars let out a guttural cry and collapsed to the ground, prostrate before the man he had wronged.

Monte Cristo's voice remained steady, almost detached. "Rise. Your life is not in danger. Your accomplices have met their fates—one mad, the other dead. You, however, will leave here alive. Keep the 50,000 francs you have left; it is yours. Tonight, you will eat and drink to your fill, and then you will be free."

Danglars remained motionless as Monte Cristo turned to leave, his shadow vanishing into the corridor as the bandits bowed in reverence. That evening, Vampa served Danglars the finest delicacies, a cruel reminder of the luxury that had once defined his life.

By dawn, Danglars stood by a stream, disoriented and broken. He stooped to drink, his reflection in the water stopping him cold. His once-dark hair was now completely white, the transformation a testament to the torment he had endured. The man who had entered the dungeon as a greedy banker emerged as a hollowed figure, forever marked by the specter of Edmond Dantès.

Chapter 117: The Fifth of October

As the autumn sun cast its opalescent light over the Mediterranean, a soft breeze stirred the tranquil waters, carrying the mingled scents of coastal vegetation and the sea. The heat of the day had given way to the cooler embrace of evening, and the vast expanse of ocean stretched endlessly, a canvas painted with golden hues. A graceful yacht glided across the waves, its white sails resembling a swan's outstretched wings. The vessel moved swiftly, leaving behind a trail of glittering foam.

On the yacht's prow stood a tall, dark-complexioned man. His intense gaze was fixed on the horizon, where a conical island began to emerge like a silhouette against the darkening sky.

"Is that the Isle of Monte Cristo?" the man asked, his voice tinged with melancholy.

"Yes, your excellency," replied the captain. "We have arrived."

"We have arrived," the man repeated, his tone laden with indescribable sadness.

The traveler, Maximilian Morrel, was soon ferried ashore in a gig manned by four rowers. The waters lapped at his waist as he waded to land, disregarding offers to be carried ashore. As he reached dry ground, a hand touched his shoulder, and a familiar voice said, "Good evening, Maximilian. You are punctual. Thank you."

"Count!" exclaimed Maximilian, his voice tinged with relief and joy.

Monte Cristo smiled warmly. "You are wet, my friend. Come, let us get you dry. I have a place prepared for you where you can rest and forget the trials of the day."

Monte Cristo led Morrel to a grotto illuminated by a brilliant light. The room, rich with the scent of exotic flowers, was adorned with luxurious furnishings. As they sat, Maximilian gazed at the Count with a mixture of reverence and sadness.

"You are not the same man here as in Paris," Morrel remarked. "Here, you smile."

Monte Cristo's smile faded. "You are right, Maximilian. For a moment, I forgot that happiness is fleeting."

"Oh no, Count," Morrel replied earnestly. "Please, do not lose your joy. If you are happy, then perhaps I can learn to find some peace."

The Count's brow furrowed. "Maximilian, let us speak plainly. Do you still feel the anguish that drives a man to seek death, or has time softened the sharp edge of your grief?"

"I have come to die in the arms of a friend," Morrel replied solemnly. "I love my sister, Julie, and her husband, Emmanuel, but they would not understand my resolve. You, Count, who stand above mortal concerns, will not try to stop me."

Monte Cristo regarded him with a mix of sorrow and resolve. "You are mistaken, Maximilian. I do not stand above life's trials. I have walked its darkest paths, and I know its greatest joys and deepest sorrows."

He rose and retrieved a beautifully carved silver casket. Opening it, he revealed a golden box filled with a greenish substance. "This is what you have asked of me."

Maximilian took the offered dose, his hands steady, his heart resolute. Before consuming it, he looked at the Count. "You have been more than a friend to me. Thank you for everything."

As Morrel swallowed the substance, his body relaxed, and his vision blurred. He felt himself slipping into a serene torpor, the weight of his grief lifting.

"Friend," he cried, "I can feel that I am dying; thanks!"

He made a last effort to extend his hand, but it fell powerless beside him. Then it appeared to him that Monte Cristo smiled, not with the strange and fearful expression which had sometimes revealed to him the secrets of his heart, but with the benevolent kindness of a father for a child.

The count now opened a door. A bright light filled the room, and a figure appeared in the doorway.

It was Valentine.

"Valentine, Valentine!" Maximilian cried out in his mind, though no sound escaped his lips. Overwhelmed by emotion, he sighed deeply and closed his eyes. Valentine rushed to his side, noticing his lips moving faintly.

"He's calling you," said the Count gently. "The man to whom you've entrusted your destiny—the one from whom death nearly tore you apart—is calling for you. Thankfully, I overcame death itself. From now on, Valentine, you will never be separated on this earth. He faced death to find you, and without me, you both would have perished. May God accept my atonement for preserving both your lives."

Valentine, overcome with joy, seized the Count's hand and pressed it to her lips in gratitude.

"Thank me again!" the Count implored, his voice betraying an unspoken need. "Say it until you're weary—that I have restored your happiness. You cannot know how much I need to hear it."

"Oh, yes, yes! I thank you with all my heart," Valentine exclaimed earnestly. "And if you ever doubt how sincere my gratitude is, ask Haydée! Ask my dear sister Haydée, who has comforted me every day since we left France. She spoke to me of you, filling my heart with hope for this day."

"You love Haydée, then?" Monte Cristo asked, his voice soft but tinged with an emotion he struggled to conceal.

"With all my soul," Valentine replied.

"Then, Valentine, I have a favor to ask."

"Of me? Oh, how blessed I must be for that!"

"Yes," the Count continued. "You've called Haydée your sister—make her so, truly. Give her the gratitude you believe you owe to me. Protect her, for…" His voice broke, heavy with emotion. "From now on, she will be alone in this world."

"Alone?" came a voice from behind. "Why?"

Monte Cristo turned to see Haydée standing motionless, her face pale and filled with dread.

"Because tomorrow, Haydée, you will be free," he said gently. "You will reclaim your rightful place in the world. I cannot let my fate overshadow yours. You are the daughter of a prince, and I return to you your father's name and wealth."

Haydée grew even paler. Lifting her trembling hands toward the heavens, she whispered through tears, "Then, you're leaving me, my lord?"

"Haydée," Monte Cristo replied softly, "you are young and beautiful. Forget me, and be happy."

"So be it," she said, her voice quivering. "I will obey your command, my lord. I will forget you and find happiness." She stepped back, her face a mask of quiet despair.

"Oh, heavens!" Valentine cried, holding Maximilian close. "Can't you see how pale she is? Can't you see how much she suffers?"

Haydée spoke again, her voice filled with anguish. "Why should he notice, my sister? He is my master, and I am his slave. He has the right to ignore me."

The Count shuddered, her words piercing his heart. Meeting her eyes, he could barely endure the raw emotion in her gaze.

"Haydée," he asked, his voice unsteady, "would you rather not leave me?"

"I am young," she said softly, "and you've made life so beautiful for me. I don't want to die."

"Then if I leave, Haydée—" Monte Cristo began.

"I would die," she interrupted. "Yes, my lord."

"Do you love me, then?"

Haydée turned to Valentine, her voice trembling. "Oh, Valentine, he asks if I love him. Tell him—tell him as you love Maximilian."

Monte Cristo's heart surged with emotion. He opened his arms, and Haydée, with a cry, rushed into them.

"Yes!" she sobbed. "I love you! I love you as a father, a brother, a husband! I love you as my very life, because you are the noblest, kindest soul I've ever known!"

"Then so be it, my angel," the Count said softly. "God has guided me through my trials and granted me this reward. I thought I needed to punish myself, but He has pardoned me. Love me, Haydée. Who knows? Perhaps your love will help me forget all I wish to leave behind."

"What do you mean, my lord?" she asked.

"I mean," he replied, "that your love has taught me more in a moment than twenty years of reflection. Through you, I have found life again. Through you, I will suffer, and through you, I will rejoice."

"Do you hear him, Valentine?" Haydée cried. "He says he will suffer because of me—when I would gladly give my life for his!"

Monte Cristo stepped back, his expression somber. "Have I found the truth at last?" he whispered. "Whether it is a reward or punishment, I accept my fate." He turned to Haydée, taking her hand. "Come, my love." Wrapping an arm around her waist, he clasped Valentine's hand in gratitude and disappeared with Haydée by his side.

An hour later, Valentine sat quietly, watching over Maximilian. At last, his heart stirred, and a faint breath escaped his lips. His body shuddered, signaling the return of life. Slowly, his eyes opened. At first, they were blank and unfocused, but as clarity returned, so did his grief.

"Oh," he groaned, his voice heavy with despair, "the Count deceived me—I'm still alive." His trembling hand reached for a knife on the table.

"Maximilian," Valentine called softly, her radiant smile breaking through his anguish, "look at me."

He froze, his despair giving way to awe. Dropping the knife, he sank to his knees, overcome by what seemed to him a vision of heaven.

As dawn broke, Valentine and Morrel walked arm-in-arm along the shore, listening as Jacopo, captain of Monte Cristo's yacht, delivered a letter.

It read:

My dear Maximilian,

There is a ship awaiting you. It will carry you and Valentine to Leghorn, where Noirtier wishes to bless your union. All that I own—the grotto, my home in Paris, my château at Tréport—is yours. Valentine will find her happiness with you, as she gives to the poor the fortune left by her family. Pray for me, Maximilian, for I am but a man who once thought himself equal to God but has learned that only He holds supreme wisdom.

Live and be happy. Remember that all human wisdom is contained in these words: Wait and hope.

Your friend,

Edmond Dantès, Count of Monte Cristo.

The world around them seemed brighter, the horizon wide with possibilities.

"What do we do now?" Maximilian asked, looking out at the endless ocean.

Valentine squeezed his hand gently. "We live, my love. We honor his gift."

In the distance, a white sail disappeared over the horizon, carrying Monte Cristo and Haydée away.

"Do you think we will see them again?" Maximilian asked.

Valentine smiled through her tears. "Perhaps. But until then, let us remember his words: *wait and hope.*"

Made in the USA
Las Vegas, NV
03 May 2025

63990304-6b38-4785-87a3-67e72294e36eR01